Copyright © 2023 by Katie Stine

Published by ScarabSkin Books

Cover design by Fiona Jayde Media. First paperback edition March 2023. First digital edition March 2023.

ISBN 978-1-7344397-7-9 (paperback)

ISBN 978-1-7344397-6-2 (ebook)

For my husband, who would never behave so poorly.

From award-winning author of
A Lady's Revenge and
The Boxer and the Blacksmith

a
VISCOUNT'S
VENGEANCE

EDIE CAY

CAST OF CHARACTERS

James Wallingford, Lord Andrepont, viscount,
cousin to Lydia and Agnes

Lady Andrepont, viscountess, mother of Lord
Andrepont, sister to Lady Lorian

Lord Andrepont (deceased), father of the current
viscount, husband to Lady Andrepont.

Lady Lydia/Mrs. Arthur, eldest daughter of Lady
Lorian, first cousin of James, married to John Arthur.

Lady Agnes Somerset, youngest daughter of Lady
Lorian, first cousin of James, widowed, lives with
romantic partner, Jack Townsend

Jack Townsend, a finder of lost things, romantic
partner of Lady Agnes

Margaret Miller, half-sister to James Wallingford,
daughter of the deceased Lord Andrepont and a
maid. Taken in by Lady Andrepont, married to Lord
Elshire.

Lord Elshire, earl, married to Margaret Miller, half-
sister to James Wallingford, cousin by marriage to
Ladies Lydia and Agnes

Mr. John Arthur/Corinthian John, a prizefighter
who has become a successful stockbroker. Continues
to box for the joy of the sweet science. Husband to

Lady Lydia, father of her child. Friend of Andrepont and Bess Abbott.

Miss Pearl Arthur, younger sister of John Arthur, lives with John and Lydia, had previously boarded at Mrs. Tyler's Boardingschool for Ladies.

Miss Mathilda Perry, friend of Pearl, boards at Mrs. Tyler's Boardingschool for Ladies.

Mrs. Tyler, owner and chaperone for Mrs. Tyler's Boardingschool for Ladies.

Bess Abbott, a female prizefighter, acknowledged to be the best in London, John Arthur's best friend.

Mrs. Coldcroft, one of the women whom Pearl stayed with as a child.

Henry Parks, Lord Kinsley, marquis, good friend of Andrepont and Jack About Town. Married to Rose, Lady Kinsley

Rose Parks, Lady Kinsley, marquess, married to Henry. Has had an affair with James, Lord Andrepont, which her husband approved.

Lady Haglund, a baroness, friend of the dowager Lady Andrepont, thrower of parties. Her husband belongs to the same club as James.

Lady Teeton, countess, new friend of Pearl's, politically active and motivated.

Lord Teeton, earl, politically active, not known for having a brilliant mind.

Mr. and Mrs. Aguilar, friends of Lady Teeton, wealthy, ethnically Spanish

Mr. and Mrs. Shumaker, friends of Lady Teeton, wealthy, ethnically German

Freddy, school friend of Andrepont, now inherited a Scottish earldom

Mrs. Foraker, the longtime housekeeper at the Andrepont home.

Mr. Barton, the longtime butler for the Andrepont home.

Lily, lady's maid to Pearl
Philip, valet to James
Smithy, driver at the Andrepont home

Mr. Parsons, butler at the Arthur residence
Roger, footman at the Arthur residence
Vasily, driver and friend to Lord Lorian from their war days.

CHAPTER 1

Lord Andrepont strode into the drawing room as if he were a ship being tossed ashore in a storm. His dark hair—never in careful arrangement—was ruffled, like he'd spent the morning running his hands through it. In contrast, his clothes were neatly pressed, as if he hadn't sat since donning them. His demeanor, the way he strode to the chair without awaiting his cousin Lydia's welcome, signaled to Pearl that something was amiss. And if Pearl knew anything, she knew that a man unmoored was dangerous.

Lydia, the mistress of the house and Pearl's sister-in-law, smoothed over Andrepont's rudeness and rose to her feet. She echoed the refined air of the room's décor, dark and foreboding, but edged in gold. "I suppose I shall ring for refreshments, then."

Pearl studied her darning instead of the man who was sprawled in a chair four feet away from her. He seemed like the Thames on a foggy day, thick, poisoned, and putrid. It made her want to scoot to the far end of the settee. Before she could so much as twitch, he turned his startling green eyes on her.

"My dear Miss Arthur, I apologize for not

greeting you. How do you do?" Andrepont straightened for a moment, baring his teeth in approximation of a smile, mimicking the manners—if not the intent—of his class.

Pearl sat frozen under his gaze. Blimey, he was handsome. It was unfair, really, for a man to be that good-looking. It made her want to forgive all manner of trespass. His dark hair, the strong jaw, his eyes so piercing and bright, as if they were pieces of green sea glass catching the sun just so.

He wasn't handsome at all when he sneered at people, which she had seen him do, though he had never once sneered at her. Old habits made her tuck away bits of kindness like that, ready to be loyal at all costs. It was a trait she couldn't quite shake.

Most looked down on her for being Corinthian John's little sister, or for being raised in questionable circumstances, but not Lord Andrepont. He didn't comment upon her red hair, draw attention to her crooked tooth, or even note the unreasonable width of her hands and feet. He was kind—at least to her. And it was obvious to anyone that this bloke was hurting right now, backed into a corner like an injured dog in an alleyway.

Pearl answered him. "I'm doing very well, my lord. And you? Have you had an eventful morning?" She smiled back, blandly polite.

"Eventful? Yes. Pleasant? I'm afraid not. Hence my calling upon this house. I was hoping to persuade your brother into some pugilistic pursuits, but he claims he must work."

"How tedious," Lydia said, joining them back in the sitting area. Lydia had met Pearl's brother, John, due to their common love of prizefighting. John continued sparring, but Lydia slowed her pursuits after producing their first child.

For a flash, Pearl considered telling Andrepont she would spar with him in the downstairs gymnasium, but she bit her tongue. She'd told no one in the household of her training, not even Lydia, who had fought in the ring. More than Pearl had done. Pearl's training with Bess Abbott had been different than Lydia's. For a purpose. Pearl's exploration of the sweet science had been necessary at first, and then more of an intellectual pursuit.

"John suggested that I come visit with you and spar verbally instead." Andrepont looked at his cousin, and in that moment, the sardonic brow arch echoed between him and Lydia, reminding Pearl of the family resemblance.

"What has you in such a state?" Lydia asked, stowing the contents of the portable writing desk she'd been working on before his arrival.

Pearl continued her darning. She couldn't look Andrepont full in the face any longer. It was too much. She focused on the turbulent painting of a ship at sea that hung next to the window, visible over Lydia's shoulder.

Instead of answering Lydia's question, Andrepont turned the full force of his gaze to Pearl and said, "Miss Arthur, have you had a pleasant Season?"

"Of course," Pearl said, fighting the urge to squirm.

"Soirees and assemblies and whatnot keeping you occupied?"

Lydia sighed.

Pearl kept her head down. She was busy with her stitches. Very occupied. "Not many, but I find my own amusement." She did not receive many invitations, having no standing whatsoever. Oh, thanks to her brother, she had plenty of money, which she'd once assumed would lure at least some fortune hunters. But those seemed scared away by John's reputation, and the impoverished aristocrats stayed away because John's marriage into the aristocracy galled them. They didn't want to uplift two street urchins if they could help it.

"That's a pity," Andrepont said, seemingly sincere. "And such a waste of youth."

Lydia sighed again, this time louder. "What's your point, James?"

"My point? I have none. I'm merely making conversation."

"By reminding Pearl of her social status? How callous. And if not callous, then cruel."

Pearl could practically smell Lydia's protectiveness. There was something about Lydia that Pearl reveled in, though at times it also repelled her. The aristocratic lady was unsettled, moody, constantly shifting. Pearl found it intoxicating but also unnerving. "I'm perfectly all right, Lydia. I don't mind."

"You may not mind, but I do." Lydia looked as if she might spit. "I know what their snubs mean, having committed them myself."

"I've never dreamed I would be elevated enough to earn a snub, so I do not suffer." As if Pearl would cry into her scented pillow if one rich young lady didn't look her way. Pearl had known hunger and loneliness. Nothing could be done in a ballroom that would hurt her.

The footman, Richard, entered carrying a large tray stuffed with a teapot, cups, and an array of honeyed seed cakes that Cook only offered when Andrepont was in the house. Richard settled the tray. He kept aloof as training bid him, of course, and Pearl also engaged in the tradition. Sometimes she snuck down to the servants' hall when she was particularly lonesome. Her time at Mrs. Tyler's Boarding House for Young Ladies had taught her all she need know about running a house and being a lady, but she missed people that felt like *home*.

She'd grown up in homes of poor families—

handed from one cramped set of rooms to the next as John grew through his own boarding school education. Pearl swept floors, pulled water, looked after little ones. She cooked and darned and filled in the gaps of housekeeping to ensure her stay with those families would continue as long as possible. She'd learned a few other lessons as well. Things no young lady ought to know.

Richard left without a backwards glance, but Pearl could tell he was still limping. He and another footman had tussled the other day—no one would say why, but Pearl suspected there was one of the new housemaids involved—and Richard had not fared as well as the other bloke.

"Shall I pour?" Pearl asked Lydia. It would give her a task while the cousins conversed, their sharp wits nothing but arrows Pearl would rather avoid.

Lydia gestured her assent and Pearl set to her task, listening as any dutiful young lady ought.

"Let me be horrendously rude and ask once again, what has you ruffled this morning?" Lydia stared at her cousin.

"Thank you for the warning regarding your manners," Andrepont parried.

"You haven't answered my question."

"Ah, yes." Andrepont scooted forward in the chair, readying to accept a teacup from Pearl. "Because it is none of your fucking business."

According to Mrs. Tyler, the curse was a warning of violence and should have sent a cold chill down Pearl's spine. Although she'd heard the curse so often that it didn't affect her, she wasn't sure how she was supposed to react in this setting. Thankfully, Lydia laughed. Pearl unfroze and breathed a sigh of relief. She didn't bother lifting the cup and saucer to Andrepont after she finished pouring. He didn't seem to mind picking it off the tray.

"My thanks, Miss Arthur," Andrepont purred.

The rumble of his voice warmed her, and she didn't like that at all, but she had more control than most. Instead, Pearl fixed her tea, giving a bright, polite smile to no one in particular. Some animals had armor, some had teeth, and others had camouflage. To each their own.

"Ah yes, ever the bachelor. Hold yourself apart from the rest of us, James, since that seems to be the way you like it."

"Oh, would you stop prying if I married?" Andrepont teased.

"Of course. Then it would be your wife's business, not mine, and she would have the onus of dragging you out of your horrible moods." Lydia sipped at her tea. She was beginning to resemble the old Lydia— the boxer who wasn't yet a mother, who had a vicious sense of humor, compassion hidden beneath the sharpened wit.

"Such advice. What do you think, Miss Arthur?" Andrepont asked. "Should I marry so that my cousin stays out of my affairs?"

Pearl looked to him, extending herself to feel the mood of the room, and sensed a dangerous undercurrent. His green eyes glittered and there was a dark amusement in them that had her mind flashing warnings. "I think a person's business contains a certain amount of overlap with family, though who is family and who is not is an everchanging prospect."

"How very diplomatic," Lydia grumbled.

But Andrepont didn't look away from Pearl, holding her gaze. It wasn't a challenge, exactly. She kept her face schooled in pleasant neutrality.

Finally, something in his expression set. "And how would you like to become family?"

"She's already family," Lydia said, her voice flat.

"My family. Miss Arthur, would you like to become my viscountess?" James asked, his voice low and calm, rumbling with untold promises.

"Pardon me?" Pearl nearly spit.

"Stop it, James. That isn't funny." Lydia put her teacup down with a clatter.

"I'm perfectly serious. Miss Pearl Arthur, would you do me the honor of becoming the next viscountess Andrepont?"

Her mind spun like a top. Pearl couldn't obtain an invitation to a ballroom full of second sons, let alone a marriage proposal. But of all the things Lord Andrepont was, a liar wasn't one of them. He'd never been cruel to her.

A flurry of questions and concerns whirred through her head, clicking like an automaton. She didn't know Andrepont terribly well. But she certainly knew him as much as she would know any other man she might marry. She didn't love Andrepont, but that was rarely a concern for those elevated in rank. Andrepont had the reputation of a rake, but to his family, Andrepont was fiercely loyal.

Lydia exploded to her feet. "No. No, no, and no. Absolutely not. You are too closely related. Absolutely not."

Living with her brother and wife in extraordinary luxury was a dream so lofty Pearl couldn't have imagined it as a child. But it meant spinsterhood. It meant no children of her own. It meant no life of her own, always living in service to John and his family. Andrepont was offering her something entirely for herself, and meager as it was, it was more than she could have ever imagined. She was still that dirty young girl, cheeks streaked with tears as she shuffled on to yet another over-burdened family's rooms.

Andrepont rolled his eyes towards his cousin. "Lydia, you and I could be married, let alone your sister by marriage. There's no consanguinity issue here."

"Yes, thank you, my lord," Pearl said, putting

down her teacup, hoping to beat Lydia to the punch. "I should like to become your wife."

Andrepont flinched as she said the word *wife*. Lydia bolted to the door and rang for a footman before choosing an alternative path. She stepped out the door and looked as if she might actually *raise her voice* to summon her husband. Just then, the footman arrived. She said, "Fetch Mr. Arthur at once. Right now. Immediately!"

Pearl realized that he had not said *wife*—he had asked if she would like to become his viscountess. He offered her a job that came with a title, not a partnership of souls. Which would be silly, of course. She knew Andrepont's stance on such things; it wasn't as if he'd ever hidden his opinions. His plan had been no wife, no children. She knew his family's secrets. Or at least, a few of them.

What had changed in this morning of mussed hair?

The feeling of tension, that fist of danger that had filled the room, dissipated. She regarded Andrepont, who was now watching Lydia's antics with amusement. A handsome husband was a prize. A rich one, a bonus. A titled one? She'd never expected that. But a husband as moody and brooding as her sister-in-law? Well. T'was better to set up her own household than always live on her brother's good graces.

❦

JAMES FOLLOWED John to his study. Lydia was positively livid—predictably so—and John's face a dark cast of his normally carefree expression. Miss Arthur seemed surprisingly neutral, accepting his proposal calmly and rationally, as if it wasn't at all surprising for a suitor to show up unannounced and ask her to marry him without even courting her first.

If Miss Arthur had truly been brought up as a proper lady, he would not have had such access to her, never been able to be so forward. Really, it should be considered rude. But, he hadn't known he would be bloody proposing. Having had one's heart broken first thing in the morning tended to make for an unpredictable day.

John ushered him into the study and slammed the door. "What is your game?"

"Game?" James strode towards John's liquor cart. It typically contained some fine smuggled whisky or at least decent gin. John's palate had been molded by alley-distilled gut-rot and had barely refined since. Perhaps it was early in the day to indulge, but these few hours had been trying, and now he had nuptials to celebrate. First, he'd been dumped and summarily dismissed by the love of his life *and* his best friend. And now, well...now he was engaged to be married. Was it even noon yet? "There's no game."

"If you do this to shame her, to mock her, by God I will—" The fury in John's voice was real and lethal. He had the ability to kill with his bare hands, and only his temperament and sense of fair play ever kept him from doing so in the ring. He was the best prizefighter of his generation. Maybe two.

James held up his hand. "I asked her to become the next viscountess Andrepont. She accepted. Name your terms. I don't need a dowry. I shall court her in public, or not, whatever you prefer. We shall have an expensive church wedding with a lavish breakfast, or we can have a small ceremony with only family. Whatever Miss Arthur would like. I don't care."

Honestly, all of that courtship business would keep him occupied so that he wouldn't pine after Rose and Henry. It would keep him busy so as not to feel the void that her absence—and frankly, his too—had already torn inside of him. And given the life that he was offering Miss Arthur, her wedding preferences were the least he could do for her.

John was shaking as he walked in circles. James knew he was trying to work out the anger coursing through his veins. He was notoriously protective of his younger sister, and rightly so. Any man of honor would be. "If you needed money, you would tell me."

"Of course, and I do not." James had sold off every bit of unentailed property he could in his efforts to collapse his title—and pay off his father's debts. He made no secret of his disdain for his father, the dead viscount, and how he hoped any future Andrepont would inherit nothing but his father's shame.

"Why Pearl? Why now?" John demanded, coming to a stop in front of him. The prizefighter stood eerily still, the way he did at the beginning of a bout.

John knew something of James's arrangement with Henry and Rose—their triangle. But even that was a poor descriptor, as if geometry could explain their entanglement. James threw back the bit of whisky, even though he knew he should savor it. Something needed to gird his loins. He was about to tell John the truth about Rose and her rejection when Lydia burst in.

"Have you told him absolutely not? I forbid this, James. I forbid it!" Lydia stormed over, ready to knock the glass out of his hand.

"Love, give me a minute. She's my sister." John said the words quietly, his own reaction to Lydia's temper.

Though James and his cousin Lydia were nearly ten years apart in age, they were two of a kind, never able to rein in their innate fury. But James had the benefit of being born male, and his anger was viewed as acceptable. Given his father, even undeniable.

Lydia stuck a finger in his face, as if she were a

fishwife down at the docks. "I know you. This is for you, and not for her."

"Is any marriage truly for the bride?" James asked. Rose had given him countless lectures about how married women had rights on par with horses or dogs. How women were people, as fully realized as any man, and as such, they deserved the ability to make their own decisions.

"Good God, man." John looked at him in horror.

During this morning's final lecture, when James had abased himself by pleading with her, she had reminded him that her body was her own, and she did not want him to know hers anymore. To help sever the link of her bed, he must not see them. *Either* of them. He'd lost his mistress and his best friend in one swipe of her autonomy.

"I would not mistreat her. She'll be as respected as she is here in your house," James assured him. He did not want John to think he had suddenly become the real heir to the Andrepont title, forcing himself onto unwilling women.

"Pardon me," Miss Arthur called from the threshold of the study. "I feel as if my opinion should be aired, if we are talking about whom I will marry."

Lydia and James both looked to John. He was her guardian. She was not yet twenty-five years of age—but honestly, James had no idea how old she was. Dear God, he knew nothing about her, not her favorite color nor her favorite flower. Well. It was still a better basis for marriage than many had. Fair enough.

"Yes, Pearl, please." John ushered his sister into the room. The change in him was obvious—gone was the quiet threat of violence. He was now solicitous and careful, the papa-figure he had become earlier that year with the birth of his own daughter.

"Shall we sit, then?" Lydia suggested with an arched brow. "If we are to be civilized about it."

James followed her lead to the sitting area near the fireplace. "Will that keep you from screaming at me like a common—"

"Only if you cease being such an imbecile," Lydia interrupted with a saccharine smile.

Miss Arthur sat in one chair, John hovering behind her. Lydia took the other chair, leaving James to stand in the middle as if he'd been called to the carpet at the headmaster's office.

"Lord Andrepont has asked me to marry him." Miss Arthur swung her wide-eyed glance around the room.

Now that James was taking notice of her, she was kind of a strange-looking woman. Not unpleasant, and certainly not unattractive. But she didn't fit the parameters of what the young ladies of the *ton* deemed correct. Her pale-blue eyes were large—their coloring prized by society, as if that mattered. But they were wide and angled in a way that accented her high cheekbones. Her coppery hair, the same light fiery color as her brother's, was definitely not in fashion. She was small as well. Something always sought after by ladies, in James's experience. But she was small in a way that suggested a skittering mouse. As if she wasn't always quite present. It was likely that essence that made it easy for James and any other man to overlook her. She appeared ever-ready to bolt.

"You needn't marry anyone," John said, gripping the back of Miss Arthur's chair.

"I needn't, but I should like to," Miss Arthur said, turning to James with those pale eyes.

Now that James was examining her, those eyes made him want to fidget. Like she saw more than she let on. Probably the whisky finally doing its job. He'd always intended to remain Society's mysterious bachelor, but his swift decision to propose was made so a new viscountess would run his house. And let him be totally unhindered. And also to show Rose that he wasn't the uncontrollable lovesick pup that she'd accused him of being.

"I need your word that this isn't a joke or some careless whim," Lydia warned.

James held his hand over his heart. "As I was saying to John, this is no joke. I have never proposed marriage before, and would never do so callously. Whatever courtship and ceremony Miss Arthur desires, I shall provide. I intend to extend whatever shreds of respectability I have to her."

Lydia narrowed her eyes. "And what of bankrupting your title?"

"Miss Arthur surely knows of my desire to have no issue of my body. I am not shy of my disdain for the title I hold. If she is to receive a dowry, I respectfully ask that she remain in control of it and that it shall not become part of any holdings of my estate."

"Done," John said without hesitation.

"Who is your current heir?" Miss Arthur asked.

It was a valid question, though one most would not ask. "He is a decent man, a scholar in Edinburgh. A fine man, several years older than I am. A distant relation. He would not turn you or my mother out, if that's what you are asking."

"This is no basis for a marriage." Lydia crossed her arms.

"I should think that anything can be a basis for a marriage," Miss Arthur said. "It's up to the two people entering the contract what the marriage itself shall be like. That is unknown territory for even the most prepared."

James couldn't help but smile at her tactful reprimand. He'd never noticed the iron in her spine. She hid it well.

"I should like a public courtship, if you please, my lord." Miss Arthur returned her steady gaze to him.

He bowed. "Of course. We shall begin right away, as the social season is almost at an end."

"And for the ceremony itself?" John asked.

"It may be open to the public, but I should like for some of our less fortunate friends to feel welcome, should they like to attend," Miss Arthur said.

"Of course," James said. At the same time, John said, "Is that wise?"

"If I may do nothing else for the women who allowed me into their homes while you were at school, then I think a lovely morning spent amongst flowers is the very least I can do." Miss Arthur looked to her brother as if a hothouse worth of flowers was a simple thing. But with Corinthian John's money, it was.

"Shall we have them for the wedding breakfast as well?" James asked.

She shook her head. "No, they would be uncomfortable. I'd rather we sponsor a breakfast for them elsewhere, and leave ours for family."

Ours, she said. It made him blink. He hadn't been part of an *ours* for something as wholesome as a wedding breakfast.

"Whatever you wish," he said, catching John's glare, as if John was the one who wanted to give his sister permission to have whatever she desired.

"I'll draw up the contracts in the next few days," John said.

"I'll contact my man for that as well," James said.

"Good," John said.

"Splendid," James returned.

Lydia sat shaking her head. Miss Arthur remained neutral and impassive. How did she do that? Surely this warranted an expression of joy from the girl. He knew what might make her smile.

"May we begin our courtship this week?" James asked Miss Arthur. "There is a private ball for which I received an invitation." The first olive branch that he could extend. His mother had harangued him to attend, if for no other reason than to maintain her friendship with Lady Atherwood. A friendship that was often kept quiet, given his own antics.

Lydia's eyes narrowed. "Whose?"

"The Atherwoods."

"*They* invited *you?*" his cousin challenged. The Atherwoods were an old family, proper, and Lady Atherwood was a sponsor for Almack's. She was a gatekeeper for all young ladies seeking good matches.

"The benefit of being titled and wealthy," James said.

"And a man," Lydia huffed.

"A viscount," he reminded, needling her further.

"I will have my mother write and ask to extend an invitation to my betrothed so that we might announce our engagement." James knew that was exactly the sort of bait a woman like Lady Atherwood would find irresistible. And if his new hobby was to force Society into accepting a former street mouse like Miss Arthur into their folds, then that sounded like jolly good fun.

If they would turn a blind eye to the horrors of his father, then they could turn a blind eye to the unfortunate early luck of a young lady like Miss Arthur. And he would relish their discomfort.

CHAPTER 2

James's mother put down her teacup. It was late, but that didn't seem to matter. Neither one of them slept on a schedule, and it was just as easy to catch her near midnight as it was near noon. The drawing room was her domain, the converted music room his.

"I didn't think you could surprise me anymore," she said. Her dark hair was swept up from the day's coiffure, but she wore a dressing gown, as if she were readying for bed and had merely forgotten to go to her room. "I am proven wrong."

James grinned and leaned against the door jamb. "That's satisfying to know."

"May I know who your bride is? The woman that has come to oust me from my rooms?" The words sounded harsh, but her tone was playful.

Still, James frowned. "Why would you move out of your rooms? I assumed you would continue living here."

It was her turn to laugh. "As the dowager, I should not be taking the suite meant for the viscountess. And it's time for you to move into the suite meant for the viscount."

James pulled himself away from the wall. It made his skin crawl—the idea of moving into his father's rooms. He sat in the chair across from his mother. "What if I stay where I am and give her another one of the rooms? We have plenty."

"James." It was rare that his mother reprimanded him. "You cannot expect that. If she's marrying you, she will expect her rights as viscountess, and that suite is one of them."

He didn't want to think about what rights a viscountess—and especially a viscount—might expect. The whole house still reeked of his father, despite the intervening years and his mother's redecoration attempts. "What if we demolish the house and rebuild from scratch?"

His mother gave him that same indulgent, affectionate look as if he were still in leading strings and had presented her with a worm.

He sighed. "Very well. But I'm having it scrubbed before I get in there, top to bottom."

She retrieved her teacup and sipped. "That's perfectly acceptable. Now, who is this girl that has so upended you that you are willing to give her your name?"

There was no way around his affections. No one had found a path inside his shell, with the exception of Rose, and he couldn't pretend otherwise. It would be no secret once Miss Arthur moved in. "I wouldn't say this is a love match."

Her mother's eyebrows arched, not dissimilar from his cousin Lydia's. Their mothers were sisters, after all. "I admit that if this is a political match, I'm mildly offended I was not given an opportunity to voice an opinion."

"Not precisely a political one either." He pulled himself up straighter.

A flash of hurt crossed her face before she schooled her expression. "Please don't tell me you've ruined some poor girl."

"I would never! Of course not." He tried to shake

off the disgust that he could be like his father, forcing himself on anyone. "It's merely that circumstances seemed to dictate I should marry, so I picked one."

"You picked one?" His mother blinked at him. "Did you have criteria, or did you choose some poor girl as if she were a pair of gloves?"

James snorted. "She isn't poor, for one. And I insisted she remain in control of her dowry so that it cannot be entailed to the estate."

His mother gazed off into some middle distance, nodding her head as if sorting through facts. He knew that when she had finished thinking, he would be sent to the nursery without supper. Or at least, thirty years prior he would have been. This might be worse. He'd rather go to bed without supper, allowed to cry into a pillow. Now, with the weight of so much on his shoulders, he was expected to soldier on, do his duty, slot into the Empire. But he'd been clear: he would do no such thing.

And then she said the worst possible thing. "This is about your father." Her green eyes snapped back on him, middle distance be damned.

"This is about me." He crossed his legs, immediately cursing himself for fidgeting.

"Her own money. You've been plain about the idea of children. You do realize there were other Lord Andreponts who were unlike your father in every way?"

"It does not matter. He was my father. I look like him. When I encounter certain persons, I watch them recoil in fear. I'll not pass that along." He hissed the words, trying hard to rein them in. His mother didn't deserve his wrath for expressing the truth.

His mother looked into the fireplace—anywhere, he supposed, but at his own face. The face that resembled the man who had inflicted so much pain. It was such a strange thing—he was vain and knew he was attractive. He had inherited his mother's green eyes, which sat alluringly stark against his dark hair. His nose was finely sculpted, thanks to his father. And no thanks to the rounds he'd spent pitted against every pugilist he could find, it remained unbroken. He'd tried to ruin it, but it always came back straight, no matter the beating.

"Your father is dead. He has no legacy if you choose to ignore him. But by hobbling yourself like this, you ensure he haunts us all."

James was on his feet before he could think, wanting to flee. He covered it by pacing the room, finally resting his hands on the back of the chair. "What do they say? Blood will out? Well, this blood will be kept firmly in check." He stalked out of the room, but before he left completely, his mother called after him.

"And who is your bride-to-be? I should invite her for tea."

James stopped in his tracks. He'd forgotten about the finer points of etiquette in his brooding. "Miss Pearl Arthur," he called over his shoulder.

"Corinthian John's sister?" She didn't sound surprised. But could anything surprise that woman? She was as much a mystery as his dead sire.

"The very one." James stomped out of the drawing room, heading for his den of relief: the piano and the brandy snifter. It was the only place in the house from which he'd managed to exorcise his father's ghost, and the only place James felt comfortable. He spent days in there, playing the instrument his father had bought only because James had tricked him into it. The only time he'd managed to get one over on the old bastard.

❧

PEARL KNEW she should feel ashamed for how much she enjoyed this new attention, but she didn't—not one bit. When Jack and Agnes—Lydia's younger sister, and legally a widow—arrived, they both commented on the dramatically over-large bouquet of white lilies that sat perfuming the drawing room. It took all of Pearl's control not to gloat and giggle.

"For you, Miss Pearl?" Jack asked, looking pleased. It had only been a few months since Jack had moved from the molly-house to Agnes's new townhome in Marylebone. His dark hair and thick, enviable lashes added to the contrast of his pale-yellow waistcoat and white cravat. Jack wore a skirt instead of trousers, which made many people pause, but Pearl had grown accustomed to Jack's unusual fashion and heady charm.

Only when Jack called attention to the ridiculously stuffed vase did Pearl allow herself a smile—and did she smile because the bouquet was from Andrepont? Or did she smile simply because it was her turn to have flowers delivered? Or was it knowing that her finishing school friend Mathilda Perry would be out of her mind with jealousy when she saw them?

"In fact, they are for me," Pearl answered, extending her hand to the sitting area. Tea had already been sent for, and Lydia had not quite made it out of her rooms yet. Pearl got to be the hostess here, perhaps for one of the last times before she moved into her own home. Well, her home with Andrepont.

"Those must have cost a fortune." Jack whistled.

Agnes caught Jack with her elbow. "No whistling. It's rude. Pearl, those are very beautiful." Agnes was taller than her sister Lydia, yet until Jack came along, Agnes had always appeared smaller. Now she radiated a happiness that could have easily convinced Pearl that Agnes was ten feet tall.

"Thank you," Pearl said, flushing with pride. She could get quite used to being courted. Suitors had never been her strong suit, so to speak. There had been kisses, and even a serious beau, Gabriel. But Gabriel could have never afforded a bouquet like that.

Richard arrived with the tea tray, bedecked with Jack's favorites. Cook knew everything they liked, and Jack went out of his way to compliment the staff.

"Oi, Richard, bit of a shiner, yeah?" Jack said to the footman.

"Jack! We're working on this, please! We can't go round to call if you keep this up. One doesn't speak to the staff while they are working. It's rude. And distracting."

"Thank you, my lady," Richard said to Agnes, his deep voice rumbling. "Bit of a row downstairs," he said to Jack.

"Have you a poultice for it? I would be glad to make one for you," Pearl said. She'd meant to go downstairs yesterday to ask after him, but the proposal had drastically changed her plans.

"Pearl, not you too? How am I to train either of you to fit in if you keep this up?"

"But I've known Richard for a long time," Jack protested. "It would be rude not to ask after his eye."

"I'm quite good at poultices for that sort of thing." Over the years, Pearl had made so many for her brother and London's Invincible Championess, Bess Abbott.

Agnes looked at the ceiling as if she could recruit aid from the plaster. "This is not the proper venue for such discussions. I do not begrudge you your familiarity, just not when you are entertaining guests, nor calling on a friend."

Lydia appeared in the doorway. "What. Are. Those."

"They're for Miss Pearl!" Jack said in a tone that Pearl couldn't parse. "Aren't they beautiful?"

Lydia looked as if she would knock the bouquet over as she stalked to the sitting area. "This is unacceptable. He cannot do this. I will not allow this to continue."

Jack looked at Pearl with a conspiratorial grin. "Who is it? I can't wait to hear."

Even Agnes looked at her sister askance. "Who could be so unsuitable that could afford those?"

"James." Lydia sat next to Pearl and began to pour the tea. She dismissed the hovering Richard with a wave of her hand.

"What about James?" Agnes asked, clearly not understanding. "Does he know the gentleman?"

Pearl couldn't help but look at her hands. Was she such an unthinkable choice? Was it her status as a former orphan? Or her status as John's little sister? She understood that the *ton* might feel that way, but it hurt to hear these people—her friends, people she'd considered *family*—put her aside. She didn't particularly care why Andrepont had asked her to marry him. The fact was, he had. And now she had an absurdly large, ridiculously expensive bouquet in her drawing room to admire. Well, Lydia's drawing room anyway.

When Pearl looked up, she saw Jack had understood and was doing his best to remain neutral. Andrepont had not supported Jack's desire to be with Agnes. He'd done everything to prevent it, but Andrepont hadn't understood the situation fully. When he realized Jack would do anything for Agnes, he had facilitated the match, as it were.

"Don't be thick, Agnes," Lydia complained.

"Have your tea, Lydia." Agnes ignored her sister's rudeness. "You'll feel better."

"Is it true, Pearl?" Jack asked. "Andrepont is courting you?"

Agnes gave Pearl a sharp look. And Pearl couldn't help but smile as she nodded. She liked surprising them. Of all people, it was her that would be a viscountess.

"Yes. Lord Andrepont sent me the bouquet."

Agnes looked to the bouquet, her expression closing in on itself. Lydia stared at her sister, a cool brow arched. "Do you see now?" Lydia asked Agnes.

Pearl caught Jack watching her. She knew Jack observed more than most, knew what it was to be forgotten and shuffled about, a weed in a garden of daffodils.

"Congratulations, Miss Pearl. I think it's smashing." Jack gave her a grin and toasted her with his teacup.

"Thank you, Jack," Pearl said, pulling herself up. She was to be proper now, even more so than before. Mrs. Tyler, proprietress of the finishing school Pearl had attended, would be ever so proud. All those hours of practice: her posture, her smile, her hair, her manners, all for this.

"It's not that it's you, Pearl," Agnes said, wringing her hands. "It's that it's James."

"What's wrong with Lord Andrepont?" Pearl asked, although she already knew the objections. She lived in the same house as Lydia, after all. She knew he was broody, knew he'd sworn to never have children, sworn to leave his title in shambles. She knew.

But to have her own money, to have a *place*. Her own rightful place. For the first time in her life, her bed would be her own, not subject to the whims of other people. It was worth the sacrifice.

"You've met him," Lydia said. "The man isn't a mystery."

"He's...a bit of a mess," Agnes said.

"Who isn't?" quipped Jack.

"Quite right, Jack," echoed Pearl, turning her attention to her teacup, as if she might find loyalty to Andrepont inside it. "Who isn't?"

LYDIA AND JOHN stood behind Pearl. The heat of the crush in front of her was stifling even before they waded in. Andrepont had her arm, and they were announced into Lady Atherwood's ball as if she were just the sort that belonged there. It was the end of the Season, the gossip was tired, and everyone would be looking to pounce on something new, Lydia assured her. Her. They would pounce on her. Being bland Miss Pearl Arthur might no longer be the camouflage she needed.

The ballroom seemed to turn all at once towards them, like a column of soldiers. Pearl no longer thought Lydia's ideas about gossip were comforting at all.

"Steady on," Andrepont murmured to her, looking smug and handsome and somehow apart from all of this. His black trousers fit him in a way that barely kept Pearl from staring. His black-on-black damask waistcoat accentuated his broad chest, and the stark white linen shirt underneath was a shocking contrast. He wore an emerald cravat pin that twinkled in the same hue as his eyes. His beauty was almost cruel.

"Now is the time, my lord. If you wish to back out, do so now, I beg you." Pearl was dressed in white, the type of frock with just enough ruffle at the hem. The muslin overskirt was so fine that Pearl had been scared it might rip as Lydia's lady's maid settled it over Pearl's slender hips. The underskirt had a slight cast of pink to it, so as not to turn Pearl's pale, ruddy complexion sallow. She wore a strand of pearls at her throat, and they sat cool against her skin, reminding her that none of these people knew her.

"Once I strike a bargain, I keep it. Are you having second thoughts?" He steered her effortlessly to the side of the ballroom, nodding at men he knew and smirking at the women who stared.

There had to be over a hundred people here. The amount of food they had to lay in for something like this. How many footmen must be on hand for the carriages, the serving platters? While the cooks and the maids must be downstairs, frantic to keep up the pace of the demand. *No*, she reminded herself. It wasn't her party to throw. She was no servant here.

The title of viscountess dangled in front of her. She could have it, if she wished. She'd be a fool not to. The look on Mathilda's face if she told her she could have had Lord Andrepont as a husband. "No, my lord. No second thoughts. I'm happy to announce if you are."

He nodded his dark head. "We shall allow Lady Atherwood the courtesy of knowing first. May I fetch you some ratafia?"

Pearl nodded, parched. Lydia came up on her fast as Andrepont departed. "We can leave as soon as you want," she hissed. "Don't let him say anything to anyone."

It was Pearl's turn to give Lydia a cool, assessing look. "Why not?"

"Pearl," Lydia said, all but begging her.

Pearl licked her lips, something she knew she shouldn't do. Because dear God, one shouldn't remind anyone that a woman had a *tongue*, but she was parched. Her stays felt tight as her heart hammered against them. "You cannot know what I want because you have not asked. I want to marry Lord Andrepont, and so I shall."

Lydia's face shuttered closed, and her mask melted into place—the terrible one, meant for outsiders. They had taken their stances, for the first time opposite one another. Pearl tried not to take her sister-in-law's disapproval to heart.

Lydia's cold imperialism took over, and she linked her arm with Pearl's. "Then you shall marry him. Let me make the introductions."

And so Lydia took Pearl around the ballroom, introducing her to matrons and debutantes alike.

Pearl nodded and curtsied, pleasantries exchanged as they moved from circle to circle. No promises of calls were made, but no snubs either. Lydia's face was set like granite, but Pearl felt optimistic. This felt like a measure of success to her: no one gave her the cut direct. And even if they did, Pearl would still return to a warm bed with a full belly. How bad could it be?

Andrepont found them and handed them both cups of ratafia. Pearl gratefully choked down the overly sweet punch, feeling her stomach rebel. She wasn't accustomed to so much sugar—it had been too expensive when she was a child, and she found it too morally corrupt as an adult.

"Shall we?" Andrepont asked as the next dance was called.

Pearl looked over her shoulder at the dance floor, where couples were lining up. She glanced back at Lydia, who was still grim-faced. Where was John? He must be in the back rooms already, doing business with whoever caught his attention.

Dancing here was not the same as dancing at the parties in Paddington. There, with Mrs. Coldcroft and her family, people would spill out into the night, from a tavern or a dance hall, or someone's adjoined rooms. Pearl would scamper up to the dancers, a fiddler or two keeping the time, hoping she could make the line before the song started. Then the caller would start the dance and she wouldn't think anything of grinning at the person across from her, her skirts whirling, her mouth gaping, laughing. Someone would spill their ale, and shrieks from children who should have been in bed hours ago would cut through the air.

The music here was familiar. It was the same rhythm. The movements were similar, but bloodless. No, Pearl corrected herself—the movements were *proper*.

Lydia took her empty cup. "Go on. You must have

the first dance if you are to have the second. No one will believe an engagement without at least two dances together."

Pearl stared at the empty cup, now cradled in Lydia's gloved palm. And then she looked to Andrepont's open, gloved hand. "We shall," Pearl said, forcing herself to meet his green eyes. Her heart pounded. Was it from his proximity? Or was it from knowing what a ridiculous thing it was to dress a Paddington girl like a princess?

He smiled and led them to the parquet, lining up with the other couples. She acquitted herself well, steps precise and careful, and she saw the approval flash on Andrepont's face when he realized she wouldn't make a fool of herself. She was glad they could be partners in this, at least.

He believed she could be the viscountess. And so she would be the very best viscountess there ever was, she thought, handing herself through the dancers before returning to the line on the other side. A great lady was not born, she was forged. And if anyone could remake themselves, it was Pearl.

❧

SO THIS IS THE RUBICON, James thought, watching pale skirts swirl amongst dark trousers. He was in some ways surprised that Lady Atherwood allowed trousers instead of mandating men wear breeches, but fashions changed, and to be fashionable, one must change with them. He followed his partner, changing hands as the music dictated. He didn't mind dancing, and he'd been told he was adept.

He spotted his mother in the crowd of people, moving amongst the bystanders. She was easy to spot in her dark burgundy gown, the color of old blood.

If he were a more polite and doting suitor, he would engage Pearl's attention as they moved.

Conversing, telling humorous anecdotes, whatever it was that men did when they wooed a woman. That had never been his forte. Frankly, he'd never needed to woo anyone. Prior to Rose, there had only been dalliances based on the physical. And after Rose... well. Rose was unlike any other woman he'd ever met. Her mind constantly churning, working through the world as if it were an equation to be solved, an answer lurking in every corner of the earth.

Her curiosity had been intoxicating. When presented with something new, she would positively glow with delight, and he wanted to bring her the world so she would glow for him. He'd almost convinced himself she would find some answer to a problem he'd never considered, if only he followed her long enough.

And he would have if she hadn't dismissed him. Shame smoldered deep inside, but he kept himself light and neutral as the dance came to an end. The company applauded, and he held out his hand to escort Ro—no, Pearl. Pearl. He was marrying Miss Pearl Arthur.

Miss Arthur took his hand, trusting. He felt a twinge of guilt. This wasn't the right thing to do, not for her. For him? Did it matter? Did anything matter? Rose had admonished him to marry, so he would. She was smarter than anyone else he knew.

Hopefully his marriage would allow him to be close to her again. And it wasn't as if Miss Arthur got nothing out of the deal. Lydia had said the girl had virtually no prospects. This would elevate her, and with her own money from her brother, the world was hers. If she had the gall to take it.

Miss Arthur was asking him something—he needed to pay attention. "Pardon?" He pretended the crush of people had kept him from hearing her.

"I said, did you enjoy the dance?" Her expression remained neutral and guarded.

Perhaps they were the same, she and him. Closed, secretive, calculating. Or perhaps she was another shallow young miss who wanted fancy dresses and beautiful flowers. That, he could provide. "I did. You are an excellent dancer. You must have had quite the dedicated instructor."

A cloud crossed her face, and he heard it then, his unintentional insult: as if a girl like her wouldn't know how to dance. He needed to watch that.

"I attended a very good finishing school. Though it was for daughters of the common people of England." Miss Arthur shook her head once and put on a dazzling smile.

There was a parry right back. *Good girl*, he thought. He deserved a dig in return. She was merely highlighting his birthright, knowing it rankled him. Good. He delivered her to Lydia at the edges of the ballroom. John was now at his wife's elbow, talking to some matrons. They must allow some other young man to ask for Miss Arthur's attention, and then James would swoop in for dance number two.

It wasn't that he cared overmuch whether she could acquit herself well on a dancefloor, or at the dinner table, but it was nice not to be embarrassed. Not that he cared about that particular emotion, either. If he did, he certainly wouldn't have shown his face here. As he retrieved the ratafia earlier, he'd heard the whispers about himself and Henry and Rose. How could he not?

The gossip was merely speculation about what schism may have happened. The three had made no great secret of their closeness—he'd accompanied them on their honeymoon cruise. As they'd said then, who cared what these tossers thought? These were the same ilk that hid his father's sins for him.

"Cousin," James greeted Lydia. "I return Miss Arthur to your clutches."

Lydia turned to Miss Arthur and said, "May I

introduce our hostess for the evening, Lady Atherwood. She's anxious to make your acquaintance." This was the moment. Caesar's boots in the river Rubicon, crossing towards Rome, his army behind him.

"I understand you have some news which you would like to share. You and Miss Arthur," Lady Atherwood prompted James. The older matron gave a polite smile of encouragement, and he could see she was thinking it was somehow a reform for him. Another wayward young man returning to the fold.

James's mother arrived to their group, but Lady Atherton's attention could not be ripped from him for anyone's sake. She knew what was coming. Everyone knew what was coming.

"Yes," James said, looking again to Miss Arthur. This was it, her chance to be free of him, should she wish it. Her wide blue eyes met his, and he found that he could read nothing in their depths. She was a blank piece of paper. To Rome it was, then. "We would like to announce our engagement."

Lady Atherton clasped her hands together and gave him a patronizing smile. "Lovely. Let me be the first to extend my congratulations to you both. Shall we announce as we go in to dinner?" Lady Atherwood now glanced to Lydia as the reigning maternal figure for Miss Arthur. *Dear Lord,* James thought, *Miss Arthur didn't have a chance in Hades if Lydia was her guiding light.*

"Delightful. Thank you, Lady Atherwood." Lydia continued with the small talk, greeting James's mother, her aunt, now that the announcement had been communicated. Lady Atherton turned to his mother as well.

"It's done now," John muttered. The prizefighter fidgeted, which only made him seem like an errant schoolboy. A thought that entertained James to no end.

"Cold feet?" James teased him.

"For my sister? To you?" John challenged him. His hands curled into fists, probably of their own volition. "I got some problems wif' it."

Lydia stepped nearer to her husband, excusing herself from the older women.

James leaned towards the couple as if he were making a conspiratorial jest. "Compose yourself, man. Your accent is slipping." James turned to Miss Arthur. "May I retrieve another cup of ratafia for you?"

"Thank you, my lord, but mayhap—" she said with a polite smile. One would never know she was not to the manner born. "If you will excuse me for one moment first."

He bowed to her, playing the felicitous suitor. As soon as she turned away, the prizefighter was on him.

"So help me, James, you hurt her, you harm her—"

"Tut tut, John. We're friends." James stepped back. The heat off the other man was positively stifling. "You and I, we're mates, aren't we? I should be insulted."

"Darling, let's take a walk, shall we?" Lydia pulled on her husband's arm, but she still shot daggers at James.

Henry would have had something droll to say right then. Something incisive and witty without being insulting. James missed him. Rose would have launched into a lecture about a woman's autonomy. Miss Arthur had agreed to wed him of her own volition. It wasn't as if he were some gothic novel blackguard, kidnapping her from a carriage on a stormy night.

A cloud of perfume suddenly enveloped him from the side. A signature scent. "How lovely to see you, my lord," tittered Lady Daniella. "It looks as though you have a new plaything."

James bowed in courtesy. Lady Daniella had married a wealthy textile factory owner a few seasons ago, but she'd kept her honorific. She was a woman who, after the birth of her first child, began to look for excitement elsewhere. Not unlike many other married women of the *ton*.

"You have a keen eye for where I place my attentions, Lady Daniella," he said, keeping his voice neutral.

"So you've finally tossed over your previous virgin? She was no longer virginal after you were done with her, I'm sure. But if you ever get tired of the innocent type, you know you may always call on me." Lady Daniella gave her best seductive smile.

He had no intention of correcting her belief that he'd pursued Rose because she was a virgin. And he certainly didn't care if Miss Arthur had spread her legs before or not. It was frankly none of his business. Instead, he gave Lady Daniella a terse smile and bowed his head, signaling her that she could leave. She flounced away, giving his mother an opening to lay her hand on his arm.

"Be kind to her, James." She had that motherly look about her, the kind that meant she was speaking to him as if he were a small child, not a man who controlled a dwindling fortune.

"Lady Daniella?" he asked, staring after the part in the crowd. But he knew that's not what his mother meant.

"This isn't Miss Arthur's world. She's trying very hard." She squeezed his arm.

It reminded him of school, where boys would grab each other and twist the skin furiously back and forth, making the flesh burn. He glanced at his mother. "I know."

His mother gave him a searching stare and then excused herself, leaving James to stare out the panes of glass to see lovers absconding into the darkened garden. Suddenly, Miss Arthur was beside him.

"I could not find my brother nor Lydia," Miss

Arthur said. "I'm afraid of what it will mean if I cannot find my chaperones."

Another dance was called. He should let another man cut in, ask for a dance, but as there were no other takers, only men milling about amongst the skirts, staring, whispering. He knew what they were saying—variations on Lady Daniella's theme. Well, they could go to hell.

"Another dance, then, Miss Arthur?" He offered his arm.

Relief flashed across her face before she took it. "This will surely make the announcement for us, won't it?"

"Indeed. We will let them whisper, and then confirm their suspicions. It will endear them to our cause," he said, maneuvering her through the crowd and onto the dance floor.

"How so?"

"For they love nothing more than to be right." The music struck as they took their places. When she smiled, he thought for the first time, *It's us against them.*

CHAPTER 3

"I can't believe I had to find out from a scandal sheet!" Mathilda hissed. Another bouquet of flowers, a voluminous collection of pink roses this time, sat plumped and aromatic on the table in the drawing room. Mrs. Tyler and Mathilda both stared at the extravagant display, unable to even make polite greetings as they stumbled in.

"It was very sudden," Pearl admitted. Was sudden the word for it? It was an escapade, a romp, or rather, it would be if there were more joy in it. She could barely admit to herself that she had wanted a whirlwind romance. The kind where she was so caught up in her love for her husband-to-be that she couldn't eat or sleep, where that faceless man had the same feelings for her. It had never occurred to her to give the man an occupation or even a coloring that she might favor. It was simply the idea that someone might be so enamored of her that he couldn't see straight.

Was that too much to ask? Yes. Yes it was. Instead of romance, she would receive a title. It was better than receiving neither.

"Is he so very handsome in close quarters? How did he dance? What does he smell like?" Mathilda asked, practically falling off the chair as she scooted closer and closer.

"MISS PERRY," Mrs. Tyler admonished. Her hearing had clearly not improved since Pearl's time in her boarding house. "DECORUM, GIRL."

Mathilda sat back in her chair, straightening her spine, but her expression was no less eager. Mathilda could fall in love with a storybook villain, let alone a man from a scandal sheet. It was no wonder that her parents kept her at Mrs. Tyler's. The rules were strict, and Mrs. Tyler had never allowed a single one of her charges to engage in unbecoming conduct. A challenge, to be sure, but the locks on the doors helped.

"I shall have you to tea once we are wed," Pearl offered, and even Mrs. Tyler looked pleased.

"He's so handsome from what I've seen," sighed Mathilda, which earned her a sharp elbow to the ribs from Mrs. Tyler.

"LOOKS ARE NO MEASURE OF A MAN," Mrs. Tyler said.

"But they don't hurt," whispered Mathilda, giving Pearl a conspiratorial grin.

"I'M SURE THE VISCOUNT WILL BE AN EXCELLENT AND PROPER HUSBAND."

Pearl nodded her agreement and took a sip of tea. It was all she could reasonably hope for, though it might take time to stow away those childish hopes of wanting more. But then again, it was not unheard of for a man to fall in love with his wife after they'd wed. Physical relations encouraged that sort of feeling; at least, Mrs. Coldcroft had said so. Given that the woman knew quite a lot about physical relations, her word had merit.

The image of Mrs. Coldcroft flashed in her mind. She looked as she had when they pinned up the wet wash. Her hands were wrinkled and red, and she wore a comfortable weight about her middle. *"I was a great beauty, I was. Not that you'd know it now. I picked the wrong man, and look at me. Be smarter than me, girl. Make your choices with your brain, not what's between your legs."*

Pearl didn't want anyone to know—her brother included—what she had seen, heard, and learned while living those months with Mrs. Coldcroft and her children. By then, Pearl had already started her monthlies. It wasn't Mrs. Coldcroft's fault what was said about her, not at all, even if John wouldn't hear otherwise.

Pearl had enjoyed living with her the most out of all the places she was shuffled to. Mrs. Coldcroft had been the best at mothering her children, always giving each one her attention when most needed.

"When is the wedding?" Mathilda asked, glancing at Mrs. Tyler, hoping for approval on this line of questioning.

"It shall be just before Michaelmas. I do hope you'll come." Pearl said it as a matter of politeness but then felt it settle deep inside her. She did hope for the attendance of a few friends that were hers and hers alone. Besides Mrs. Coldcroft, her childhood had kept her isolated in rooms full of people, never belonging, never able to be more than merely the lone Miss Pearl Arthur, interloper.

At Mrs. Tyler's, she had been the same as the other girls—an upwardly mobile young woman hoping to marry well, have a family, run a household. She and the others had enough education to converse well on a number of topics, but the focus had been on running a household, balancing a ledger, and hiring and managing staff. When Pearl left to live with Lydia and John, she felt quite capable of running a household. But she had not trained for anything else. Would it be enough to be a viscountess? Perhaps.

"OF COURSE WE SHALL ATTEND THE

WEDDING," Mrs. Tyler said, her plump arms crossing over her ample lap.

The mistress of the boarding house smelled of powder and cheap lavender soap, Pearl knew. There had been infrequent embraces, but Pearl cherished every one of them, and it felt as if there was an air of affection right then. She needed to grip it in both fists to hold on to it. She would take affection wherever she could find it.

❧

"Is this to your liking?" James asked, turning around as the tailor continued to scoot about his ankles, checking measurements.

"Trousers? In a church?" John said. "That cannot be considered correct."

"Times are changing, friend, and fashion changes with it." James held back a frustrated sigh. John had managed every aspect of the wedding thus far and had become a complete arse about it. Nothing was good enough for his sister—a sentiment that James respected, but he disliked being on the receiving end of the man's demands.

"I think I preferred the dove gray. It is a morning wedding, after all." John looked to the tailor, who nodded and backed off the tucking of James's cuffs.

"When else would we have a wedding?" James asked, doing his best to hide his growing testiness.

"In a rainstorm, with a special license, in front of an archbishop."

"What kind of nonsense have you been reading? Good God, man." James thrust the sleeves down. The tailor rushed over to collect the clothes as James shucked them. "And you're in luck. I don't know the archbishop, so I certainly could not roust him out of bed for a special license."

John looked offended. "You're marrying my sister and you don't even know the archbishop?"

James looked at him in disbelief. "What are you on about?"

John relaxed, showing a wide smile. "I'm joking."

"You don't seem like it," James grumbled, taking the next set of clothes from the tailor. "What's this now?"

"It's another set I thought might work better."

"It's the same bloody set as the first one."

"That was dove gray. This is slate gray," John explained.

"You know my measurements, yes?" James looked at the tailor, who nodded in response. "Then make whatever this popinjay has chosen fit me. I'm getting dressed. This is ridiculous."

John sputtered some excuses.

"You are ridiculous," James said, pulling on his own trousers.

"You wouldn't feel that way if it was your sister."

"Yes, I would still think you're ridiculous. My sister was married to a man twice her age. Me? I was fine about it. Small wedding, family chapel, she's happy, he's happy, it's done."

John looked skeptical.

"What, you want a badge to show what an arse you're being about this? You think you will show her how much you love her by fussing like this? You won't. Let her make her own choices."

The tailor packed away his tools and fabrics. "If you will excuse me, my lord. Sir."

"Thank you, Mr. Tavish." James dismissed him with a nod.

"She deserves to be fussed over," John grumbled.

"And from the looks of it, you and Lydia are doing just that. My God, does the *ton* know about your wedding planning? They should hire you for the next big event. You're both out of your minds."

"Do not minimize her James, or help me God, I—"

James did his best to not roll his eyes. Instead, to steady his friend, he gripped the man's forearms, which were tightening as he spoke. "I shall take care of her. She shall not want for anything. I swear it."

"On pain of my fists." John gritted his teeth.

James released him. "Which are far worse than death. At least with death, it's over. Your meat hooks take months to recover from. I remember." James turned to leave his dressing room and head to his study for a finger of brandy. "Dear Lord man, you make me want to start drinking early."

"I know about Lady Kinsley. So does at least half the *ton*."

Hearing Rose's name on the prizefighter's lips made James's heart seize. He would have rather John had knocked him with a belly-go-firster. He stopped in the doorway. "Then I'm sure you know that it is over."

"Is that why you proposed to Pearl? To appease your mistress?"

James hated the way it sounded coming from John's mouth. It made him sound weak and controlled. He struggled to find words that would make John stop worrying, but he couldn't.

"Will you go back to her? After you and Pearl are married?"

"If Pearl wishes to take a lover, I won't stop her." James turned to face his friend. He meant it. "I want Pearl to be happy. At least, as happy as she can be when shackled with the Andrepont title."

John shook his head. "The rest of the world doesn't see it as a burden. Not your name, and certainly not your person. Do you know how many shrill cries of 'he's so handsome' I've heard coming from the drawing room this past week? It makes a man physically ill."

James grinned. His good looks had never been in question, and he had never doubted them. The fact that his handsomeness was always equated in the next breath with his father was what bothered him. He didn't understand why the women of the *ton*—and some men for that matter—didn't run when they saw him. His father had wreaked havoc for long enough. Amazing how money and a flawless smile erased memories.

"Are you jealous those shrieks aren't about you? Do you miss the adulation from the ring?" James said. John had been Corinthian John, the champion prizefighter. There had been hordes of women eyeballing his muscles for years, dreaming of what it would feel like to be pressed up against them. Aristocratic women, barmaids, it didn't matter. In the ring, everyone loved a bare-chested champion.

John harrumphed. "Your cousin and my child are more than enough to keep me occupied. You think I have time for a flight of fancy? Besides, if you think what I would do to a man that wronged Pearl is bad, unleash Lydia on an unsuspecting flirt. She would destroy not only the person's face but their entire bloodline."

James laughed, and his shoulders relaxed. He and Lydia had always been a pair: the same dark temperament, inability to forgive, and gnawing need to unleash their inner demons. They both took to the boxing ring for it—though Lydia had managed to win herself a husband, even if she couldn't win a prizefight. James lifted his arm, ushering John towards the door. Hopefully marrying John's sister would make the family closer, not ruin his friendship.

❦

THOUGH THE WEEKS PASSED QUICKLY, Pearl had thought being engaged would be more exciting than it was. Flowers came at regular intervals. She and Andrepont walked in Hyde Park with Lydia as a chaperone. Pearl called on Lady Andrepont for tea. Both Andrepont and Pearl performed the steps, but she felt no closer to being wed and moving into a house with two strangers—two people she would live with for the rest of her life.

The banns were read. No one objected in church, and Lydia shielded her from any objections in the ballrooms. The dress was made. Lydia commandeered a cathedral for her. The scandal sheets gossiped about her gown, the flowers, how handsome her husband-to-be was. But it felt as interesting as plain porridge left out on the table.

In fact, the whole affair felt like something out of a theatrical put on by the girls at Mrs. Tyler's boarding house. She half-expected Andrepont to be a shadow puppet that she would mime kissing while holding a posy of frayed ribbons.

But this was her last night at her brother's house, and she lay in bed, feeling as if an entire cargo crate had been lowered onto her chest. She sat up just to breathe easier.

Tomorrow she would be a married woman. Her whole life would change. She would have authority; she would be the wife of a Peer. What did that even mean? She was so glad he was a viscount and not something loftier. There was likely a great deal more responsibility for a duke or some such. She didn't want to think about it.

There was a scratching at the door.

"Yes?" she called, pulling up the sheet to her neck. Is this how Andrepont would come to her tomorrow night? A scratching at the door? Or would he burst in? Or would he seduce her slowly in front of the fireplace? Hopefully it would be nothing like Mr. Jowls—not that she knew his name—who visited

Mrs. Coldcroft every three weeks like clockwork. He never spoke except to grunt out "thank ye" after he was done.

At least he thanked her. Did a husband thank his wife? Or would her husband be as disgusted by her as Gabriel had been?

But would Andrepont visit her bed? He'd been clear about not wanting children, and, well, there was only one way to ensure that didn't happen. But, if the marriage wasn't consummated, he could put her aside at any time. The marriage could be annulled. Pearl frowned. She didn't like that idea one bit.

The door opened and Lydia entered, holding a candle aloft.

"Did you need something?" Pearl asked.

Not long ago, Lydia had been a spongy, hollow-eyed version of herself. After a visit from a medicine woman, she improved by eating properly and following the prescribed treatments. She'd been doing so well that Pearl had stopped her daily inquiries after Lydia's health. In the whirlwind of planning, she hadn't thought of anyone but herself. Blimey, she hadn't even gotten up to the nursery to hold the baby in days. Guilt blanketed her.

"I don't need anything," Lydia said, completely contradicting Pearl's thoughts. Her sister-in-law left her candle on the nightstand and perched on Pearl's bed. Pearl scooted over to make room. "But it did occur to me that since you don't have a mother to tell you what to expect on your wedding night, you might need someone to explain it to you."

Pearl felt heat rush through her, head to toe. She blushed, not because she needed an explanation of marital relations, but rather, because she knew far more than she ought. How should she tell this to Lydia? She shouldn't. Because then Lydia might tell John, and then John would feel bad that he hadn't shielded her as well as he believed he had. What could she even say? "Oh."

"I thought I had some years to perfect this speech. But, here we are." Lydia cleared her throat. Her dark brows drew together, an almost comical contrast to their usual use as demonstrations of Lydia's disdain.

"Don't feel like it is necessary to—" Pearl said as Lydia began.

"Marriage is a contract," Lydia said. She looked up at Pearl as if she might stop, but Pearl gestured for her to continue. Lydia cleared her throat and straightened her shoulders. Pearl couldn't help but imagine a younger Lydia, one not so self-assured, not so bold. It didn't seem possible. "Part of that contract is reproduction of the family bloodline. Families like James's require an heir to inherit the estate and secure the financial needs of the women inside it."

"Did my brother prepare this speech for you?"

"No. Am I doing so poorly of a job? You must secure yourself, Pearl. When James dies, he will have no choice but to hand off the estate's money to the next heir. The properties are entailed. You will only have whatever portion you bring to the marriage, and only that which is specifically kept aside for you. No one knows what the next heir will do. Secure yourself by making the next heir."

Pearl sighed and sat back on her pillow. "You've met Andrepont, correct? Dark hair, you both do that same eyebrow thing?"

"There is no eyebrow thing."

Pearl stifled a laugh. "Andrepont is explicit about not wanting an heir. So I doubt there will be one."

"But—" Lydia's brow creased. "To make the marriage valid, it must be consummated. At least once."

Pearl leveled her gaze at her sister-in-law. "But if

he can annul the marriage and put me aside, then he gets whatever he wants. Whenever he wants it."

"But there would be no proof that he didn't. The assumption would be—"

"He's a Peer," Pearl said, sighing. Wealthy men got what they wanted. And if he acted impeccably, then who would be the wiser? "John says he made sure my dowry is untouchable in the marriage contract. I'll be fine, Lydia." Pearl kept her hands folded in her lap, trying very hard not to betray the idea that she had already thought about marital relations with Andrepont. That she'd already looked at those broad hands, wondering what it might feel like to have one gripping her hip. What it would feel like to breathe into that perfect jawline. She wasn't a saint. Of course she'd contemplated it in the darkness of her bedchamber.

"What I'm saying is, there's no way he won't give in to his...er..." Lydia looked uncomfortable.

Instead of supplying a word and smoothing over her sister-in-law's discomfiture, Pearl let the silence linger. "Yes?"

"Men have urges," Lydia started again.

"Only men?" Pearl had seen many a young woman just as randy as her male counterpart. But women carried far more of the burden of consequence, which might be why women were more likely to control themselves. Even when sometimes, they didn't.

"People—" Lydia admitted.

"Yes?"

"It has been referred to as a baser nature, but in the confines of marriage, theoretically, it becomes not base but something pleasant when both parties are adequately attracted to one another, and it often behooves a wife, in those circumstances..." Lydia trailed off. She sagged, but then her eyes sharpened. "You are letting me make a fool of myself, aren't you?"

Pearl gave the wide-eyed stare of an innocent.

"I knew it. You probably knew more about it before you got your monthlies than I did before I met your brother."

"My brother gave you that speech?" Pearl made a face.

"I'm trying to be kind!" Lydia shouted, pushing herself off the bed.

Pearl grabbed her wrist, pulling her back. "I know you are, and thank you. I shouldn't have the knowledge I have, but living in cramped quarters with married people, I've learned more than what Mrs. Tyler would deem appropriate." It was an understatement, but completely and utterly true.

"I want you to know what you need to know. I want you to be prepared. I want..." Lydia trailed off again.

Pearl knew Lydia was not good at showing emotion or letting others know she cared. It wasn't in her nature. But Pearl could see the intent behind her actions, the fuss she'd given to every detail of holding an outlandish wedding before Parliament broke for the Michaelmas holiday so the *ton* might have a chance to attend before the Peers retired to the countryside.

Pearl gripped Lydia's hand. "Thank you. I love you, too."

Lydia exhaled sharply and her shoulders dropped as if making a point. Sometimes it was like communicating with a horse, all body language and huffs.

"Tomorrow you become Lady Andrepont. I want you to be ready."

"Tomorrow I become your equal," Pearl said, knowing it would needle Lydia.

"Hardly. I'm still an earl's daughter. Nothing can take that birthright away. You'll still just be a viscountess. And married in, no less."

"Good night, Lydia."

Lydia smiled, picked up her candle, and left, softly closing the door behind her. Pearl stared at the ceiling and willed sleep to come. Instead, visions of Andrepont's strong, fine hands on her wedding night danced through her head.

❦

"JAMES," Henry said, his voice soft, as if he were chastising a child. The man's golden hair was pulled back into a queue, an old-fashioned style that somehow still suited him. They stood in Henry's study. As the host and ranking Peer, James couldn't sit until Henry invited him to do so, which he hadn't. "We talked about this."

"Let me see her," James begged. He'd had a lot to drink that day, it was true. He'd frequented his club—a rare occurrence—only to find the betting book filled with even more disgusting wagers than he'd imagined. Haglund and Tipton and likely some others bought him drinks, and he accepted every single one of them. It was stupid, and he ended up keeping company with several men he openly despised, but the lure of alcohol on the day before his wedding was powerful. Just like the lure of Rose was undeniable.

James staggered, and Henry relented, helping him into a chair.

"I'm not keeping her from you," Henry reminded him. "Rose has her own free will."

"Please," James whispered. "Will you not intercede on my behalf? Will you not act as saint and go-between?"

Henry looked down at him, and the disappointment in his crystalline light-blue eyes was as visceral as a blow to the head. James could admit that his friend was a beautiful man. It was his beauty that had gotten him into trouble at Eton all those years ago. Just as it was James's anger and desire to use his fists that made protecting Henry the easiest excuse to use them. They were opposites, and many a lady of the night had propositioned them for it. Where James was broadly muscled and dark and hard lines, Henry was golden and lithe and graceful. No wonder Rose chose him. His title was higher, his family more exulted, his beauty more classic.

"James, I..." Henry trailed off and looked away.

"Thank you, Henry," came Rose's voice from the doorway.

James's head came up with a snap so hard that his head swam. She looked precisely like herself. She wasn't ethereally beautiful like her husband. In fact, many would call Rose a touch plain. She looked every bit her namesake of an English rose in her coloring, but she had this way of comporting herself. She carried herself as if she might ascend into the clouds, or float along the water, or sit in a field of diamonds to amuse herself. She was wholly herself in a way that few people ever inhabited their bodies, and James wanted that. He wanted to be like that, to be comfortable in his skin like that, and he wanted to be near Rose to merely exist close to her.

"I've done as you've asked," James said, nearly choking on the words. "I'm to marry tomorrow."

"I know," Rose said, her hands folded in front of her.

Only then did James realize he was on his knees in front of Henry. He shouldn't show her such weakness. It was a whisper leftover from his father, his admonishments of manhood, how to present himself, how to subjugate a room to his will through charm, and if that didn't work, through force. He scrambled to his feet.

"Is this what you wanted? Truly wanted?" James demanded. He saw her sadness; he saw how weary she was. This had to be some game to her—a way to make him show his devotion. He would dance to her music; it wasn't like he hadn't already been dancing to another's tune for his entire life. So many arbitrary rules and customs, and he followed almost all of them. All of the ones that didn't feel like blatant fraud.

"James, I want you to be happy. If you are happy, then I am happy." Rose's face, the gray-blue eyes that he had seen open in ecstasy—ecstasy he brought about—everything about her was closed. Shut to him. There had to be a way to open her again.

He closed his eyes, trying to steady himself. The last bit of smuggled whisky from Sir Haglund had been a poor choice. He barely knew Haglund, and he'd been talking on and on about a reform bill. James had not disabused him of the fact that James had never taken his official seat in Parliament, nor anticipated ever doing so.

"I'm taking the steps you ask of me, Rose." James opened his eyes and focused on her. Her lips so pink and kissable. He knew her mouth so well.

"I ask nothing of you, James. Please don't sacrifice yourself for me. I won't reward you for it. I cannot."

"Rose," Henry said, his tone just as quiet.

"No, Henry. James clearly needs to be confronted with the truth. We have tried to be soft; we have tried to be kind. If that worked, he wouldn't be here now." Rose's folded hands dropped and curled into tight little fists.

She wouldn't use them. She wouldn't pummel her clenched hands into his chest, she wouldn't try to throw a facer. Rose used her mind, not her body. He braced for an onslaught of cruel words, but they didn't come, for Rose wasn't cruel. She was matter-of-fact. She was practical. She'd grown up friends with a vicar's daughter.

"Rose, why can't it be like it was?" James asked. It had been a whirlwind of fun and intimacy. The three of them traveling the world, drinking, laughing, reading books, playing chess, sketching, lounging in beautiful countrysides that were not their own. At night, James would abscond with Rose, and they would play and lounge in their own way. Sometimes Henry would join them in hopes of making an heir. But that was just a practical end to their evenings.

"Because I wasn't happy," Rose said.

"Of course you were," James protested. He could see in his mind's eye her body twisted in bed, arching under his hands, his mouth.

"Don't, James," Henry said.

"Don't what? I know she was happy—I saw it! I made her happy. I know that I did."

Rose folded her arms across her chest, accenting her gown's lace-covered bodice. It finally dawned on James that he had interrupted their dinner. They were dining together as a married couple. As befitted their rank, their social status, their class. "Please don't make me say it."

"Say what? Rose, tell me."

Her blush-tinted skin turned even pinker. "An intimate climax is not happiness, James. You place too much importance on fornicating. That alone can't make me happy. Or anyone."

James could do nothing but stare. He placed too much importance on fucking? That wasn't possible. It wasn't how the world worked, it wasn't how men and women worked. Everyone knew that women put the emphasis on the emotions of coupling while men were the ones who were able to fornicate without finding a deeper meaning.

He felt as if he'd been slapped.

"It would be better if you took your leave," Henry said. "I'll see you out."

"But—"

"We will attend tomorrow, James, but know we attend as the Marquis and the Marchioness, not as

Henry and Rose." Her eyelashes fluttered, but there was not a hint of a tear anywhere on her pale face.

She had stopped being Rose to him, hiding behind her title to make herself unreachable. Henry guided him by the elbow, as if he were a dazed young miss. This couldn't be happening. James found himself bundled into his carriage. Rose had dismissed him to his fate.

CHAPTER 4

St. George's was covered in an array of white and yellow and orange hothouse flowers. Pearl held a heavy bouquet of white and bluish-purple blooms. She felt as if she should identify these flowers, but her mind would only work at its most shallow depths. Her blue gossamer gown was dripping with so much lace and beading that she felt the weight of it even standing still. The words droned on, and she knew people stared at her back, but she barely felt present, though her body went hot and cold at intervals of blinding speed. She and Andrepont turned away from the bishop who had just blessed them. The pews were full of faces she didn't know, but she knew she ought to recognize them. Andrepont kissed her chastely. Her lips tingled at the brief, colorless contact. The organist began playing. They were supposed to walk down the aisle, but she couldn't move her feet. They felt as if they were encased in slippers made of ice blocks.

Her husband, this man standing next to her, felt unfamiliar and strange. He tucked her arm under his and whispered, "Look happy." He led her through the church, everyone staring. There were Lydia and John, both looking concerned. Next to them, Lydia's parents and the now Dowager Lady Andrepont.

There was Mrs. Tyler, who looked proud. She would be able to tout this marriage as the influence of her boarding school for years to come. Mathilda was nearby with her parents, which was the first time Pearl had ever seen them. As they reached the back of the church, she saw the staff from Lydia and John's house, and even a few friends from childhood, including Mrs. Coldcroft and her children, the youngest one's hair slicked back and still wet.

Outside, Andrepont handed her up into his carriage, a beautiful, sleek black thing with the crest painted on in gold. A large man closed the door behind them and whisked them away from the church, the crowd, God. She was numb.

"Are you well?" Andrepont asked her.

She nodded but still couldn't bring herself to speak.

"I apologize for being a bit of a brute and pushing you out of there, but I was worried you might faint."

London passed in a blur. She shook her head, hoping to communicate that all was well, she didn't mind at all.

"We'll get you a cup of tea when we get home, and you'll be good as new to change for the wedding breakfast."

Another event. She should be grateful. She was grateful. She looked down at her gown, the culmination of so many hours of painstaking work. It was gorgeous and the palest blue with silver bangles stitched in intricate patterns. She'd never worn a gown so incredible—never seen one on anyone else, for that matter.

Her husband was the same: incredible, and never what she'd imagined. He wore a dove-gray coat and a brilliant blue damask waistcoat with fine stitching that matched the pale blue of her gown. He was tailored and fitted, looking brooding and not at all joyful as his green eyes bored into her. As if he might just see through her.

"Husband," she said aloud, testing out the word.

"You may call me James if you like, but if that's too familiar, continue to call me Andrepont. I shan't mind."

She nodded.

"Would you prefer I address you as Lady Andrepont? Or would you prefer I use your Christian name?"

"Please, refer to me as Pearl," she said, trying hard not to blush. She wanted to hear that gravelly timber curling around her name. Flashes of acts she'd heard and seen danced through her mind, replacing the original participants with herself and *James*. She wanted to hear him say her name.

Why her mind flashed to such a subject at this inappropriate juncture, she couldn't fathom. But then, nothing about the day had made sense.

"Very well, then. Pearl. If you are feeling up to it, my housekeeper would like to meet with you and introduce the staff before you change. They would like to welcome you to your new home."

She had a home, finally. A place that she couldn't be forcibly torn from by money or capriciousness. She vowed that this manor would be her last residence, no matter what it took to stay. She glanced at her husband, gazing out the window. They would consummate this marriage, for Pearl wouldn't allow him to put her aside.

They pulled into the driveway of the Mayfair estate and Pearl felt her stomach drop. She'd been here before—recently, even—to take a polite tea with Lady Andrepont, but now, entering it as her own felt beyond her understanding. The staff lined up outside the front door, the footmen wearing the red-and-black livery of the Andrepont title.

The carriage stopped and the driver came around,

again the large man who seemed overly familiar with her husband. With James. Her stomach turned over. This was her life. She'd made her choices.

She wondered what Mrs. Coldcroft would say to her now, in this moment. Pearl swallowed hard and took James's hand to step out of the carriage.

James escorted her to the man and woman standing in the center of all these people. The housekeeper, whom James introduced as Mrs. Foraker, was a kind-looking woman with fading auburn hair. She was compact in her build and looked efficient and competent. There was no gleam of familiarity or friendship there, but Pearl supposed that wouldn't be becoming when meeting the new mistress of the house. Next was the butler, Mr. Barton. He was much older, stern, his hair completely white and thinning. He eyed her with his rheumy gaze and nodded his respect to her.

James took his leave, instructing Mrs. Foraker to continue the introductions, including a young Miss Lily, who would be her new lady's maid. She was a pretty girl with dark hair and dark eyes. There was a stab of jealousy in Pearl's heart, for she had always wanted thick, dark tresses like Lily's, not the fine reddish-gold ones that plagued her.

This would be the girl who would help Pearl dress and undress. The girl that would know the secrets of Pearl's monthlies and pregnancies. She would be the temptation that would dangle in front of James every day.

Pearl caught herself. There was no reason to be jealous of her lady's maid's beauty. How absurd. Pearl silently chastised herself and smiled at the staff that surrounded her. She could perform this role, lady of the house. She smiled at them, gave a few quick words that she didn't remember, and urged Lily and Mrs. Foraker to show her the rooms that were meant for her.

She needed several cups of tea before the guests arrived.

❧

JAMES ALREADY HAD MORE than he'd bargained for. It was his wedding day and he was fighting a pounding headache. He'd already taken some headache powder and dashed down some terribly burnt coffee. His staff still hadn't the hang of roasting the coffee beans, but it had helped. He'd done his duty. He had made a pledge, in a church, in front of a man of God. He was married, obligated, and shackled.

But his bile threatened to come up again when he thought of last night's confrontation with Rose. How dare she say she hadn't been happy? How could she not have been happy? Her husband gave her every indulgence in the world—travel, books, wine, food—and James had given her everything else—sweating nights, bellows of pleasure, devotion with every part of his body.

She'd been at the church. She and Henry both, sitting up front, near his mother. They were the highest-ranked Peers in attendance, and by God, they looked perfect. Their clothes, their hair, even the subtle diamonds that glinted from Rose's ears. He noted that she hadn't worn the rubies he'd given her. Rubies because his family's colors were red and black. She hadn't wanted them when he'd gifted them. He had been earnest, wanting some way to lay claim to her. In the end, she'd accepted, but he'd never seen her wear the earbobs.

Glancing about his private study, he realized it was a mess. He should have asked the maids to straighten up. He allowed them in a few times a month—just to keep things tidy. But he didn't want them disturbing the piles of music near the piano or noting how much he drank from his decanters. This was where he was himself, and no one could watch him or judge him or make him playact a role meant for his title or his social status or his wealth. He almost poured himself a finger or two of whisky but decided against it given that he was to have more people in his house than he preferred.

Instead, he sat and played Mozart sonatas. He liked them for the mornings—Mozart was fresh and light, given all the scale work included. Really, James was a bit of a snob about it. If musicians did their daily major and minor scale work, they could practically sightread anything by Mozart. Know the patterns and the music unraveled itself like one long thread. Without realizing how much time was passing, James worked his way through several sonatas.

A soft knock on the door alerted him to the next bit of his day. The family. The brunch. The speeches. The marriage. Couldn't he just go back to his piano? Everything made more sense when he was at the instrument. It was a place where he had always been the absolute master. The only place where he could make a decision that didn't feel as if he was imposing his will on others.

Music was the first and only way he had made his father bend to his bidding, not the other way around. Music had been his version of striking back at the suffocating brutality of the former viscount. The man whose title James wore like a coat he had to thrust his arms into every morning.

But no. Obligation first. Duty was something he instinctively shrugged away from, escaping it as he had escaped his father's fists on more than one occasion, though he had lighter punishments than likely everyone else in the house. Going off to school was a relief and also a source of unending shame because he'd left his mother and half-sister unprotected with that man.

James stood and swung his coat back on, covering his shirtsleeves. The mirror by the door allowed him to check his cravat, and deeming himself presentable, he opened the door to find Barton.

After a few last-minute checks about the wine, James found his way to the drawing room, where they would be escorted into the dining room once it was fully ready. But for now, James needed to be the host. The husband. The viscount. His nightmare.

❧

PEARL WAS the first person in the drawing room, seconded by Lady Andrepont. The older woman looked beautiful and harsh. The angled cheekbones she shared with her son looked somehow sharper on her. She was elegant in her pale-yellow gown, different from what she had worn at the church ceremony. Of course they would all change clothing. They had so much wealth to show off, it would only be fitting.

Pearl couldn't help the feelings that bubbled inside her. The unfairness, the pomp. She was supposed to look at the aristocracy and view them as her betters, she knew that. But now that she was on the inside of the rarefied set, living in their homes, eating at their tables, it was impossible to view them in any other way than exactly like the people in humbler circumstances. Would this woman be so beautiful if she'd had a lifetime of uncertainty about where her next meal would come from? Or even less than that, would she be this beautiful if she were not adorned with jewels and decked in the finest fabrics?

Well, that comparison was unfair because this particular woman would be breathtaking no matter where she stood. One minute she appeared strong and commanding, but with the shift of her head, she appeared meek and biddable. Pearl needed to learn that skill. She only knew how to appear meek and biddable, and as a viscountess, she needed to appear to be in command of at least herself.

Lady Andrepont came forward and grasped her hands. "Welcome to the family. May I call you Pearl?"

Pearl swallowed hard. Family. She was in a family. She had a mother. Her stomach clutched in anticipation. Words got stuck in her mouth, unable to move. So she nodded instead.

"We have much to discuss, you know. I've run this household for many years, and I am more than happy to hand over the reins if you are comfortable."

Pearl swallowed the lump in her throat. "Whatever is best for you, my lady."

Her mother-in-law gave her a warm smile, and again her bearing transformed, now into a Madonna-like painting. "Ah, we are the same rank, you and I. And we share a title, no less. I hope you will be happier wearing it than I have been."

"What should I call you?" Pearl asked, not realizing until the words were out that she felt desperate to call this woman *mother*, if for no other reason than she'd never known her own.

Lady Andrepont cocked her head to the side. "What do you think would be appropriate?"

Realizing the woman's surname was Wallingford, she said, "Mother Wallingford?"

But instead of creating a bond, the other woman flinched. She dropped Pearl's hands and stepped away.

Before either of them could speak, the butler entered, announcing a stream of guests.

Pearl still didn't have a mother then. She steeled her heart and smiled, performing the part of the perfect bride to the best of her ability, ignoring the throbbing void Lady Andrepont's unwilling flinch had created.

The wedding breakfast proceeded without any

hiccups. Pearl couldn't remember what she ate or drank, but it was likely exquisite. They adjourned to the back garden, Lady Andrepont's domain, and took tea and cake out of doors, as it hadn't rained, by some miracle. There were still some autumn blooms in the garden, and the chill felt invigorating after the crush of the day.

By the time the clock in the drawing room struck four, the guests had all left, leaving the three of them together. They returned to the drawing room.

"Sherry?" Lady Andrepont suggested.

Pearl glanced to James for permission, but he wasn't paying attention. She should decline since she didn't know the rules of this household.

"You're a married woman now, Pearl. Do as you wish," Lady Andrepont said, watching her glances.

Pearl nodded, embarrassed to be caught out. She only wanted to do what was right. What would please James. She'd already made a hash of it with Lady Andrepont, suggesting that she might call her *mother*. It was a mistake, and she didn't know how long it would take to recover their relationship from her blunder.

"You needn't have any on my account, either. I'm perfectly well acquainted with drinking alone."

Pearl looked up in shock at the woman's admission. James's head lolled in their direction.

"One might say it's a family pastime," James said with a sardonic smile.

His expression curdled her stomach. She'd assumed his lip-curling sneer was a front for everyone else. But it appeared here, where the only audience was herself and his mother. Which one did he wear it for? Now that they were married, would he come to resent her? Did he already? Had she made a mistake tying herself to this man?

Well, she'd a title out of it. She had a home that was hers. She had stability and an erstwhile parent and some semblance of freedom. It was more than she'd ever had, which made it a good choice. A smart choice. Mrs. Coldcroft would no doubt give a nod of approval.

And he was handsome. There was no question that his jaw, which could cut glass, was striking. His eyes, the color of emeralds, were mesmerizing. Even with a loathsome personality, many, many women would be happy to bed him. Pearl would. And she knew enough to enjoy it. And damn him, she *would* enjoy it, just to spite him. Even if he was disgusted with her, as Gabriel had been. They were shackled now and she wasn't about to give up a home.

"Sherry for you, too, darling?" Lady Andrepont asked, rising to ring the for a footman.

Pearl hoped he would say yes. She wanted to know him better, spend time with him. They could make this union work well, if only he would try. Love was absolutely on the table, if he was interested. She could turn a sarcastic personality into something she could bear, even enjoy. She'd become friends with Lydia, hadn't she?

Instead, James stood. "No, thank you. I think I will go divest myself of some ill-gotten whisky down in my study."

Lady Andrepont nodded and rang for the servants.

"My lady," James said, bowing to her.

Pearl wanted to hear possession in his voice. She wanted to hear an emphasis on the word *my*. But there wasn't. It was the same intonation he'd used on every woman who deserved the phrase.

He went to his mother and bowed again. "My lady mother."

His mother smiled indulgently. "There are two ladies in the house now."

"Indeed," James said.

Pearl waited for a snide comment about being a

man outnumbered or burdened or somehow put upon. She braced for it, waiting for a joke to show the truth of how unwanted she was. She'd heard that joke her entire childhood, and nothing she contributed had ever changed that horrible humor.

"I'll be fending off hordes of adorers once they hear of so much beauty in one household." James inclined his head towards Pearl one more time and took his leave.

At least his joke hadn't been at her expense. Pearl's shoulders relaxed.

Lady Andrepont didn't speak once the sherry arrived. They both accepted a glass, and Lady Andrepont stood at the window, watching storm clouds roll in and the autumn sky darken.

Pearl finished her sherry and, feeling pleasantly fuzzy, was about to take her leave when her mother-in-law broke the silence instead.

"This hasn't been a happy household, Pearl. I hope you can forgive us our anger and our sadness." Lady Andrepont turned to look at her. Rain began to fall outside, the sound beating a steady rhythm.

Not knowing what to say, and distracted by the sound of splatters against the windows and the slate outside, Pearl stood, fluffing the skirts of her beautiful gown one more time. "I hope that whatever made you feel that way is gone."

Lady Andrepont chuckled wryly. "Most assuredly gone. But we are a bit strange because of it. I want you to know that we are trying. We want to welcome you. I am very pleased my son has chosen someone to marry. I hope you can remember that."

Pearl curtsied, the only thing she could think to do in that moment. "Thank you, my lady."

Instead of chastising her formality or giving Pearl a hint of how she should address her, Lady Andrepont crossed the room to put her empty sherry glass on the tray next to Pearl's. "Good night, Pearl."

And with that, Pearl was left in the drawing room alone. On her wedding night.

※

BEETHOVEN FELT good in his hands. The Waldstein was a frenetic piece, but it felt right for a day like today. His wedding day. It was as if the most absurd thing that could have happened had actually occurred. What life was this?

The octave path in his right hand fell into a light-hearted trill. And then the meandering path of sixteenth notes. His left hand was fatiguing with the repetitive motion of the bass. It was challenging to go at tempo and not let the rhythms sweep him away and ultimately fall apart. Even if that's exactly what he'd allowed to happen.

He stopped and stretched out his left hand, allowing himself another swig of the whisky that he kept on the shoulder of the piano. His passion for Rose had gotten away from him. And that lack of control had...what? Scared her? Repulsed her? He had always held that passion was good—it was the opposite of what his father had tried to instill in him. His father, the monster who had cold-bloodedly assaulted women of all stations across London for decades. Whom no one would stop. No man dared confront or refuse. He'd held power and secrets and the ability to charm those who didn't know what kind of demon lurked underneath his chiseled features.

James looked exactly like him, he knew. What he inherited from his mother only sharpened his father's features. When he was younger, he would attend parties or enter taverns and women would gasp or outright flee his presence. All because he looked like the demon, and who knew if the son was strong enough to refuse the legacy of his blood? His father had been charming and proper, needing the armor of good manners in addition to his title and money to keep his atrocities covered.

But James had no intention of such trespasses and instead cultivated a lackadaisical air, which seemed to charm his own generation even if it did nothing but irritate the older one. Which was fine with him, as the older generation was complicit with his father. And to be perfectly frank, fuck every single one of those weak cowards.

But that was how he'd ended up here, on his wedding night. He had no intention of visiting Pearl tonight or any night. Her bed was her own, and he would be damned if he forced her or even suggested he share it. That was his father. He was his own man, and outside of the boxing ring, he wouldn't hurt anyone. Well, unless they absolutely deserved it. He thought of when he'd shot Lord Denby in the leg to prevent Lydia from doing something reckless. But that had been to save Lydia.

He'd witnessed older boys try to prey on Henry when they were children, and he'd gone down swinging. It was too much like what he'd witnessed at home, but he was more of a size with those aggressors. Both Henry and he had bruises to nurse for a bit, but no real harm had been done. Henry stuck close to him after that. And that violence—that had been to save Henry.

There was a sharp two-knock rap on the door, which signaled his mother. No servant would knock unless absolutely necessary, and even then, it was a soft scratching, not the confident and succinct *knock-knock* that his mother favored.

"Enter," he called, picking up his glass and swiveling around on his stool. He lowered the lid of the keyboard so he could recline his elbow on it. He felt one of her speeches coming on.

His mother entered, doing her customary survey-at-a-glance of his domain. Her nose wrinkled, as it typically did. "When did the maids last come in here?"

Two weeks ago, he knew. But instead, he shrugged and sipped his whisky. He knew it needed to be cleaned, and he would order it tomorrow, or perhaps the next day, depending on how drunk he got tonight. "Did you require some assistance?"

She sniffed and stiffened her spine. No one but a queen could out-regal his mother. She'd endured all manner of humiliation and pain and yet was still compassionate. Not warm, as no one in their service would ever describe them as a loving duo, but his mother was kind, even thoughtful. Aloof, yes, but given her life, who wouldn't be reserved? It was a badge of honor, as far as James was concerned.

"Your wife is quite young."

Ah. He was in for her tangential attacks this evening. She wouldn't speak on what she actually meant, so he'd have to guess at her motives. "Is she? I hadn't noticed."

"Very eager to please."

James raised a finger to point at his mother. She hated that. "That I agree with. Excellent observation, Mother."

"Sparring with me gets you nowhere with her. Be gentle with her, James. She's trying very hard." Her hands relaxed and interlaced.

"You've mentioned. Besides, I didn't intend to get married."

Her eyebrow quirked up, a family habit. "And yet, you have. The bishop asked if you wished to, and as I recall, sitting there from the front row, I distinctly heard you say that you did."

He shook his head. "You know what I mean."

"Do I? What I know is that my son, a wealthy, titled landowner in his thirties, married a young girl with money and no family. I doubt she could have forced the circumstances on you."

Ire built in James. "It's not like I could have backed out without ruining her reputation."

"Then why did you ask her? Did her brother force it on you?"

"Of course not," James said quickly.

"Was it a drunken bet?" Her voice went cold.

She thought so little of him. "I would never."

Her arms folded across her chest, a sure sign he would get an earful. He flinched preemptively. He hated when he truly upset her. Working her into a huff was one thing, but the full force of her anger was terrible when unleashed. Her truths were brutal, knives that could never be sheathed.

"You have every advantage. Not just in life, but in this house and in your new marriage. Smiling at her and letting her keep access to her own dowry is one thing, but treating her like an actual person is another. This is your mess and your responsibility."

James set his jaw. As if he wasn't entirely aware of his advantages. He had never been unaware of them. No one would let him forget. Not unless he was in the ring or at the piano.

"And this is about your mistress? That bluestocking marchioness? She already has a husband, James. She has what she needs. That girl sitting alone upstairs in that drawing room has nothing."

"Don't talk about Rose. You know nothing about it." It was all he could do not to growl at his mother.

"I know plenty about infidelity. And that girl deserves to know what sty she's entered, but I have a sneaking suspicion that she doesn't."

"What do you want of me?" James stood and threw back the last of the whisky. "What would you have me do?"

She stiffened again. James knew she'd never fought in the ring—nothing so unladylike for her—but she would have made one hell of a fighter. "I want you to at least try to be a good husband. And sleep in the master bedroom, not sprawled out here like some kind of wastrel." She waved in the general direction of the couch he'd spent many a night on.

"I'm not sleeping in that bed." His father's bed. His father's room. He'd never moved in, and for good reason.

"I replaced the bed long ago. It isn't the same one. None of the furniture is the same. Make it yours and erase him," his mother commanded. "And take care of your wife." She whirled around, her skirts spinning as she left.

James stalked across the room and slammed the door shut behind her. Back to the Waldstein he went, grateful for one of the most technically challenging pieces Beethoven had written thus far.

❦

THE LOVELY MISS Lily helped Pearl undress and tidy away her beautiful clothes. Pearl knew that the very rich and fashionable didn't wear a gown twice in one season, but the clothes were so exquisite she wanted to don them again. Lily had taken Pearl's hair down and brushed it until it shone like fresh copper.

The bedchamber was much more than Pearl had expected. Lady Andrepont had asked if she liked it, and Pearl could barely keep her mouth from hanging open at the splendor of it. The walls were papered in a jewel-toned floral pattern on a dark-green background. A heavy walnut bed frame dominated the room, with velvet curtains gathered at each bedpost ready to shut out the world if need be. The dressing room was bigger than some of the flats she'd lived in as a child. This room had been designed as a sanctuary, full of cozy hiding places.

The bathing area had a tub that was permanently left there, just for her own private use. Servants had hauled hot water up in anticipation of her desire to bathe, and she had slipped in lavender oil and rose petals.

After Pearl put on her wedding night lingerie—which embarrassed her, no matter Lily's assurances—she sat in front of the fire with a novel, waiting. She picked at the silky robe, a blush color that made her skin appear more luminous than its typically freckled pink. The gown went past her feet, which was her own insistence.

The seamstress had told her it wasn't wise to have so much fabric, as it could trip her or her husband on a night that should go without clumsiness, but Pearl knew she needed to be covered. James need not see how overly large her peasant feet were. And not in the idyllic painting-of-dairymaids way. In the way of actual dairymaids hauling heavy pails of milk through London with yokes across their shoulders.

The book should have been engrossing. But when Pearl looked up, she realized the fire had dwindled and she had no memory of anything that had happened on the page. There was a fine clock on the mantel, and it was almost midnight. Pearl hadn't heard so much as a stirring from the master bedchamber next to hers.

She crept over to the adjoining door. This was the conjugal door. The one where, in some fantasies, James would sweep through wearing nothing but his breeches and lawn shirt, professing his insatiable desire for her. She listened at the keyhole, glad she would be able to lock it if she wanted. But there was nothing to hear.

There was something to be said for etiquette, so Pearl scratched at the door. Having absolutely no response, she boldly pushed the door open and crept in to find nothing but darkness. Glowing embers in the fireplace. The bed crisp and made up. There was nothing in there. No piece of James. No sign of anyone. The cold of the room was assuredly pushing into hers, and so she quickly returned to her own domain.

Well. Perhaps he was nervous. After all, she was Corinthian John's little sister. James wouldn't be the first man scared off of romance because of her brother. But wouldn't that change since they were married?

It had been a long day. An arduous day, really. There would be plenty of nights ahead for them to consummate their marriage. And if he wasn't looking forward to it, then neither was she.

So she banked the fire, snuffed her candle, and crawled beneath the bedcovers. Wedding night be damned.

✿❧

CHAPTER 5

James awoke to a crisp *knock-knock* on his study door. He raised his head, which caused his neck to cramp. His head throbbed, his mouth was dry, and he felt like his eyeballs might pop out of their sockets. His stomach turned over as he pulled himself upright.

"What?" he croaked. The instant he spoke, his head clanged like a bell, as if he were back in that damned drafty church. There was a stash of headache powder in the desk, if only he could cross the room. It might as well have been on the Continent, for all he could get to it.

His mother swept in, looking fresh and well-rested. "I see you didn't take my advice."

He grimaced, hoping it was a facsimile of a courteous smile.

"Motherly instincts would insist that I take pity on you, but at the moment I cannot seem to bring myself to it."

"Charming," James managed to say. He stood and the room swam. His bowels clenched. He had a chamber pot in here somewhere. "So you've decided to come and...what exactly? Mock your only child?"

"Part of parenting, not that you would know, is doing what is best for your child, even to his detriment." She walked over to the desk, far too quick for any human at this hour. It seemed that she knew exactly where the headache powder was. She held it up for him to see and, glancing about, found only a dry ewer that had once held water. "James. This is beyond a broken heart."

"Is it? And how exactly would you know? You'd have to love someone first."

Her expression tightened, and he knew he'd hit a mark he should have avoided. She rarely spoke of her life before his father, and he knew she'd been quite young when they married. It's possible she'd had some love before him, but there was no way his father would have tolerated a love during their marriage. And God knew she hadn't done anything since his father's death.

Instead of responding to his insult, she pulled an envelope from her skirt pocket. "This has been sitting on your tray, awaiting your attention for a week." She slapped the envelope down on the desk. "It's an invitation to a ball tonight. For you and your bride. Pearl seems the type that would enjoy a ball. Take her. Be kind."

"How do you know what is inside a sealed envelope? Are you clairvoyant now?" He managed to stumble over to the desk and wrested the packet of headache powder away from her. Water be damned.

"Because I've received word from Lady Haglund. She attended the wedding yesterday, not that you would remember. She was hoping to persuade the newlywed couple to join them as a celebration. She needs to know if she should order extra champagne for a toast."

James poured the powder directly into his mouth. It was bitter and turned to paste.

"That's not how you take that," his mother said, folding her arms across her chest.

He coughed, unable to respond. The powder

stuck in his throat. In fact, he might not ever be able to open his mouth again. He thumped his chest with his fist. His mother just stared at him until he managed to generate enough saliva. As he struggled, he wondered if Rose and Henry would be at the ball. He could at least see them across the room, anything to make him feel whole again. "Please send a note to Lady Haglund that Pearl and I will attend. And thank her for her generosity."

"Wonderful. I'll ring for some water." She stepped over a portion of rug that had rolled up and past a pile of music on the floor. "And the maids. Really, James. This is untenable."

৩৯৩

AFTER PEARL DRESSED and dismissed Lily, she peeked through the adjoining door. As she suspected, the room had not been disturbed. Now, Pearl sat expectantly at breakfast. She figured that Lady Andrepont would take a tray in her room, as many married women did. But Pearl had hoped she might see a glimpse of her husband.

There was a small buffet set out, and Pearl enjoyed the lovely morning light streaming through the windows. Despite the room's obvious opulence, the chandelier's glittering crystals, the heavy, polished furniture that contained displays of silver and porcelain, Pearl found it a pleasant experience. Some of the worst flats she'd lived in had no windows to let in light and air. Strange how something so universal as the sun was still a luxury.

Mr. Barton, the butler, attended her himself, bringing a pot of steaming hot water for her tea. Lydia had very fine morning tea, which she'd promised to send along if Lady Andrepont's choices were lacking.

"Thank you, Mr. Barton," Pearl said, doing her

best not to rub her hands together like a greedy child. Nothing was better in the morning than a dark brew.

Knowing that eventually she would be the keeper of the tea chest key, Pearl asked Mr. Barton to find the housekeeper, Mrs. Foraker, so they might go over household duties and traditions. Lady Andrepont should also be present, but perhaps that was not necessary, as the dowager seemed to be as scarce as Pearl's new husband.

"Mrs. Foraker usually attends to her duties and then meets with Lady Andrepont during the mornings, but I will see that she knows you require her services, my lady." Mr. Barton bowed to her, which made Pearl blush.

She shouldn't blush when a servant was showing respect. She was a viscountess. Perhaps not the most well-bred one, or well-prepared, but she was here now, and this was the respect conferred to a title such as hers. It was one of the many things she would have to get used to. "Thank you again, Mr. Barton."

Finishing her meal, Pearl grew restless alone in the large dining room. There was furniture on one end, holding some exquisite teapots. Taking her cup and saucer with her, she decided to explore. It was her house now, of course. She had every right to poke around, even if it felt as if she would be scolded at any moment.

Pearl set her tea on the table behind her and opened the glass front cabinet. Several pieces were of typical English make, but with exquisite decoration, including a smooth, cream-colored Wedgwood Queen's Ware teapot. Displayed next to it was a smaller teapot, glazed blue with a quail pattern of the Kakiemon style, another in the blue and white décor typical of Delftware. Had the Andreponts received these as gifts? Or had Lady Andrepont traveled and obtained them? It would certainly be a conversation starter with her mother-in-law, and Mrs. Tyler would be pleased that the details of serving ware that had been outlined in Pearl's education were coming to fruition.

Towards the back, tucked in the second row, as if there weren't enough room to display it, was an odd mud-green ceramic teapot. It lacked the high quality of the other vessels and had no lacquer or shine to it. Surely, they didn't use a teapot that had no finish to it? Pearl pulled it from its place and opened the lid to see if there were tea stains from use.

Curious. There was a divider inside the teapot. Two separate compartments. What kind of tea would be served in such a way? Perhaps one compartment held the tea leaves and the other held hot water, so that the tea might not over-steep? She looked at the mechanics again, and there wasn't a way for the compartments to mix. How peculiar. She would definitely bring this up to Lady Andrepont. How fascinating.

There were even holes in the handle. They were small, and easily overlooked, but why on earth would a teapot need holes in its handle?

She replaced the odd vessel in the cupboard and continued her turn about the room. Finally, Mrs. Foraker joined her.

"My lady, you needed me?" The keys on her belt jangled from her sudden stop. Mrs. Foraker looked like competence. She was likely a handful of years older than Lady Andrepont, and her hair was pulled back into a tight and business-like chignon. This was the woman who knew the household backwards and forwards. Someone Pearl should befriend.

"Only when you have a moment. I would love an introduction to the household books from you and Lady Andrepont. At your convenience, of course." Pearl gave her best smile, trying to transmit that she accepted Mrs. Foraker's expertise and authority in the matter.

"Certainly, my lady. My convenience is at the beck and call of yours."

"But not at the expense of Lady Andrepont. If she has further needs of your time, then please attend to her first."

Mrs. Foraker's eyes softened, which meant this interview was already a success. "Yes, my lady. And I was asked to pass this along to you, as well." The housekeeper pulled an envelope out of her skirt pocket and handed it to Pearl. "It is for this evening. I've already alerted Lily. She's upstairs now sorting your wearable gowns."

Pearl didn't bother to hide her surprise as she scanned the invitation. "Tonight?"

Mrs. Foraker inclined her head.

"That seems sudden, don't you think?" Pearl scanned the invitation and saw the postmark was from a week prior. "I should hope for more warning than this in the future." Pearl grimaced at the words as they came out of her mouth. This wasn't the housekeeper's fault, but her words implied that it was. Whatever goodwill Pearl had managed to evoke earlier evaporated.

Mrs. Foraker looked at her shoes.

"Well, then. It seems I must forego our household meeting and instead make preparations for a ball." Pearl gave Mrs. Foraker a smile that she hoped seemed genuinely happy. Pearl wanted to feel that way. It was her first day as a married woman, after all.

Mrs. Foraker left the room, and Pearl did her best not to grind her teeth in frustration. Opportunities. These were all opportunities, and she should be happy. So she would be.

※

PHILLIP HARANGUED JAMES about his cravat. "It needs a pin, my lord, or else it won't stay."

James fidgeted. He needed something, but he had no idea what. He felt like he was crawling out of his skin. This was when he needed to stay home and train in his private gym. Instead: Lady Haglund's soiree and Miss Arthur. Or rather, Pearl.

He couldn't bring himself to call her his *wife*. The idea that he possessed a wife was…unimaginable. But here he was. He felt like he was falling into his father's mold inch by inch, no matter how hard he kicked. He needed Rose's pragmatic perspective on his predicament, Henry's gentle teasing. He was like an opium addict, craving his next hit of their company. "Fine. Cravat pin."

Phillip picked up a tray with three pins laid out. One was a deep red jewel, the next was a simple gold with an "A" stamped on it, and the third was covered in small seed pearls.

James raised his brow. "Are you going for obvious, or is that truly a stylistic choice?" His waistcoat was a red damask, and he wore black trousers and a black coat. He was already in family colors. He felt as if he should be clad in all black. Mourning for who he'd been, which was, namely, not his father.

"Pardon me, my lord, but I don't believe anyone had ever described you as subtle." Phillip smiled politely as he delivered his insult.

James harrumphed at his valet's wit. "Valid point. Then let's support the family, shall we?"

Phillip looked down at all three choices, and James realized that any of those pins could be construed as supporting the family. What his mother had said earlier echoed in his mind. *Be kind to her.*

"Pearl it is," James said, and Phillip looked inordinately pleased. There was some validation there, knowing that at least one person was glad he was nice to the new viscountess.

Phillip deftly retied the cravat, a complicated

knot that James didn't know the name of. There were too many fashions, and he certainly couldn't keep up.

That must be the way around this Andrepont destiny. James already had his father's looks, his remaining wealth, his title. The change he could control was his marriage. He'd courted Pearl with extravagant flowers and his time. He could support his viscountess in the same means. Lydia had long ago counseled him that effort was what women truly wanted.

Money and good looks were helpful, which he also had, but Lydia had been correct about effort—at least, that had borne true with Rose. When he had courted her, he read the books she'd recommended, visited the museum when she'd asked. He was terrible at chess, but he'd allowed both Henry and Rose to wallop him time after time because it was a way to spend time together.

Thinking back on it, more often it was Henry and Rose playing chess with him lounging nearby, occupying himself with a sketchbook or some such. Even stranger, he didn't feel resentment during those times. It was part of Henry and Rose's marriage, their connection to each other. He searched for a sense of rejection now, looking back on it, but could find none. Why would he be jealous that they could enjoy a game together?

Selfishly, he had always viewed himself as the center of their trio, the man who could satisfy Rose. But perhaps, it hadn't been that way at all. Henry had married Rose out of necessity, and Rose was given no choice in the matter. That she'd been able to forgive Henry at all was one of the extraordinary things about Rose. Henry had once accused James of only wanting Rose because he could never marry her: she had been safe. And she was easy to love—agreeable, pleasant, kind.

When she wasn't any of those things, James

merely left her presence. Not always something you could do with a spouse. He wondered what Rose would say about his pearl cravat pin. Too on the nose? No, Rose wasn't aware of such subtleties.

Phillip inserted the pin, working it snugly through the fabric. He stepped back and brought a mirror for James to inspect his handiwork.

"Very fine," James said, hoping the encouragement made Phillip want to keep his job. James had been through a few valets over the years. Admittedly, he had not always been nice to the men who spent their time caring for his person. Perhaps because he also had not been good at caring for his own person.

Phillip's eyes roamed up and down, checking every crease and buttonhole. "Anything else?"

"If you deem me presentable, then I'll go down to meet my—" He tried to say *wife*, but he couldn't. He cleared his throat. "Carriage."

"Very good. Enjoy yourself, my lord." Phillip backed away, tidying the brushes and trays of cufflinks and pins.

James exhaled fully. He could enjoy tonight even without Rose and Henry. He could enjoy dancing with Pearl, flirting with her. Hopefully she would be able to laugh at his jokes.

He descended the stairs to find Pearl waiting for him. She already had her pelisse and gloves on. He hadn't realized he was late. Her expression looked worried, which he supposed was nerves. This would be her first party as a married woman. It was bound to be different. Would she dance? Would she play cards? She was Corinthian John's sister, so she might even overly imbibe.

"Good evening, Pearl." He greeted her as he stepped across the tiled entryway.

She inclined her head in greeting. "My lord."

"James," he corrected her. Being kind was to invite

intimacy, and that meant using names, not titles. *See, mother?* He wanted to call out, as if she were still in the house at this hour. He was being nice to Pearl.

"James," she echoed, her smile lighting up her face. She was quite pretty when she smiled. Her skin was like milk, fine, clear, and luminous.

Barton stood by and helped him slip on an overcoat before opening the door. The carriage with the family crest on it awaited. "Shall we?"

"Is your mother coming?" Pearl asked as they stepped into the cool autumn air. Night had fallen some time ago. James watched her breath puff out of her mouth and disappear.

"I believe she has already departed. She has her own carriage." His mother liked to have her freedom, and he was happy for it. She had suffered enough already for three lifetimes of marriage.

Smithy stood by the carriage door but stepped aside, allowing James to hand Pearl up into the carriage. James thought he detected an air of approval in the man's bushy brows. Being gallant apparently counted for something.

Once James clambered inside, Smithy closed the door behind him, and the carriage swayed as the big man found his perch.

James rapped on the roof and the carriage lurched into motion. Pearl sat facing front, the preferred seat for most riders, but James didn't mind.

"Have you had a pleasant day?" James asked.

"A surprising day," Pearl answered, though her expression did not seem to agree with her words.

"I find surprises delightful. Do you?"

Her eyes flickered over him, as if judging whether she should speak her mind.

James dropped his solicitous tone and fell back into the relaxed sardonic wit she was likely accustomed to. It was how he behaved at every dinner he had taken at her brother's house. "Do speak your mind, Pearl. We are chained in the holy bonds, after all. Being silent would be tedious for us both."

Her smile was more of a grimace, and he found he didn't like that one bit. She should be mooning over him, trailing a hand down his arm, whispering sweet sentiments in his ear. At least, his assignations with women other than Rose had been of that ilk. Perhaps Pearl was more like Rose, needing to be pursued and assured.

"I was surprised to find out we would be attending a ball so suddenly," Pearl finally said. She held his gaze with her blue eyes, and he didn't like the judgment he saw there. Would Pearl turn into a shrew now that marriage papers were signed? Not that it mattered overmuch. There were plenty of couples who rarely spent a day in the same town. They would merely add to their number. Tiresome, but not entirely unpredictable.

"I, too, was surprised. My mother brought it to my attention this morning."

"I'm glad she was able to find you," Pearl said, clamping her mouth shut as soon as she spoke.

"I beg your pardon. Are you..." He cocked his head, trying to parse her complaint. "Displeased with me?"

Pearl shook her head, eyes firmly on her reticule. A line creased between her brows that made him want to huff. When Rose had behaved like this, he just took leave of her and gave her time to regain her faculties properly. Is that what one did with a spouse?

Pearl looked up and no doubt noticed his annoyance. "It will take time for us to become accustomed to one another, I'm sure."

There now. He inclined his head, grateful that he didn't have to end his first full day of marriage rolling his eyes at Pearl's foolish expectations. Not that he knew exactly what they were, but no doubt they were the same tired ideals of the rising class. Affection, attention, gentility. They didn't want a husband, they wanted a puppy. Sadly, James was no puppy, and the sooner Pearl realized it, the better off they would both be.

⚜️

THEY WERE ANNOUNCED into Lady Haglund's ballroom amid a crush. Pearl didn't think anyone heard their names, but enough people turned to stare. Suddenly she was uncertain of her dress choice. There hadn't been time to ask for Lydia's opinion, and no one could find Lady Andrepont to garner hers. Lily had been invaluable, taking out each dress that Pearl asked for, smoothing it, even finding ribbons to match each one before Pearl ultimately decided against them in favor of a deep-green beaded gown.

The décolletage was lower than any gown she'd ever worn in public, but Lily assured her that her pale skin was all the rage. They powdered her shoulders to cover some of her freckles, which appeared despite her skin never having seen the sun. Lily had advised against jewels, said Pearl had no need of any. Rather, a single red ribbon around her neck was enough to offset the gown. Pearl had argued that perhaps she should wear green to match the gown, or even black? But Lily was adamant. Red. Blood-red. It seemed ghoulish, but Pearl acquiesced. When she watched James come down the stairs, his waistcoat a blood-red damask, she understood Lily's insistence. She'd wanted them to match.

Pearl had never had quite so many eyes on her at once. James urged her off the landing to descend into the milieu, but Pearl was rooted to the spot. Her mind blanked, her body screamed danger. She had been taught all her life to run from peril. She was fast, she was agile, and she should hide. But here was her *husband* urging her into the fray. She took a breath to steady herself and descended the staircase, her hand aloft in his.

Finally she could admire the room. Blimey, it was hot—beeswax candles fitted into two massive chandeliers, and the crowd was shoulder-to-shoulder. Women's gowns were flowing over onto each other's skirts and flirtatiously onto men's trousers. Jewels, likely not paste ones, either, glimmered in the candlelight at necks and tucked into coiffures. Pearl felt naked with her single red ribbon. Where was her finery? Where was her token?

James guided her to his mother and Lady Haglund. He bowed to them, and Pearl instinctively curtsied. She had no idea of rank or protocol, but she was sure she was beneath them.

"No need to show deference to me, Lady Andrepont." Lady Haglund smiled, reminding Pearl of the cook at her brother's house. She had been kindly to Pearl, even as she would turn and bark orders at the maids and footmen. "My husband is a mere baronet."

Pearl stood confused for a moment before realizing that Lady Haglund was addressing her. *She* was Lady Andrepont. How utterly confusing. She glanced at James's mother, who appeared serene as could be. Pearl said, "I have been trained my entire life to show deference to my elders."

Lady Haglund laughed and James's mother, the real Lady Andrepont, smiled broadly. "That line will work tonight, my girl. But I warn you that some other matrons of society will not be pleased to hear that you consider them your elders, even if they absolutely are." Lady Haglund let out another peal of bell-bright laughter. It somehow sounded dainty and heartfelt all at once. Pearl would have to learn to laugh like that.

Mrs. Tyler once referred to Pearl's laughter as the braying of a donkey. Pearl had tried very hard not to laugh in company ever since.

"My—viscountess is yet unaware of whom she may encounter at these events. I'm hoping my lady mother will be able to assist her in the coming weeks." James's words were formal, and his eyes were already above their heads, scanning the crowd.

Pearl tried not to feel insulted. Again. He wasn't even present for the conversation, his mind elsewhere. She glanced at his mother, who was watching her in return, that sardonic black eyebrow raised with interest. Blimey, the whole family held the same tick. Was Pearl expected to paint kohl on her own brows to see if she could match them?

"Lady Andrepont, may I retrieve some punch for you?" James asked, and without waiting for an answer, excused himself. From behind, someone jostled her.

Pearl felt James's cut deeper. She'd clearly been abandoned. Both of the other women schooled their expressions into blankness. Pearl hoped she was doing the same.

"If you'll excuse me, I'd like to find a place to freshen up." Tears were beginning to form, which was entirely silly. There was no reason to cry. She hadn't cried in ages—ages! And certainly not from something as impossible to control as a man who abandoned her in a ballroom. She should be quite used to any form of abandonment by now. Her father left them before she was born. John abandoned her to various families, and so of course her husband would choose to sign some papers and forget her as well. What were men for, except to leave?

She pushed her way through the crowd with small, polite smiles and excuse me's, shorter than most, finding herself at armpit level with many men before she finally located the women's retiring room.

She sagged against the wall, hidden by a massive potted fern that heralded the entrance to the room.

"Did you see her?" one woman said from inside the room.

"Andrepont's new wife? Yes. My goodness, what a mouse!" another woman said.

"A buck like that, and he chose her? The man could have had the pick of unmarried ladies, just like he had the pick of the married ones."

"Maybe because she wouldn't object to his affairs. What became of his prolonged tête-à-tête with Lord and Lady Kinsley? When you get on a boat with a newly married couple, you're not there for her ridiculous lectures."

Peals of laughter. And not the kind that sounded like bells. This was the sound of vultures, scavengers awaiting a kill.

"Really, I feel sorry for her. She couldn't have known what she was getting into."

A sick feeling settled into Pearl's gut. She didn't want to know this, yet she needed to.

"Especially if he turns into his father." Both women hooted.

"But do you think he has any of those... proclivities?" One of them asked.

"Why? Do you like it rough?" More laughter.

"At least I might notice it. The only way I know it's over is that he grunts. Other than that, I'd have no idea." A heavy sigh.

"Come on. Maybe we can get some young stallion to dance with us. It's the only thrill I get these days." The rustle of fabric was the alert Pearl needed to slip around the fern and escape detection by the women leaving the retiring room.

She couldn't say she wasn't glad of the knowledge. Glad to know more of her new husband. Of what she faced. But still, she wished she could have been told before finding out while hiding next to a potted plant. All the years she'd believed she was impervious to words.

She slipped into the retiring room, which was now thankfully empty. She sat down at the dressing table and studied herself in the mirror. No wonder they called her a mouse. Her red hair was coiled in curls and artfully pinned. But it was simple and without artifice. She wore no kohl or blush—on her pale features, cosmetics looked harsh. Her eyelashes were the same color as her hair and eyebrows, giving her an unusually bare countenance. Her blue eyes were her best feature—or so she had always thought—and they stood out in bright contrast to the rest of her.

This was not the look of a woman who could contend with a man like James. A viscount. Someone worldly, with a string of married mistresses. A man who, on a whim, hopped on a boat for months on end. But her? She was from nothing. She knew the smell of livestock. Of living in rooms shared with pigs —who were cleaner than many gave them credit for. She'd witnessed respectable women—mothers and caretakers—visit a tavern to find a kind gentleman who would give her bread money in exchange for intimate favors. A man who wouldn't expect more than what was offered and wouldn't try to take it for nothing.

Pearl knew what it felt like to have chapped hands split from the washing. She knew the smell of a freshly tilled garden. She knew the sound of a mother's heart breaking when the baby she delivered didn't cry. These were the things those other women didn't know. The things James would never understand. The ways in which she was alone, and would always be alone, now that she owned a lofty title of viscountess.

The tears that had threatened earlier dried up. She'd spent her life hiding her strength, showing only kindness and meekness in an effort to be accepted.

Helping first, expecting nothing, hoping for kindness in return. Foolishly, she'd hoped that marrying meant she would have a place of her own and would no longer struggle to belong. It was always thus for her. She knew this—and she knew how it ended: with her being sent off to be someone else's problem at some undetermined date. But this time, she had money. She could make her own fate. Her own security. And that was securing her marriage bond so that it was undisputed. She vowed not to leave that house. It was hers.

"Pardon me," a handsome blonde woman said, sitting down at the dressing table next to her. "Are you by any chance the new Lady Andrepont?"

Pearl nodded first and then caught herself. Verbal answers were expected; speak when spoken to. She was no longer that abandoned child. But could one speak to someone to whom they'd not been introduced? Considering this was a retiring room and not the ballroom at large, it seemed necessary. "Yes, I am. And you?"

She smiled warmly. "I'm Lady Teeton. I was hoping I'd get to meet you tonight."

"How do you do?" Pearl had no idea of Lady Teeton's rank. She needed to get a copy of Debrett's to study. How woefully unprepared she was.

"I know this is a bit forward. But let me say, I do hope we can be friends. You are very possibly the most interesting person here." Lady Teeton examined her face in the looking glass, angling it this way and that, checking the security of her hairpins.

"That really ought to depend on the eye of the beholder, no?" *Never contradict, never contradict.* Mrs. Tyler's words blasted in her ears as if the woman herself were standing there.

"You have me there. Why you are most interesting to me is that you married Lord Andrepont, and I've been after him for years." Lady

Teeton tore her eyes from the looking glass to smile at Pearl.

The sourness of Pearl's stomach appeared in her mouth. She'd heard about the poor manners of men, but these women were positively predatory.

Lady Teeton's eyes widened. "Oh my goodness, no! Not like that! Oh, how dreadful. I do beg your pardon." The woman leaned over and clasped Pearl's hands. "No, no. I didn't mean it in such a way. I am no adulteress. Rather, I have been after your husband to take his place in Parliament. We want his vote. My husband and I. We need to build a coalition to lift the extreme punishments for small offenses, and I think if Lord Andrepont ever made the effort, he could charm his fellow Peers to see our side."

Pearl shook her head. "I'm so sorry, but I know nothing of politics."

"Politics is the business of people, Lady Andrepont. I'm hoping that with your help, we may get your husband to at least take his seat. It has sat empty since his father's death. The country only runs if those who can, participate."

Pearl smiled. "Then may I understand that you—"

"Believe in women's suffrage?" Lady Teeton interrupted. Her lips thinned. "Of course I do. I'm at least half as much smarter than most of Parliament and far smarter than the rest of it. If those utter nincompoops can run this country, can you think of how much better it would be if the rest of us were allowed a say?"

Pearl smiled. "You know, Lady Teeton, I think you were right."

"Splendid. But do tell me what I've gotten correct." Her blonde hair glinted, drawing the eye away from her simple gown and white gloves. It was her person that was animated and spectacular, not her appearance. Take the woman's excitement away and her beauty no longer held.

"You said that you thought we would be friends. I believe we shall." This was a woman who could show Pearl how to be a proper wife. Not the carnivorous kind that hunted her husband.

❧

ROSE WAS HERE. He couldn't believe she would deign to attend such a party. She'd not wanted to attend the Season for two years, and now she was a woman who went to balls? She was, of course, dressed beautifully. Dark blue and mauve twined up her skirts, almost like peacock feathers, spilling across her décolletage in a most alluring manner. James almost laughed. She would never realize the effect of her gown.

Men would be staring at her bosom, with the exception of Henry, her church husband, who stood next to her. He looked well. He looked happy, actually, which seemed surprising. Next to him stood Lord Teeton, a massive bore who prattled on about nothing but the law yet never seemed to see its nuances. James hated even playing cards with the fellow because his table talk put everyone to sleep.

He approached Rose, wanting just to be near her. He said her name quietly, not wanting to interrupt Henry and Teeton.

Rose startled, as if he'd scared her. One gloved hand flew to her throat. A column he'd kissed before, her head thrown back. How could she not want that again? He'd promised to honor her wishes, and never kissing her again was one of those. He didn't understand. He couldn't.

"James!" She took a breath to collect herself and then pasted on a polite smile. She was getting better at those. He knew how hard those niceties had been for her to learn. Then she corrected herself: "Lord Andrepont."

"I'm so glad to see you." His hands were sweating,

but still, he wanted to reach for her fingers, hidden in the swirl of skirts.

"Is your wife here? I'd love to make felicitations to the new Lady Andrepont." Rose had this talent for tone of voice. She said everything as casually as if she were asking for a sip of water. Everything was the same level of solemnity.

James shook his head. "I need to talk to you." He had no agenda, but the need to speak with her felt insistent, nagging even. He had followed her instructions. He'd married. There. Done. Now could they go back to the way things had been? Now could he kiss her throat?

"I'd scan the room myself, of course, but I'm afraid Henry insisted I not wear my spectacles tonight. Better for our appearance if I don't seem too much a bluestocking. Would you point her out to me?"

James frowned. She'd never worried about such a thing before. Her spectacles were for her vision, not for her vanity. Of all the asinine things to insist upon. "Why would Henry ask you to forgo your sight?"

Rose's cheeks colored. She blushed prettily, but James found he was irritated by it tonight. His blood thrummed harder in his veins. He knew this feeling, and where it would lead. Either to a boxing ring or a bed. And right now, he had access to neither.

"Well, I suppose I may have mentioned that I look less a bluestocking if I don't wear them. Henry wants to make a career for himself, and as his wife, I must do my part."

Despite his valet's earlier ministrations, James raked a hand through his hair. "A career? Dear God, what has happened to you since you pushed me out?"

Even the fake smile faded from Rose's lips. "Nothing. We are the same as we always were. Perhaps you are finally paying attention." Irritation permeated the air. Henry risked a side-eyed glance at

James, never displaying any useful emotion but making James aware that Henry knew what was happening.

And because God hated him, Lady Teeton approached with Pearl. Fuck.

"Here you are! I would desperately love to introduce you. Lady Kinsley, this is the new Lady Andrepont. Lady Andrepont, this is Lady Kinsley. She and her husband have been instrumental in strategizing for this term."

Instrumental? James struggled. *When?* He swung his gaze across their small cluster, taking in Rose and Henry, Lord and Lady Teeton, and then Pearl, looking lost and small and out of place. She didn't belong here. The Teetons had been powerbrokers for the last decade, hounding him to take his father's seat in Parliament, hoping to win him over to a pointless morality.

All of those bloated lords said one thing in session, heckling and goading each other, only to walk out and commit the very sins they attempted to legislate against. Hypocrites, liars, thieves, rapists all. He hated them. They loved his father, and therefore they were worthless. Like hell he'd join their lot.

James's ears felt as if they were stuffed with cotton. The women talked amongst themselves. Pearl leaned forward to greet the others, projecting herself towards them as if she could match their status, their height. It was laughable. He was laughable.

He stumbled away without excusing himself. There was plenty of liquor at the card tables. It was time to find some money.

❧

LADY TEETON STEERED Pearl from the women's lounge to the small cluster of Lord Teeton, Lord and Lady Kinsley, and James. Pearl spotted her husband as he raked his hands through his hair. It reminded her of that morning he'd proposed. Ah. It was this woman who had caused him the distress. She was the reason Pearl was a viscountess.

Pearl knew her husband was propositioning Lady Kinsley. It was obvious. She couldn't pretend it didn't hurt. Her stomach felt like a fist, clenched and hard. This was marriage, then. Watching someone else receive the attention you were supposed to receive. James's regard should be hers, as his bride, but alas, it belonged to Lady Kinsley. How silly Pearl had been to think otherwise. She should have known that at best she would be a placeholder.

Everyone thought Lady Kinsley was a lovely person. Even Bess had once remarked that she was among the few gently bred ladies that could have a real conversation.

And now, snugged against other people, clad in their best finery, Pearl could pretend that everything was absolutely fine. Better than fine. Wonderful. Blimey, what that title of his bought: obedience, conformity, silence. The fist twisted harder, and Pearl forced herself into a small curtsy of introduction to Lady Kinsley.

She looked different without her spectacles, which is how Pearl had known her previously. Pearl reminded the marchioness of their previous meetings, and they reminisced until James abruptly turned tail and fled. Coward. There was dodging and weaving to get away, and there was flat-out running off.

Pearl watched a parade of emotions flicker across Rose's face. She felt for him, that was certain. If Lady Teeton was correct that politics was about people, then Pearl ought to be tip-top.

☙❧

CHAPTER 6

Another hangover greeted James before he opened his eyes. Of all the unholy beasts in the world, a hangover was the worst. His mouth felt like the floor of a sawmill. Even his eyes felt like dried persimmons. If opening his veins would cure it, he would do it. He pried an eyelid open, trying to find his bearings. Ah, yes. Familiar territory, and someone had kindly left water nearby along with some powder. Excellent. Whoever did that deserved an extra five pounds at Michaelmas.

His neck hurt, cricked to the side as it was on his study's couch. There was a soft scratching at the door, which meant a servant wanted access. His mother would have barged in, and Pearl, well, he had no idea what she would do.

"Enter," he called. He pushed his hands at his temples, relieving pressure that throbbed more regularly than the chiming of the bells at St. George's.

"Hullo, my lord," he heard. The voice sounded muffled through his concentration.

He pried that one eye open again. *Ah, double fuck.* Pearl smiled politely at him. She was wearing a walking dress, her hair tucked primly away. Dear God, would she start wearing one of those horrid matron caps? He groaned.

"Good morning, my lady."

"Checking on your progress." Her tight smile was echoed by her hands twisting together in front of her.

"Progress?" He fumbled for the ewer and managed to almost tip it over.

She scrambled towards him, saving the water pitcher and his cup from spilling. Was she truly that quick, or was it just the hangover distorting his reality? And more aptly, who the fuck cared? He grunted his thanks as she poured him a cup.

"You clearly don't remember earlier." Pearl held the vessel for him to take.

He stared at it a moment, letting his thick tongue flatten against the roof of his mouth, a feeling that could only properly be found when extremely hungover. He took the cup from her and fumbled for the envelope of headache powder. When he gained purchase with it, he found it slipped from beneath his fingers. Huh. How strange.

"Drink the water first, my lord. Chemicals after water."

"They aren't chemicals," he grunted.

"Water." The woman would have made a decent governess with that commanding tone of voice.

He drained the glass and held it out for another round. He felt the cool water inside him, snaking through the hot, arid emptiness of his body. "More."

She obliged, and he drank it down. Again and again, and slowly, while he felt soggy as a sock on washing day, his mind began to clear. Ah, yes. This morning. He considered her for a moment. "You came in earlier with a tray."

"Indeed." She tore open the envelope and handed it to him.

Her flat expression told him everything he needed to know. "I apologize now, but I am quite curious what names I may have called you."

She nodded, and a crease appeared between her

brows. Was she trying not to cry? His mother would have his head. "I believe you accused me of being an unbuttered parsnip. And then a potato-faced polecat. Oh, and my personal favorite was the hellhound of sunshine."

"A thousand apologies for my comparison of you to root vegetables." He swallowed.

"Please do not apologize for the last. I believe it is my favorite of all the endearments I have earned in my lifetime."

"Hellhound of sunshine?" His head was clearing, and it no longer felt as if an entire field of cotton had grown in his body overnight. "Glad to be of service."

"Pardon me, my lord." Barton entered the room carrying a flat parcel. "This came for you."

James, recognizing the package, scrambled up, eager. "Thank you, Barton."

The butler left as James tore open the parcel. It was the latest music from Tipton's Music Shop. His head had cleared enough that he could play. Not just could, but desired to do so. Now, new music could occupy his churning mind.

"I didn't realize you were such an avid musician," said Pearl from over his shoulder.

He turned in surprise—he'd forgotten she was there. "Yes, quite. It occupies the hours. If you'll excuse me."

He sat down at the piano, shuffling the music, eager to see what was there. The notes swam a bit in his vision, but that would iron itself out. For now, he could just close one eye.

"I also wanted to ask if you'd like to attend a dinner party at the Lord and Lady Teeton's Mayfair house two days hence."

It was hard to concentrate on her, like she was already disappearing from view despite standing in the same room. Couldn't she see he was busy? "The

Teetons? God no. Those people won't shut up about politics. Tiresome people. Utter bores."

He opened the first page and looked through the key signature. Easy enough, just a few flats, which he preferred over reading key signatures full of sharps.

"One other thing, my lord."

James tore his attention from the sheet music and turned around to look at her. When would she be gone? His stomach roiled and he wanted to forget himself.

"I'm concerned about our marriage being valid." Pearl twisted her hands together as if she were nervous.

Good God, he did not have time for a timid woman. "I assure you the bishop was ordained. And there are plenty of witnesses."

He made to turn back to the keyboard, but she took a step forward to halt him. "I mean that it is unconsummated. It would be simple for you to annul it and for me to be left with nothing."

"Nothing?" he snorted. "Why, I think your dowry made you richer than I am. And your brother made sure the marriage contract was ironclad. Besides, why would I seek an annulment?"

His hangover was not so bad that he missed the narrowing of her eyes, but he didn't have the temperament to care. He returned to his music and let her leave on her own time. He had no use for worrying over actions that were already completed. What was the point?

⚜

PEARL HAD FUNCTIONED as a servant in many households, despite having never been paid as one. Being dismissed from company was a familiar occurrence, but never in her life had she been so horridly discharged from someone's presence as she had from her husband's. She stomped out and slammed the door. When the first few notes of a scale wafted through the door, she knew for certain he hadn't taken notice of her at all.

Shame filled her. She had basically raised the question of physical intimacy and he hadn't even noticed. Was she so unattractive? So utterly horrid that he wouldn't even consider marital relations with his own wife? Him, with the reputation of a rutting stag?

Oh, he'd made it utterly clear last night, as she'd collected his drunken person from the card tables, that this was a marriage in name only. He didn't know her, didn't want to know her, and didn't want her interfering with his previous life. The life he was so goddamned happy with that he had to marry a complete stranger to fix something. Something that went by the name of Lady Kinsley.

Her cheeks burned with shame. She hadn't felt like this since Gabriel mocked her after that night in the warehouse loft. It had been a warm summer evening, and she'd thought him so handsome in the long golden light of the late sunset. He'd brought her a flower, and she'd felt so stupidly special. She'd let him take her up there, knowing what he expected, knowing what would happen. He'd lifted her skirts and made a perfunctory exploration between her legs, but that's all it took for her. She'd already been so ready for him, happy to be with him, wanting him to declare his love. She'd long dreamed of this moment. And when it came, so did she. And Gabriel laughed. His hands still slick with her, he laughed.

She shook the memory away. It had nothing to do with the situation at hand. For Andrepont would never know her body and said as much. What use was a man, anyway? That's what Mrs. Coldcroft advised: *get to know your own self best*. And she did. Which was why Gabriel needed little skill to make Pearl soar.

Fine. If he wanted separate lives, she would give him a separate life. Furious, Pearl blundered out into the passage, heading right instead of left, which would have taken her to the public rooms and the staircase. Instead, she found the servants' stair tucked next to the silver closet, the locked door she had been informed led to the dead viscount's study. She crept past it, taking another passageway meant for the public, and she wandered into the ballroom. Except, it wasn't a ballroom anymore.

The cavernous room still had chandeliers and opulent gilded sconces ready to receive beeswax tapers. But none existed there now. The beautiful parquet floor was scuffed and marked up with chalk. A sawdust-stuffed bag hung from a pulley in the corner. A straw man was not too far away. Mufflers and wrappings hung from pegs hastily hammered into the wall. A jumping rope coiled on a table nearby. Clean towels were folded neatly, awaiting an athlete.

Across the large room was a raised boxing ring, as good as anything Pearl had seen at actual bouts. It wasn't large, but the platform looked solid and had two guide ropes so unsuspecting fighters wouldn't fall out.

Pearl knew that James boxed. John had hosted James at the gymnasium in his house numerous times. But she hadn't understood that James trained at his own home as well. An old longing overtook her, the familiarity of the equipment, the smell of sweat and sawdust mingled together. Without questioning her impulse, she went to the straw man and began a slow routine: jab, jab, cross, uppercut, uppercut. She'd missed those sensations.

John would have let her train at his gymnasium if she'd asked. He would have never denied her, especially since Lydia had begun training again. But Pearl felt confined—Mrs. Tyler had drilled them in etiquette, essential to finding husbands, and husbands were the ultimate goal. Pearl hadn't wanted to depend on John forever, so a husband was necessary, and women who fought didn't get husbands. And now... now she had a husband. Perhaps she could be free once again.

Her knuckles jarred against the straw man. Beginner's mistake. Her wrist needed to snap straight, otherwise she'd risk breaking a finger. And how was she supposed to explain an injury like that?

As her arms burned with exertion and her back worked in concert, the rest of her body urged her forward. She hadn't just trained with her arms, the way some of the new fighters had. Pearl missed her old training skirts, looser and coming just below the knee, which allowed her to swing out and kick from her hips. It felt so good to stretch and move in that way.

She untied her slippers. The soles were supple leather and would easily slip on the parquet floor. But then, as soon as she got them off, she realized her satin stockings would be the same. She hitched up her skirt, tucking it into the hem of her pocket hole. Still in her way, she rucked it up further and untied the garter around her thigh.

☙❧

JAMES HEARD the thump of fists hitting straw in between sightreading his new piano pieces. Curiosity got the better of him, and coming to investigate the noise, assuming one of the footmen had taken some liberties, he instead found Pearl, with exceptionally good technique, working the straw man as competently as any young fighter. Why she was disrobing, he did not know. And while a gentleman would signal his presence, James was too intrigued to think on propriety.

When she rucked up her skirt, a strangled noise

came from his throat. Her bare thigh was a tantalizing sight. She rolled down her satin stocking —beautifully crafted, with ornate patterns along the back of the leg. The kind of decoration only the lady and her lover would see. The garter was a simple green ribbon, and he could practically feel the smooth satin of it between his teeth.

Of course she would feel comfortable in a boxing gym. Corinthian John was her brother, Bess Abbott her friend. How had he not realized Pearl would be at ease using her body in such a manner?

John. Her brother. He'd promised John he would respect his sister. And James did respect her—when he remembered her. But now, he didn't know how he couldn't remember that bare skin, smooth like cream, even while doing the most onerous of tasks.

With one leg bare, she undid the other garter.

James had not been one to find women fighters particularly attractive. In fact, the ones he knew had the opposite effect for him. He preferred the idea of a masculine brotherhood of fighters. Although he liked and respected Bess Abbott, she always made him feel out of sorts somehow. He was never sure how to treat her and followed John's lead by treating her as he would any man.

Watching Pearl work with confidence through his gym, with tantalizingly smooth bare legs, he reevaluated his prior convictions. The lady moved to the heavy, straw-filled bag hanging from the ceiling. He'd hung it himself, with the aid of several footmen. He hoped she didn't hurt herself on it.

Her leg rose and kicked the bag, and he almost fell on his own arse in surprise. His hangover had been temporarily forgotten, but it reared its head with a vengeance. Pearl moved with grace and agility, balancing as she moved around the bag, dancing almost. A kick there, then a shift of her weight and a kick from the other side. He'd never seen anyone fight like that before. And he'd never seen a woman hitch up her skirts in that manner. His mouth was dry and his trousers tight—his weakness must be from the hangover and not from this taboo display.

This was a sight he could not tear himself from. This was more than mouth-watering. Seeing her destroy the straw man made him want her from a depth that surprised him. Her slim muscles flexed and worked as she moved, and he was rooted to the ground.

He had so many questions for her, but he certainly couldn't announce himself in his current state. Even aside from his promise to her brother, it was unseemly to approach a woman who was not one's paramour with a cockstand. Misunderstandings would no doubt result, and he was in no condition to be clever. With as much willpower as he could muster, James slunk back to his study, unsure of how to perceive his viscountess.

❧

PEARL HAD NOT INTENDED to work up any sort of heat while exploring the ballroom-turned-gymnasium. But it allowed her to vent her anger and come up with a way to make herself feel better. And that scheme largely rested on having options. Options to punish her husband for ignoring her, options to secure her marriage, and options to leave should that be required once she was done annoying the man she was bound to. Not wanting to bother Lily, Pearl cleaned herself and changed into a better day dress suitable for calling upon Lady Teeton.

But she also pulled out the small carpet bag she'd hidden from Lily when she'd moved in. It was a talisman of sorts, battered and threadbare, the constant companion from her childhood that she couldn't bear to be separated from.

Some children had dolls, or wooden ponies, or even a certain ribbon. But Pearl had a carpet bag, and in it she packed an escape, shoving it under her bed for safekeeping, just as she had a thousand times before. Nothing excessive, just an extra shift, walking dress, woolen stockings, and an envelope with a few banknotes. She didn't know if James had a temper or not, but if she truly irritated him the way she planned to, she wanted an escape route.

It was a habit that had taken months to break when she moved in with John and Lydia. But now she was in a new house, and there was the bag, stuffed and hidden, hopefully out of sight of any servants.

She was haunted by her earlier vow. She wanted to stay here for the rest of her life, if only for the stability it promised. She never wanted to move again. This should be hers, this place. She could have wept for the war inside of her.

But the bag was packed despite herself. And it did make her feel better to know that it was there. A measure of safety in an unpredictable household. But it was time to forge a life for herself, her husband's attentions be damned.

❦

PEARL CALLED ON LADY TEETON. She was shown into a drawing room that reflected the oldest art and latest designs of pastel colors. Carefully curated gilded frames enclosed paintings of pastoral scenes and frolicking ancient Greeks. A painted pianoforte was at one end of the room while Lady Kinsley and Lady Teeton sat across from one another at the opposite end. Seeing Lady Kinsley made Pearl go cold. She hadn't wanted to face her husband's former mistress again—especially given that James's rejection still stung.

Lady Kinsley wore her spectacles, looking far less

intimidating than she had at the ball. She looked an approachable bluestocking, the kind of woman that Agnes and Jack might befriend. Both women rose to their feet as Pearl approached, a courtesy Pearl knew she didn't merit.

"Lovely to see you again so soon," Lady Kinsley said, extending a hand. Pearl reached out to clasp her hand in greeting.

"And you," Pearl echoed.

Lady Teeton seemed to view the interaction with approval, as if they were children performing manners appropriately. They all sank into their cushioned seats. Pearl felt utterly out of her depth.

"Refreshment?" Lady Teeton suggested.

Pearl knew refreshments were only offered to callers who might stay longer. She knew it was on account of her husband's political potential, but any kindness at this point would be welcome. And besides, if her husband didn't like the Teetons, then Pearl liked them even more. "I would love some."

"Grand. Cream or sugar?"

"Splash of cream, if you would." Pearl risked a glance over at Lady Kinsley, who seemed anxious to talk once again.

"Sugar is one of those resources that seem diabolical," Lady Kinsley said.

"Oh?" Lady Teeton encouraged while pouring Pearl a cup of tea.

"Think on it: the way it is extracted is utterly inhumane, but the taste of it is sweet. It is, quite honestly, the way a vicar discusses the devil himself."

"Are you quite religious, Lady Kinsley?" Pearl asked, wondering how she would have squared her piousness with her adultery.

"Oh, no, not at all. Quite the opposite, but I grew up in the country, and I had very few friends. The only girl my age was a vicar's daughter. Naturally, I heard many, many sermons."

"How edifying," Pearl said.

At that, Lady Kinsley gave a snort. "Edifying indeed. It gave me ammunition for the next dinner party to call her father on the inaccuracies of his platitudes. I'm surprised he allowed his daughter to remain my friend."

Pearl smiled. Lady Kinsley was charming in her own way. Sweet, really, like honeysuckle, not like sugar. And given her hair was the color of honey and her eyes grayish-blue behind the spectacles, she was pretty enough to find pleasing, but not enough to evoke envy or spite. Her air invited informality and ease. Pearl could see why James had gravitated towards her. The woman felt so very safe, somehow.

And wouldn't it gall James if she became friends not just with Lady Teeton but also his ex-mistress? That would be lovely, too. However, she still had to decline the dinner invitation. Attending alone wouldn't be proper, as the intent was to have couples.

When Lady Teeton mentioned the dinner party, both women looked visibly disappointed as Pearl declined.

"I do so apologize," Pearl stammered.

"I know it isn't your doing," Lady Teeton said as Lady Kinsley looked out the window at some unknown point of interest.

Pearl shook her head.

"If we cannot entice your husband, perhaps we can still entice you. Would you care for a pamphlet my husband wrote? I'd love to share his proposal. I don't wish to be rude, but knowing a little of your background, I would be most interested to hear your thoughts. All the lofty musings of an aristocrat can never match the actual lived experience of one from limited means."

"Are you...asking for my opinion?"

"Of course. How silly would I be in pushing for legislation that had never been reviewed by someone who might understand how it might truly change the world?"

Between the tea and some bland cakes, Pearl found herself opening up even more to both women. They were interesting and thoughtful, asking for Pearl's ideas—and not just on something as inconsequential as the location of lace on a gown, but on whether a tariff might be removed from imported goods from the former colonies. How the grain tax had been such a dramatic failure. How hunger fueled a rebellion faster than gunpowder.

After both Lady Kinsley and Pearl had overstayed, Pearl excused herself, as if she had so many other social calls to make. She still intended to make her way over to Marylebone to call on Lydia, as well as Agnes and Jack.

"If I may be so forward, once again," Lady Teeton announced, "where will you go during the Michaelmas recess?"

Pearl blinked. The holiday had not been one she observed, and thus it held very little meaning for her. John had a break from school when he was young, but he hadn't always the time to visit her.

"We have an estate just north of here, not far, that is very restful. I think we'll retire there for a few weeks," Lady Kinsley said.

They both looked at Pearl expectantly. Was there a country estate hidden somewhere that they would go to? With a name as old as Andrepont's, likely there was, but neither her mother-in-law nor her husband had mentioned leaving town. And certainly their lives were not governed by Parliamentary sessions. "I don't believe Andrepont leaves London."

Lady Teeton made a face as if Pearl had just admitted that they didn't eat with utensils at dinner. "Then permit me to extend an invitation to ours. Give me a week or so to plan out the details and invite a few other couples. We can have it all, leisure and legislation all at once."

"A working recess?" Lady Kinsley asked. "How interesting."

Pearl stood awkwardly, not knowing how to extract herself. The chimes of nearby St. George's struck the hour, startling her.

"Don't let me keep you," Lady Teeton said, rising from her chair. "But, if you are still interested, Lady Andrepont, I would like to send you my husband's pamphlet at the very least."

Pearl nodded. "Of course. I'd be happy to read anything that you deem of interest."

A short walk from Mayfair to Marylebone shook the nerves from Pearl. As a matron now, Pearl no longer required a maid to trail behind her as a chaperone. How odd. She was deemed a person now —at least in one sense, as she had become an extension of her husband. Though, one supposed, she should be with a footman for protection.

It was odd to be ushered in to her brother's house. It had been her home just last week. But still, as the maids and footmen encountered her on her journey upstairs to the drawing room, they gave happy nods of acknowledgment. It felt like home. Like she should go stow her bonnet and gloves in her room, rather than hand them off to Mr. Parsons at the entryway.

"To what do we owe such a visit, my dear Lady Andrepont?" Lydia proclaimed, standing from her usual seat in the drawing room. She held out her hands, and Pearl entered the embrace with her whole heart. She had missed having someone who wanted her nearby. Someone who saw her, appreciated her.

Pearl sighed and almost let the words *I missed you* spill out of her mouth. There was no need to embarrass Lydia with her earnestness.

"If our parents could see us now," came John's

voice from the threshold. It was his turn for an embrace. Pearl buried her head against his familiar chest. She didn't have any memories of their parents, but she understood what he meant. How far they'd come.

Pearl finally stopped squeezing her brother's broad torso. She dropped all of her learned tones and open vowels, adopting the flattened and nasal accent of their youth: "A rich man and an aristocrat. How could it be, when our blood runs as pure as the gutter?"

"Yes, yes, we all know that we are all terribly backwards and that the rabble of the Earth are superior to the bloodthirsty pedigreed families that conquered your island," Lydia drawled.

"Can I get a proper cup, please? I've been going round on a call and the refreshments were sorely lacking."

"Just the tea or...?" John teased. The spark was back in his blue eyes, and he had that coiled energy in his body. When he was younger, it would cause him to fidget side to side, as if he were prepping for a fight. Now he kept himself still, but his energy was palpable.

"Oh, as if I could say no to any of Cook's treats," Pearl admitted. The trio arranged themselves in their usual places—Lydia and John on the couch, Pearl in her chair. Richard, the footman, brought up a tray.

"Richard, you're looking well," Pearl said, noting his blackened eye had faded.

"Yes, miss." He colored, and then paled. "I mean, my lady. I am so sorry. It slipped out."

Pearl gave him an indulgent smile as she reached for the teapot. "Not to worry. It's so new that I've forgotten at least twice."

Lydia slapped away Pearl's hand. "What are you thinking? I am the mistress here. I shall pour."

Shaken, Pearl retracted her hand. Lydia was all

smiles, and Richard withdrew, but it reminded Pearl that this was no longer home. She was no longer the Pearl that belonged here with her brother. She belonged in that other place. The empty house with a drunken husband and an absent mother-in-law. The one where she once again had a packed bag waiting under her bed.

CHAPTER 7

His body ached from playing. He loved that feeling in his hands: well-used, accomplished, strong. Tipton's had sent yet another parcel of music. Nothing terribly profound—no new Beethoven—but it had been a joy to work through new pieces. It kept his mind focused, his body floating in a limbo where it couldn't tempt him or lure him or hurt him. He sat back and stretched his back and shoulders.

Since the wedding, over a week ago, he hadn't visited his in-home gymnasium, and he could feel his weakening gut. Granted, he had also avoided the room for fear he would find Pearl once again in a state of undress. He would never admit that she had sparked his interest, nor that her utter confidence in her body had shaken him.

Or admit that he listened for her now. That awareness of her in the house prickled his skin. In a complete reversal, he'd gone from forgetting she existed to knowing the moment she walked out the door to call on her friends. Or Lydia, or Agnes—both of whom were *his* cousins. Not hers. Not that it mattered, since he'd refused to see anyone since the wedding.

In his confused and wounded state, he hadn't

taken good care of himself and had holed up at the piano, hoping the pain of losing both his best friend and his lover would lessen. What would he even say to Pearl, or Lydia, or John, when they would all want some piece of him and he had nothing to give? Just his pathetic self, who couldn't even maintain his loyalty to his ex-mistress because he'd figured out this woman in his house was far more interesting than he'd been led to believe.

The light had faded into night, and his stomach finally protested loudly enough to make him pay attention. He strode to the door, thinking to visit the kitchens, but upon opening it, he found a tray waiting for him. Mrs. Foraker knew his proclivities. He retrieved the tray, scarfing down the hunk of cheese, the buttered bread, and the watered-down beer. The beef broth had gone cold long ago, but he swirled it like brandy to break up the congealed surface and drank it down. The meal was the recommended training food for any athlete. Mrs. Foraker knew his habits, clearly, or perhaps she was hinting that training was better for him than drinking.

Sated, he stretched and looked around his lair. The maids had been in yesterday, so the room wasn't in terrible shape. Things felt good and the mud of despair he'd wallowed in was slowly washing away. He meandered to his gymnasium—a location that had been the ballroom in his father's day. A place where deals were brokered, wives gossiped, and a few danced. It had been a busy room when he was young. And those nights often ended in tears for some young woman—usually a maid who was caught unawares as guests left and the rest of the staff was busy attending to other matters.

James shuddered in the cavernous ballroom. Not him. Never him. His cravat had disappeared sometime during the day, and now he peeled off his shirt. Windmilling his arms, he finally felt himself again after the charade of courting Pearl and the agony and embarrassment of Rose. All that was done now, and he could return focus onto himself.

This was his domain. Like the music room, he'd commandeered it and made it his own, the world be damned. And it was here that he could forget everyone else, including the redheaded mouse who'd invaded his territory.

The heavy bag hung suspended in the corner, freshly refilled with sawdust. James wrapped his hands with strips of cloth. He owned mufflers for heavy bag work, though he didn't often wear them. Neither John nor Bess put any value on mufflers since fights continued bare-knuckled. They contended that mufflers only made a fighter's hands weak and soft, unable to withstand the punishing blows of bone against knuckle.

But James had never brined his hands like them. Never had to fight for money—only glory. It was different when desperation was born from a need to fight rather than a need to eat. James slipped the mufflers on over the wrappings. No one was here to judge him, and he had no fights pending, so he would indulge himself. Besides, between piano and prizefighting, he would choose music every time.

He started slow, jabbing the bag and circling, practicing footwork and clearing his mind. He pushed the image of Pearl's bare legs out of his mind and thought only of the work in front of him. The focus was blessed relief, just as the sheet music had been. To not feel or think or talk. Just move. Left. Left. Left, right.

Before long, sweat was beading on his temple. He gave his shoulders a break and removed his mufflers. Moving to the next designated station, he skipped rope like a child since running through London without a shirt on at this hour would attract too much attention. He could see the next day's gossip rags: Newly Married Viscount Runs in Terror from His New Bride!

The rhythm of the rope skimming across the floor was another calming metronome for his beleaguered soul. Skip, skip, skip. He let the rhythm remain relaxed, then sped the tempo little by little until sweat began pouring from him, sliding in drops between his shoulder blades.

Time was irrelevant. His body floated, his blood thrummed, and his mind was blessedly still. He increased his speed further, pushing to finish himself off. It wasn't unlike being with a woman. Whether pushing to climax or pushing to exhaustion, the result was the same: gasping for breath, waves of pleasure crashing through his body. Faster and faster he went, blood pounding, and then finally he could stand it no longer. On his last skip, he threw the rope aside and walked off his panting.

Whatever liquor had lurked in his veins had been thoroughly purified. He rang for Phillip. He needed a bath, some water, and an orange, if they had any.

***

ONCE AGAIN, Pearl took dinner alone. In the cavernous dining room, she ate her fish course bite by bite. Utensils down. Chewing. Swallowing. Glancing about the room. Mrs. Tyler would be proud of her manners even in her solitude. Pearl tasted none of Cook's labor.

Mr. Barton appeared with a small parcel in the dining room. "Pardon the interruption, my lady, but this just arrived for you. Would you like this now, or shall I have it placed in your dressing room?"

"I shall see to it now. Thank you, Mr. Barton." Pearl was glad for the distraction. When she opened the parcel, she found a note from Lady Teeton.

My apologies for the lateness of this reading material. Do call when you've read it, or at least send your thoughts. You are more important than you know!

—T

Enclosed was more than the single pamphlet Lady Teeton had promised. Indeed, there were newspaper clippings, handwritten speeches, and what appeared to be a draft of a proposed bill. Lady Teeton had sent an entire policy platform, and though Pearl was woefully underqualified to even read the material, she felt obligated to do her part. When she'd agreed to receive the pamphlet, she thought it might be above her comprehension. This was more than she'd bargained for. Pearl was the type for an occasional gothic novel, not political philosophizing.

She finished her meal, picking through the stack of papers. How on earth was she supposed to accomplish this? And when would Lady Teeton expect her response? Pearl was not aware of any guidelines, and she certainly didn't want to disappoint. At least Lady Teeton's penmanship was legible, which made the perusal easier. When the footman cleared her plate, she instructed for a cup of chocolate to be delivered to her rooms in hopes that the drink might aid her comprehension.

Once upstairs in her room, Lily helped her undress and brush her hair. Pearl's reading material awaited her on the table near the fireplace. She was dreading it, which wasn't helpful. It would only make reading it harder. But that was what the drinking chocolate was for. To help her concentrate.

Through the adjoining door, Pearl heard buckets of water being poured in the bath. Bucket after bucket. The footmen must be exhausted, for it was a large tub. If she could but luxuriate in a bath instead of languishing over political tracts.

"Would you like me to ask for you to bathe first? Since the water is here?" Lily asked, meeting Pearl's eyes in the mirror.

It was tempting. "But if the bath is for my lord..." Pearl trailed off, still looking at Lily. Pearl wanted that bath. The hot water turning her pale skin pink, hot enough for sweat to bead on her face. And it would alert her erstwhile husband of her occupying the house. He would finally be forced to face her proximity, to acknowledge her existence.

"And who knows where he may be?" Lily said.

Quite right. He hadn't bothered to show up for any meals or be available for callers. He'd abdicated his position as lord, merely living in the house and allowing his mother and Pearl to run it. As far as Pearl was concerned, that abdication also ensured he bathed second. She could put off her reading and irritate her husband all in one move. "Please, Lily. Inform his lordship's valet that I will be taking the first bath. Please add extra rosewater."

"Of course, my lady," Lily said.

"Even more rosewater than is reasonable. Spare no bottle." Pearl grinned. Hellhound of sunshine, indeed. He wouldn't forget that he had a wife again.

◈

JAMES FINISHED his exercises and wound his way to the master suite. If he wanted to sleep in a bed tonight, he ought to get used to the one in there. It was supposed to be his. And that's where the bath was readied. He wiped at his brow and his chest with a towel, enjoying the scrape of rough fabric. If he'd engaged a trainer, they would scrape the sweat from him, just as any professional athlete. Both Bess and

John had admitted once that it was the best part of training—when the trainer took care of you at the end, after you had nothing left to give.

James didn't want a trainer to push him when he didn't want to be pushed. But having enough wealth meant a quality bath to keep his limbs from cramping as they cooled. In some ways, James agreed with John and Bess's assessment of the best part of an exercise. The relaxing bath at the end.

Phillip waited for him at his door. "Ah, my lord, I need to—"

James walked past him. Whatever the issue was could wait. James had woken with a hangover, and he'd managed to wrest the day into productivity despite it. He'd earned this. He yanked off his shoes, tossing them across the room. His father's room. It felt bland and impersonal, which was an improvement. He unbuttoned his trousers and yanked them down, still moving towards the bathing room.

He stomped the trouser leg and stepped out of it, leaving the garment crumpled behind him. He flung open the door to the bathing room, anticipating the hot water, the steam in his face, and he found...a woman.

She luxuriated in the bath, her eyes closed, pinkness blushing the apples of her cheeks. Her red hair piled messily on top of her head, as if she had been in the middle of brushing it out when it was pinned back up. Her milky skin was marked a shocking red where it dipped below the water line. Pale breasts floated, ripe and full. Her legs were bent, but through the water, he could just spy a thatch of gold between her legs.

James knew his mouth hung open like some kind of rube. It finally occurred to him that this sensuous creature was Pearl. The Pearl he'd come to know as quiet and dutiful, not the lounging Siren before him.

The Pearl who took her exercise with a straw-filled mannequin and her bare fists. Now there was so much more that was bare. So, so much more.

He expected her to cover herself or run or stammer some excuses. But she didn't. Her arms spread wide along the rim of the bathing tub, as if his presence was absolutely no bother. Slowly, she opened her eyes, pinning him with her blue gaze. His mouth went dry. This was very different from spying her bare legs. This was...everything. Her attention, her confidence—it heightened his awareness all over again.

"Yes, my lord?"

James wouldn't stammer like some kind of schoolboy. He'd seen naked women in his life, and he wouldn't be cowed by this one. Though it was very difficult to keep his body in check. Only his persistent fatigue prevented an obvious and embarrassing display on his own very nude body. He managed to keep himself at half-mast. "You are in my bath."

"Is it yours? I was under the impression that we shared the bathing chamber."

He ground his teeth. "You know perfectly well that I had this drawn for me."

Her arms came off the edge of the bathing tub and she leaned forward. The motion obscured the sight of her breasts, but he found the graceful expanse of her back to be just as alluring. "And how would I know that, my lord? You keep to yourself. You don't join me for meals, and you certainly don't respond to invitations. You don't sleep in your own bedchamber. How am I supposed to know what is for you when it is a domain only I occupy?"

The heat in her voice was palpable. She was angry with him. He knew it. His own temper flared in return—he'd spent all day drowning out the disrespectful ideas and thoughts he'd had about her.

Could she not see he was trying? "Why do you care where I eat and where I sleep?"

Her jaw set. "You brought me to an empty house and abandoned me."

"We signed a contract. You're a grown woman. It isn't as if I've barred you from leaving the house, or kept your friends from visiting. Now *you* are in *my* bath."

"You may have it when I am done. And I am not done." Pearl leaned back and resumed her position, eyes closed.

James was so angry he felt like he could pull the entire tub up and throw it across the room, water and naked Pearl and all. He growled. As if *she* could dismiss *him*.

"And do put some clothes on."

He narrowed his eyes. "The same could be said for yourself, *my lady*."

"Except I am the one who is actually in the bath. You are the one standing there in the altogether."

"The what?"

"You heard me."

"I don't believe I've heard that phrase before. *The altogether*." The steam built up condensation on the walls, and James felt the dampness seeping onto his skin.

Pearl opened her eyes, the irritation plain on her face. "You asked me to marry you. I did. Don't claim ignorance of my background."

His anger morphed into frustration. His half-sister, Margaret, would have pointed out that Pearl had lived a very different life, and that as the person possessing more power, he should be sensitive to that. He gritted his teeth. "I wasn't mocking your background, I was merely—"

"It is awfully difficult to enjoy this bath with you standing there waving your pole about."

"My *pole?*" James laughed. He liked the reference,

and said anatomy was garnering energy from the fact that she'd noticed it.

"Get out, please." Her eyes closed again.

"I don't believe I will. I think me and my pole will stand here and wait our turn."

One of her blue eyes cracked open. "Your pole will stand, too?"

An off-color joke from Pearl Arthur, mouse of Marylebone? He wasn't quite so put out by losing the hot water. His cock jumped as she shifted in the tub, the water dipping low on her body. "Why, Miss Arthur, do you have a dirty mind?"

Her face fell and she closed her eye. A drip of condensation fell from the ceiling onto the tiles below. "Miss Arthur no longer exists."

Her words felt like a door slammed in his face. The condensation pooled in the grouted lines of the black and white tiles. Real shame crept into him, unable to be kept at bay by the walls he'd erected in his youth.

She was right—he'd made her into a viscountess. Miss Arthur ceased when they said their vows in front of that bishop. It still didn't feel real—at least to him. But she was correct. He had brought her here and ignored her. Even his mother had said so. He slipped on a banyan robe that hung on the wall and waited until he heard the water slosh out of the tub as she exited. He felt like a cad.

❦

PEARL'S SKIN burned from the water, or at least that's what she told herself. She was proud of herself for standing her ground, not covering her body, letting him see what he'd married. He thought he'd married a mouse—the women at the Haglund's ball had said as much. It's how they viewed her, and she had let them. Mrs. Tyler had taught them meekness and amiability, and Pearl wanted to be a good student. She'd never gone to school before, and from what John had described, the rewards were there for the taking.

The posture and walking had been easy. The lessons she'd had while John sparred in Tony's boxing gym had given her a grace and agility other girls lacked. Her body was not foreign to herself, as some of the girls had described it when learning the same techniques. Her body was hers. Her own. The idea that somehow her mind was separate from her limbs seemed strange at best and asinine at worst. She'd always been in her skin. That was what Gabriel had discovered and made her feel ashamed of.

But no more shame. No more men telling her how to feel about her own body.

Now this body was steaming and red from her husband's bath. He had been livid, which pleased her. She was glad to get a reaction from him—it made him acknowledge that she existed. And the bath had been lovely, if she'd been given the opportunity to enjoy it thoroughly. Lily had added the entire bottle of rosewater, which made the bath aromatic, but not as gaggingly floral as she'd hoped. She wanted James to stalk out of the bath smelling like a perfumery.

She would have stayed in longer, but she was thoroughly unsettled by their exchange. It had never occurred to her that he might enter the room without a stitch on. And he was a fine sight. Having just exercised, his muscles were in full display. The ridges of his stomach, the thickness of his thighs. And then there was that dark thatch between those powerful thighs.

That was a revelation. Pearl had seen naked men. She'd seen hundreds clad in only breeches, as she'd been around training gyms in her girlhood, and she'd watched John in his early set-tos. And she'd seen Mrs. Coldcroft's clients, who were not the sort that Pearl would have preferred to see. And then, she usually only saw the bottom halves. They rarely fully disrobed. Their bottoms had been flabby, pale like fish bellies, muscled just below the beltline only to fall like an emptied pig's bladder.

But Pearl's husband was—her mind went unexpectedly blank. Her husband was not like an emptied pig's bladder. Her blood thrummed with the memory of him. As she wrapped herself in her nightgown and robe, she heard the splashing of the water in the tub, no doubt as he sank himself into it.

She had an urge to spy at the keyhole like she had when she lived with Mrs. Coldcroft. But no, she'd antagonized him enough for tonight. Instead, her imagination went wild, picturing him pouring water over his head, his wet hair dripping down those sculpted shoulders. She shook her head. Those thoughts would only lead to her throwing herself at him, which would obviously end poorly.

The sting of her maiden name on his lips cooled her blood. She knew she was invisible, but to have him so unaware was painful. He'd made these life changes happen for her, and then he just...forgot?

Gabriel had shown her what happened when she wanted a man more than he wanted her. But if she could tempt James into wanting her, then she would, if for no other reason than revenge for making her feel so bloody insignificant.

She checked under the bed. Her pack was still there, hidden up between the front posts of the bed and the bed table. Dark and inconspicuous, no one should notice it. She tamped the candles in the room and crawled into bed, unhappy. She curled up like a bug, pretending to sleep, but really, she was listening to the water shift in the bathing room, listening to see if she could discern the movements of the man inside.

It could have been minutes or hours that she dozed. When she awoke, she felt as refreshed as if it were morning. Tossing and turning gave her no relief, so she lay in bed and listened. The house was quiet. She got up and felt her way to the bathing room, and listened. Nothing. She struck a match and lit a candle from her mantle, taking it with her as she peered into the room to find it empty. She peered through the adjoining door's keyhole to see that her husband's room was pitch black as well.

And then she heard it. Faint piano music. She wrapped herself in her dressing gown and slipped out of her room. Lit by a single candle, she descended the stairs, following the sound, as if the strains of music were sung by Odysseus's Sirens. Standing in front of James's study door, she listened as he played.

It was almost delicate, the piano sounding more like a woman dancing than the man who had stood naked and angry, fists clenched, just hours before. She sank next to the door, letting her head rest against the doorframe. She tucked her feet under the hem of her dressing gown to keep herself warm.

Perhaps there was more to this man than just the selfishness that she had experienced in the last few days. The music he created was so much more than his apparent narrow desires. Not that it excused his behavior towards her. Staring into the darkness, Pearl chose to think of the music as a private concert.

She listened as he worked through the same passages over and over again before moving on to the rest of the piece. Finally she grew cold enough that she returned to her bed, her feelings more disordered than ever.

CHAPTER 8

J ames could make an effort, as his mother had requested. Originally, he'd thought attending to Pearl in public was enough, but apparently he was incorrect. Since Pearl complained of being abandoned—particularly while lounging nude in the bath—he would bring it to his mother's attention so she could also make an effort to welcome the new viscountess to their home. At least he could prove it wasn't just him doing damage.

Thus, James woke earlier than he had since voyaging with Rose and Henry. They were both ghastly morning people, waking with the dawn, eager to start the day, and to talk. God, how they talked. They preferred coffee in the morning, cups steaming, and chattering like magpies. James wanted a gentler morning filled with dozing, warming tea, stretching, and looking at the sky.

Not wanting to bother with his valet, James pulled on trousers and a waistcoat over his linen shirt. He heard nothing from the room next door, which meant Pearl was either sleeping or had already gone down. James shook his head. It was hard enough to get up so early in this strange room. Last night after his bath, he'd gone down and played his new sheet music until his hands stiffened. He needed the extra exhaustion after his encounter with Pearl. He couldn't bear to toss and turn in the master's bedchamber. The viscount's bed.

When he'd finally pulled himself away from the keyboard, his shoulders felt tight across the yoke, and his legs had cramped. He stretched some, then slipped into bed, his mind dampening like a doused wick. He hadn't the time to fret about the room, or his father, or any of it. His body was worked, his mind fatigued.

Pulling on his boots, he readied to face the day, with the exception of his cravat. That would have to wait for Phillip. But he was at least ready to face Pearl. To make amends with his viscountess. Within reason. The bath had still been cold and smelled pungently of rosewater. He supposed he'd invited that with his "hellhound of sunshine" comment.

Descending to the breakfast room, he encountered a maid who seemed so surprised by his appearance that she squawked with alarm and flattened herself against the wall as he passed. Was he such a beast this early? It did nothing to reassure him that he wasn't turning into his father. When he arrived in the dining room, Pearl looked up in shock. Her fork clattered against her plate. At least she hadn't squawked.

"Is all well?" she asked, eyes wide as if she were expecting disastrous news.

"Shouldn't it be? Unless my rumbling stomach is too much of a plague for you." A lie—he wasn't hungry, even though he knew he ought to be. He couldn't remember a time when his stomach didn't churn, especially first thing in the morning.

She gestured to a seat nearby. "It is your house, my lord. Do break your fast."

He gave her a courteous bow and headed to the banquet, where dishes of eggs and ham and toast were arranged. "They do this every morning?"

"They do," Pearl said.

James grunted. Surprises never ceased. He filled his plate and sat next to Pearl, who also had a steaming pot of tea. Of all the things on offer, that sounded the most appetizing. "How do we get another cup for me?"

Her eyes rounded.

Ah, yes, he could see how silly it might seem. It was his house, after all. He should know. But the last time he attended breakfast in this room, he'd been in leading strings, and that was just to allow his father to eat and berate him at the same time. "I don't usually take meals in this room."

"Apparently not." Pearl rose and rang for service.

Mr. Barton appeared, looking much fresher than James had ever seen him. Perhaps Mr. Barton was a morning person, too.

"Another for the tea service, Mr. Barton," Pearl instructed. She seemed to the manner born suddenly, again, not as James had expected. He hoped she wasn't overly chatty this early.

The butler bowed slightly, giving James a judgmental glance. "Of course, my lady."

James had the disconcerting suspicion that the servants were taking to Pearl more than him. He was the one who paid their wages. Shouldn't Barton have addressed him? But then, Pearl had jumped to it, while James sat there contemplating his ham.

"I wouldn't worry," Pearl said.

"I beg your pardon?" James said, looking up.

"Your ham," she said, pointing to it. "It won't come back to life."

He smiled at her. She was making an effort, too. "You have put my mind at ease." He cut into it. "Truly."

She smiled and returned to reading the papers in front of her. He watched her, slowly raising her teacup to her lips, sipping as she looked intently at whatever occupied her. He'd assumed that it was a newspaper at first. Whatever else did people read at the breakfast table? But upon closer inspection, she was reading some kind of handwritten copy. He couldn't quite make it out, but her face was screwed up in concentration. A small furrow deepened between her brows.

She was adorable, like a baby deer, all scrunched up like that. Her red hair was pulled back into a loose and low chignon, which she had probably done herself. Somehow, seeing her unguarded at the breakfast table felt intimate in a way that seeing her in the bath hadn't. Well, that had been different. A different type of intimacy. He took another bite of ham. They were married, after all; some type of intimacy was likely expected. His stomach rebelled. Ham was not a morning food. Whose idea was that?

Barton appeared with another pot of tea and a cup for him.

"My thanks," James said, eager to move away from the ham. Barton bowed and left. James fixed his tea—bracingly strong with a bit of sugar. Contemplating the woman next to him, he did his best to keep the amount of her skin he'd seen at bay. That she was surprising him, shocking him, even now—James couldn't keep to himself any longer. Apparently he would be the chatty one. "May I interrupt your reading?"

Pearl looked up slowly, tearing herself from the page and dropping a finger on the line to retain her place in the text. It reminded him of Rose. Except perhaps that Rose was always irritated when he interrupted her reading. "Of course, my lord. What do you need?"

The question stopped him short. She sounded like a servant. No longer to the manner born with him, then. It irked him. He didn't *need* anything. "I am curious as to what has your utmost concentration."

Her expression melted into relief, and she bestowed a smile on him. A real one, not a polite one. "Lady Teeton gave me some texts to read, and I have to admit that it is more intellectual than I am accustomed to, but I think I'm understanding it."

"Lady Teeton?"

"Yes, after you said we shouldn't attend their dinner party, I called round and she asked me to look over the bill her husband wrote."

"I guarantee you that Lord Teeton didn't write any bill."

Pearl glanced down at the papers. "Well, surely the reason it is in a feminine hand is because she does his copying for him. She's very dedicated to him and his work."

James scoffed. "Dedicated is one word for it." He watched as Pearl's spine straightened. Ah, there it went. All that soft, unguarded intimacy evaporated again. Who knew that this was his real talent in life? Alienating other people.

"I don't believe Lady Teeton is disingenuous."

"No, she is very earnest." Silence stretched between them as Pearl stared at him. He sipped his tea, letting her stare. He knew this power play. Whoever spoke first lost. So he didn't. But he was also very careful to not notice her chewing on her delectable lower lip.

"She is my friend," Pearl said very quietly.

"That was a fast progression. I thought you just met her." James didn't know why the Teetons irritated him so much. Forbidding a friendship with them was a sure way to push Pearl towards them.

"What is the time frame required to make a friend?" Pearl asked, her gaze narrowing to a point that made him squirm in his seat. Oh yes, she should have been a governess. No schoolboy could have withstood that kind of disapproval.

"Surely more than half an hour of discussion is

required before you declare your friendship?" He disliked the idea of anyone else getting close to her. Not that he would get close to her. Obviously.

"She's interested in my opinion." Her tone was still subdued, but there was more to it than just her words. "And it's been more than half an hour. You disappeared early at that particular assembly. I doubt you remember much of that night." She gave him a level stare that made him squirm.

James was reminded of the science of harmonics, where the reverberations of sound could incur more and more intervals above those pitches struck, if one could but parse them. Here Pearl said little, but her meaning echoed above it all. He just didn't know the context.

He switched tactics. "And what is the new bill about?"

"Repealing the death penalty for minor criminal offenses."

"Why? It's not like they enforce the death penalty now that they can ship them off."

"But they can sentence anyone to death for such petty offenses. I knew a boy, once——" Pearl shook her head, withdrawing her memory from the conversation. "Apparently there is a growing movement to make fewer offenses punishable by hanging. However, repeal laws have been short on votes every time. Even though it's been proven that harsher punishments don't work. People steal for all sorts of reasons, and given a desperate person, they'll steal regardless of the penalty. The intention behind those laws is punishment, not correction."

"Seems like something that should have been fixed long ago."

Pearl stared at him again, though this time she seemed surprised, or expectant somehow?

Time to switch topics once more. "Do you have

any needs today? I plan on continuing in my study this afternoon."

"I'm at home for callers today, so I shall be in the drawing room. I'll meet with Mrs. Foraker first to go over the household accounts, and then I'm expecting Miss Perry to call today, and perhaps Lydia or Agnes and Jack."

James was impressed. He hadn't thought about her applying herself to her new position as viscountess since his mother still lived with them. Good for her. She returned to her reading. He did his best to not notice where the square neckline of her gown gaped just below her clavicle, before the rise of her breast. He did not think about what that inch of skin would feel like on his bare palm. Or what it would be like to worry her bottom lip with his teeth. Because that would be disrespectful. And he'd made a promise.

He swallowed his scalding tea and excused himself.

"I'D LIKE to hire another maid to replace the one who left us last month. The others have been making up for the shortfall, but they are not happy about it, especially since Mary went and hurt her foot." Mrs. Foraker took another sip of her tea.

Pearl was having a hard time focusing on this interview, even though she was the one who had insisted upon it. A lady needed to keep the pulse of her household, and no one knew the household better than the housekeeper and the butler.

Mrs. Tyler had instructed them to keep the housekeeper on task, the conversation business-like, and absolutely not indulge in tea and biscuits with them. Pearl, however, was of the opinion that nothing cemented loyalty and friendship quite like a good snack, so Mrs. Tyler's rules could be damned. In fact, this way, meeting with the housekeeper was far more pleasant than Mrs. Tyler had estimated. Mrs. Foraker was knowledgeable about so many aspects of the house, the staff, and the family itself.

Pearl knew the stories—or at least some of them. She knew the previous viscount had harmed Lydia. She knew that he'd harmed other women, and had planned to harm Agnes if he'd gotten a chance. It was morbid to be curious, but she was now living in the man's house. Not that she believed in the occult, but could a man so cruel linger?

"Lady Andrepont?" Mrs. Foraker prompted. "May I hire on another maid?"

"Oh!" Pearl blushed, knowing that it would make her seem young and inexperienced. Mrs. Foraker would likely feel more apt to help her when Pearl needed her. "I hadn't realized you needed my approval to do so."

"You are the lady of the house now, are you not? Unless you would prefer I continue to consult with the dowager Lady Andrepont instead?"

"No, no," Pearl said. Not all her fluttering was an act. It had been hard to concentrate when thinking of James's appearance at breakfast. Even so early in the morning, he was shockingly handsome. The way the light seemed to lay against his cheek in the breakfast room was worth artistic study. She could barely keep her thoughts on Lady Teeton's political tracts with him so near. And now, well...now, focusing on household business was a challenge. "That is, do consult with the dowager if it seems necessary, but I would like to oversee the house. It only seems appropriate to take on my responsibilities."

"Very well, then. Would you like to conduct the interviews, or shall I?"

"What did Lady Andrepont do?" Aside from wanting to induce Mrs. Foraker's feelings of friendship, Pearl also wanted to give the housekeeper the correct answer. She wanted to be good at this assignment of viscountess. How different could this occupation be from hauling water, tatting lace, or making matchsticks?

"She would have me conduct the interview and then introduce the new maid once she arrived." Mrs. Foraker betrayed no sign of irritation with Pearl's inexperience, but also no sign of affection.

Pearl suspected that the tragedy of the former viscount's presence caused a different sort of loyalty and friendship in this household. Bound by adverse conditions, not unlike soldiers, they had survived a horrific master.

"Then that is what I will do as well." Pearl sighed with relief and took a sip of tea. At least she had one correct answer. It made her bold. Now was the time, when she was still new and could excuse her curiosity as innocence. "May I ask what happened during the previous viscount's running of the household?"

Mrs. Foraker's expression flattened into complete blandness. "I don't know what you mean."

Pearl debated in her mind, but then decided to push on. Answers might help her navigate both her husband and her mother-in-law. "He clearly wasn't a kind man. And his study remains locked and untouched. Since he is dead, should we not open it and refurbish it to our own use?"

Mrs. Foraker stiffened at the suggestion. "I would not presume."

Pearl tried a different tack. "Perhaps you wouldn't mind telling me what happened to him? He was still somewhat young to die so suddenly, wasn't he?"

"The magistrate ruled it a case of a robbery gone afoul. Many a wealthy man has been the victim of such an attack." Mrs. Foraker pushed her teacup and saucer onto the table. "My lady, thank you for your time. I must attend to my duties."

The questions had clearly provoked her, so Pearl decided to warm her up with a different topic before she left. It would do no good to leave her feeling so disconcerted. "One more thing before you go. What does my lady mother do with her time? I have not seen her during the day here. Nor at dinner."

Mrs. Foraker contemplated her teacup for a moment, as if it would reveal the nature of her loyalty. Finally, she relented. "I don't wish to speak out of turn. It is not my place to keep track of her whereabouts. However, if you were desiring to speak with her, she often spends her time in the potting shed outside."

Pearl frowned. How many times had she looked out on that very garden and seen no one? "Where does she prefer? I have not seen her."

The lines in Mrs. Foraker's forehead disappeared. "There is a potting shed and greenhouse towards the mews. You'll find her in there." Mrs. Foraker stood. "I have much to do. If you need nothing else, my lady?"

Pearl smiled. They weren't friends yet, but if Pearl could manage it, they soon would be. "No, Mrs. Foraker. Thank you for taking the time. I look forward to our next chat."

The housekeeper took her leave, and Pearl went to the drawing room window that looked over the gardens. Off in the corner, near the mews, indeed stood two small buildings. Pearl would have never thought to look for the former viscountess there. She seemed far too sophisticated to be in a greenhouse.

But she hadn't seen her mother-in-law in many days. Hopefully she wouldn't deem it an intrusion for Pearl to go after her. She glanced down at her day dress. It wasn't a particularly expensive one, so she might as well risk it. In fact, she'd been dismayed that she was wearing this dress when James deigned to attend breakfast. She had far more flattering day gowns, things that didn't clash with her hair or skin.

Now that the housekeeper was gone, Pearl let herself indulge in thoughts of her husband. It was impossible to remember all the ways in which he'd abandoned her when she now had seen James's naked thighs and the ridges of his...stomach. Even now, her heart tripped faster. If commandeering his bath got him to attend breakfast with her, what did she need to do for him to come to dinner?

She left the drawing room, descended the stairs, and stopped. She had no idea how to get to the garden. Would she need to go down through the kitchens? Undoubtedly she could get to the garden from there, but surely there was a better way.

When she'd been in the ballroom-turned-gymnasium, she recalled French doors that opened onto a garden. Retracing her steps from yesterday, she found herself back amongst sawdust-filled bags. It was too tempting to let pass. This time, however, she didn't bother removing her shoes and stockings. She wouldn't indulge in full exercise; she had things to do.

Of course, some of her training was lost to memory, but there was so much that remained in her body. Movements that felt good in her hips, the twist of her lower back.

Now, if she could get her hands on a sword. She smiled at the thought of her husband finding her with an ancient cavalry sword in her hands. The technique might as well be ancient, for all it was used in modern fights. But learning the techniques of an older time had spoken to her. There was something about those older stories, of swords and fighters being chained to the floor by their ankles as if they were wild animals being baited.

A fight using only her bare knuckles didn't interest her. With her smaller size, she wasn't sure she could compete. But if she could use everything at her disposal—kicks, a sword, or even a long staff, she could extend her reach and be competitive. That's why both Bess and John had advised her to learn the old rules, even if they weren't welcome in a contemporary set-to.

Pearl was good at all the things fighters weren't supposed to be good at now, like weapons, yes, but also wrestling. Critics hated fighters that dodged blows. And Pearl was fast. Very fast. She'd learned pickpocketing as a child, and somehow it had translated into her feet as well. Outstepping an opponent was easy for her even though it was something frowned upon by the general audience. As a child, no magistrate had ever collared her, no merchant had ever caught her. When she wanted to be invisible, she was. Too bad that was the case outside of her criminal endeavors as well.

The sudden jolt of reality brought her back to herself. The lure of the gymnasium had been enough to pause her efforts in making overtures to her mother-in-law. Pearl walked the perimeter of the large room, feeling the size of it, learning its edges for no other reason than to cool her body and mind. It was easy for her mind to stay frantic and heightened after training, always scanning, wanting to dodge and duck and run.

But she had to return to her role as viscountess. Breathing low and slow, as if she'd been running, calmed her. This was the price of stability. Decorum. Gentility. Meekness. The Pearl that Mrs. Tyler had sculpted reemerged, and the Pearl of her girlhood receded. She would seek out her new lady mother and inquire after dinner plans. Perhaps they might enjoy some camaraderie. Would tea and seedcakes do the trick with her as well?

Finishing her exploration of the gymnasium's corners, Pearl used the ballroom's terrace doors to access the garden. It was a bit overgrown, as if there weren't enough gardeners to manage. Should she recommend hiring a gardener? Just outside the ballroom was a proper sort of garden one might expect of Mayfair, with shrubberies and flowers, all planted tidily, but in need of shaping. As Pearl continued, the formal gardens gave way to more flowers and a stone path, and finally she reached the kitchen beds, full of vegetables and herbs. The two garden sheds were in front of her, and the wall to the mews beyond them.

The greenhouse was made of glass, and while the panes weren't exceptionally clear, she could see someone moving inside it. She tried not to be nervous, but how was she to approach her? What would she say to the older woman? *I'm lonely, so I interrogated the housekeeper in order to find some company?*

Blimey, she was a mess. But there was naught to do about her turmoil. Mrs. Tyler would advise to be patient and meek, and soon enough she would draw attention from her mother-in-law because of her modesty. But this house didn't seem to work the way Mrs. Tyler believed a great house would. If Pearl wanted relationships with anyone here, she would have to force the issue. If she waited any longer in her tenure, her loneliness would become even more awkward and she might expire from embarrassment.

Pearl squared her shoulders and approached the door. She raised her hand to knock, but the door swung open to greet her.

"I thought I saw someone lurking on the path," Lady Andrepont said. Her face was lightly powdered with dirt, and she wore a smock over her gown. She looked more refreshed and relaxed than Pearl had ever seen her.

"I wasn't sure you wanted company," Pearl said, entering the warm shed. She was glad she'd found the courage. Turning to leave as Lady Andrepont opened the door would have been even more embarrassing than forcing her presence upon her.

"Not at all. I assumed your curiosity would get the

better of you eventually." Lady Andrepont offered a faint smile and turned back to the workbench.

Pearl froze. Had Mrs. Foraker informed her about the questions she'd asked? "My curiosity?"

"After all, the mistress of the house is tasked with caring for all its inhabitants. Medicines and poultices, tisanes and tinctures. All of those can be found in these gardens. I worked very hard to keep my family and my staff healthy and strong."

A blush crept up Pearl's neck, burning as it crawled. "I, I—" she stammered. "I know nothing of medicines." Mrs. Tyler had mentioned it, but it seemed somehow unimportant. Like learning Greek in order to read and converse with an intellectual husband. Lord knew she didn't have one of those either.

Lady Andrepont laid a hand on her arm. "Since I now live in this house at the generosity of you and my son, I would be happy to teach you what I know. Should you be interested to learn."

"Please." Pearl was surprised at the dowager's sudden warmth. It was as if an entirely different woman stood before her: generous, kind, thoughtful, and...covered in soil. Not to mention, this was a gaping hole in Pearl's education. Helping the people who relied upon her was essential to becoming a great lady. How embarrassing that Mrs. Tyler had glossed over these necessary facts.

"Where to start? There is so much to it. Do you know how to dry plants?" Lady Andrepont's brow arched, the same as her son's, the same as Lydia's. Pearl almost laughed aloud.

"I do know how to do that. I just don't know what to do with them afterwards. Or what to give to whom."

Lady Andrepont's beautiful face was like marble, unlined, uncreased, as if she rarely made an expression. Only here in the greenhouse did the woman's emotions seem to bubble to the surface. It struck Pearl as sad. The women she'd known in her girlhood had bouquets of wrinkles by the time their children were grown. Crow's feet at the eyes from squinting in the sun or smiling at their babies. But this woman had no smile lines. No frown lines even. As if she had lived in purgatory—neither good nor bad—only existing. Was this to be Pearl's fate as well?

"Let's start with the simple things. Peppermint." She held it aloft and sniffed at it, then held it out for Pearl to sniff. "Good for calming a roiling stomach or excessive gas."

Pearl dutifully sniffed the sprig, not wanting to admit that yes, she had known that. But some things didn't seem like medicine, just common sense. "And that goes in a tea?"

Lady Andrepont smiled. The transformation of her face was shocking. She was striking without smiling, but when she smiled, it was as if the world cracked apart and true beauty showed through. Pearl found it to be an even greater tragedy that she had no smile lines.

"You do know your medicines," Lady Andrepont said.

"I never thought giving peppermint tea for an upset stomach would be considered medicine."

"Give yourself more credit, Pearl. You're likely wiser than you know." Lady Andrepont gave her a sidelong look that seemed to imply she knew more about Pearl than she was letting on.

They worked side by side, chatting amiably about the plants and where and when to cut them.

"I meant to ask you about the many teapots in the dining room. They are all so different and beautiful. Are they gifts?" Pearl asked.

Her mother-in-law smiled. "Some are, yes. Others, just things I have collected. London has the luxury of variety."

"That is what I noticed about your collection." Pearl looked over to connect with the other woman. This was her opportunity to pull her mother-in-law into some semblance of friendship. "The different styles I recognized thanks to Mrs. Tyler's exacting education on ceramics, all except one. It was so strange that sitting amongst the Queen's Ware and Delftware, there was a clay teapot. It had been fired, of course, but didn't have the high gloss of the others. It was such a strange addition to the collection. The interior was like nothing I'd seen either, as if it had two separate chambers inside."

The other woman's expression hardened and Pearl felt her pull away. "That's interesting that you mention them. I don't remember them very well. I'll have to revisit them sometime." She looked around the room. "I would love to start teaching you about how to combine medicines, but I find that receipts can be quite mentally taxing. Why don't we continue tomorrow, and you can bring down a notebook to record them?"

Pearl felt the same distance as when she'd questioned Mrs. Foraker about the late viscount. "Of course. Whatever you like." They hadn't finished hanging all the sprigs to dry, but clearly, she was dismissed.

Filthy now, covered in fine soil from the workbench, Pearl wasn't even sure where to wipe her hands. Tomorrow she would ask for a smock to protect her gown. She left her mother-in-law in the greenhouse, and whilst shaking out her skirts, she found an entrance to the house that wasn't in the ballroom. She crept in, and when she approached the ballroom from the passageway, she heard someone working the heavy bag.

Her muscles echoed in pleased acknowledgment of the work. She peeked in to find James, shirtless and sweating. He looked up, catching the heavy bag as it swung back towards him.

"Good afternoon," he said as he caught his breath.

"Good afternoon," she returned, unsure of how to respond since her mind had stopped functioning. Something about the way his forearms flexed as he gripped the bag caused every nerve in her body to flare. She should turn away. She should not look. She should run.

"Have you had a good morning?" he asked, casually, as if he were strolling in Hyde Park and not in a state of undress. And what a state it was.

Her mouth was dry and she couldn't think of what to say, so she nodded instead. She was covered in dirt and not at all presentable. "And you?" she finally managed.

"Indeed. I enjoy my time in the gymnasium."

She dipped into a shallow curtsy and turned, hoping to make her escape in her soiled gown.

"Don't you?"

The words stopped her cold. She turned back towards him. "Pardon me?"

"Invigorating, isn't it?"

She whirled back towards him, frozen to the spot. He stalked towards her. Every muscle seemed to ripple as he moved.

"The gymnasium. The sawdust bags can almost feel like a real opponent sometimes, don't you think?"

She wanted to flee. Every bit of her was crying to run—well, almost every bit. There was one very loud bit that was keen to be captured. She stood her ground, heart thumping like a rabbit's.

He reached her, his body close enough to touch. "You, viscountess, have secrets."

Her nerves heightened beyond control, Pearl burst out in anxious laughter. The idea that *she* had secrets, when this whole house was positively built of them.

James looked annoyed and confused, which she didn't mind at all.

"I beg your pardon, my lord. I have no secrets." Her mirth broke his spell over her.

"I think you do," he said.

Pearl shook her head. "Oh no. It's impossible to have a secret if no one wants to know it. Then it's merely minding one's business." She curtsied low and left him. And because she couldn't help a good parting shot: "I'll be the first having a bath before dinner."

When she glanced back over her shoulder, he was grinning.

৩≹৯

CHAPTER 9

The little minx. He finished his routine and went upstairs to find the bathing room already vacated, disappointing but understandable, and the water refreshed. It was scented this time with halved oranges, which he tolerated better than the gallons of rosewater. He'd wanted to burst in on her again and even wore his trousers into the room, just in case she was lingering.

He wanted to spar with her—verbally, of course. Or perhaps, he could admit to himself, he wanted to see her outline in the water, the top of her breasts bare, the spread of her elegant shoulders on display, the red-gold hair teasing out of that hastily pinned mess. He shook his head and shucked his trousers.

This was not the control he usually displayed. He needed to be respectful. Corinthian John had once killed a man with his bare fists, and that had been a fight in the ring. God knew what the man would to do someone who ruined his sister.

The sister who had skills of her own. Something about that must run in their blood. James had been impressed with her speed while she worked the straw man: she was fast, so very fast. Though, that could have been his hangover making her seem much faster than she truly was. Even so, how could she hide herself behind that bland exterior? He sank into the lukewarm water.

He was willing to cede her the point that she couldn't have a secret if no one cared to ask. He had been guilty of it. Who would think that woman had anything remotely interesting to say, let alone do?

Lydia had been the focus of his family, and her boxing was scandal enough for all of them. And then the business with Agnes. Dear God, he'd almost lost his mind over it. He was glad he had been wrong about Jack, but he'd been ready to tear the lad apart with his bare hands for taking advantage of his cousin's soft disposition.

Turned out that wasn't Jack's intent, so James humbled himself and facilitated the match between Jack and Agnes. It wasn't a pretty day for his ego, but he would do anything for Agnes. Or Lydia. Or Margaret. Or his mother. Marrying milquetoast Pearl seemed reasonable when the rest of his family required so much of him. But, like with Jack, James appeared to be wrong again. There was more to Pearl —including acres of milky skin to be tasted—no. No. He wasn't an animal.

Soaping himself, he reveled in the moment that she hadn't been able to speak due to the sight of him. As if he hadn't noticed. His vanity was healthy enough to enjoy it when a woman liked what she saw. It wasn't the first time, but something about ruffling bland Pearl's feathers—forcing her to reveal the passionate woman underneath—that was fun. A game he might continue. Why not? Where was the harm in preening for her?

He would dress for dinner in his finest. Perhaps he was a peacock, as Rose had once accused him of being. But was there not value in that? Why not look his best? Why not tease one's wife—

The thought stopped him. *Wife*. It was the first time he'd even thought the word and meant Pearl.

He hadn't meant to call her that, even in his own mind.

He swallowed hard. Self-loathing cloaked him. He wouldn't be like his father. He wouldn't. Women were not possessions. They were not meant to be used and discarded without thought.

A wife is like this piano, his father had told him on the day they acquired the large instrument that was now in James's study. *Useful on occasion, beautiful to look at, and impossible to get rid of.*

Music had not been what his father wanted James to focus on, but James had managed to talk him into lessons and a piano by convincing him it would make James seem more powerful. Displaying rare skill and commanding a room were the most important tools in dominance. And music commanded any room. Of course, recitals and the like were not to be engaged in—too much akin to a young lady's display of talents—but James hadn't wanted to pursue music because of the performance aspect. His father had acquiesced, a rare occurrence, and ordered the most expensive pianoforte he could find.

His father had been a nightmare, and he would not emulate that monster. James needed to dismiss all thoughts of Pearl, and any idea that might lead him to believe she was, in all truth, his wife. Others might use that word, but he would not. It wasn't safe. For either of them.

PEARL SAT with her darning in the drawing room, waiting for dinner. Lady Andrepont had seemed happy to turn over this particular domestic chore. Regardless of station, a wife's duty was to darn her family's socks and shirts, and at least Pearl knew how to do that. There was no pleasure nor resentment at such a task; it was a job to be done. She appreciated the feeling of accomplishment as the pile shrank.

Mr. Barton would fetch her when dinner was served, the only break she allowed herself from her evening ritual. It had become the only rite she could rely on in this house, where no one spoke unless spoken to.

When the door creaked open, she didn't bother looking up, only finished her stitch and stuck her needle in to finish later. But Barton's words never came. Puzzled, Pearl glanced up to find her husband staring at her, equally bewildered.

"What are you doing?" he asked.

"What are *you* doing?" It was perfectly obvious what she was doing, and completely expected. He, on the other hand, was not expected here. And looking quite dashing in all black. His waistcoat was a fine ebony satin, shining beneath his jacket. The white cravat was simply knotted, held in place with a jet pin. His Hessian boots shined like a mirror, accenting how very form-fitting his breeches were. She'd heard stories of Beau Brummell when she was a child, but surely, he could not have competed with James.

"I'm waiting for the dinner gong," her husband said, taking the seat furthest from her.

"May I ask why?" Pearl removed her needle and resumed darning. She didn't need to look at him if he wouldn't look at her.

"Because if I went chasing my dinner into the kitchens, I'd likely end up with spit in one of my soup." James looked at her as if it were perfectly obvious.

Pearl burst out laughing for the second time that day—and the second time because of James. She couldn't help but look up from her task. "You don't think any of your staff would spit in your soup, do you?"

"Mrs. Foraker?" He raised his eyebrows.

"Absolutely. Crafty, that one, and she's known me since leading strings. Has absolutely no patience for me."

Pearl gave a teasing harrumph. "I can see why. You are positively infuriating."

James gave her his own teasing smile. "I have been a gentleman to you every step of the way. How could you deem me infuriating?"

Pearl swallowed her words. The question had gone deeper than flirtation. This felt like an earnest question, and he was right: he'd left her alone, given her freedom to come and go, allowed her to have her own money at her discretion. And, for some, refraining from her bed would seem the most gentlemanly thing to do. Especially since children were not expected. It was generous, from the standpoint of many.

She dared not admit that she'd hoped for more. Not of his generosity, but of *him*. That the sight of him in the bathing room had occupied her thoughts all afternoon. That seeing him shirtless in the gymnasium drove her to distraction. That she could barely refrain from touching herself in the bath, knowing he would be in the same water soon after. She practically squirmed, but managed to keep still.

Barton entered, saving her from explaining. "Dinner is served."

James stood, offering his arm. A proper gentleman. She took it, leaving her darning in the basket near the fire, her sole domestic responsibility available. He smelled of the oranges she'd instructed Phillip to put in the bath. It covered the scent of rosewater, and it reminded her of the fights. Oranges were the preferred food during and after set-tos since they gave the body fuel and water all at the same time.

"Thank you for having the bath refreshed for me, by the way," James said.

He must have noticed her smelling him. Her cringing blush was predictable and she hated it. "Of course," she said, doing her best to tamp down the heat. "Since I knew you would likely be needing one."

"Having caught me at my exercise."

"Precisely." Pearl let go of his arm as they entered the dining room, taking her usual seat at the side of the table so she could look out the windows. They had troubled to light the chandelier tonight, no doubt because the master of the house deigned to show himself.

"And you needed a bath because...?" James asked.

Her body went cold. He knew about her training. Somehow he'd found her secret. But she refused to let him feel like he'd won something. "Because I'd been out in the potting shed with your mother. We had a lovely afternoon together. I had no idea she was so adept at the herbal sciences."

James rolled his eyes as he subtly leaned back, allowing the footman space to serve the soup course. Pearl gave him a beatific grin, as if she had no idea what he was speaking about. Let him ask. Let him be direct. Let him show an interest in her. She had married the man, thinking, naively, that it meant some type of camaraderie. So if he wanted her, he could come get her.

"I had no idea you'd spent the day with my lady mother. I wonder why she has not come down to dinner." James finished his soup, as if the family not dining together was somehow strange.

The clear broth was tinged with ginger. Barton paired it with a crisp white wine. Pearl remembered what Lady Andrepont had said about ginger: good for nausea, and helped to amplify the blood. "When was the last time you dined together?"

"When we had that dinner party. The Townsends were here."

"That was months ago," Pearl pointed out. The

footman removed the soup. She took a sip of the white wine to appreciate it, then vowed to leave it be.

James drained his glass. "So it was."

"Do you not find excessive alcohol consumption to harm your training regime?" Pearl blurted.

James tilted his head and looked at her expectantly.

"I've noticed that you seem to consume quite a bit of it. At least, of late, you seem to. I don't know what you did prior to our—that is—my...I mean...since I've moved in." Pearl thanked the heavens when the footman returned with a cream and potato course. In her haste to stop herself from speaking, she took a bite. No, it was decidedly not potatoes. It tasted rich. Mussels perhaps?

"I didn't realize you were monitoring me." His movements were far from smooth as he stabbed at his bowl.

"I wasn't."

"Because it isn't any of your business, of course."

"Of course."

They chewed in mutual silence. Amazing how from one moment to the next they could be friendly, and then she would say something to anger him. Would it always be this between them? Tiptoeing one way, only to offend, and then tiptoeing the other way, hoping to finish a conversation?

But Pearl couldn't leave it alone. She hated this sort of tolerated silence. At the homes she grew up in, people fought and threw things until peace descended. This business of no apologies and bloodless contention was foreign to her. How could peace be brokered if negotiations never occurred?

"I happen to be quite familiar with training regimes," Pearl said, then realized what she was freely admitting—exactly the knowledge that she didn't want to give him. "My brother and all of that."

That dark arched brown raised. "Yes. Vaguely aware of your brother. And all of that."

"I'm not trying to control your alcohol consumption. I'm just—" She huffed in frustration. "Making conversation."

"In that case, your finishing school should be fined for its spotty education. Condemning one's vices is terrible for conversation. Condemning one's virtues, however—now there is a way to conduct oneself." He offered her a smile of reconciliation.

She smiled in return. "In that case, my lord, your appearance is dreadful."

"Only my appearance?"

"I don't know you well enough to insult you much more." Pearl blushed again, appalled that it was true. They didn't know one another—not that it was necessary. It would just be nice. She risked a glance at him; he looked chastened as well.

"Very well, you do have a point. Perhaps we should make an effort in our conversation."

She wanted to shake him. Between their courtship and now their marriage, all she was trying to manage was one single genuine conversation. Her temper roared to life, knowing she'd been the only one to put effort towards communicating. But she tamped down her annoyance. "Excellent, my lord. Conversation it is."

They finished their cream dish in silence. He cleared his throat as the dishes were removed. A claret was poured for them. She was tempted to finish her wine. Abstaining from alcohol was one of the virtues Mrs. Tyler had taught them. Alcohol consumption decreased one's inhibitions, and a woman needed every single inhibition she could get. Women were more natural, Mrs. Tyler said, having moon cycles. They could not elevate themselves in the way men could, to live in their minds only, as they were reminded of their bodies once a month.

Of course, that had not been Pearl's experience, but she hadn't Mrs. Tyler's knowledge of etiquette to tell her otherwise. Pearl noted once again that Mrs. Tyler's advice had not helped her thus far. She took the remnants of the white wine glass and downed it. James looked on in amusement.

"Am I that charming of a dinner companion?" he asked.

She shot him a look that would have gotten knuckles rapped. "There are times to follow the rules, and there are times to ignore them."

"What, not to break them?"

"Breaking them means you give them credence and credibility. If I ignore them, the rules don't exist." She smiled at him. "And there are a great many rules for women, have you noticed? It's positively exhausting."

"I can only imagine. But please, do relax."

The footman arrived with a meat course, what looked to be roast beef. When Pearl cut into the meal, she was pleased to find that she was correct. Something she could predict, at least. "I can't relax entirely."

"Why not?" James put his utensils down, choosing instead to cradle the wineglass. "This is your house."

Pearl could feel the pleasant warmth in her feet from the wine. "No, this is *your* house, and *your* staff, and *your* mother."

"Ah, yes, but we are bound in the eyes of Heaven and Earth. You are me and I am you. This house is yours, as is the staff, and apparently, my mother is yours as well. She's never given me plant lessons."

Pearl put down her utensils. The beef sat heavy in her stomach. She was accustomed to much lighter fare, and much less of it. "I do prefer your interpretations, my lord. But in the eyes of Heaven and Earth, you are incorrect. You are not me. I am you. That is the difference."

"What God brings together, let no man put asunder?" James quoted.

"But the woman is to be subsumed into her husband, not her husband equally altered by the presence of his wife."

James's face froze, a mask settled into place. It was unexpected, and Pearl didn't know what she could have said to upset him. She was merely teasing. If anything, she was taking the man's part, arguing for the erasure of herself.

Somehow the topic must have reminded him of Lady Kinsley. He had loved her, and likely loved her still. Pearl lost her appetite.

"I don't believe I will stay for the pudding course. If you'll excuse me." Pearl left the table, all but fleeing his presence. She had blundered, and she didn't even understand how. He stood and bowed, a formal acknowledgment. Was it so necessary? She cringed again.

Perhaps she could try her hand at Lady Teeton's reform bill again, a way to distract herself and not think about every way she seemed to ruin her marriage before it could begin.

❧

THERE WAS no reason for James to stay at the table after Pearl left. He'd eaten more than he typically did, and strangely enough, his stomach didn't hurt for his efforts. Perhaps Pearl had been the distraction he needed—pleasant conversation and good food. What a novelty in one's own home.

The footman cleared the dishes, and Barton appeared to offer another course. James waved him off, retiring to his study. For once, though, he didn't want to pour himself a brandy or a scotch, or anything else. Pearl's notice had been enough to dissuade him from another drunken night. She was right—the alcohol did interfere with his training. And with his music. It made him sluggish, both in thought and in body.

He sat down at the piano. There was something about Beethoven that felt right tonight. The first movement of the Waldstein matched the intensity of his feeling.

He'd driven Pearl away. When she spoke of being subsumed, it reminded him so much of his father's beliefs that he couldn't breathe. That a woman was less a person and more a hunting dog. There for a purpose, nothing more. And the purpose, well. An image flashed in his mind, home from school on a holiday break, coming upon his father assaulting one of the maids in the stairwell, offering him a chance to do the same. It turned his stomach.

Dinner was suddenly so very noticeable in his body. This is why he didn't eat much in a single sitting. If his mind was allowed to wander, it made his entire physical being difficult to bear.

It hurt him to think Pearl believed he felt that way about her. That he expected her to disappear from view, in favor of becoming his pet. He much preferred the idea that in a marriage—a real one, anyway—both persons would swirl together, becoming a new kind of alloy. Mr. Worley, the blacksmith, would be pleased with that sort of metaphor.

James dug into the chords, shaking his thoughts from the dinner conversation in order to concentrate on his music. The pattern started in the left hand, far down in the bass, an optimistic roiling, then echoed in the right hand, both quiet, a level of control difficult to maintain. The main theme returned, another quiet section with a bass pattern that could easily get out of hand and fall out of rhythm.

The key change felt a relief when he arrived at it. As if to say that while the rest of the piece was hopeful, not all of it was without strife. He worked the transitions until he could play it without issue.

His hands felt tight from not having properly warmed up. He stood and walked the room, shaking his arms. What many didn't understand was that the harder one tried to control one's hands, the less dexterous they became. Relaxing was the key to control. Confidence. He returned to the piano and played his scales, allowing his hands to settle into the familiar patterns. He closed his eyes, letting the practice take over.

He returned to the Beethoven, choosing the third movement instead, a rondo. While he played, some of the candles sputtered out, making it difficult to see. Tired of straining his eyes, he stopped, hoping it was early enough to ring for more candles.

But no, when he checked the grandfather clock in the corner, it was well past midnight. He wouldn't be so callous as to force anyone up for this reason. There were likely some stashed in the room somewhere, but James didn't feel like discovering them. Instead, he gathered a single candle to light his way to bed. Enjoying how the candle flickered and lit the shadows, he let himself go still.

His bedroom. The one that adjoined Pearl's. Why was it so hard to take the house as his own? The lease wouldn't be up until the end of his life, or perhaps after. They were stuck with it. Unless they decamped for one of the country estates, but his mother would never agree to that.

This was his house, his bedroom. Pearl had no idea what hornet's nest she disturbed when she moved in. It forced both him and his mother out of their routines. It occurred to James that both he and his mother lived as if his father were still alive. It was as if the monster had merely stepped out and would return at any moment with more threats and punishments to mete out to them both. But the man had been dead for well over a decade. His ghost had haunted them long enough.

Those months ago, when Jack About Town had broken into his father's study, a locked room that was meant to remain so for all eternity, James had felt like he might lose his mind. That his father would return, discover the intrusion, and hurt them all—not just a beating, for no, the man was cleverer than that. And his mind believed that not only James and his mother would be punished, but also Lydia, Agnes, their parents, everyone. All of London would burn for the infraction. It took days for James to believe there would be no retribution. That the room held only artifacts and not his father.

Perhaps it was time to move on, but not tonight. When he opened his door, he found a surprise. His wife, in her nightgown, sleeping in the passageway, her head resting on the doorframe. A candle sat nearby, merrily flickering. She'd been listening to him play.

Her long red braid cascaded over her shoulder, and she was curled up, cold no doubt, her feet covered by her thick dressing gown. Before he could change his mind, James returned his candle to its place, snuffing it out. In one movement, he scooped up his wife and her candle. She was warm against his chest, burrowing her hands against him, not fully awake.

As he mounted the stairs, he realized it hadn't felt wrong when he thought of her as his wife. He hadn't been considering her a pet; he'd used *wife* as a benign term to describe a relative. He had his mother and sister and cousins, and now, he had his wife. She snuggled closer to him, causing him to smile. It had been a long while since any creature took to him in this way, let alone a person. He renewed his vow to John that he would take care of Pearl.

He carried her to her bed, tucking her under the

covers. She murmured something in her sleep, but he couldn't quite understand it. He didn't want to ask for clarification, lest it bring her around to consciousness.

Using the adjoining door, he took the candle to his own room. It was the first time he'd used that portal. And it might be the last, for all he knew. But what surprised him the most was that the physical memory of her perfumed head resting against his chest helped him fall into sleep without trouble.

CHAPTER 10

Lady Teeton's reform pamphlet was not ignored exactly, but it was subjected to benign neglect. Pearl dutifully carried it to her meals, in case she might be alone, but James now met her for breakfast and even accompanied her to dinner. They traded subtle barbs and far more smiles. Pearl might even go so far as to say she was becoming friends with her new husband.

The second two weeks of Pearl's marriage passed in a far more pleasant manner than the first. On her days at home, Mathilda Perry and Mrs. Tyler came to call. Each time, Mathilda grew bolder about asking after her marriage, until finally Mrs. Tyler had to put an end to the interrogation by threatening never to return.

Agnes and Jack called as well, later in the afternoons. Given his own recent change in households, Jack asked how Pearl found her surroundings.

"Strange, innit?" Jack grinned. "In a good way, I mean."

"I lived with my brother, so it hasn't been that strange, but you know we didn't have the family heirlooms. Here, there are so many things clearly left by previous generations."

"I hope it is all to your liking," Agnes added, concern showing in her expression.

"Of course, yes. In fact, there is a cabinet full of teapots in the dining room that I would love to show you. Between the two of you, I bet you would be quite knowledgeable."

Pearl led them into the dining room. "There was one teapot that I admit was extraordinary in its engineering. Two compartments! And it was so blandly decorated."

"Two compartments?" Jack asked. "Inside the pot?"

"Yes! But only one spout. I couldn't figure out what it was for."

"Perhaps holding back the leaves, so as not to over-steep the water?" Agnes suggested. She peered over Pearl's head as Pearl searched the cabinet, pulling out the Queen's Ware and Delftware pots but unable to find the small ceramic one.

"I don't suppose you see it back there, Agnes?" Pearl asked. Her cousin-in-law towered over her.

Agnes shook her head. "I'm afraid I don't."

"How strange. I know I saw it."

"When was the last time?" Jack asked.

Agnes returned the teapots to the shelf and shot a warning glance at Jack. "This isn't a case."

Jack shrugged and returned his dark gaze to Pearl. "Last week?"

"Thereabouts, I guess. Longer, probably. I haven't checked on it. It isn't even mine. I shouldn't worry. I'm sure it's being properly taken care of."

"Of course," Jack said, holding his hands up. "But—"

"Not a case. Not everything needs an answer," Agnes said.

"You know I don't believe in mysteries," Jack said.

Pearl waved Jack's concern away. "No matter. Besides, I believe Cook is trying a new kind of cake this afternoon, and they should be ready shortly. I'd hate to miss it."

Agnes's eyes lit up. Jack executed a bow. "Lead the way."

PEARL CONTINUED VISITING Lady Andrepont in the greenhouse, learning more about herbs and various ways to apply them to the body. She even introduced Lady Andrepont to the single poultice she knew well —the one to reduce swelling and bruising. Mustard seeds, mostly, which Lady Andrepont was glad to know about. She added it to her own small book of receipts.

Pearl took care not to mention the missing teapot. Some intuition insisted that Lady Andrepont wouldn't want to discuss it. Aside from which, what was the use of raising the alarm? It had belonged to Lady Andrepont, and she likely moved it to her private rooms as a keepsake.

"You never know when the time will come to use these remedies. If you are called upon in the middle of the night, your head might not be thinking clearly." Lady Andrepont had a streak of dirt across her cheek and looked right at home.

Pearl felt a kinship with the woman; they were both different under the surface. First impressions could not be trusted. She wondered what else lay below the surface of her mother-in-law. They exchanged a smile as Pearl hung cuttings upside down to dry.

"How have your evenings been?" her mother-in-law asked, her tone far too conversational to be exactly that.

"Restful," Pearl said. "The bed is very comfortable. Thank you for letting me have the room."

"Of course—it's only right. You are the mistress of the house and deserve all the trappings of such. I'm sure my son would allow you a stipend to redecorate it to suit your own tastes."

The very idea of decorating a room to her own specifications caused her mind to blank. Pearl felt the older woman's eyes on her. She hadn't meant her sleeping regime, and the change of décor was likely meant to suit both Pearl and James. Did her mother-in-law not realize the true nature of their marriage?

"And dinners? Is the food to your liking? I took the liberty of planning this week's menu, but please alter it however you wish going forward. Mrs. Foraker will be happy to assist you."

Dinners. Suddenly, it dawned on Pearl that the meals had been quite purposeful. The ginger, the fortified wines, oysters. Along with leeks, and then the next night they'd been served parsnips and aubergine. All known aphrodisiacs. Pearl gasped. "You are...are...you—"

"Matchmaking?" Lady Andrepont laughed. "My own clumsy attempts, yes. I thought I might try my hand at it, but so far it doesn't seem to have made that much of a difference. Has it?" The woman lifted an eyebrow at Pearl.

Pearl shook her head, exasperated at this family. "Is that why you haven't been in the house hardly at all? It seems as though no one can find you."

"I have a life that keeps me busy. However, I did make an effort to make more commitments out of the house. I wanted to give you and my son your privacy." The woman smiled to herself, as if she were exceptionally pleased with her espionage.

Pearl stilled. She opened her mouth to tell her mother-in-law that all was not as it seemed. There would be no children of this union. They needed no privacy.

Lady Andrepont swept away with her shears,

humming to herself as she trimmed. Pearl couldn't bring herself to dispel the woman's fantasy. Was she already naming grandchildren as she waltzed down to the rosemary bushes? No matter. Many people were unable to have children for one reason or another. They could easily sidestep those sympathies as the years passed.

As for now, she should expect a steady diet of ginger, leeks, aubergine, asparagus, eggs, and plenty of wine. If she didn't start carving some time for herself in James's gymnasium, her dresses would no longer fit. She checked the watch she kept pinned to her smock. There was still time before dinner. Should she risk it, knowing that James might leave his study at any time?

A thrill ran through her. He knew she wanted to use the room. Just like he knew she fell asleep outside of his study door every night, listening to him play. The first few nights, she hadn't stirred at all, waking in her bed embarrassed and alone. But James hadn't mentioned it, so neither did she. Then, last night, she did awaken as he scooped her up in his arms. She fit so nicely against him, and he smelled of oranges and wood polish and the sweet, dark port they'd shared after dinner. As the autumn deepened, the house grew very cold at night, and being pressed against him, feeling the heat of his body while she was drowsing, was one of the best feelings she'd ever experienced.

It far outweighed the kiss from Billy Richards. Or the one from Manfred Stevenson. Or that cheeky sailor whose full name she never caught, who'd whisked her into his arms for the show of it in a crowded square one day. She still believed he was trying to pickpocket her but had been disappointed to find she had nothing on her person. She'd already handed off her small stash to a friend before the sailor's overtures.

And what she'd done with Gabriel. Even that

wasn't as good because of what happened in the end. How he'd left her feeling ashamed. But Gabriel had disappeared into London, and his words couldn't hurt her.

She finished tying up the last sprig and removed the twine and shears from her smock's pockets. Pearl called out her regards to her mother-in-law and untied the smock as she walked to the door. Lady Andrepont's lone arm popped up amongst the rows of plants to wave her dismissal. Pearl hung her smock on the nail by the door, surprised at the excitement building inside her.

Pearl walked faster than she ought past the garden entrance, down the footpath, and into the not-terribly-well-kept gardens outside of the ballroom. She slowed as the terrace windows came into view. Of all the ways she could seem uneager, this was the most obvious. As she strode up the stone terrace steps, she heard the sounds of the sawdust figure being hit. There were many sounds associated with the gym, and this kind, where the figure was hit squarely with a solid force behind it, made a satisfying thump. There was something proper to it, as if the sound itself was saying *well done, you.*

Pearl loved those sounds, and she was gratified to hear that James could make the figure sing in the same way. Nothing was quite so attractive as competency. Green eyes, a teasing wit, and a muscled physique didn't hurt either.

Peering through the windows, she saw him deep in concentration. She recognized that feeling in her body and wanted the same. Unfortunately, the door creaked as she opened it, ruining all chances of surprise. No level of concentration could block that horrific screech.

He turned, pausing his exercise. He looked as if he was expecting her. He was in the middle of his training—sweating but not yet exhausted. It was a time when every bad idea sounded like a good one. Pearl knew that from experience. In those moments, when blood ran hot and fast, a fighter felt invincible, powerful. Even her.

"More gardening?" James asked, his breath faster. He shook his arms out. Sweat flew off in a small arc.

"I'm learning a great deal from your mother," Pearl said. They watched one another carefully. He flexed and preened for her, and she couldn't help but notice and admire him.

He chuckled. "Careful, that woman borders on the occult sometimes. No need to be excommunicated from the church."

Why would he say that? "Soothing a rumbling stomach seems less occult and more of a remedy."

He shot her a look that spoke of her naivety before turning back to the sawdust figure. He began to work the bag.

"Snap your wrist more in the jab," she said. "It's your weakest point."

He stopped. "How would you know what my weakest is?"

"I've seen my share of fights. And fighters."

He turned back to the bag and slowed his technique, focusing on his wrist. The first jab was the same as his others, but the second attempt honed the skill.

"Yes, good," she murmured, stepping ever closer. "Again."

He raised that eyebrow, but continued. The sound of the figure resonated time and again, more and more solid.

"Excellent. Ten more times to keep it in your body."

He nodded and obeyed, eyes never straying from the figure. He landed his jab ten more times in the figure's face. After the tenth blow, he turned to her. "And now?"

"You kept on the figure's head. Are you thinking of changing your fighting style?" Facers were dangerous. They broke fingers and hands. There was no way he could protect his hands for piano and engage in this style of pugilism. If it was the old style, where he could use a quarterstaff or a cavalry sword that had a guard to protect the hands, then it wouldn't bother her. But how could he do both?

James dropped his head. "I wouldn't, unless I was using mufflers. Or unless it wasn't an actual bout."

Pearl wasn't sure she heard him correctly. "Not a match? Who would you be fighting? Where would you be fighting?"

He exhaled loudly, as if she were asking prying questions, but to her, it seemed a very reasonable conversation. He said, "There have been times in the past where being able to deliver a well-timed facer is highly effective."

"James." She spoke his name quietly. "Who are you fighting?"

He shook his head. "In the past? Many. The boys at Eton. My father. In the past few years? Enemies of Lydia, rude blokes on the quays in Spain. There are just times when I need to protect those I love."

"Ah." Pearl went quiet. She could guess who he'd protected in Spain, as he'd been off in the world with Lady Kinsley. Would Pearl ever be included in that group of people to protect? Or would she always be on her own? Not that she needed him, because she could protect herself. But still.

She recognized the drive in him. It had nothing to do with the love of fighting, the need to hone technique. Those needs and pursuits existed in his music. She'd noticed while she'd listened to him in the middle of the night, repeating a single passage time after time until it was perfect. He was like an automaton, never ceasing, striving for perfection. She'd been impressed with his doggedness—a doggedness that translated to the gymnasium as well.

Yet that which drove him to the straw man was not the same as that which kept him on his piano stool. The need in this room was fear. He was here because he didn't want to get hurt or let those whom he loved be hurt. Music was passion. Pugilism was protection.

Everyone did it for different reasons—money, which had been John's motivation, or because they were good at it, which had been Bess Abbott's.

"Do you have mufflers here?" Pearl asked.

James pointed to the shelves.

"They don't help you if you don't put them on your hands."

James grinned—not one of his sardonic, teasing smiles but the kind that lured a woman to her doom. "They make my hands sweat. And they smell bad."

She laughed. It was one of the reasons Bess Abbott refused to use them. And because Bess didn't use them, John refused. Her brother may have had better renown, but Bess was the one who'd led the way for John's training at every step. Pearl walked over and sniffed them. "This set has never been worn."

He put his hands on his hips, stretched his shoulders. "How can you tell?"

She held one glove up. "The ribbons aren't stitched on. Just pinned."

"I think you know more about this than you let on."

"About mufflers?" Pearl set the glove down, not meeting his eye.

"About boxing. Pugilism. Fighting." He sauntered closer to her.

She shrugged. Mrs. Tyler would be displeased with her digression. Young ladies didn't shrug. But her former sass was emerging. "That's not a question."

"Pearl. Have you trained?"

"Trained? Be specific." She was being coy now, and they both knew it.

He stalked closer. "Have you been a student of the sweet science?" Invoking the nickname of pugilism was a further test.

She wasn't a liar. This was her best-kept secret. But fine, let him have it. Just the one. "Yes."

ॐ

HE NARROWED HIS EYES. He knew it. Taking a risk, he slapped her. Or tried to. He certainly wasn't going to throw a punch at Corinthian John's sister.

She ducked out of the way and gave him a look of utter disdain. Not because he'd tried to hit her, but because he was slow. He grinned and threw a jab, faster this time, but still not at full power. She blocked it with her forearm, deflecting it easily.

He threw a cross, but she ducked it. He jabbed again, but she danced back. Faster and faster he moved, but she either blocked or danced away. She was better than he'd expected. This was serious training. He hadn't seen any muscles on her, and he could admit it, he'd looked, so it had been a while since she'd really worked.

This was her ability while she was out of practice?

She was small and agile, moving faster than he could anticipate. It was as if she could read his mind and knew where he was going before he did. Losing patience with himself, he stopped checking his speed or his strength.

Before he could figure out what was happening, she'd maneuvered him to the ballroom doors. She danced across the threshold and into the passageway, laughing as she left him, dancing off towards the stairs.

He collapsed, resting his hands on his thighs, catching his breath. How did she do that? Her laughter echoed in his mind. That wasn't bloody fair. He hadn't been able to lay a hand on her. Not even close.

Well, the woman would be going to dinner tonight, and he'd find out then. He should call round to John and ask him about her training, her technique. What was her weakness? Well, obviously, it had to be her strength. She was barely larger than a child. But it didn't matter if she could run him all around a ring.

No wonder John had been such a champion, if this was his blood. James shook his head and straightened up. He needed to walk this off and clear his head. Imagine what that woman could do if she was in her peak form! He walked the circuits of the room, cooling his blood and his body. This was a very intriguing development.

Surprisingly, he didn't mind being outwitted by her. This time. And he certainly was glad none of his jabs had connected. He didn't want to hurt her—he'd meant only to test her. And she'd exceeded his every expectation.

Once he'd given her sufficient time to get a bath in, he headed upstairs, half-hoping she'd be still be in the tub. Instead, the bath had been used but clearly refreshed, the oranges once again added for his benefit. He wondered if she preferred the smell.

He sank into the bath, scrubbing more vigorously, hoping to erase his ungentlemanly awareness of her. She'd been in this water. She'd let it rise around her body, heating her, turning her skin from pale to flushed, and—

And he had to stop. John's sister. Respectful. But his loins didn't care about respect, and his cock was being very loud about it. How he wished this water were colder. He got out, hoping the brisk air would likewise cool his loins.

He couldn't go down to dinner like this. If he did, his cock would take over and he would do something he'd regret. Better to be done with it now, rub one out, and join Pearl for dinner like a man, not a howling wolf.

Not wanting to risk it in the bathing room, he dried himself roughly and wrapped the towel around his waist. He ached for her, suddenly. The curtains were open, allowing the soft evening light to spill through. Darkness came earlier and earlier, and he knew he should savor these twilight hours. He went to the fireplace, willing himself under control. It wasn't the first time he'd lusted after a woman. There had been many a wank for Rose before they'd worked out their arrangement.

But this was different. Pearl was, by law, his. He rested his arm on the mantle, letting the towel drop to his feet. The draft from the fireplace made his skin prickle. The thought of her face, laughing at him as she stepped just out of reach time and again. God, what he would do if he caught her. The fantasy was too much to bear, and he began working himself as he imagined her ensnared.

He'd pull down her hair first, fisting it in his wrapped hands. He imagined the shocked look on her face, pleased, though, that he'd caught her. He'd pull on her hair to lift her chin and kiss her. Their first real kiss—not the one in front of their wedding audience, but the one where he would show her what passion was. Then that wrapped hand would stray to her décolletage to pull down her dress, exposing her small pink breasts to him. He could barely get to the idea of sucking on her hard nipples before his mind jumped—him thrusting inside her, the feeling of her surrounding him, enveloping him, hot and moaning—

God, what if she was next door, knowing what he was doing? To know how badly he wanted her, how this is what she pushed him to. The idea thrust him over the edge.

He shuddered, mumbling curses under his breath. Even in his fantasies, he couldn't wait. Calming his breath, he felt the flush subside, the drowsy pleasure sink in. Hastily, he grabbed the towel from the floor to clean himself and then the fireplace.

৩৯৩

SHE SHOULDN'T HAVE LOOKED.

But she did.

Peeping at keyholes was bad form for a child, let alone a full-grown woman. But there had been something about hearing him finish his bath. Peering through the keyhole of their adjoining door, she found him by the fireplace. And then the towel dropped, and there was his beautiful arse, rounded and high, then his thick thighs, muscled no doubt from all his jumping of rope.

She'd nearly gasped when he began working himself. His face was shielded in the crook of his arm. When he grunted and stood on his toes and came, she almost moaned herself. He was beautiful.

Imagining him thinking of her while he did that, let alone gripping his muscled thighs as he thrust into her, made it hard to breathe. Retreating, she moved to her chair in front of the fireplace. If he were the sort to peep at keyholes, he would be able to see her. She snaked her hands between her legs, desperate to find release. It took only moments until she tensed and finished.

But Pearl couldn't go to dinner having the smell of her excitement on her. He would know it instantly. And then he would know she had watched him, and she had liked it. She felt shame, not because of what she had done but because she knew better than to believe James had been thinking of her.

As for her own pleasure, Mrs. Coldcroft had advised her about the act. That it was far easier to find release with oneself, and it was far safer to find it alone. Men couldn't be trusted, and the sooner a girl knew, the better off she'd be. Touching oneself wasn't dirty, it was necessary. It kept her safe from the charms of men who would make her believe only they could make her feel good, when it was anything but the truth.

As long as the one release was enough to keep her mind clear through dinner. She didn't want to abject herself before him like that; begging for intimacy would only lead to humiliation and heartbreak. She knew he would tell her no, resist her. And she hadn't the fortitude to be rejected any longer, marriage bond be damned.

He'd probably thought about Lady Kinsley. Their last time together. It was probably magnificent, and she probably knew all sorts of wild things from their trip around the world together. Pearl was just a dirty guttersnipe who'd peeped at a handsome man through a keyhole. She swallowed hard. That was enough to cure her lust. It was wrong to look. It was wrong on so many counts, and how would she feel if he'd done the same?

Chastened, she returned to her writing desk. She still hadn't finished Lady Teeton's bill. But how was she supposed to think about reform laws when James was naked next door? Gloriously naked. She shook her head and gritted her teeth. Reform. Legislation. Important matters, and someone must attend to them. Because James wouldn't. He had neglected his seat in Parliament. Refused his seat at the table. Muffled his own voice, and subsequently, the voices of those he loved.

Few men could vote, and no women. Who would

speak for her and John? Her brother didn't own land. He leased the Marylebone house, though his wealth exploded from every orifice. The image of sovereigns shooting out of her brother's ears made her giggle. At least that made the heated thoughts of James dissipate. Pearl needed to focus on her role as viscountess since she had no role as James's wife.

JAMES WAS ABOUT to ring for Phillip to help finish dressing him when he heard Pearl giggle. The noise was faint, given the walls and doors and plaster between them, but it cut him. She sounded girlish and happy, not at all the proper young miss with a mysterious past. He wondered if there was a young man she had loved—before meeting him, of course. There was no doubt in his mind that if she'd had a chance with another man, she wouldn't have agreed to this bloodless pact. Especially now that he knew more about her. A woman who could move like that, dodging and twirling away from him with ease, had passion in her. And she deserved to be with a man who could make her giggle. That man wasn't him.

He kicked himself all over again. What a fool he'd been to allow Rose to goad him into marrying. He should have known it would change nothing between them, serving only to ruin the life of another.

Not hearing another giggle emanate from the other room, James rang for Phillip to assist with his cravat and cufflinks. He would be above reproach tonight. A perfect gentleman. And perhaps he could hint that he would be accepting if she took a lover. A young man who could make her giggle.

But his stomach knotted up at the thought of it. Could he really see Pearl escorting another man into her chambers? Sit at his piano while she was upstairs, allowing another man to—

"My lord?" Phillip entered the room. "I beg your pardon. You must have not heard me at the door."

"Yes, come in, Phillip." James shook out the rest of his tangled thoughts. The point of having a wank was to get her out of his mind. Like a bloodletting. Instead, the thoughts were worsening now that his imagination had awakened to the possibility of her.

Phillip retrieved the box of cufflinks and pins.

"The rubies? Truly, Phillip?" They were reserved for formal occasions. "As far as I know, royalty isn't dining here this evening."

Phillip took the jibe in stride. "Pardon me, my lord, but judging by your clothing, you were maintaining a higher standard than a leisurely at-home dinner."

Before he could stop himself, he blurted out, "What is the viscountess wearing?"

"I'm sure I could consult with her lady's maid."

James nodded vigorously, somehow invested in the idea of a war of attrition in fashion with Pearl. Phillip disappeared, shutting the door to the bedroom. Alone, James paced. He wanted her to worry about her gowns. He wanted her to fuss with jewels. Did she wish for his approval? By God, he hoped so. As desperately as he now sought to have hers. What was wrong with him? Throw a few jabs, have a hot bath and a wank, and suddenly he was losing his mind?

There must be some kind of fever going around. This was preposterous.

Phillip returned, barely stifling his excitement. "I have spoken with the lady's maid. Your viscountess will be wearing red."

His valet's breathless state was amusing to watch. A grown man getting into a fuss over dinner wear?

"*Red*, my lord. Red." Phillip looked at him as if this were an obvious cause for excitement.

"As in my family colors?" James said, still unsure as

to why the dress would be the cause of so much excitement.

Phillip nodded and kept bobbing his head. "And other things. It is truly a splendid gown."

"Noted." James felt like he was missing something, which at least allowed him to shove his tangled feelings off to the side and never think of them again. "Shall we dress to match, then?"

Phillip gave him a look as if he were just above a village idiot and charged to the wardrobe. In the end, James traded out his black waistcoat for a blood-red one and changed the cufflinks from brass to gold. His cravat was styled with a pearl.

"A pearl for Pearl," sighed Phillip, who then looked up at James utterly terrified at the liberty he had taken with the viscountess's name.

James held up his hand. Once again, he wasn't his father. No need to beat any of the manservants. "It's fine, Phillip. The sentiment is clear, and I'm sure the viscountess will appreciate your thoughts."

"No, no my lord. *Your* thoughts. You must reassure her that *you* thought of this." Phillip patted and tugged at the cravat, getting the fabric to lie just so.

"Why would I not give credit where it's due?" James asked with suspicion. The servants were matchmaking. His father had once had a man horsewhipped for gossiping. James wouldn't go that far, but his irritation with the meddling of others was beginning to chafe.

Phillip pulled himself upright. "As you wish, my lord."

Having no further need to be fussed at, James dismissed the valet and headed to the drawing room. His mouth was dry and his palms felt clammy. Was he nervous? How absurd.

The drawing room was empty. Fortunately, his mother kept sherry hidden away in the corner. He investigated, only to find her sherry stash removed. Ah. Because this was no longer her drawing room, and therefore, it had been removed to make room for Pearl. He rang for a footman. But hadn't Pearl just spoken about cutting back on alcohol, for fear it would tarnish his training abilities? He felt damned no matter what he did.

He sat in one of the chairs and brooded. Not long ago, he had been a single and sane man. Now he was fussing over his clothes and his alcohol, and his *wife*. He stood in frustration.

A basket near the fireplace caught his attention— this is what she had been working on the other day when he'd first joined her for dinner. What was it? A pillowcase, a sheet? He pawed through it, careful not to be stuck by the pins that may hold stitching in place. But no, it was embroidery. Those were his shirts. *His* shirts. What was she doing with his clothing?

He turned when he heard her come into the room, which caused his brain to puddle into hot wax. Her dress was indeed red. The décolletage was a daring plunge. Beadwork shimmered as she stepped, and his mind went utterly blank. *Thank you, Phillip*, was all he could manage. At least now he could understand the valet's excitement. The workmanship of the gown was probably very fine. Stitches and beads and bobs and all he could think of was how it fitted her body so well, showing off the lean curves and displaying her breasts in a fashion that he was happy not to share with anyone else.

Dining alone, please and thank you.

"Careful with that—you might get a prick," Pearl said.

"I beg your pardon." He looked down at the shirt he still held in his hands. Right. Prick of a needle. On his hands. Dear God, what was he doing? He tossed it down into the basket. "What are you doing with my shirts?"

Pearl smiled at him, seeming completely unaware of how very much skin he could see. And her skin was tantalizing. She had freckles, it turned out. It wasn't all milk. And he was certain there were trails to follow, winding this way and that, like a deer path cut through the countryside. Except instead of a deer, he would follow like a—

"James, can you hear me?" She was even closer to him.

"Perfectly."

"Then I'm glad you haven't noticed the difference between your mother's mending and mine. Or at least that your valet hasn't mentioned. I admit that darning is not my best skill."

"And what is your best skill?" he purred. Thoughts of her mouth on his body skittered through him. He took a step back and raked his hands through his hair. He had to stop. The idea of Corinthian John delivering a powerful facer cooled his lust. "I beg your pardon. That was most inappropriate."

She tilted her head and looked at him, opened her mouth as if to speak, but then shut it again. Was she going to chastise him? Berate him for foul thoughts and filthy words? Because she ought to. Her brother wouldn't allow her to stay here if he abused her. And he wanted to abuse her in a very, very specific way. The kind that would have her clutching him, crying out.

Barton interrupted it all. He could kiss that man. Or plant a facer on him.

"Dinner is served."

CHAPTER 11

Pearl was pleased that Lily had recommended the red dress. She would never be bold enough to wear it outside the house, but if making James unable to look above her clavicle was the result of it, good. She wanted him to pant after her like a stray dog. He deserved it if he was still thinking of his time with Lady Kinsley.

As Mr. Barton left the drawing room, James approached Pearl with his arm out to escort her. She took his arm, noticing then that his cravat was pinned with a pearl. How could she not believe it was for her? He was dressed to match, with a red waistcoat in the same exact shade as her gown. Lily must have conspired with his valet. His arm was warm, and she could feel it all the way through her white gloves. She hoped he was outright sweating.

"I wonder what is on the menu for tonight?" she mused aloud. Did James know about his mother's meddling? The aphrodisiacs stuffed into every course?

James shook his head, clearing his throat as they processed. "Haven't the foggiest."

No, he had no idea. They entered the dining room in silence. She didn't know what to say any more than he did. She might be showing off more skin than she normally did, but entering the drawing room, seeing him holding the mending in front of him, all she could think of was him in front of the fireplace, finding pleasure in his fist. It was all she could do to keep her mind in the current moment.

Instead of remembering the curve of his thighs, the planes of his stomach, she catalogued what she saw. The banquet that had once held the curious teapot, the chandelier lit with beeswax candles, the table set with silver, and her husband. Her husband who had every right to put his hands all over her, hands that could perform marvelous things on a piano. What could they do on her?

She stripped off her gloves, and she could swear James was watching her. Did he want her? He'd spoken that double-entendre in the drawing room. But then, he only just left his mistress. Men likely went through some kind of withdrawal. She didn't know that for certain, but from the way Mrs. Coldcroft talked about it, some men were addicted to bodily pleasures just as some were addicted to opium.

The footman delivered the soup course, revealing it to be another ginger broth. Of course it was.

"More ginger," James commented.

"Indeed," Pearl said, dutifully eating.

James stared at her, working his jaw. That silly, square jaw that could cut paper. "I like ginger."

Pearl swallowed. She didn't think he was talking about the spice, and rather talking about her hair. All she could do was blink. His words weren't aligning with what she had thought he wanted. Maybe she was wrong? "I see."

He seemed chastened, and she could have pinched herself. How did a woman encourage her husband to flirt at the dinner table? How did any woman anywhere manage a man? There were reputations all over London of women who could do precisely that. Indeed, Lady Kinsley had fairly bewitched James for a period of several years. How could she do it while Pearl was nothing but prudish responses? Was that something a wife could ask the mistress? Was that done? Add another question to ask Lady Teeton when she got a moment to respond.

The footman cleared the soup course, and a platter of hardboiled eggs and asparagus in cream was presented. The eggs were halved and arranged in such a way to highlight the asparagus in a manner that was suggestive of a man's parts. Pearl glanced up at James. How was she supposed to maintain her decorum?

A grin was breaking through James's face. They really did look like a cock and balls. It couldn't possibly be just her. She swallowed a snicker. This had to be his mother's doing. It had to be. Her mother-in-law had stopped being subtle. James broke out in laughter, and Pearl couldn't hold it in any longer. She burst out laughing, and merely looking at James made her laugh even harder.

The poor footman stood stock still, his face so red his ears seemed to be aflame. Pearl tried to reassure him that he was not in trouble, but she couldn't get out any words.

"Dear God, they look like—" James laughed so hard he couldn't finish his sentence.

The footman shook his head as he considered the platter. His thoughtfulness only made Pearl roar harder.

"Put it down. We'll manage," Pearl wheezed. The egg-and-asparagus arrangement on fine silver made it even funnier.

The footman scrambled out of the room just as Mr. Barton returned with the first course of white wine.

"Is there a problem, my lord?" Mr. Barton asked, seemingly genuinely concerned, which only sent the two of them into more peals.

"Look," James said to the butler, gesturing to the

plate of halved boiled eggs, paired with rather thick asparagus.

Pearl snickered. Aspirational asparagus.

Mr. Barton pulled himself up, as if he could save the house from irredeemable bawdiness. "Well. Your lady mother requested it."

"My mother?" James blasted, practically falling from his chair. "Oh my God."

"Wine, my lady, my lord?"

"Bloody hell," Pearl said, finally coming out of her last fit. She wanted wine more than anything else in that moment.

Mr. Barton froze. James stared at her for a moment.

What had she just said? All that training, all of the corrections from Mrs. Tyler, and she had cursed right in front of her husband and the butler. Shite. Her embarrassment was far beyond a blush. It was the opposite—cold seeped into every corner of her bones.

Instead of shaming her manners, James broke out laughing all over again, waving Mr. Barton to pour the wine. The butler poured, then beat a hasty retreat. James picked up his wineglass to toast her.

"This is the absolute best dinner party I have ever been to," he said, waiting for her to pick up her own glass. He wiped his eyes.

She picked up her own, her marrow thawing. "But there are only two of us," she whispered.

He nodded, drinking up. "And I haven't laughed this hard in ages."

She felt oddly pleased about that compliment. "I think your mother is trying too hard."

They both chuckled, taking a sip of the cool and crisp white wine.

"Oh?" James's expression relaxed into seriousness, as if he truly were puzzled. "Do you think it's a hint of some kind?"

Pearl wanted to play along, but she couldn't keep a straight face. "Would you like to try some and find out?"

James looked her dead in the eye with a smolder blazing harder than she had ever seen in anyone before. "I would very much like to find out."

She swallowed hard, feeling suddenly very exposed and vulnerable. Delightfully so, in fact. He wanted her. He did. She reached her hand across the table.

James suddenly pulled back, straightening in his chair, severing their connection.

Startled, Pearl covered her reaching for him by pretending to pick up the platter. "Then may I serve you, my lord?" She winced at her words. Could she be any more pathetic? In truth, she was the wretched, abandoned street urchin floating house to house, living off John's prizefight winnings and whatever she could skim from the purses of unsuspecting marketgoers. Desperate. Always desperate. She hated being desperate.

But this was her house. Her title. Her place. She wouldn't run, and she wouldn't be run off either. She deserved to be here.

James cleared his throat, gesturing to his plate. "Please."

They ate the eggs and asparagus in silence, humor dissipating from the room. When the footman returned to remove the dishes, he seemed puzzled by their sudden stoic demeanor. The second course was a roasted bird of some kind. Pearl barely tasted it. Mr. Barton poured more wine, but Pearl didn't touch it.

Pudding came, a trifle topped with sweetened cream, which was her very favorite thing. There was no putting that aside, no matter how miserable she felt. She dug in, ignoring all the advice Mrs. Tyler had drilled into her over the years about not seeming too eager. Despair seemed to shrink in the face of the layers of fluffy sweetened cream, and she devoured it, leaning back in her chair, her spoon still in her mouth, close to moaning with pleasure. This was heaven. If she couldn't have a husband who even remotely liked her, couldn't have a family to keep her company, then at least she could ask the kitchen to serve her sweetened cream on a regular basis.

She opened her eyes to find James staring at her.

"I beg your pardon," she said, straightening up and returning the spoon to the table. Once again, he was appalled by her manners. This house was a confusing place. She should maintain her decorum at all times, yes, of course. But there had been times when showing her true self had been advantageous, like when she engaged in light sparring with James. But clearly, her accidental cursing and her poor posture was a step too far. Truly, she knew better.

She wanted to go to bed, pull the covers over her head, and disappear forever.

"Would you care to join me in my study for some port?" James asked.

"Oh." She blinked. This would be the second invitation to have port in his study. Last time had been interesting. They had talked about family and music. It wasn't deeply personal, but it had been friendly. He still wanted her company after tonight's debacle? "Of course."

⚘

HE WAS DYING. All the blood in his body was below his waist and he couldn't breathe. It wouldn't be an entirely unpleasant death, watching her lick cream from the spoon with a full-throated enjoyment he had never witnessed in a woman. Oh, to be that spoon.

But one did not suggest such a thing to one's wife. He cursed inwardly. There was that word: *wife*. He invited her to his study, a dangerous proposition. He shouldn't be this close to her, not after witnessing that display. At least in the study he could play for her and be distracted by the intellectual exercise of the technical passages courtesy of Herr Beethoven.

Her arm lay tucked against his as he escorted her to his lair. He was the spider, guiding in an unsuspecting fly. Pearl's brother would murder him if the man knew his thoughts. A husband shouldn't even think those thoughts. Barton had thoughtfully placed the fresh bottle of port and two glasses in the middle of the room for ease of serving.

James's heart pounded. They wanted this—the whole house. The servants, his mother. Did they not understand the agreement? Would Pearl have ever agreed if she knew she would have had to capitulate to his basest desires? The kind that made him go blind from lust?

"Your mother—" Pearl began as she took a seat.

James waved her off. He couldn't speak about his mother while he was concentrating on not being visibly attracted to Pearl. He poured the port and handed her the dainty glass. She'd put her gloves back on, but the barrier just incensed him. To pull off that glove. Or to feel that glove in other places. To ruin that glove.

"To an unusual dinner," James said, holding up his glass as a toast.

"I'll grant you that." Pearl's tone sounded disappointed.

Had she been able to tell what he'd been thinking? Is that why she was disappointed? He believed he was good at hiding his innermost thoughts, but apparently he was wrong. He was so thoroughly and rightly fucked. He sipped the port, resisting the urge to down it all. If he got too inebriated in front of her, could he properly trust himself to not throw himself at her?

"Do you have plans for tomorrow? I believe it is your day to call around to other ladies." Not that James kept track of her schedule. But he could tell when she was in the house. The whole place felt different. Lighter, somehow.

"I had thought to call round to your cousins and Lady Teeton."

"I imagine you miss the camaraderie with Lydia quite a bit." James tried to imagine what they possibly could have talked about. Lydia was not an easy person to get along with—nor was he. Which was why they'd always been close.

"I do, but I miss Agnes's company as well. The three of us really. After the business with Jack, we all came together in a way that felt…" She hesitated and gave a shrug. "Special somehow."

"We could have them all over for a dinner." After the business with the sparring match, which yes, he had intended to beat Jack into oblivion, he felt guilty. In his defense, he had thought Jack was deceiving Agnes to take advantage of her dowry.

Interestingly enough, he considered, there were probably some gossips in the *ton* who thought precisely the same thing of him wedding Pearl. The exact nature of his relationship to Henry and Rose was never public knowledge, but Henry's proclivities were not unknown. There had been a scandal the year before Rose's debut—the entire reason Henry had pursued Rose was to have some kind of reasonable deniability of the man who blackmailed him.

"Do you remember that night? At John and Lydia's? We were all there, you and your mother, all of us, and Lydia had the baby with her?" Pearl sighed, resting her cheek on the back of the sofa. Her red hair glinted in the firelight. She looked like a Botticelli painting—the one in Florence—if only she would let loose her hair.

When they'd gone—Rose, Henry, and he—they'd

traipsed all over the Italian peninsula. Visiting Florence, then Rome and Naples, then Venice before turning back. It was in Venice where James thought he could never be apart from Rose. They drank sparkling wine at a party and chased each other through the warren of streets, getting lost as they ran over the canal bridges. His one clear memory of that night was Rose looking back at him as he found her, laughing and smiling. He'd thought that was love. He'd thought the look on her face in that moment was everything he could hope to find in this life.

But here was Pearl with a dreamy look on her face in his study. There was no drunkenness, no running. She was here in his domain, with no intention of leaving. "I remember that night," James said. "All of us, together. When I was a child, we were often together, both of our families. After—" James cleared his throat. "After my father—" He tried again. He couldn't.

Pearl sat up, stretched her arm out to him. "You don't need to say it for my sake."

Good. Because he couldn't manage the words.

"Do you think we could try it again? Getting the families together?" Pearl asked. "Just for dinner, nothing extravagant."

He nodded, the knot untwisting. "I'd like that."

"And maybe your mother would stop putting aphrodisiacs in our food," Pearl said with a giggle.

James froze. "What was in our food?"

"Did you not notice all the ginger? I mean, the eggs and asparagus were obvious."

"Ginger is an aphrodisiac?" He didn't remember that one. Oysters, yes. Which were served the first night he'd joined Pearl for dinner. The woman was conniving. "I thought ginger was for seasickness."

"It's supposed to help the blood move. I think it works for both."

James shook his head. Then perhaps he wasn't all

to blame for his lustful thoughts. If he had been getting all this medicine, maybe he wasn't out of control and Pearl wasn't the alluring Siren she seemed to be. Was she not?

He moved to sit in the chair next to the sofa. He rarely sat in the chair, given that he was either playing the piano or sleeping on the couch. She adjusted her position to see him better, and that small move hit him square in the chest.

Someone was willing to change themselves to better accommodate him. Not ignore him or challenge him or make him keep up. He'd not known that such a small thing could mean so much.

His father had taught him that there was the way of things: men like them would inevitably be in control, dictating whims to servants, spouses, lovers, children. But those orders would be obeyed to the letter, and while a good servant might be able to anticipate a need, explicit instructions were required.

His mother taught him that all people, regardless of status, were still human, and therefore fallible. All people were lonely and greedy and hungry. Expecting another to change in order to suit his needs was not just folly, but childish. They'd lived in the shadow of his father's terror for so long that once the man was gone, they went their separate ways. She continued her own life, and he, as a young man, had no interest in knowing what his mother was doing. He had his own wounds to lick.

Yet Pearl was interested in him without demanding anything of him. Not asking him to change to suit her needs, nor changing herself to suit him. It felt extraordinary. He leaned his elbows on his knees and looked up at her. He wanted to tell her how unusual she was, how this time they spent together felt special.

He couldn't get the words out. She was looking into the fire, ignoring him completely. What could she be thinking about? Lofty things like Rose? Ask Rose what she was thinking, and one had to be prepared for an entire scientific lecture. The woman was incapable of pillow talk.

"What do you have planned for tomorrow, my lord?" Pearl sounded tired, her voice barely above a whisper.

He shook his head. The same as always. Get drunk, play piano, punch some sawdust. It wasn't a bad life. He missed his friends, though. He couldn't go see Henry, and now it felt wrong to visit John. He avoided his club for fear of the comments he might receive from the lads there. Nor did he want to be ambushed by Haglund or Teeton. "Same as always."

"You don't sound as if you enjoy your 'always.'"

He contemplated the empty glass in his hands. "It was enjoyable for a while. And for a while, all that was intermixed with courting you, and that was enjoyable, too."

"Courting me was enjoyable? It always seemed like you were doing your duty." Pearl shifted, pulling her legs up on the couch and tucking them underneath her long skirts. The angle of her plunging neckline shifted and the expanse of revealed rosy skin distracted him.

James quickly looked down at the floor. If he watched her any longer, he'd forget how to speak. "I enjoyed playing prince charming for you. Sending large bouquets that I knew would infuriate Lydia. Dancing at those balls where the other young ladies couldn't figure out how you'd landed a confirmed bachelor."

"Ah. So you enjoyed courting me because it made other women mad?"

He risked a glance at her, realizing now how his words must have sounded to her. "I meant that I liked the idea of playing a hero and not a villain. I was taking an action that would delight you, make you feel special."

"Do you think that I would only feel special if it made other young ladies upset?" Pearl said the words carefully, as if she were tiptoeing through mud.

He shook his head, baffled. "Isn't that how it works with young ladies?"

Pearl gave him a rueful smile. "I wouldn't know."

She couldn't have hurt him more if she'd stabbed him. The reminder of her rough upbringing—the extent of which he didn't understand—was enough to show him he'd been a thoughtless cad. He nodded. "Point taken. Point taken very seriously."

She reached out, placing her hand on his wrist. "We're both new at this it seems."

He covered her hand with his. *Stay*, was all he could think. Keep touching him, keep reaching out to him, keep seeing him. He wanted to keep this moment sacred and safe, but he didn't know how to maintain it. What was the secret to making someone want to be there?

"I—that is, I want—" What did he want? Wildness flooded his veins again, thinking of what he wanted. Everything. He wanted everything. The world, and more than that, he wanted time. He wanted to reverse time, change the world, erase his father, even at his own expense. He would have never pursued Rose and made her unhappy. He would have never proposed to Pearl and condemned her to a life of misery. He wanted Pearl to look at him with love—the way Lydia looked at John. He'd never seen it up close. Not like that.

"Yes?" Pearl asked.

"Would you train with me tomorrow?" He blurted out. That was not what he meant to say. Training had been the furthest from his mind. "After you finish calling on your friends, of course. Before dinner?"

Pearl sat back, removing her hand. Clearly, that

wasn't what she was expecting either. She furrowed those nearly invisible red brows together. "Are you expecting me to train you?"

"No," he said quickly, hoping she would understand that he didn't want anything from her. He only wanted her company. Her wit, her jokes, her ability to make him feel as if each day was a little less of a burden.

Thankfully, she agreed. "Then I should get some sleep. I have a big day ahead of me. Calls and then training." But she didn't get up to leave.

"Would you like to relax on the couch while I play? Or would you feel more comfortable outside, sitting on the floor?" It felt good to tease her. Not quite so at sea.

"What would Mrs. Foraker say?" Pearl teased back.

"Does she know?"

"I'm fairly certain she has replaced my candle while I slept. I distinctly recall one night going down with barely a nub, and when I awoke, it was a full candle again."

"The house is magical," James said, rising. "Any requests, since you're here?"

"I like the ones with the fast notes."

"Ah, so you are a music aficionado. Fast notes, and all." James pawed through his stacks of music. Mozart would fit, as would the latest Beethoven.

"Yes. Mrs. Tyler made all of us girls learn the basics of piano. Sorry to say my basics are knowing there are high notes and low notes, and black keys and white keys."

"An expert."

"Undoubtedly. I would have been a great proficient, if only I'd learned how."

James couldn't help but chuckle. "Of course. How dare the universe strip you of your acclaim?"

"I'm sure it's because I'm a ginger. We are truly discriminated against. At piano playing most of all."

He sat down at the piano, his heart much lighter than it had been. Everything lighter than it had been. "Then have some Mozart. It'll make you feel better."

CHAPTER 12

Lady Teeton embraced Pearl as if she were an old friend. "I was positively terrified you decided to snub me!" This time, the Teetons' drawing room was empty of other callers.

Pearl knew it was an exaggeration, and that any excuse would smooth over the situation. "There are many things vying for my attention. I apologize for having not put you at the forefront." Pearl meant it casually, but visions of James flooded her mind. Naked at the mantle in his room; looking up at her, his elbows on his knees in front of the fireplace; wiping tears of laughter from his eyes in the dining room. He was dreadfully handsome. It almost hurt when that green-eyed gaze landed on her.

"Of course," Lady Teeton replied with a coquettish smile as she gestured at Pearl to sit. "Newly wed. I remember."

Pearl winced. If only a marriage bed was what vied for her attention. The delights that might happen if James reached for her. A weight settled on her chest. But he wouldn't. And no one knew that better than her. "But I have been reading through your reform bill, lest you think that I have entirely forgotten you."

The spark in Lady Teeton's eyes returned. This was her passion. James was probably right—Lord

Teeton likely hadn't written a word of the bill. Some people loved painting, others fashion, and apparently some loved political policy. Who was Pearl to judge? "Excellent. We missed your presence at dinner the other night. Your insights would have been invaluable. Lady Kinsley, for instance, grew up in the country and has no firsthand knowledge of any of these plights."

Pearl gave a faint smile at the mention of her husband's mistress. Former mistress?

Lady Teeton put her hand on Pearl's wrist, clearly realizing her faux pas. "I'm so sorry. I'd quite forgotten. Tea?"

"Please." Pearl wanted to slip out of the woman's grasp. It was an easy gesture, a quick flick of the wrist. She would be sparring this afternoon with James and no doubt would use the maneuver at some point.

"I assumed you knew." Lady Teeton poured the tea, looking up at Pearl, clearly referencing Lady Kinsley's affair with James.

The adepts of tea-pouring no doubt could perform this trickery, not looking at a cup and still not spilling a drop or allowing the teapot lid to shift and grate. Pearl had learned the technique, of course, and performed adequately genteel pouring, but she would never perform like a natural. "I know."

"Then you must not hold it against Lady Kinsley. After all, her husband is a wonderful man. She's very lucky to have landed him."

If her husband is such a wonderful bloke, why'd she step out with mine? Pearl wanted to ask. And she wanted to ask it with all the sass of the young street urchin she'd been. But instead: "Of course. Lady Kinsley is blameless in this respect. I was not married to Lord Andrepont at that time."

Lady Teeton sat back, pleased with herself. "Oh, good. Lady Kinsley truly has an incredible mind.

While she is lacking in experience, she remembers everything she reads, and she reads whatever comes her way. The three of us would make such fast friends, I know it."

"Three of us?" Pearl asked without thinking.

"Yes. My influence, Rose's brains, and your experience. We would be a force to be reckoned with." Lady Teeton seemed to grow three inches as she described it.

Pearl liked the idea of being a force to be reckoned with. Instead of being waved away, thought unimportant, or left as an afterthought. Then it dawned on her: Lady Teeton was courting her. Not for a marriage, but for a friendship, or perhaps more. She wanted power, and she thought Pearl was the missing ingredient.

"I would like you to consider coming to the country with us. We spoke about it, and I do apologize for not sending details. What with the reform bill, I haven't had time to arrange our calendar. But when I do, please promise me you'll come. With Lord Andrepont, of course."

"Will Lord and Lady Kinsley attend, do you think?"

"Don't worry about that. They'll attend, but her tryst with Andrepont is absolutely over. I've had reassurances from Rose personally. She has no interest. Biscuit?"

Pearl nibbled on an oat-filled shortbread while her hostess prattled on about the best times to visit their country estate in some place Pearl couldn't even remember. Would James thank her for taking him to a place where he could be alone with Lady Kinsley? Would he want a chance to win his mistress back?

Well, that wasn't really for her to decide. And she wanted friends. Since her husband spent his time doing precisely what he wanted, then she would as well. She would invite him to attend, and if he didn't, that was his fault. She was going to Lady Teeton's country estate, and she had a fair idea of how to make James attend along with her. He wanted to spar, and what was a prizefight if there were no prizes?

"I beg your pardon, Lady Teeton, but I really must get on. I have a few other calls to make. It's been lovely to see you, and I look forward to your invitation." Pearl stood smoothly, proud of herself for making her wishes known.

She left Lady Teeton's Mayfair home and walked to Marylebone to visit Lydia and Agnes. Really, she went to ask John about James's weaknesses in the ring. She'd seen a few of his tells—he was easily distracted and easily inflamed. He fought on instinct, not on intellect, which made him easier to trick.

By the time she arrived at her brother's house, she was out of breath.

Parsons opened the door, looking very pleased to see her. "My lady," he said with a formal bow. "It is a pleasure to see you again. Won't you come in?"

She handed over her hat, gloves, and pelisse. "I am here to call on Lydia, of course, but I'd like to see my brother first, if he's in."

"He is engaged in his exercise," Parsons said, gesturing down the hallway.

"Thank you. I hope everything is settled downstairs with Richard and Paul?"

"Indeed. Paul has decided to take his leave."

Pearl frowned. Paul had been an excellent footman. Perhaps she could poach him for her own household. "Poor Anne Marie. How is she faring?"

Parsons walked with her towards the purpose-built gymnasium. "The girl is slower than she's ever been, which is a remarkable feat. I didn't know a human could be so utterly snail-like."

Pearl laughed. "Heartbreak is such a difficult thing. Can Richard help her repair her heart at all?"

Parsons shook his head. "I'm afraid he's washed

his hands of her now. He won't even look at her during mealtimes."

"You know, replacing Paul will add new blood downstairs. It might solve itself. Or even hiring another upstairs maid for Anne Marie to train. It would distract her. Both would be best, in my opinion."

Parsons brightened. "Excellent suggestion, my lady."

"I will mention it to Lydia." They reached the closed door. "I'm so glad we can solve these problems together, Mr. Parsons."

He bowed to her again. "You are a credit to your new household."

The familiarity felt good—like sinking back into a warm bath. She'd felt too awkward at her new house. Especially where baths were concerned. Banishing James's naked fury from her mind, she entered the gymnasium without knocking. Her brother had information she needed.

John whirled around, sweating. He and Bess were sparring in the elevated ring, and the championess took the opportunity to wallop him in the side. John danced away from her. The air was humid and smelled of their sweat.

"Wot you want?" he asked, letting his flat accent emerge. The one they shared with Bess. He snorted and spat into a towel lying on the floor.

"Expertise."

Bess snorted. "Then you'll need me."

"Piss off," John tossed over his shoulder at Bess.

Pearl knew her questions wouldn't hit right at first, so she just started in. "Tell me how James fights."

John narrowed his eyes. "Why? He hurtin' you?"

Bess tried to kick him one, but again he danced away. "He couldn't touch her if she didn't want it. You know that."

"Don't mean nuffin' if—"

Pearl planted her feet, huffing to stop John's insult. "It ain't like that. I'm to spar with him this afternoon, and I ain't leaving it to chance. So how's he fight, yeah?"

"He knows you've trained? You said you weren't never going to let anyone know. Not ever," Bess said as she shouldered past John.

Bess was right. Pearl had said that. She'd sworn John and Bess to secrecy. How would Mrs. Tyler have treated her if she'd known what Pearl had seen? How would Mathilda have reacted? And Lydia? Lydia was a wild animal sometimes, and she clearly felt that prizefighting was her territory. She wouldn't have wanted to share with Pearl. Not when Pearl's style was so at odds with hers.

"It just happened," Pearl admitted.

"Nuffin' just happens." John put his hands on his hips. "Is something—is something going on?"

"No!" Pearl flapped her hands out, completely at a loss. "That's the problem."

John frowned, but Bess looked like she might understand.

"He wants to spar this afternoon before dinner, and I aim to make a wager to get what I want."

John's hands flew to his ears. "Don't wanna know."

Bess thumped in the chest. "Don't be an arse."

"That's my sister!"

Bess gave him a look of disdain. "So you listen to her problems, you pigwidgeon. Fer fuck's sake."

John lowered his hands. "He can be sloppy. Especially on his left. Footwork's not solid as some, so when he gets tired, it's bad. Watch out for his right cross and his uppercuts, they can knock a grown man out. He's got the speed when he wants, in short bursts, but can't sustain it. He might seem like he's an emotional fighter, but he can be cunning-like when he wants. Got a sense of humor and he likes to play games wif' you. He'll change it up if he finds he don't have the advantage."

Pearl pulled herself up and restored her learned accent. "Sounds like he's quite the opponent."

John smiled at her, no doubt swallowing the extra spit in his mouth to do so. He mimicked her accent. "Indeed. Careful there though. When he shatters, there'll be pieces of him everywhere."

"Noted," Pearl said, turning to leave.

"And I don't mean in the ring."

Pearl turned, curious if John really meant what she thought he did.

"He's a man without a mission right now. His mum's safe, his sister is safe. Lydia's safe, Agnes is safe. He's no one left to take care of."

"What about me?"

"He doesn't think of you as his yet," John said. "When he does, mark my words. That man will crash at your feet like a glass bottle. Be careful."

Pearl contemplated that. James clearly didn't view her as his wife, as he hadn't even attempted to be in her bed. Was it Lady Kinsley stopping him? Was she under his protection, and that was why he was so changeable?

"C'mon." Bess nudged John. "Get back to it." The two circled back to their stances and Pearl slipped out.

She didn't understand James. But she wasn't about to change her mind about getting what she wanted, because what she wanted was so very reasonable. A life. Friendship. She was inviting James along with her, but he had to participate.

MORNINGS WERE HELL. James had always hated them. He'd missed breakfast with Pearl because he didn't know if he could see her and then let her out of his sight to go calling. Not that he would prevent her from leaving, but rather, he worried he would stare after her like a lovesick puppy. That was pathetic, and James Wallingford, the viscount Andrepont, was pathetic in many ways, but not that one.

Instead, he dressed late, and when Pearl had left, he went to find his mother to confront her about her meddling. Aphrodisiacs were one thing, but a complete display of cock and balls in the form of boiled eggs and asparagus was just a touch over the top. Predictably, Mrs. Foraker tried to dodge the question when he cornered her.

"I'm not my father, Mrs. Foraker," he explained. "I want only to speak with the woman who birthed me."

The housekeeper gave a weak, apologetic smile. "I know you're not, my lord. Habits, and all."

She might as well have spoken aloud the real reason: *you look so much like him.*

Finally, Mrs. Foraker yielded to his gentle interrogation and signaled the greenhouse out by the mews. While the formal gardens needed pruning, the wild gardens that his mother cultivated were doing well. The stepping stones were oases for him amidst thigh-high bushes of flowers and herbs. He entered the greenhouse where his mother was tending her strange garden, with its strong smells and an array of drying herbs ready for whatever potions she concocted.

"Practicing your witchery, Mama?" James called as he entered the humid place, smelling of loam and manure and a touch of peppermint.

"It isn't witchery, just remedies. You know that." She peered round the corner of the plants. "You'll get yourself muddy if you don't put something on over your nice clothes."

"I'm not going to help you plant."

"You say that now." His mother smiled at him.

"There are some smocks by the door. Slip one on and come back over here. Grab that basket, too."

James rolled his eyes and scoffed, but he did what he was told. Something about mothers compelled him. He noticed one of the smocks still had a watch fob attached, and given its size, it had to be Pearl's. She must have been out here more than he'd thought. He grabbed a different smock and tied it around his waist. "Are you indoctrinating the young woman who lives here with your herbal witchery?" He grabbed the basket off the workbench and wandered over to his mother, who already had clippings waiting for him.

"The young woman? You mean your wife?"

James squirmed. "You shouldn't call her that."

"I was there when the bishop announced it. What else would I call her?" His mother pushed back her bonnet to look at him better. She looked younger these days. More at ease.

"You could call her by her name, for instance. Or, the viscountess. Or Lady Andrepont," James suggested, tucking an errant sprig of rosemary back into the basket.

His mother chuckled. "You are so skittish. Like a deer in a hunting park."

"Where else are there deer?" He said it as if his mother had explored the world.

"Is this about me?" she asked, looking up at him, all humor drained from her face.

James tilted his head, confused. "Are you making some kind of metaphor?"

His mother gave him a puzzled look. He hated being in the greenhouse; all the bending gave him a crick in his lower back.

"I'm talking about your wife!" His mother said, straightening as well.

"Is she the deer?" He was genuinely confused.

"You don't listen," she said, fidgeting with her

small basket of tools. "That's my fault. I should have done a better job. I didn't know how."

James shook his head. The entire conversation was over his head. "I listen perfectly well. But if you don't speak in coherent sentences, I don't think I should be expected to read your mind. The only thing I've come to understand is that while we are talking about deer, you have no intention of referencing actual deer."

"Very astute," she said drily, walking past him to the workbench. When he didn't immediately follow, she gestured. "I believe that you are not getting along with your wife because of how you saw my marriage."

"Who says we aren't getting along? We're getting along famously."

She gave him a look he recognized from childhood. "Servants talk. You know that."

"As I recall, we all talk."

"You know what I mean. There is plenty of talk downstairs about how you and your wife—"

"Her name is Pearl. I'm quite sure she's given you leave to use it." James set down the basket hard enough to hear the fibers crunch.

His mother glared at him. "I don't understand why you are being so difficult."

"Shocking. I'm shocked that you have found a situation you don't understand."

She put her hands on her hips. "I'm not above boxing your ears if you need it. Right now, it seems you might. Now are you going to listen to me or are you going to be smart with me?"

It didn't matter if he was five or thirty-five; some things never changed. "I'm listening," he grumbled.

"I may be incorrect, but I think this—whatever is happening between you and Pearl, or not happening, as the case may be..." She gave him a look as if he ought to be happy she'd used her name. "You've not seen a good marriage, not up close anyway. And that is my fault. I should have remarried after the death of his lordship, but I just couldn't bring myself to do it."

She might as well have skewered him with those gardening shears. "Mama, don't. I would never ask you to marry someone for my sake. It's cruel."

"But..." Tears formed in her eyes.

It broke his heart. He'd come out here to tease her about the cock-and-balls dinner plate, thinking he might get a laugh, and instead she was crying. Crying because of his father. He put his hand on her arm, hoping it would give an ounce of comfort. "No. He broke us all. But he's gone now, and we've picked up our pieces. Don't ever apologize for him."

"But you don't know how it's supposed to be, James. What you saw wasn't the way marriage works. You don't know how to be a husband, or how to have a wife. It's not the same for everyone, but it certainly isn't what I had. Being a wife isn't bad. It's only bad if the husband is bad. And you aren't. Because you aren't him. Do you hear me, James? You are not him."

The words sank in slowly, water in an already flooded terrain. He didn't want to hear this. He didn't want to talk about this. His whole body began to shake. He tried to calm the rising panic. "I can't," he said, blinded by the darkness he felt invading from everywhere. He needed air. He was suffocating in the humid greenhouse. He couldn't let her see his weakness—she'd already suffered too much. It was his fault. He couldn't protect her, couldn't protect anyone.

He stumbled out of the greenhouse, shucking the smock somewhere near the door. He threw off his coat, striding through the garden, stripping off every bit of himself. He was raw and hurting and wild.

When he reached the ballroom, all he had left was his shirt, which he threw off in one swift movement. Wraps be damned. He went to work on the sawdust bag, throwing combination after combination, not thinking about warming his muscles, not worrying about strains or sprains or what made sense.

When he couldn't bring himself to punch any longer, he found the rope and skipped. The steady *chuff-chuff-chuff* of the rope on the ballroom floor calmed his mind. He wanted to think of nothing. Not his past, not his future. Just his body. What felt good in that moment. If only something could make him feel good when everything else felt bad.

Pearl crept in. God, she was a mouse. He hated timidity. So why had he wanted Rose? She wasn't timid, but she certainly wasn't the bold temptress he'd found amongst the married women of the *ton*. So why Rose? Because he couldn't have her. Because she didn't know him well enough to judge him for his past actions, and she couldn't judge him for his father's. James was so angry he could barely see straight.

"I'm here for a sparring match, but it looks like you're already deep into your exercise," Pearl said.

She was dressed oddly. Shorter skirts ending just below the knees, with white stockings. Her calves and ankles were visible like a schoolgirl's. Instead of a dress, she wore a short white jacket that crossed in the front and tied in the back.

"What are you wearing?" he growled, slowing his pace but refusing to stop altogether.

"This is a proper women's boxing uniform. Or, it had been, anyway." Pearl looked down, as if she might want to cover her ankles and calves.

"Not from what I've seen," he spat. She had shapely calves, he would admit that. He let his lust riot unchecked. He hadn't the strength to rein in his baser thoughts. His hand clutching that ankle for instance.

"It's because women's boxing isn't what it used to be," Pearl said.

Even James was not so oblivious to miss the wistful tone. But he had no patience for it. Not for dreams or hopes or any of that. They were a waste of time. He stopped his rope. "How long before you're ready to begin?" He stalked over to the shelf where a fresh ewer of water sat ready for him. The perks of being the master of the house.

"Is there something wrong?" Pearl asked.

"How long will it take you to be ready?" He asked again, pouring a cup of water and guzzling it down.

"Moments, really," she said, starting to windmill her arms. "But I'd like to put a wager on our fight."

"Done." He slammed the cup back onto the shelf, causing Pearl to jump. "What's your wager?"

Pearl tilted her chin up. "If I win, you go with me to Lady Teeton's house in the country for a week."

"No," he growled. There was nothing on God's green earth that would take him there to be harassed for a week.

She frowned. "Four days, then."

"No," he said.

She narrowed her eyes. "Every round I win, I get a day of you there. And every round you win, name your prize."

"You do what I want." He didn't know what that was. Something. The animal inside him roared. It knew exactly what he wanted Pearl to do. "For a day. No complaining, no scheming, no nothing. I'm selfish, and I don't want to feel guilty about it."

She put her hands on her hips. "And how is that different from every other day?"

Anger flared, but to control it, he stalked over to the ring—a small platform built up, the scratch marked hard into it. "Are you saying I'm selfish?"

"Extremely so. I've never met someone so entirely selfish in my life." She stomped over to the ring. His anger was contagious, apparently.

He held out his hand and she slipped under the rope into the ring. "Everything I've ever done has been in service of someone else. My mother, my sister, Lydia, Agnes—"

"Rose?" she countered, putting her toe on the line.

It embarrassed him to hear Pearl say his lover's Christian name. He didn't want to be reminded of Rose when Pearl stood in front of him. It was like being in the ocean and being told the desert existed. It was irrelevant at best and unhelpful at worst. "Don't ever say her name."

Pearl winced, but crouched into a posture. "Then let's get on wif it."

He barely registered that her accent had changed as he, too, crouched into his posture, toes on the line.

"Countdown on three," Pearl said.

He grunted his assent, his rage still blinding him. Was he really going to try to hit this woman?

"Three, two, one."

He struck out, a wide, sweeping right cross, only to miss her entirely. She was across to the other side by the time he figured out he'd missed her by a mile.

"Nice swing! Don't drop your elbow," she taunted.

He went after her, only to find he couldn't get near her. The swiftness he'd seen in her before only became more obvious. Every jab, every step, she didn't bother countering because she was too far away. He was already tired from his previous work, and she was running him from corner to corner.

"How are you going to win a round if you don't come near me?" he panted.

"Round ends when someone drops. That will be you," she said as she danced away.

"A one-round fight?" His feet felt heavy and hot.

"That's up to you." It didn't look like she was even breaking a sweat. No wonder she didn't need to warm her muscles. After what felt like years of running around the ring, he knew he needed a different tactic.

He stopped and put his hands on his knees to

breathe. His anger abated through sheer exhaustion. "How about a draw?"

She laughed. "I have no need to stop. And unlike you, I want to win."

He straightened. "I want to win."

"Really? Because getting this prize and your everyday life is different, how?"

He inched closer to her, a devious plan blossoming in his mind. "Because *you* would have to obey me."

She narrowed her eyes. "That implies you have paid attention to me enough to request something."

"I've spent the better part of three weeks doing everything I can to not pay attention to you." He inched closer. On a whim, he stretched his arms up and out, letting his pectorals flex and lift. Her eyes flicked down. Distraction.

She said nothing. It was gratifying to know she noticed his body. Perhaps she was more aware of what went on between men and women given her upbringing. He stepped ever closer to her. He wouldn't strike her, of course. But he could pin her, and feeling her squirm against him in fury, well, that would improve his day.

Suddenly, she skittered backwards. "And I you."

"Pardon?"

"You think I'm not keenly aware of the water you sink into at the end of your training? Where the water touched me, where the water will touch you?"

His blood drained from all useful parts. All he could picture was her in the bath, that red-gold hair pinned up, spilling down. Her breasts sitting plump and open in the bath. How close he had been to her—

And then he was sitting on his arse.

How had he gotten here? Pearl was already dancing into her corner. "Thirty seconds, my lord," she called. "That's one day at Lady Teeton's!"

"How the bloody hell did you do that?" He looked around himself, seeing all his limbs intact and attention blissfully away from his groin.

She smiled sweetly. "Distraction. Apparently, it's a game we can both play."

CHAPTER 13

Pearl graciously allowed James to take the first bath. The only bath, really. She hadn't worked up much of a sweat. She'd clean herself, of course, but only with a cloth. In her room, she didn't need Lily to help disrobe from the boxing costume. It was the old style, from the previous century even, and the women who'd worn clothes such as these couldn't afford the help. Everything was easy on, easy off.

She untied the jacket, shucking it off, leaving her in a sleeveless chemise.

Had he meant it, she wondered, *when he said he'd spent days trying not to pay attention to her?* Or had it just been a distraction technique, as her brother warned he might attempt? He was cunning, that much was true.

She heard the water slosh in the bath. It was totally inappropriate to spy through the keyhole. Knowing he was undressed, soaking in the tub. Considering what a mess he'd looked when she arrived, his poor muscles certainly deserved a hot bath.

Before she could stop herself, she was standing by the door to the bathing room. She heard him sigh. The sound of his voice echoed strangely in the small room, and she could feel the heat seep through the crack under the door. Suddenly, her body was uncomfortably warm.

"I can hear you out there," James called through the door.

"It's my bed chamber. I'm allowed to be here." There was a thrill of being caught by him, she could admit.

"Your floor creaks."

"You mean *your* floor creaks. Your name is on the lease of this place." She would not bend down and look through that keyhole. Would not. She could hear him splashing. He was likely washing himself. Running a soapy cloth along his arms, down his chest.

"What's mine is yours," he said. "Or something like that."

She cleared her throat in order to clear her thoughts. "Something like that. But really, what's yours is yours and what's mine is yours, too."

Water rushed and sloshed, and she heard him exhale. He must have dunked his head.

Was she goading him by returning to this argument? "I took your name. I'm no longer Pearl Arthur. I'm Lady Andrepont. Or, if you hadn't a title, Mrs. James Wallingford. Silly, really. Because if I died and you remarried, the next woman would be named the same thing. It's very confusing."

There was silence on the other side of the door. She'd managed to put him off with her radical points. That was no surprise.

"You aren't dying."

"Well, no, I hadn't planned on it."

"So I will not be taking another wife. End of discussion."

Interesting. He was surprisingly mercurial about such a topic, considering he didn't seem to think of her as his wife. At least, according to her brother. But then again, John hadn't been in this house. Perhaps it had changed James in some way to live with her. To have married her. Altered by her.

"Duly noted." More splashing behind the door kept her thoughts occupied. She willed herself to move away, but she was rooted to the spot.

"Are you still there?" His voice was pitched much lower. It made her belly twist.

"I am."

"Are you still wearing that ridiculous boxing costume from four hundred years ago?"

"Why?" It wasn't ridiculous. It was historic. And more to the point, it was *accurate*. It was from a time when women boxers were taken seriously. There was a mentor, a training regime, an amphitheater. Now, they were expected to strip down in public and waggle for the louts shouting curses in the corners.

"Because I would very much like it if you weren't in it."

Her inner running monologue shut down as if it had been tripped. "But you lost."

"Which is why I said I would like it very much. You are under no obligation."

"Unlike you and Lady Teeton's country house."

"You get one day." There was more splashing, but it was slow.

"What are you doing?" she asked.

"Aren't you peeking through the keyhole?"

Oh, blazes. Did he know? "I am not."

"I would be."

"Would you now? I had the idea that you didn't care for short redheads."

"I don't have a type," he said. "It's demeaning to women."

She snorted. "I didn't think that mattered all that much to you. To men at all, really."

"Then you have greatly underestimated me, Pearl. I look forward to the day when you decide to get to know me."

His words left her weak in the knees. She couldn't speak. Finally, she managed, "That makes two of us."

"Does it?" He growled. "Because you could get to know me right now, if you wanted."

Heat pooled in her body and her mouth went utterly dry. "How?"

"If you want to take it slow, look through the keyhole. If not, you can always join me. Are you the type to jump in with both feet?" The tenor of his voice was rough, and the sound of the water was taking on a methodical rhythm. She knew he was touching himself. But the way he said it, this was a different James. The kind of man who played the game in the ring. It wasn't him, or at least, not the part of him she had seen so far. This was the dangerous, risky viscount, the role he played to get what he wanted.

But she didn't want the role. Who was the man she would live with for the rest of her life? She wanted the man who played piano for her at midnight.

Both men inhabited the exquisite naked body on the other side of the door.

Pearl sputtered nonsense before her thoughts ordered themselves. "I don't like morsels."

"If you join me, it will be a feast."

He was right, and they both knew what would come of it. But he hadn't yet kissed her outside of the marriage vows in the church. He hadn't shown any love of any kind. And if there was a choice for her, she would wait. She would wait for him—the part of him that didn't toy with her affections.

She cleared her throat again. "I'll wait for you to come to me. Then I know you'll be honest."

"You think I'm lying? Walk through that door. I promise you I'm very, very sincere." The water sloshed, no doubt as he sat up.

He wouldn't make this easy for her. Her attraction

to him was obvious, and he knew it. "I don't think you're lying. But I don't think you're earnest."

He laughed, but it was an ugly sound. Not at all the free laughter of last night's dinner. "I'm sorry, Pearl. Did you want sincerity or did you want fucking?"

She winced. Men had been crass with her before. It was part of being a woman—regardless of age. Expect the crude language, the rude propositions. But there was disrespect in every single one of them. The sound that echoed around the words, not the words themselves. And she heard it here, too. "When I want something," she said, steeling her voice. "I get it. You know what I want. And when you can give it to me, I'll take it."

He heard a low whistle on the other side of the door, and she stomped away to make it known she was done with their conversation. She redressed quickly, escaping the bedroom before he would be done with his bath. Or be done with himself.

Before she left the room, she checked her bag under the bed. Still there, still packed. It wasn't much, but it was hers.

She would go down to dinner because she couldn't let him win. But she didn't want to face him when he was ugly like this. What had happened that he'd changed so drastically? It wasn't her business. She had her victory: he would join her for one day at Lady Teeton's country house. At least one, because he'd already agreed to a rematch tomorrow.

❦

ORGASMS WERE STRANGE THINGS. Sometimes, they filled one with delight and joy and peace. And other times, like this one, it was nothing but shame and self-loathing. He came roughly in a towel as he heard Pearl leave her room. He'd been awful to her. The fantasy that had finally brought him relief was him kissing his way up her thighs, apologizing for being a cad.

Not his best moment.

Today had not been good. And he didn't want to subject her to his abominable behavior, so he rang for Phillip, dressed, and went to his club. The club he rarely visited but managed to keep a membership to, as it benefited him for a number of reasons. Mostly for the gossip.

He entered its hallowed halls, though they shouldn't be, considering the debauchery that was allowed. He sat in the lounge area and took up a newspaper, one of the hundreds that seemed to be in circulation. He perused the gossip pages and found the salacious news of different aristocrats, all with the thinly veiled initials after their honorifics.

It was noted that Lord and Lady Kinsley had made themselves more public lately, attending balls and even gaining entrance to Almack's. James had no clue why they would possibly want to do such a thing, or how much they must have paid to a charity to get Rose into that group of matrons, but whatever worked for them. Was Henry really vying for political power?

He had the breeding, the money, and the clout for it. But Rose would be on display. James could have sworn she said she didn't want to be in the public eye like that. Hence taking the six-month cruise where no prying eyes would see them. Rose would get to see the world, they would get to be as they wanted, and no one would write about them in columns such as these. Why on earth would she be courting these vultures?

"Andrepont! Haven't seen your ugly mug around here in ages." Lord Hawthorne dropped himself into the chair next to James. "Heard you finally got marched to the vicar."

"Bishop," James corrected. The waitstaff finally brought his claret, which he appreciated even more now that he had company. At least it wasn't Haglund or Teeton that had accosted him.

"I beg your pardon?"

"As far as I'm aware, no vicars attended my wedding, but thank you for your interest." He'd never liked Hawthorne. Knew him from Eton. He was a few years older and had the intellectual capacity of a dairymaid's milk bucket.

Hawthorne made an appreciative noise. "Heard you might finally be taking your seat."

A chill ran down his spine. "My seat?"

"Yes, House of Lords. You know the one."

"Yes, I've heard of it." This had Lady Teeton written all over it. Hawthorne was a gossip and an idiot. He bumbled through life good-naturedly and horridly lucky. It was annoying.

"So you are! That's deuced good news. Nice to have a friendly face about the halls, you know."

"What are you talking about?" James rustled the newspaper, trying to signal to Hawthorne that he couldn't care less.

"Oh, you know, there's just a bit of meanness left in some of the blokes. Jeering and whatnot. Bloodthirsty, seems like."

"My apologies Hawthorne, I've no idea what you're on about." *Nor is it my concern*, he thought.

Hawthorne patted his knee and then stood. "As long as you're there for the vote."

"Let me reiterate: I've no idea what you're on about."

Hawthorne raised his glass in a toast that, had it come from any other man, James might have believed to be a mockery. So Rose was not the only one who was being gossiped about. He flagged down a servant.

"Is Teeton here, by any chance?" James asked.

"Billiards room, my lord."

James tossed aside the newspaper and downed his claret. "I'll be joining him. Another of these, if you would." He stalked down to the billiards room. He'd get to the bottom of this mess. He didn't like being talked about; he didn't like being involved in other people's conflicts. His family had enough conflict of its own, and it had consumed his life. Why would he invite more?

Teeton was playing billiards like he did everything —distracted at best. The man himself was inoffensive, like walking blancmange: bland, unobjectionable, and welcome only to break up the boredom of a sick bed. The billiards room was thick with smoke and idiots. Teeton stood in the corner talking with some of said idiots while the billiards table lay fallow.

James wanted to call him out in front of the rest of them, but other than being utterly unremarkable, there was nothing about which James could confront him. Instead, he stalked over to Hawthorne. Good God, most of these men he'd known in short pants.

Several men gave him a nod of acknowledgment, which he returned because he wasn't entirely rude. They might have been arseholes, but so was he. He'd personally bloodied at least five of their noses for some reason or another. Likely, it had been Henry.

"Andrepont! Fancy seeing you out of the house," Teeton said in greeting.

"Or out of bed," another man snickered from over James's shoulder.

"Who are you losing to this evening, Teeton?" James asked, not wanting to have any of them at his back. He wanted all of them where he could see them.

Suddenly he was embraced, his arms full of another person. "Good God, man, it's been fifteen years!"

James pushed back his mysterious hugger only to

find the no-longer-unwhiskered visage of Freddy Partridge. Freddy had been one of Henry's many younger hangers-on. Henry, when not being pushed around by the older boys, was idolized by any boy who had an ounce of appreciation for beauty. Freddy had been one. James had delivered a particularly harsh beating to an upper-class boy on Freddy's behalf once, though for the life of him, he couldn't remember the boy he'd ravaged.

"Freddy! They let you into this place?" James asked, stunned into utter inaction.

"Show some respect to your betters, viscount," Teeton leaned in to say with a grin.

"You inherited?" James asked, cataloguing the man's features: a dignified amount of whiskers along his sideburns, his shoulders filled into a man's size, no longer the scrawny child.

"As did you, Lord Andrepont," Freddy grinned, showing James how he'd even grown into his massive front teeth. The boy had looked like a rodent. It had been unfortunate.

"Forgive me—I've had too many prizefights. Remind me again of your title," James said. He really should be able to remember. But he hadn't seen Freddy since before he inherited. Since everything that happened—his cousin William dying, Lydia at the country house, his father's rage, and then his death. It had been such a spiral.

"You are looking at his lordship, the Earl of Rosblair." Teeton beamed as if he himself had crowned the boy.

"Isn't that Scotland?" James asked.

"Well, yes, it is but—" Freddy couldn't get a word out without these other blokes butting in.

"A Scottish title doesn't mean you live in Scotland, Andrepont!" Another voice came from the back of the room, prompting lower chatter that was likely ribbing the speaker for his interruption.

"I'm trying to talk to Freddy, you cunts. Don't make this a time to relive the past by me putting my fist in your faces." James growled at them, which shut them up for the moment. "Now Freddy, catch me up on the last fifteen years."

When the manservant arrived with his claret, James ordered a carafe to share with Freddy. Whatever he'd gone in to talk to Teeton about could wait. They found a small, unoccupied reading room and took seats away from the crowd of absolute blowhards.

"And what has happened with you, Andrepont? I read in the newspapers that you just celebrated your nuptials. My felicitations." Ever so polite, Freddy.

James thanked him, but he didn't want the reminder. He didn't want to think about Pearl at that moment, not when Freddy was there to talk about the past. The past and the future weren't connected for him. The past was the nightmare, and the future was repentance. There was so much to atone for, and James didn't know how to do it.

He'd given his half-sister Margaret what she wanted: marriage to a man twice her age. He'd helped engineer Lydia's hopes: crippling Carlisle both physically and financially, and convincing their family to weather the scandal of marrying a prizefighter. He'd even repaired the damage he'd caused in Agnes's life. And so where did he sit now? How could he make it up to his mother? The countless maids he didn't even know about in and around London? Were there other mistresses, prostitutes, or offspring he needed to help? "Let's just say that after I left school, my family absorbed all my attentions. It has been that way ever since. And you?"

Freddy recounted the intricacies of his father's protracted illness. "He lingered, but it wasn't a death I'd wish on anyone."

James could think of one who would have deserved a malingering death.

"After you left, life was hell. At least Henry left around the same time, so he was safe, but... Andrepont, I'm telling you, it was bad."

James shook his head. Another failure. "I'm sure it was."

"I learned to defend myself, but I was no match for the bigger lads. But I got through it. I can't thank you enough for what you did for me."

"Anyone would," James said.

Freddy gave him a faint smile. "Quite the opposite, really. There were those who beat me and those who stood by and let it happen. You were the only one who bothered with a nobody like me."

"Nobody? Freddy, you're an earl! Why didn't that alone protect you?" It wasn't foolproof, having a title, but it certainly helped.

"You really don't remember?" Freddy looked up through a fringe of hair. He sported the foppish look of a dandy, long hair included. "My father was a second son. I was third in line to an obscure Scottish title. Who cared?"

"But your father—" James frowned. Hadn't there been the whole story of his father's lingering illness?

"My father inherited because both he and his brother became ill. His brother died early. Then, while my father hung on, the paperwork was done. My father became earl. Then me, after his death. It's been a long road. And it's also why I haven't been in London."

"If your estate is up there, why are you here?" James poured more wine into each of their glasses.

"I was supposed to find a wife, but I admit I had a difficult time navigating the Season. If I had success, I would stay and court my bride and then take my seat in Parliament in the next session."

The boy—no longer really a boy—would take his

seat. If only he knew the snakes that lived in that reptile house. "I'm not sure the House of Lords will be any better than Eton."

Freddy's eyes went wide. "How do you mean?"

"They're the same men. The very ones. Just like in the billiards room back there."

Freddy laughed. "Oh, I know. Some things can't be helped. I've made my peace with them, and them with me. In fact, I hope to use some of their cruelty to me against them in negotiations. And I cannot wait to jeer them when they propose something I don't like."

James shook his head. "Freddy…"

The man put his hands on his forearm. "There's no need to coddle me. I'm looking forward to this. To give people like me a voice. The ones who were on the receiving ends of those fists. I get to make the rules now."

There was something about his speech that stirred James's sympathy. "I won't be there to protect you."

Concern creased Freddy's boyish face, giving insight into what he would look like another twenty years from now. "What do you mean?"

"I never took my seat."

"I beg your pardon?"

"In the House of Lords. It sits empty. I never took it." James had never felt anything about the fact before. It had been fifteen years, and yet, it hadn't bothered him until now.

Freddy shook his head. "But you are the viscount Andrepont, are you not?"

James nodded. "I am."

"Then how could you not take your seat? What about your responsibilities, your obligations, your people?"

"I've tended to my obligations." What could Freddy know of how seedy power was? How it corrupted men, made them believe they were above the law?

Freddy drew back from him. It was the same look he'd seen in the eyes of those who saw his father in his face. "It isn't my place to condemn you." Freddy got up, downing the wine in a skilled gulp. "But I do hope you change your mind."

He left, leaving James with his carafe of claret in an empty room. There was nothing to keep James company but his own terrible mood.

❦

PEARL WOKE to the faint strains of piano music. James had returned, then. She hadn't known where he'd gotten to, but she'd eaten dinner alone. After dinner, to amuse herself, she'd changed into her boxing costume and trained in the gym, hoping he might come upon her. She worked until exhausted, but still she was alone. Finally, she retired to her room where she ignored Lady Teeton's tracts and gave herself a rag bath. Lily had come to brush out her hair, but Pearl hadn't felt like talking. When sleep came, it was in fits and starts.

Unable to help herself, Pearl grabbed her wrapper and headed down to the music room. She tucked her feet underneath her to keep warm, listening as he flew through some very complicated-sounding pieces. He missed several notes—not that she could tell—but his mild cursing made the errors obvious.

Before long, a single candle flame approached her from down the hallway. Mrs. Foraker appeared, holding a tray with a small teapot. Her hair was down, and she was in a night rail and wrapper, too.

"How did you know I was here?" Pearl asked.

Mrs. Foraker smiled kindly at her as she set the tray on the ground next to Pearl. "There are no secrets in a house like this, my lady. Compliments of

Lady Andrepont, a tea blend from the garden, good for the middle of the night."

"You're both too kind." The thought that every servant knew she sat outside her husband's study every night, pining after him like a forlorn child, embarrassed her.

"Don't fret, my lady," Mrs. Foraker said, tucking her arms in front of her. "He's a had a harder time than it appears. And he's got it in his head that he's no good. It's not true, of course."

"Why would he be no good?" Pearl asked. "Whatever gave him that idea?"

"His father. I don't know how much you know about him, and it isn't my place to talk. But I will say, even my heart stops sometimes when his lordship approaches. It takes me a moment to recover myself and remember this is the son, not the father."

"Could he have really been that terrible? I've known terrible men." Pearl could catalog the men she'd met and the ones she'd been warned about. The men who'd beaten wives to death, the ones who'd smothered their own children in a rage.

Mrs. Foraker took a breath and surveyed the darkness around her. "The difference between the men you've known and the man whose title ran this house is power. The previous lord Andrepont had power, and he wielded it with a vengeance only he understood."

Pearl felt ashamed for not realizing it earlier. There was a difference between men who let their fists get out of hand once a fortnight and a man who could summon the favor of the law. Morbidly, she wanted to know more. What had the man done that was bigger than a common criminal? Or perhaps the crime lay in the idea that he knew he had no comeuppance at the end of his trespass.

The music stopped. Mrs. Foraker looked at the door, scooped up her candle, and scurried down the hallway. Pearl smiled after her. Matchmakers to the end. Leaning against the wall, Pearl cradled the cup of hot tea. There were hints of peppermint and an earthy smell she couldn't quite place. She took a sip and gagged. It was horrid. Bilge water tasted better. She was all but spitting when the door swung open.

"How long have you been out here?" James demanded.

Pearl coughed and put down the cup. "Not long," she croaked.

His cravat was off, and she could see the notch where his neck met his collarbone. In the dark illumination, he was all hard angles and shadows, the image of a devil. The bare skin made her body buzz in response. He glanced at the teacup. "That one of my mother's concoctions?"

Pearl nodded.

"Come on, I've got some whisky that'll clear the taste. There is something deucedly wrong with that stuff. I'd rather eat a rancid dog."

Pearl followed him. He took her cup and poured it into a planter next to the drink cart.

"Won't that hurt the plant?" she asked, concerned.

"No," James said offhand, his words sounding loose with drink. "It's silk."

She laughed, and he smiled as he handed her a tumbler with a finger's worth of whisky. "Are you joining me?"

"I'm already drowning in liquor. A dram now would just make my hangover worse."

Pearl sipped the illicit whisky, letting it burn on the way down her throat and sting her eyes. She'd had plenty of the stuff before. It crossed her mind to pretend otherwise, but it was late and there was no point in keeping up a façade of propriety. After all, he could now see her bare feet if he looked down. She was past shame. Her peasant feet were not nearly the worst thing about her. It was time to drop the pretenses that kept them bound. Mrs. Tyler would not approve, but Pearl only seemed to founder when relying on the advice of others. She needed to follow her instincts, the ones that told her to be honest and true with him.

"Are you upset that I didn't accept your invitation to enter the bathing room today?" Pearl asked, not daring to meet his eyes.

James plopped himself into the chair nearby, letting out a big sigh. As if he were relieved that the curtain of propriety that hung between them was being torn down. "No. I'm rather glad you didn't. You were right—I wasn't being nice. I was inviting you in for all the wrong reasons."

Pearl sat on the couch near the chair, just as they had the other night when they'd stayed up talking. "What are the wrong reasons?" The word she thought of caught in her throat, but the whisky loosened it. "Lust?"

James chuckled. "Lust is a very good reason to invite a woman into the bath."

Pearl swallowed hard. Of course he didn't lust after her. She knew that; men didn't lust after a woman like her. And he had been very clear about his disinterest. She'd thought otherwise during the ring, but that was just his cunning distraction. Well, it had worked. She'd believed he noticed her. The realization knifed her pride to ribbons.

"No. Rather, my reasons were vanity and vengeance."

She resolved to have a better sense of humor about his lack of interest. What else was there? She was tired of being disappointed. Her life had been full of disappointments, and choosing to have no expectations was nothing new. "Hm. An alliterative pair of bad reasons."

"Which is how you know it is a definitively bad idea."

Pearl laughed, bold enough now to meet his eyes. Even if she couldn't bring herself to say it, she was happy that at least he could make her laugh.

"You have no idea how glad I am that you see fit to laugh at my jokes. At least our marriage has that."

His acknowledgment sent a tingle down Pearl's body, following the trail of the whisky's burn. Their marriage. "What do we do about our marriage?"

"How do you mean?" James asked, furrowing his brow. He looked even more attractive with a quizzical puzzle to his features.

Perhaps it was the whisky, but Pearl touched his arched eyebrow, sliding a single finger around the quirk, then touched those glacial cheekbones. Dear Lord, why did he have to be so handsome? His skin was so smooth until halfway down his cheek, where the evening's dark stubble took over. "I mean..." She trailed off. Disappointment was too familiar an emotion. There was nothing to say. Just her touch outlining his face.

He grasped her hand as she tried to pull it back. "Pearl—"

"Yes," she said, hoping to make clear that she meant it. There was so much in this world to want, and she hated to give it up. It was late and she was tired. Why couldn't he try to be her husband? Why couldn't he try to want her?

In turn, he used his opposite hand to trace her cheek. "You are very beautiful. Do you know that?"

She couldn't bring herself to smile or even acknowledge it, because it simply wasn't true. There was something about her amalgam of features that made her striking, interesting to look at, but not beautiful. Not like Lydia, or even like Lady Kinsley. Pearl was too odd—her hair too red, her mouth too wide, her eyes too angled.

She watched him stare at her in apparent fascination. She would allow that as long as he wished to do it. His finger traced from her brow down to her cheek, cupping her jawline, and then he placed his thumb on her lower lip.

"Pearl," he breathed, leaning closer.

"Yes," she said again, trying to show him how much she wanted everything. The whole damned world. How miserable she was with the desire of it all. He brushed his lips to hers, letting go of her hand and using both of his to gently cup her jaw. She lifted her chin to meet him, wanting more, wanting to deepen a kiss she'd been longing for.

He brushed her lips again, firmer this time, and Pearl shifted forward on the couch, meeting him. His hands went to her unbound hair. He deepened his kiss, and Pearl sighed into him, melting into the rightness of it all.

James pulled back, leaving her unbalanced.

Pearl caught herself, stunned and suddenly cold. Bereft. Silly. Ridiculous.

"My apologies. I quite forgot myself."

"Quite all right," Pearl said.

"I do my best to maintain control of myself, and I've been drinking. It's late and—" James stood, cutting off his speech. He ran his hands through his hair. "There are no excuses for losing control. I do apologize." He bowed to her, effectively dismissing her.

Pearl stood, feeling a swirl of embarrassment and shame. It had been so good to be in his arms. To feel his touch on her bare skin. To have tenderness, even for that brief moment. "It is late. Good night, my lord." She curtsied and hurried out of the room, forgetting her candle. She didn't realize she was without light until she reached the hallway and kicked the tea tray that Mrs. Foraker had left, injuring her toe. She couldn't very well go back and retrieve the candle. Stifling her embarrassment, she put her hand on the wall and limped her way back to the stairs and up to her room.

Unable to sleep, Pearl opened the windows and watched the half-moonlight brush the roofs of Mayfair denizens. Finally, she crawled into bed and watched the sunrise, unable to feel much of anything.

CHAPTER 14

J ames lay in bed, straining to hear any
movement from the next room over. Obviously,
he needed to get ahold of himself. A carafe of
claret had him out of his senses, which was to
blame for him kissing his wife. He shook his head.
No, Pearl. Kissing Pearl. He couldn't think of her as
his wife without thinking he had rights to other
things, and that was thoroughly unacceptable.

Knowing Pearl was in the room next door had
kept him from sleep, but he didn't want to creep
down to his study and be farther from her. While he
lay and watched the sun crawl into the room around
the curtains, fretting over his life choices, she was no
doubt fast asleep, content to know she was safe from
his predatory advances.

He dressed, calling Phillip up hours before he
normally even got out of bed. Respect needed to be
his thought whenever he saw her. Respect her, just as
he'd promised her brother he would do. He hadn't
even gone to visit John since the wedding, scared that
the prizefighter might read his mind and see his illicit
thoughts. The last thing he needed was John Arthur
demanding a grudge match.

Phillip appeared in James's room, seeming out of
breath.

"Something wrong?" James asked.

Phillip shook his head, rushing to the drawers with cufflinks and cravats. "No, my lord. You merely caught me unawares." Phillip coughed.

"Not getting sick, are you?"

"No, my lord. Just had a mouthful of breakfast when I heard the bell. My apologies."

James frowned. He didn't want his valet to starve or choke. "You could have finished your meal."

"Thank you, my lord." He brought over the fresh-pressed cravat and the box of cufflinks. "I was surprised you rang so early. I wanted to hurry up here in case you need something special."

"Nothing special." James lifted his chin to allow his valet access to tie the cravat properly. The only thing special was to share a meal with Pearl. To explain. Or merely endure the awkwardness that would no doubt settle between them since he had taken liberties the night before.

"Will a simple knot suffice for today, or would you like something more ornate?" Phillip rarely asked, but since James had rung so early, perhaps Phillip was anticipating a meeting of some sort.

"Simple is fine. I'm only going down to break my fast with the viscountess."

Phillip frowned, but said nothing. James knew there was more going on than he knew. Servants talked, as his mother reminded him. Had her lady's maid talked?

"What is it?"

Phillip shook his head.

"Should I not take breakfast with the viscountess?" Had she been crying? Had he truly been such an oaf that she found her life here untenable?

Phillip winced. "The viscountess decided to go for a walk early this morning. Shortly after first light."

"What?" How had she managed to sneak out

without him hearing? "Did she take a footman? She shouldn't be out alone!"

"No, my lord. She took no one."

James sputtered incoherent furies, but Phillip finished the knot with expert patience. "Smithy took it upon himself to follow her."

James let out a breath of relief and nodded. Smithy was a savior. The large man drove his carriage, cared for the horses, and had a knack for discreet behavior. "Thank God. Smithy will be getting a large bonus this quarter."

Once Phillip was dismissed, James no longer had a reason to get to the dining room. He stared at the door between his room and Pearl's. What would it be like to just...walk through it?

She wasn't there. She wouldn't know.

But perhaps after last night, she'd locked it against him. If she'd known his thoughts, she would have. The brass doorknob gleamed now that the curtains were open. The sky outside was grayish, but it was enough to illuminate his folly. He tried the door.

It opened without a squeak. Her room lay beyond, the curtains thrown open, a small fire keeping it warm. He shouldn't cross the threshold. This was her room. Her sanctity.

But nothing in here looked like her. It was still decorated to his mother's taste, with papered floral walls and dark furniture. Pearl wasn't full of artifice. Not that his mother was either, exactly, but his mother had a secretive side that welcomed this sort of aesthetic. Pearl was different. She was light as air, nimble, agile, she—

He had to get ahold of himself. Instead of closing the door and keeping her privacy sacred, he stepped in. This close to the fireplace, he didn't smell her, just the crackling fire. He took another step and another until he passed the sitting area, the writing desk. He certainly wouldn't violate her privacy by looking in there. No doubt there were notes back and forth with Lady Teeton, and the less he thought about that woman, the better.

There was something under Pearl's bed. He could see it stuck way up next to the wall. Could the maids really be so lazy? Well, he could fish out whatever was squirreled away, bring it to Mrs. Foraker, and she could deal with the staff appropriately.

When he reached the bed, he could smell her, finally. Talc and rosewater, and something else, that very sweet essence of her. He laid down on his stomach and reached under the bed, fishing out the bundle. It was a carpetbag. Odd. Shouldn't this be stored with the rest of the household luggage?

He opened it, finding hose, two simple dresses, a chemise, and a bundle of bank notes. He opened a drawstring pouch to a pair of gold earrings. What was this? His stomach clenched. He hadn't noticed that his daily stomach pains had abated since he and Pearl had started getting to know each other. But the physical hurt now returned, assuring him the pain was his lifelong companion. He was mature enough now to know its name: dread.

Pearl was planning on leaving. Leaving this house, leaving him. There were bits of dust surrounding the bag, so it had been under there for long enough. She hadn't packed it in reaction to last night.

He shoved the bag back under the bed, back into its corner. He stood, dusted himself off, and returned to his room, closing the door firmly behind him. This complicated things considerably. It forced him to admit that he didn't want her to leave. He liked hearing her in the house. He liked knowing she would be outside the door, listening to him play. He liked knowing she spent time with his mother in those ridiculous greenhouses near the mews.

Running away—could it be so terrible to live here? Was he so overbearing? Or his mother?

He went to his study instead of the dining room. There was no way he could eat feeling like this. And if Pearl wasn't there, what was the point? His mind raced. What could make her stay?

Instead of playing, he paced. What did she enjoy? He drew a blank. Dear God, was he such an arse that he *still* didn't know anything about her? No wonder she wanted to leave. She'd accused him of being selfish, and he'd blown up at her. But she was right. He was selfish, and getting angry with her for accusing him of being so only proved her point.

He needed to do something for her, but he didn't know what. Greater than just sharing meals with her, which he enjoyed, he needed to really listen. Ask questions, learn—then he would know what she needed. Because the truth was, he *liked* her. Not just because she was beautiful, which he had said last night. He winced. That was definitely over the line. He had kissed her. Twice. Tangled his hands in her hair, which had been so silky, so soft. He'd wanted to pull that hair, urging her towards him, pull her onto his lap, and—

His body responded to the memory, but he quelled it. No. He had to think, and not with that.

❧❦❧

THE COOL AIR helped Pearl clear her head. She'd noticed Smithy not long after she left the house, trailing a few blocks behind. Once she got to Hyde Park, she debated purposely losing him in the trees but decided against it. The man was just trying to keep her safe, and she appreciated the sentiment, even if it was unwarranted.

There were plenty of cutpurses out, even this early. But Pearl had been amongst them before and still remembered the tricks, even if they no longer recognized her. Her dress marked her as wealthy, but she carried no money. While she might be accosted for other reasons, she was confident in her ability to get away fast enough to escape harm. Though, having Smithy nearby made it easier to let her thoughts wander, rather than having to scan the avenue for problems.

Her mind played last night in a loop, like an actor stuck on a single line, unable to move on. The kiss recurred, the brush of his lips to hers, the smell of him so close, his hand reaching into her hair. But then he pulled away and her thoughts began again, with his hands tracing her face.

Why would he pull away? Why would he stop? She was nearly shaking with frustration. This wasn't how John and Lydia were, but they'd been a love match. A love-against-all-odds match. Perhaps this was her own fault for agreeing to marry a man she didn't love. Or even know very well.

Her slippers were soaked with morning dew, so she circled back to the house. Her house, she supposed. She paused across the street to study it. One of the few in Mayfair that was a true estate, with gardens and grounds. The former lord must have had a great deal of money and influence to have such a place. She hadn't ever appreciated that before.

A lump formed in her throat. There was so much she didn't know. How were they to overcome their pasts if neither knew the other's? Her mind was finally exhausted, as were her feet. She hoped James would still want to spar in the afternoon, and if he did, she needed to get some sleep.

When she entered, Mr. Barton greeted her, a relieved expression on his face. She was honored that they worried for her safety, even if it seemed excessive. Taking off her bonnet and gloves, she asked him to have Lily wake her at three in the afternoon. She stumbled up to her room, stripping off her serviceable walking gown and wet stockings, collapsing into bed in her chemise.

Hours later, Pearl woke as Lily entered the room. "It's three, my lady."

Pearl's stomach churned, but she sat up. "Oh, you've brought a tray! Bless you."

Lily settled the tray over Pearl's lap, letting her snug into a much-needed repast. There was a pot of steaming hot tea, rolls, fresh butter, and cheese. A smattering of dried fruit and nuts rounded out the meal.

"Cook says say the word, and she'll whip up some lemon seedcakes for you as well." Lily took a step back, picking up the walking dress that Pearl had left in a heap on the floor.

Pearl waved her off, already a bite into the cheese. She couldn't decide which to do first, butter the roll, or pour her tea. "Oh no," she said between bites. "This is plenty. I don't wish to ruin my appetite for this evening."

Lily had a smug look on her face as she folded the dress.

"What is it?" Pearl demanded. "You must tell me." Pearl spilled her hot tea, scalding her hand.

"Careful!" Lily scolded. "Mustn't be losing your head over a bit of gossip, my lady."

"I want all the gossip." Pearl stuffed dried apricots in her mouth. "I have no compunction nor shame regarding gossip in this household."

Lily retrieved the chair from Pearl's dressing table and scooted it over to the bed. While Pearl ate like she was once again a starving five-year-old at Mrs. Wilkerson's house, Lily told her how James had called for Phillip early. And then, when he'd heard that Pearl was out on her own, could no longer eat any breakfast even though that was what he'd intended to do.

"Do you think—" Pearl stopped herself. Gossip in

the house needed to funnel *to* her, not *from* her. That was another of Mrs. Tyler's teachings.

"Did something happen, my lady?" Lily's eyes were wide.

Pearl couldn't even speak. Did a kiss between a married couple count as something happening? Shouldn't it be expected? Ordinary, even? She sighed. If she'd known better, she would have wished for a marriage where kissing was a daily event not worth mentioning.

Lily looked at her with suspicion. "Something did happen." The maid was nodding. She stood and stowed the chair back at the dressing table. "And you've a set-to with him soon, don't you?"

"Well—" Pearl stumbled. A set-to? Did the whole house know she boxed? There went a closely guarded secret. But, she supposed servants ought to keep secrets of the house. And if they were treated well and paid well, then they would keep them. "Please don't tell anyone about my exercises."

Lily's eyes rounded. "I would never breathe a word, my lady! But may I say that I am right proud of you? Not many women can hold their own. No one wants women to have more power than they already do. I hope one day you'd be willing to show the women on staff here how to do a thing or two. Just to keep ourselves safe, if it ever came to that."

Pearl's heart lurched. She wasn't the right person to teach anyone anything, but how could she resist Lily's request? "Of course. I want every woman to be able to protect herself when necessary."

"I'll make sure there's no one in the halls when you join his lordship in the ballroom." Lily scooped up the dress and left the room, a satisfied smile on her face.

Pearl finished her meal and got out of bed. Walking big circles in the room, waving her arms around, trying to make her body settle, she felt like an idiot. Sparring was never something she'd worried about in the past. But honestly, she knew it had nothing to do with sparring and everything to do with James. He'd kissed her: soft and searching, the second one like falling into a dream. And it was as gushingly wonderful as Mathilda Perry had ever gushed.

The boxing costume might be too much. Perhaps she should costume herself as Bess did—a regular dress, pulled down to the waist and the sleeves tied round to keep it stable. Pearl was small enough that she didn't require any banding about her breasts, the way Bess did. She pulled out a clean day dress, the oldest one she had in the wardrobe, and put it on like a lady boxer.

Surveying herself in the mirror, she liked what she saw. Her shoulders were nicely curved, her biceps small, but the line of her arms was still elegant. Not like a stage dancer, but an athlete. Her linen shift was new and well-made. It was thicker than the ones she'd owned before John made his money, and not near as see-through as what she'd seen in the actual fights. Pearl chewed her lip. Was this what James wanted as his wife? Certainly not. She was coming to realize he didn't care what he had for a wife since he did not intend to pay attention to her.

It was a coup, really, to be seen by him at all. And if she wanted him to pay attention to her, then she should go down and meet him for a sparring match. Where she would win yet another day with him at Lady Teeton's retreat. If she kept winning each round, she could very well win an entire week with her new friends. Her heart swelled. Some people actually enjoyed her company.

She liked people, and it was hard not to be around them the way she had been at John and Lydia's house. Not only had the entire staff been comfortable with her, but Lydia and the baby were constant companions.

No one knew how quiet this mausoleum really was.

Her heart turned over as she left her room, feeling as if she might as well be completely naked, not wearing her stays. Lily had promised the servants would clear out so she didn't have to worry about spotting a footman on her way to the ballroom. Still. How unnerving.

Before she graced the doorway, she heard the scratch of the rope hitting the floor in quick succession. She peered around the doorway, feeling as if her linen shift were see-through.

Sweat had sprayed off of James in a circle on the floor. His bare chest glistened, and his eyes were cast up to the corner of the ballroom, lost and faraway. Many of the athletes she'd known possessed a peachy complexion, like her own, which meant that when they exercised, they became as red as a beet. But James wasn't bothered by that sort of influence. His cheeks sported a blotch of pink, but it didn't take over his entire face. He was actually rather handsome like this, his green eyes brilliant and focused in contrast to the heat of his face.

If only he would turn that focus on her again. The kiss had felt magical, and she wanted it again.

She took a bold step into the ballroom, letting her scuffed, hard-soled slippers thud against the parquet. His eyes snapped over to her figure, and he slowed his pace until he stopped.

"You came," he said, barely out of breath.

"Of course I came. It's a matter of honor."

"After last night, I wasn't sure if you would want to be in the same room with me." He turned and stowed the rope on the shelves behind him. His shame was palpable and confused her.

"I'm sure I don't know what you mean," Pearl

said. And she didn't. Why would she not want to be in the same room with him? She wanted it more than anything.

He gave a curt nod and turned to her. "Quite."

Did he think she meant to forget all about the kiss? Because that wasn't humanly possible. She could live to one hundred and not forget.

He gestured to the ring behind her. "Shall we?"

As if this were a dance. She headed over and climbed into the ring, with him following close behind. He glanced at her, and she couldn't help but notice that he took time to drag his eyes across her chest. Was her shift see-through in this light? She tamped down her embarrassment. He'd already seen everything in the bath. If he'd liked it, he would have reached for her then. He hadn't, so what did it matter? This was her. And she was his viscountess. They were bound to one another, whether he liked it or not.

He swung his arms freely in the ring, and she did the same. Shifting from foot to foot, she rotated her ankles and flexed her toes. They eyed each other.

"Same terms?" she asked.

He grunted in his response, looking at the floor.

"I'm not sure grunting is legally binding for these transactions, but by all means, if that's how you'd like to do it. Terms accepted. I win a round, we spend another day at the Teetons' country house. If you win, then I must obey you for a full day."

His eyes rose to meet hers, and suddenly there was a mix of emotion she couldn't read.

"Would you not hate me?" he asked, his voice hoarse.

"For what? For winning? I assure you, while I'm not fond of losing, I am very sportsmanlike."

"No, I mean, hate me for ordering you about."

"If it's the bargain we struck, why would I hate you for it?" Pearl frowned.

He rubbed his hands through his hair. Pearl recognized his tell.

"What if I asked you to do something you didn't want to do?"

"Like eat the asparagus and egg dish?" She joked, hoping to lighten the mood.

He gave a whisper of a chuckle. "I would never forgive myself if I hurt you. And I'm afraid you wouldn't tell me that I was doing so."

Her mind whirred like a clock about to strike. "You are worried that should you win a round—improbable, but possible—and you order me about for a day, that you may order me to do something I don't wish to do? In that happenstance, I assure you I would speak up about not wanting to do whatever action."

James bobbed his head. "But what if you didn't? Felt as if you couldn't?"

Pearl frowned, unsure of what to say. "You don't frighten me, my lord."

He put his hands on his hips and paced, his head down. "I'm not a good man, Pearl. This is a terrible bargain for you."

"I can make my own decisions."

"Not if you don't have all the facts, you can't." His head snapped up, his eyes boring into her. "Do you know what I think about? Do have any idea how I spent my night?"

She shrank back a step. Her heart skipped faster.

"While you slept soundly in your bed, safe and secure, I fantasized about you. About your lips, your hair."

That sounded perfectly fine to her, and why did he assume she'd slept at all? She hadn't. Every hour that crept by, she watched the stars move dimly in the heavens. She heard every church bell chime, every scuffle of the maidservants in the wee hours. He stalked closer, so she backed away in response.

"Does that not scare you?" he demanded.

"No," she said. "Why would it? You think you're the first man to think of me like that?" It stopped him dead in his tracks. The arrogant bastard.

"What?"

"Do you think I'm so ugly that I haven't had men telling me where they want to put a hand or a tongue or other bits since I was young? Where do you think I've been?"

"Who? Who would say such things to you?" A storm clouded over his face.

"Men on street corners, awful old priests, the dairyman once." She thought about it. "In fact, it was rarer that a man didn't say those things to me. Haven't you any idea what it's like to be a woman?"

James stared at her, clearly stupefied. "Why would they say such things to you?"

She shrugged. "They're men. That's what they do. They say ugly things to try to scare girls. Or entice them, if they think they can. They think it's funny. Honestly, every woman I know ignores it."

"But a man shouldn't say those things to a woman's face. It's ugly. It's demeaning."

Pearl laughed. "And who is going to make them stop? Other men? The more men there are, the worse it is. Other men join in on the comments and the laughter. Honestly, one man saying that bit to me, I can ignore. It's when there's a whole lot of them that they get out of control."

James rubbed his hands across his face and up into his hair.

"I know your lot likes to pretend women are delicate and precious. That's nice. Kind of. It's a pretty dream if it all works out in the end. But women are tougher than nails, James. We've been through it all, seen it all, watched our mothers and our sisters go through it. There's nothing you can throw at me that I haven't seen or heard before."

"The idea of that sickens me." James paced to the other side of the ring.

She knew it. The gutter experience was too much. This was really why the rich and the poor couldn't mingle with one another. It wasn't that the poor were too crass and vulgar for rich toffs, it was that the roughness of their lives embarrassed the protected and privileged. "Hurts, don't it?"

"What hurts?"

"To learn a new way of the world. There's a whole set of people and buildings and such that you never even knew existed. You lived in ignorance. And then, it makes you feel small to see you weren't never included." Pearl heard her accent slipping.

"That's not it at all." He turned to face her. "Why was no one protecting you from this? From those vulgar men, those awful wagtongues?"

Pearl stifled a laugh. "*I* was protecting me. I wasn't hurt. Did I want to hear those things? Of course not. Would I rather they hadn't said it? Yes, obviously. But until men hold themselves to a higher standard, what am I supposed to do? Hide?"

"Yes!" He said. "Hide from men like that! Why else do the aristocracy hold their daughters so close? We can afford to!"

Pearl retucked the sleeves of her dress. She couldn't believe the words were actually coming out of his mouth. She did her best to keep the gutter sass from her posture, but oh, she had an urge to cant her hip and tell him stories that would give him chills. "So your solution to men behaving badly is 'hide and don't be poor?'" Blood thrummed faster through her body.

"What else can you do?" he asked. "You certainly can't protect yourself."

That was it. She stalked up to him, rabbit-punched him in the face, and danced backwards.

He yelped and his hand flew to his nose. "What was that?"

"You were saying something that I found rude. I made you stop. I think I proved my point about protecting myself." Pearl fussed with her sleeves. Maybe they would get a sparring match out of the afternoon.

"I wasn't expecting it." He brushed beneath his nose.

"Don't worry, you aren't bleeding. I barely touched you."

"I wasn't ready."

Pearl put her hands on her hips. "Imagine yourself as a young girl walking down an alleyway, trying to fetch a midwife in the middle of the night for your mother. Or going to a pub to retrieve a drunken father. Or a matchgirl selling on the street corner. Think of all the ways women are exposed in the world. We get by."

He lunged forward, swinging at her. She ducked under the wide blow. "Oh, come on. That wasn't even close." Grunting, he came after her again, and she danced away.

"But if I ever got my hands on you, then you'd be sorry. You wouldn't be able to handle a punch."

"And that's why Bess always taught running away. Women don't stay and fight, we fight and then we run."

James sped up, attempting to corner her faster and faster. He gained on her, anticipating her ducking and dodging. To keep him off-kilter, she stopped and blocked a few blows with her arms.

The force of his punches reverberated in her bones. She'd have significant bruising, but her blood was up and she barely felt the pain. So she did what he wouldn't expect. She kicked him hard in the side. He grunted at the impact, dropping his arms.

She followed with a quick succession of blows to the face—unwise, given her bare knuckles. But when he raised his arms to protect his face, she stuck her foot right in his gut, pushing off to retreat again.

He grunted, wheezing, but remained standing. "Nice shot."

Pearl nodded but didn't bother answering. She needed to concentrate on watching his limbs. Where was he going, what foot was he leading with, where was he looking?

Instead, he surprised her by backing up. "I'll give you this round."

Maybe she'd kicked harder than she'd meant to. But that was two days at the Teeton country house! Why did it not feel like a victory? "I'm sorry."

He waved his hand, sitting down on the floor in the corner, cradling his stomach. "I should know better. You've proved your point."

Pearl inched closer. "Do you need some water?"

He nodded, so she got out of the ring and retrieved the water ewer from the shelf by the door. She climbed back into the ring and poured him a glass, then one for herself as well. She sat next to him.

"You're better than I gave you credit for," James said. "Smarter than I gave you credit for, too."

Warmth bloomed in her chest, no doubt flushing her skin a hideous shade of pink. When did he notice? "Thank you."

James stared at his cup, turning it in a circle. "I don't want to be a bad man."

"And you aren't," she insisted.

James cocked his head to the side as if he were thinking. "I think you just showed me that I am. I underestimated you. I am blind to the plight of those who have a life different than my own. I'm spoiled, really, by the very thing I hate."

"I'm afraid from where I sit, I can't imagine hating money and a title. It's like a fairy tale for someone like me."

James stretched his legs and leaned against the

post on the corner of the ring. "I hated how my father used the money and the title to shield himself and his cronies from the law. He used the privilege of his status and handsomeness to entice women and then hurt them. On purpose. And when they threatened to complain, or go to the authorities, he and his friends laughed. In the end, I had to use most of the available funds I inherited to pay off his debts."

Pearl listened, thinking back to Mrs. Coldcroft. James would definitely not understand the decisions she'd made. But she was savvy, good with money, and knew how to keep her children safe. Isn't that what a good person did? "So you see all power as tainted, then?"

"It is. Inherently so."

Lady Teeton's tract had pushed Pearl to think hard over the past few weeks. Given how James saw the world, she could see why the Teetons wanted his support. They wanted to remake the social structures, in some sense, by eliminating the death penalty for crimes brought about by poverty. The poverty she had seen. The desperation she'd once felt. James clearly had an urge to protect those he cared for, and everything she'd been reading from Lady Teeton seemed to bring her here, to this very conversation.

But she knew James would never listen if the Teeton name crossed her lips. And while she wasn't sure she had any ideas to contribute to Lady Teeton's political foray, maybe James did without knowing it. She said, "If all power is tainted, how else can the world work? There's always some kind of hierarchy. A parent to a child, a vicar to his parishioners. A monarch to his people."

James shrugged. "That's not my concern. I can't tell others how to be, but I cannot participate."

Pearl finished her water, still unsettled by his unwillingness to engage. "But if you don't participate, then all the ones who are abusing their power get to abuse it with impunity. There's no one standing there saying 'that's bad.'"

"Not my problem."

She put her cup down next to his foot and turned to him. "Think of it this way. When I was young and fetching the morning water for the family—"

"What family? I thought John was at boarding school and your parents had died."

"Yes, that's true. But it wasn't as if they would have let me tag along with John at school. I had to go somewhere, so I was passed around the families my mother had known. Mostly Irish ones, it just depended on where I could go. Who had room."

James frowned. "You must have gone to some kind of school. You can read and write, I've seen it."

"James. I have a point. Please let me make it."

"My apologies." He downed his cup.

"When I was young, fetching the water, and a man on the street said these awful things—the very things you abhor—I kept my head down and allowed him to yell his abuse."

James nodded, clearly unsure where the conversation was heading.

"But think. If you had been there to protect me, and you said, 'Oy! You cunts! Shut the fuck up!' Then that man would have. He would have listened because you shamed him into realizing his own poor behavior."

James blinked rapidly. "I don't know how to respect you, agree with you, all while I am surprisingly attracted to you yelling obscenities."

"A regular sunshine hellhound." Pearl smiled. "I know more vulgarities if you'd like to hear. The Irish are very creative people." His hand strayed close to hers, but stopped. She welcomed his touch, but she didn't want to derail what felt like a very important conversation. "What I'm saying is that while power is absolutely a corrupting influence, it is a slap in the face to have someone as dedicated as you, who knows how power can be abused, choose to abdicate that influence."

James recoiled. "That's a bit harsh, isn't it?"

Pearl shook her head, getting to her feet. "I don't think it is. I don't have a voice because I'm a woman. My brother doesn't have a voice because even though he's rich, he doesn't own any land."

"But he could if he wanted to. He's got the blunt for it."

Frustration flared in her breast. He was so damned stubborn. "Is that the point, do you think, James? Get up." Pearl danced away, pushing her body back to action. The only way to make her point was to make him move.

He grumbled and got to his feet. "I suppose it's been more than thirty seconds."

"To the scratch, then. It's about time we start this fair."

"Fair? I don't believe you fight fair."

"And why do you think that is, my lord?" Pearl met him at the ring's mid-point, where the scratch would have been if it were an organized set-to. She edged closer, so they stood nose-to-nose, or nearly, given their height difference. He could easily rest his chin on her head.

"Because it doesn't matter to you?"

"Because if I fought by your rules, I would never win. The rules were made for you, not for me. I don't get a vote. I don't get paid by going to work at a bank or shops. The factories I am allowed to work in pay the least." She cocked her head to the side and backed up, so her toe was exactly on the line. She raised her fists. "Here, in the ring, would you have me beaten to a bloody pulp, or would you let me use my wits to bend the rules?"

"What does this have to do with me?" James

asked, echoing her movements by putting his toe on the line and raising his fists.

"You would be the man who would help people like me—like Os Worley, like Bess Abbott, like Jack Townsend, like my brother—change the rules of this world to make happiness achievable. Not everyone gets family wealth. Not everyone gets a title. But you did."

James narrowed his eyes and took a wide, half-hearted swipe. She grabbed his fist with both hands and swirled into him as if they were dancing, not sparring. He seemed surprised as she looked up at him, snuggled into his armpit.

"What if you could change the rules? What would you do?" Still grasping his fist, she twirled out of his embrace. Letting go, she danced behind him, making him turn around, giving her time to think up her next move.

"But that's not my concern. How other people live, why would you assign that responsibility to me?" James sidestepped one of her brazen jabs.

"Who else will do it? Who else doesn't like the structure as it stands? Before long, there will be more clamoring to change the world. Mark my words, all men will want the right to decide their lives. And it won't be long until women tire of being perceived as little more than a family pet."

James scoffed and tried a combination of a jab and an uppercut. She blocked the first and stepped away from the second. "To do nothing while being part of the chosen few makes you complicit. If you love any of us, you would want to make our lives better."

He stared at her, shaking his head. "It sounds like you think I have no heart."

"Actions speak louder than words," she said, throwing jabs and crosses that he blocked with ease.

"If you think that of me, how would you ever trust

me?" He retreated a few steps, still blocking as she continued her onslaught.

Trust. What a word. It meant so much and sometimes so little. But she was bound to him in so many ways, and she found that she did trust him. His inner torment was obvious, and his blatant desire to do right, despite his inability to trust himself, spoke volumes. If he couldn't trust himself, perhaps it was time to show him that she did.

And what else could she let him have, except herself?

Heart pounding, she jumped, wrapping her legs around his waist, her arms around his biceps, slick with sweat. She pulled back as hard as she could and they fell together. She lifted her head up and out of the way, dreading contact with the floor.

He caught her. His arms braced her on either side of her head. She relaxed into it, easing onto the ground—and into her decision—fully. He stared at her with shock in his green eyes.

"I trust you," she whispered. "My twenty-four hours is yours."

☙❧

NOSE TO NOSE WITH PEARL, staring into her great blue eyes, James's heart stuttered like a great clogged steamer ship. How he'd ended up like this, caging her in, protecting her with his body, he wasn't entirely sure. But he knew she had engineered it.

The worries he'd had about her youth, her delicacy, her physical fragility evaporated. *I trust you* echoed in his mind. Her trust was everything, and her words seemed to mean so much more. "Does my twenty-four-hour period begin now?"

She bit her lip and slid her hands further up his arms, pulling him towards her. "If you like."

If any other woman had done this, he would have

read her body as an invitation. But he desperately
didn't want to ruin whatever was burgeoning between
them. Still, as he looked into her eyes, he felt drawn
into a world where he could be a hero—where she
saw that potential in him. He drew back. "You
chastised me."

"You needed it." There was no malice in her tone,
only a mere statement of fact.

"I've been selfish with my life," he said, thinking
through how he protected only those he loved most:
his mother, Margaret, Lydia, Agnes. Not the women
of the world who were terrorized by his father—or
even broader than that. He'd not tried to use his
position to help any of the powerless.

"But your life isn't over." They locked eyes, and
there was so much more said between them as she
pulled him down to her, twining her ankles around his
midsection. There wasn't enough fabric between
their bodies to shield her from him. "It's only just
now begun."

He was caught by her, in more ways than one. She
was more than he'd given her credit for being. He
searched her expression, wanting more than he dared.
But even with this fragile arrangement, he didn't want
to lose whatever faith she had in him. He lowered his
head slowly, giving her time to escape him, should she
desire. But she didn't move—rather, pressed up into
him. He kissed her. Gently at first, testing. But she
kissed him back without pretension, without caution.
For the first time in so very long, he let go, deepening
their kiss, going to his elbows, pressing the entire
length of his body against hers.

With his hands free, he tugged at her hair. She
smiled against his mouth. He opened his eyes to
watch her, and he couldn't help but smile back.
Grinning like a fool, he felt her shift underneath him,
indicating a direction, so they rolled over as smoothly
as if they'd made love a thousand times.

"I want your hair unbound," he said.

"As you wish," she said, pulling the pins from her hair.

If the kiss hadn't been enough to make him rise to the occasion, her words certainly were. Her hair fell around her shoulders, beautifully honey red. He twined strands around his fingers, fascinated with the silky color against his skin.

"For a long time, I hated my hair," she said, a bemused expression on her face as she watched him play with her tresses.

No doubt she could feel his cockstand pushed against her bum. Would she know what it was? How worldly was she? "It's beautiful. The color of butterflies."

She looked at him curiously. "No one has ever compared my hair to butterflies before."

"I'm extremely sophisticated," he said, suddenly not wanting to talk about her hair anymore. He pulled at her arms, causing her to fold herself over him. Her hair draped around them, a cage just for them. Their own world. "I don't want to push you."

"You can't," she said.

There was her youth—only the young could be so desperately self-assured. "Don't underestimate me."

"Likewise."

She pressed herself against him, her hand skating down his bare chest. She kissed him hard, tangling her tongue with his. Her hand went lower and lower, until finally, it brushed exactly where he'd dreamt of it.

His cock jumped of its own accord. He wrapped his arms around her, tightening his grip and letting his tongue explore her mouth. Her hand dragged up his thigh, drawing a maddening hot ribbon on his flesh until reaching his cock, then moving to the other side and dragging again. Her delicacy was exquisite torment.

He pulled back from their kiss, not wanting to open his eyes, not wanting to break the spell, but dear God, there were limits. "What are you doing?" he growled.

"Hmm?" She asked, as if she were thoroughly distracted by a favorite book and not torturing him blind.

"I can't—" Her hand went straight to his cock, cupping his bollocks, and all that came out was a groan.

"Say what you want, my lord. I'm happy to do whatever you wish for, but you must tell me first, otherwise I'm only guessing."

"I can't think." How long had it been since he'd last had a woman? Since Rose, and she had never been particularly active in their lovemaking. To be with a woman who was so intent on exploring his body made him unable to function.

"Pearl," he begged. Did she understand what she was doing?

She leaned forward, kissing him in light, almost lapping strokes. Her hair tickled his shoulders. It didn't help matters. He gripped her hips and pushed her down backwards, positioning her so his cock centered right at her entrance. Her dress was tucked between her legs, the barrier between them.

He ground her into his cock. "That," he said through gritted teeth, "is what will await you if you keep up with this."

She grinned and threw her shoulders back, which only pushed out her pert breasts. "Me? I think I've been quite clear about what I want." She licked her lips.

He damn near came in his trousers. "You haven't said a word."

She looked down at him, her hair once again cascading, distracting him from the muted ecstasy of her heat pressing against him through layers of fabric.

"If you'll remember correctly, I wrapped my legs around you and dragged you to the ground. If that is subtlety—"

He ground her down harder and she made a mewing sound, just as she had when she'd licked the cream off her spoon at dinner. He cursed the very cotton farmers for making clothing. "Enough."

She nodded, her eyes unfocused until she closed them. He pulled her down to him and kissed her again. After he felt as if he'd kissed her senseless, he rolled them over again. She stared up at him with a dazed look, her mouth red and swollen from the scruff of his day-long beard. He felt the pulls of obligation. He wanted desperately to fuck her until she couldn't speak, but to make sure she wasn't hurt, to make sure she could enjoy herself, he needed to know if she knew how things worked.

"Are you a virgin?" he asked, trying very hard to sound concerned and gentle—not at all as impatient as he felt.

She stiffened and frowned. He'd hoped she wouldn't take offense, but there they were. "Why?"

"Because I don't want to hurt you."

"I told you that I want this."

He rolled off of her and pulled her upright, into his lap. He took care to drop featherlight kisses along her jaw as he spoke. "I don't care if you are or aren't. It doesn't matter to me if you have the experience of a courtesan or a nun. But I want to know how to treat you."

She kissed him hard then, as if proving her passion. "Treat me as you would any other woman."

He pulled back and looked her in the eye. "You aren't any other woman. You're my wife." As soon as the words were out of his mouth, his heart thumped hard, as if, for the first time in decades, the organ's will was recognized.

Pearl blinked in shock.

He swallowed past a lump in his throat. His cock still ached for her, but he told it to wait its turn. There were other bits needing attention first. "We're a team," he continued. "And if we do this. If you allow me to—" He gritted his teeth. God, if he said what he wanted, he would end up fucking her right then and there, with no more preamble than this. And Pearl deserved more than that.

"If I let you fuck me," Pearl continued, clearly recognizing his difficulty, "then we're crossing a line that cannot be uncrossed."

James nodded. "Precisely. I want to be careful with you."

She nodded. "Then I don't mind telling you that I am a virgin. As pure as any blue-blooded girl."

"I don't care about any other girl." He ran his hands up and down her arms, his hands brushing by her breasts. So close. "Nor do I care that you are a virgin. But I want—I want—"

She smiled coyly and leaned forward, whispering in his ear. "I've never had a cock inside me. But I've seen it all. I know what one looks like. I know what you do with it. I know how to make myself come if I see it."

James couldn't breathe. Had she thought of him while she made herself come? "Fucking hell." He tore at her then, yanking up her dress until her arse was bare against him, pulling her chemise off her shoulders, desperate to get to her naked body. Enough with the teasing. He let his mouth drag down her strong, freckled shoulder, one hand wrenching the chemise until finally he was able to rip it open. He let the other hand roam over her arse, shapely and warm. He pulled at her flank and she moaned as he captured her nipple in his mouth. He bucked against her, desperate now to let his cock take root. He needed to be inside her.

"Get your fucking trousers off," she said, running her hands through his hair.

He practically threw her off him, and she snickered at his impatience. He fumbled with the buttons on his fall, finally, as she scrambled forward on her knees, trying to assist, a sight he would be absolutely fucking delighted to see again. He found the button on the inside of the waistband.

"Everything off," he commanded, whipping his trousers off one leg at a time. She stood and pushed the dress down. As soon as she stepped out of it, he pulled her ripped chemise off over her head. Gathering her greedily in his hands, he ran his fingers all over her. She was his. All his. He pressed against her naked flesh. He knew this wasn't perfect, knew she deserved to have a bed, but they were here.

He kissed her mouth and then worked his way down, spending a fair amount of time on each breast, but not overly much, in his opinion. He would be happy to revisit both later. Dragging down, he had to make certain she was ready. His hand went to her small curls of hair, a tuft of that delightful honey color. He slipped his hand between her legs as she stood there, panting, his mouth not far behind. She was already wet. Sopping, if he could be so proud to boast. He looked up at her with admiration. She was a wonder.

He bestowed a kiss on the top of her mound and then positioned himself on his knees between her legs, letting his tongue dart between her folds.

"Oh, fuck me," she sighed.

He draped her leg over his shoulder, cupping her arse so she wouldn't lose her balance. She gripped his other shoulder, talon-like. He didn't mind at all. He took another lap with his tongue and she shuddered. Again, and she arched her foot, rising away from him, whining.

"Perhaps too much right now?" he suggested, and

she nodded. He removed her leg from his shoulder and laid her down. He stayed his own needs and lay on his side next to her, his hand drawing lazy circles around the hard nub between her legs. Almost immediately, she shuddered and tightened, curiously silent. She'd clearly found her release. Her responsiveness was like nothing he'd ever seen— nothing he'd ever heard of in a woman, outside of erotic fiction, but he'd never put much faith in its nearness to reality. "Holy fuck, Pearl. You just came, didn't you?"

"What?" Her eyes snapped open, fear obvious on her face.

He kissed her cheeks and her forehead, willing himself to slow down, despite the urging of his cock. "I've just never known a woman who could come so quickly. It's incredible."

Her face and chest flushed, and it made him curious. She'd turned her face away.

"Are you ashamed of this?" He prodded, not that he wanted to have a conversation right now, but it did seem like an obstacle for further explorations. He reminded himself that it was better to take his time. He drew his finger down her arm; just touching her was sublime.

"I'm not supposed to," Pearl said, her voice near to trembling.

"You're not supposed to what?" James asked. "Enjoy yourself? That's horseshit."

Pearl faced him, giving him a patronizing look. Governess material, right here. She would scare the deuces out of children. "I know women aren't supposed to be so brazen. Wanton. But I can't help it."

"Women are human, aren't they? The beauty of us all is that we are each different. I am frankly awestruck with admiration at your ability to be so in your body."

She gave him another look that was not entirely complimentary. "You say that today because you are overcome with lust. Some day you will decide that it is improper, unseemly—"

He held his hand up, smelling of her, making him very, very distracted. "A lover who believes his partner should merely tolerate his presence is a terrible lover. You make it easy for me to believe that I'm extremely above average."

She burst out laughing. It was disconcerting to hear a woman laugh while they were both naked, but his cockstand was still maintaining hope. "It's a gift?" she said with a smile.

"More like a miracle." Her beauty was transcendent: her honeyed hair spread out beneath her like the sun, the glow in her cheeks, the flushed burn of her lips. She was like an immodest Venus. "Here's a challenge. Can you do it twice in a row?"

She laughed again. "Try me."

Desire coursed through him like he'd never felt. "Oh, I will," he said, spreading her legs wide, and what a sight that was. He would go slow, he would be patient. This was not a time to be a rutting animal. He held himself above her, his cock begging to find her slickness. Her quim was so warm and so wet and so inviting, it was difficult to remain in control. He pushed in, as slowly as he could, but he sank deeper, and the friction was unbearably good. His eyes flew open, trying to remember to make this pleasurable for her.

Her blue eyes were locked on his, and it was as if more than just his body had sunk into her.

"More," she whispered, reaching up, as if to gather him in whole.

He leaned over her, propping himself up on his elbows, lowering his chest to hers, pushing in deeper until there was nowhere else to go. He pulled out and thrust in again slowly. She threw her head back with a moan. He was transfixed by the curve of her jaw, the shape of her lip, the arch of her neck. This was paradise, this was perfection, this was home.

He felt her pressure building again. He tried to curb himself as he gave measured thrusts, but couldn't. He continued, mesmerized by her responsiveness, measuring his speed to hers until her body gripped around him and he could no longer hold it in. They came together, the pleasure blinding. He crushed his mouth to hers, wanting to capture every ounce of her essence, let nothing of her sweetness escape. He needed her like life itself. He shuddered as her quim pulsed around his cock one last time.

His heart pounded, and though he was exhausted and spent and wanted to collapse, he held himself above her, not wanting to crush her. He felt different. Mesmerized, he watched her as she panted, lifting her hands from where she'd gripped his shoulders, wiping the sweat from her face. He wondered if it had been as blisteringly good for her. There had never been a moment like this for him. Never. Not with Rose, not with anyone. This was why they called it making love.

He felt as if his soul had passed into her, that he no longer held all of himself alone. How was he supposed to live in just a single body, with a single heartbeat, when they had achieved this together?

She was so extraordinary. Her insight, her body, her humor. This was a higher level of union, a true act of love. But then, that implied he loved her. Which, was impossible. He didn't know her well enough to say that he did. Not to mention that love was...out of the question. And, quite simply, out of character for him. No, he was dreadfully mistaken. Something about their conversation before this act had made him out of sorts.

But he couldn't deny the attraction. The companionship. The laughter. Confused, he pulled out, only then realizing what he'd done: he'd spent inside her. He had crossed a line with her, yes, but he hadn't intended to cross this line with himself.

He'd vowed to never father children. He couldn't stand the idea of perpetuating the family he'd known. Cold dread slithered through him now that his lust had cooled. He'd forgotten himself, been careless. And now Pearl could be with child. Everything he'd stood for, everything he'd believed, had evaporated in a moment of juddering heat. He was paralyzed with self-loathing. No matter what he did, his father laughed at him from the grave.

He felt sick.

❦

PEARL FELT jittery down to her bones. That was why Mrs. Coldcroft had warned against losing her maidenhead to just anyone. It was utterly delightful. There had been a moment when she felt like she and James had one body, one place, as if there was no delineation between them. Who was inside of whom at that moment? She couldn't possibly tell. She'd lost herself inside those green eyes, lost track of time, everything outside the pleasure between them.

She rolled onto her side, feeling sweaty, messy, and completely wonderful. Exploring her own body was nice, but to have someone else's ministrations was beyond comprehension. "I suppose we're truly married now." She was his *wife*. They could do this every *day*.

James turned his head to the side and gazed at her. Those green eyes were more than beauty—they held depth and soul. He looked bewildered and then pained. She watched as his expression closed, like a firefly blinking out of sight.

"No man can put asunder, so they say," James said drily, getting to his feet.

He stalked out of the ring, completely naked, leaving her lying there, completely a mess.

Shame flooded her senses. What had she done? Aristocratic women weren't supposed to like it. She knew that. But James had said she was a miracle. Of course, that was before he'd gotten what he'd wanted. Pearl closed her eyes to hold back the tears that threatened to spill forth. It was as Gabriel had said— being able to find pleasure so easily was a sign of a whore. And as everyone knew, no man wanted to be married to a whore.

CHAPTER 15

I f a man could have a hangover from thinking too hard, James had one. Never, in all his most debauched moments, had he ever felt as much of a rogue as he felt now. He'd made promises to respect her, cherish her, even, and what had he done? Proven that he couldn't control his urges, exactly like his father.

The water was lukewarm, and smelled of nothing because James had ordered the bath before Pearl had left the ballroom. No oranges, no roses, just water. And shame.

And worse, he'd poisoned her with his seed. It was his honor, his sacrifice, to not bring a child into this world, to not push his blood into some unsuspecting soul. And now? James squeezed his eyes tight, as if he could will himself out of the mire of his mind. It had only been the once. And it often took more than that for a babe to take root.

But when he broke from flogging himself on that point, his mind countered with the memories of her face. How she urged him on, how she asked him to continue. Indeed, how she had physically dragged him to the ground. Lord, she was incredible. The joy of her inhabiting herself so fully that she climaxed so easily—it made him feel more than a king. It made him feel humbled to be the one bringing her to it. She was right: it was a gift. She was a gift, and he'd only now realized it.

Rose's admonishment echoed in his ears: an orgasm wasn't love. Physical acts couldn't replace the efforts a suitor must make. Ones that a husband should make.

He couldn't promise anything. What had he been thinking, allowing himself to bind her to him physically? If she truly were with child, he would be repeating that horrific cycle of Andreponts. Another generation of monsters out to terrorize London.

He got out of the bath. The one thing in life he couldn't afford was being naked, thinking of Pearl and the acts they'd committed, while she puttered around the room next door, able to hear him. Dressing quickly, he retreated to his study.

Attempting Beethoven at a time like this was foolhardy. Bach, even more so. Mozart? The scales might soothe his hands, but the delicate flitting seemed a mockery of what he felt. There was no way he could play while his stomach and mind churned. He poured himself a dram of whisky and stared at the open curtains. He couldn't be bothered to even take a drink.

Stone-cold sober, his mind turned the arguments over and over, tumbling in the empty barrel of his head. If he was in his study, he wouldn't be tempted to enter her bedroom. He wouldn't be tempted to talk—knowing full well that talking to a woman in her bedroom could only lead back to what they needed to discuss.

And what kind of degenerate husband bedded his wife on the floor of a ballroom? John would murder him with bare hands if he found out what James had done. At the end of a sparring match? It was terrible. Morally corrupt. But it had been...incredible. Better than any other of his amorous experiences.

Their bodies had simply worked together. They fit like a lock and key. Except he was no longer sure he felt like the key—rather, the other way around. He'd always felt the act itself was a purely male event. He was the active participant and the woman received his efforts. But now it felt strangely reversed. Despite their anatomies, he felt as if Pearl had somehow pierced him. As if their transgression had transcended body parts and become some other near-holy act.

Afternoon faded into twilight, and still, James could only churn. He knew he was only punishing himself, that no good came from his brooding. At least when he was heartbroken from Rose, he'd played, he'd gotten drunk, he'd ranted to her memory. But this—this was far worse.

The thought stopped him. When had he resolved his heartbreak? He didn't know the exact moment. Pearl had distracted him with her presence, and then when he next realized, his fixation on Rose had evaporated. Perhaps he hadn't loved Rose, as he'd believed. Because he'd never felt for her what he felt for Pearl. And if he'd thought he was in love before, his feelings now were somehow *more*—he was frozen, like an insect in amber. Trapped in his own downfall.

He'd believed that passion was his escape. His father hadn't had passion, he'd had cruelty. James had found love and good in his own hedonism because he could control it, make sure everyone enjoyed the acts. But here. Now. He had a wife and he'd *debauched* her.

She'd been so beautiful, that gorgeous red hair curtaining them, creating a world of two. Her face when she'd found her joy, the cry from her swollen lips, her muscles going rigid—no. No. His body strained to react at the memory, but he tamped it down. How was he going to face her without thinking of those moments? Without trying to recreate them and debauching her all over again? When he could atone enough?

For if what he feared was true—that he really did love his wife—how could he face her again?

⊗⌘⊗

SITTING ALONE in the dining room, Pearl decided pretending as if the day had never happened was absurd. They were married. This wasn't some one-time tumble.

The soup arrived, a nice ginger broth again. But James wasn't even here. He hadn't joined her in the drawing room, and the footman had cleared his place setting. What a coward. If one of them was going to be embarrassed over what had occurred, it should be her. The noises she made. Her assertiveness in the beginning. Dear Lord, her enthusiasm. She should be mortified. If Mrs. Tyler had been bold enough to discuss what happened between a man and a woman, she would have definitely counseled meekness.

But Mrs. Tyler be damned. Pearl wasn't meek, and especially not about *that*. There wasn't anything wrong with enjoying one's own body. Or how much she and James liked one another outside of their bodies. But now, he behaved as if the intimacy of their bodies had interfered with the intimacy of their friendship.

She refused to be ashamed. And she refused to let him be ashamed of what they'd done. Enough.

Throwing herself back from the table, she pulled her gloves back on. Dinner could wait. She was going to fetch her husband.

She stomped through the house, not trying to be dainty, not trying to be small and quiet. She was done with that.

Out of simple courtesy, she knocked on his study

door. Then, out of anger, she flung the door open without waiting for his permission.

He stood in front of the drink cart, a full dram of golden liquor in a glass, untouched. His clothes were impeccable, of course, so he'd dressed with his valet after his bath. But he wore all black, as if he were in mourning.

It infuriated her. How dare he pass judgment.

He turned towards her and she could see the torment in his green eyes. And it only fueled her anger.

"Enough," she said, trying her best not to ball her hands into fists.

His dark eyebrow quirked at her. "Enough?"

"*I've* had enough," she amended.

"Of what, exactly?" He crossed his arms, causing his coat to shift and tighten.

She refused to be distracted by looking at his arms. And his hands. And thinking of all the things those hands and arms had done this afternoon. "Enough of this charade."

A weary smile graced his face. "My lady, all of this is a charade."

"It isn't. *We* are not a charade." She stepped closer. Those kisses had not been false. His body next to hers, his enjoyment of her and her enjoyment of him, that was real and true.

His head cocked to the side. "Why do you think I proposed to you? Did you think I had been pining after you?"

His mockery was meant to push her away, but she refused to allow it. "You don't fool me, my lord. James. I know you. And I know today meant something to you."

"Ah, today." He moved so well, but in the wrong direction. He sauntered in a lazy circle, putting the drink cart between them. "I hate to tell you, but fucking isn't love."

Pearl cursed. And not a dainty curse that Mrs. Tyler might utter. No, it was one she'd learned from the docks, and her accent dropped away. "You fucking cunt."

He smiled. "Such language, Lady Andrepont."

"You fucking knew wot I were 'fore you wed me, ya daft, jingle-brained pig. My sympathies, really." This was a moment she wished she were tall like Bess, or imposing like Lydia. She canted her hands on her hips.

James took a beat to look her over. "I had no illusions. I don't feel cheated in the least."

Pearl gathered in her anger, straightening her spine and dropping her hands. There was no reason to lose her temper. Only a reason to win this argument. All she wanted was her friend back. Her dinner companion. "Then why didn't you join me for dinner? What makes today different than all the days before?"

James looked away.

"Take the liquor, if you need it." Pearl motioned to the undisturbed glass.

He looked back at her with a sly smile. "Drinking doesn't bother you."

Her temper frayed. She stepped forward and tossed back half the whisky. It burned going down. She held out the glass to him.

Locking eyes with her, he accepted the glass and finished it in one swallow. He set down the glass. "Pity. That was meant to be savored."

"Feel better?" The cart sat between them. She wanted it gone. If she could just touch him, draw him out.

He looked away instead. It was shame, she realized. And not for her. For him. She knew he wouldn't show his vulnerability until she did the same. Another secret, then. Whatever the cost, she knew it had to be sacrificed. "There was a boy who liked to kiss me once. His name was Gabriel."

James flushed and stiffened in response, which was gratifying.

"I liked to kiss him, too. Mostly because he said lovely things to me before he kissed me. He made me feel things. Things about how wanted I was. How he needed me."

James gave a cynical grunt, but he didn't interrupt.

"Wasn't long until he found that it didn't take much work for me to find my pleasure. When he found that out, he called me a whore." Pearl's fingers knotted in her skirts. She tried to make them stop, but couldn't.

James's face creased into a rictus.

"When you didn't join me at dinner, I thought you believed the same as Gabriel." Pearl's heart pounded and the room felt hot. She clung to the wild hope that she was wrong about James. That he wouldn't share Gabriel's conclusion. It was a risk to say it aloud, but Pearl was done with not saying that which needed to be said. No more living in darkness and ambiguity.

"You are not—" He choked.

"His words haunt me." She wanted to be in James's arms. If only he would embrace her, if only she could get around this ridiculous drink cart sitting between them. "I am nothing more than what I've always been, no matter how you dress me up."

"This isn't about you, Pearl."

"Oh, I believe it is. I was there. It is absolutely about me."

"No, Pearl. It isn't. It's about my wife."

She wanted to look around the room for another woman standing there, but she knew it would only make him angrier and shut down this tiny crack she'd managed to pry open. "I believe I am your wife."

He scrubbed his hands on his face and through

his hair. "Do you know what my father once told me? That a wife is like a piano—pretty to look at and impossible to get rid of."

"And?" It made her want to laugh. His father cut quite the figure.

"What do you mean, *and*? That's a horrific attitude to have towards any person, especially one that is dependent on you."

"I agree. But what does that have to do with me? I take both the idea that I am pretty and persistent to be complimentary." She dropped a sassy curtsy, as if his father were in the room.

James shook his head. "You wouldn't say that if you knew him."

"You want to know what my father said about wives?"

He nodded, his face stricken.

"I've no clue. He left, or maybe died, before I was born. My mum died shortly after I was born. So. I know something about how the dead hang about your shoulders, convincing you they still matter."

He shook his head again, as if she didn't understand dead parents.

"But they only matter if you let them. You've given him so much power. So much more power than he deserved."

"But—" James stopped. They stared at each other. Had he finally run out of excuses?

"He's dead," she insisted. "Say it."

"He's dead." He couldn't look her in the eye.

She softened her voice. "You don't sound convinced."

"You, of all people, should know why. He ruined everything he touched. He destroyed us." James's voice broke. "I can't do that."

"But you aren't the same man," Pearl whispered.

"They call me by the same name. I sleep in his bedroom," James insisted, finally meeting her eyes.

His green eyes glistened. "There's so much you don't know."

"Like about Lady Kinsley?"

James flinched. "Please don't."

"You aren't a bad man."

He shook his head. "I've done things that I cannot forgive."

"Do you think I could forgive them?"

He gave her a look that could not be misinterpreted.

"Asking for someone else's forgiveness is far easier than forgiving yourself." Pearl moved around the drink cart. "I can forgive you for leaving so abruptly this afternoon."

James scoffed. "You really shouldn't."

She slowly pulled off her gloves. "It's a transgression against me. I get to choose. And I choose forgiveness."

He looked at her again, as if he was slowly breaking and crumbling. "Pearl, you can't."

She laid her dinner gloves on the damned drink cart. "I can. And I do. I forgive you, James. And I forgive this Lord Andrepont for being so remote and aloof."

He shook his head. "Don't."

She grasped his hands, and he responded by gripping her in return. As if he were a drowning man, desperate for a way to float. "James. You are your own man. Be the man you admire. Not the one you fear."

"The man I fear is the one that wants to take this moment and ravish you on the couch. The one that wants to make you scream my name so loud that the stableboys hear you. The man I fear wants to lock the doors and bar visitors for weeks so that I may have you to myself."

"I don't think that's the man you fear." She searched his eyes. "The man you fear would make me scream from pain. You want me to scream from ecstasy." His mouth was so close to hers.

"I haven't had a day where I don't compare myself to my father. And I don't want to treat you as he treated my mother. Or any woman."

"Do you think he ever made a woman scream in ecstasy?"

James winced. "Not the sort of question one asks, Pearl."

"I would bet he never thought to try." She stood on her tiptoes and leaned into his chest to whisper in his ear. "Make me scream, James. Make the stableboys all the way in Marylebone hear your name."

His voice hitched as he asked, "Do you want this?"

"More than anything. Let's lock the doors for days." Her heart beat faster. Would he allow himself the abandon he'd found earlier?

He pulled back. "And you would tell me if something wasn't to your liking?"

"I promise. And you will do the same for me?"

He grinned, wide enough that she noticed a crooked tooth hidden in the back. She hadn't seen it before and it charmed her. She had one too. Suddenly, he scooped her up and deposited her on the couch.

She squealed with delight. He yanked off his cravat. There was a pinging sound as something metal bounced across the wooden floor.

"Your valet will murder you for that."

James knelt in front of her, shucking his coat and waistcoat. "He has plenty of reasons to quit. This is just one more." He removed her shoes, tossing them aside.

Pearl felt his freedom in this moment. Nothing mattered more than the two of them, here, together. This sanctuary. He grasped her ankle, circling his fingers around it. She couldn't tell why she found it so arousing, but she did. He pushed up her modest sage-green gown, exposing her knees and revealing her stockings.

She loved the white silk stockings with the black curl pattern along the back. There were so many bits of frivolity she could forgo, but this decoration of her body, she loved. James murmured his appreciation, letting his lips skirt the baroque scrollwork up to the backs of her knees. He reached her green ribboned garters and the pile of fabric that was her dress. Pearl couldn't bring herself to breathe.

James pushed her legs wider, making room for himself. He let go of her ankle and instead gripped her hips, pulling her forward on the couch. "Do you need to warm up at all?"

Pearl was already dizzy with lust. "Pardon?"

"I don't want you to hurt yourself when you start screaming." He kissed his way up her bare thigh, pushing away the fabric of her skirts.

"You self-important—" She gasped. His tongue was in a place where she'd never thought a tongue to go. It was soft and marvelous and she couldn't think, let alone speak. His hand reached up and gripped the neckline of her bodice. "Please—" she meant to ask him not to damage her clothing, but instead her hand closed over his as she rocked with pleasure.

He withdrew his face from between her legs, placing his hands where his tongue had been circling the wetness. "Whenever you're ready, my lady."

That was all it took for her body to shake with pleasure. Her mouth continued to rasp out sounds, but she couldn't have said if they were words or obscene sentiments.

"Good girl," he murmured, then bent his head between her legs once more. This time, he removed his hand from her bodice and used it between her legs, the other kneading the flesh of her thigh.

She put her hands in his hair. Beautiful and dark, though longer than she'd ever known it to be. Longer hair could be pulled in the ring. So she did it. She pulled his hair, and he made a noise that she liked.

He looked up at her, admiration clear in those bright emerald eyes.

"Did you like that?" she asked.

He nodded, his lips and chin wet with her. She used her grip to push his head down, and he grunted again in pleasure. It wasn't long until she stiffened again, pleasure crashing over her even harder than it had before. She lost the ability to control her babbling, finally coalescing around his name.

James stood, wiped his mouth on his discarded cravat. "Louder next time. That's not quite a scream."

Pearl grinned. "What about you?"

James pulled his shirt out of his trousers. "What about me?"

"I was afraid you were going to end this without..." She faltered. What was the polite word for it?

"Without finding my release?" He whipped the linen shirt off over his head. "Not to worry." He unbuttoned the fall on his trousers while looking at her unabashed on the couch. "As much as I love this view, I have another fantasy to fulfill. If you wouldn't mind."

James held out his hand as if he were asking her to dance. She took it. "Lead the way."

He escorted her to the piano. Holding his hand, she stepped up onto the stool. She held her skirts higher than needed, giving him ample time to admire her ornate stockings. He guided her over the Beethoven folio on the music stand to the long closed expanse of the piano. Her perch was not nearly so high as it seemed. Pearl settled on the top of the closed lid, James stood between her thighs. She wrapped her legs around his waist. He was still too low, to make this fantasy work, but James raised up on his toes, His hard cock nudging her. She wanted to scoot forward, to make him enter her, but if she did, she'd fall off the instrument completely.

He used his foot to pull over a stack of music books, standing on them, focused on returning to his place between her legs.

"Is this a fantasy you've had since you were a boy?"

He traced her folds with the head of his cock, teasing her, teasing himself. "Not until recently, when a beautiful ginger listened to me play. Then it became one."

"I'm your fantasy?" She was exceptionally pleased by that.

"Pearl," he breathed, slowly sliding inside her. "You're every man's fantasy."

His words ripped her apart. It took so little she should be ashamed, but when it felt like love, how could she be? He thrust into her again and again, and when she opened her eyes after her climax, she found him staring back at her. She gripped his jaw with one hand, holding the piano ledge with the other.

"Come for me," she commanded. And he did.

⚜

AT ETON, there had been rumors that a man aged prematurely if he lost all his sperm, whether from masturbating too much or whoring too much. A man needed his vitality to live. James now believed—based on empirical evidence, obviously—that it was quite the opposite. Losing all of one's semen was the best way to live.

This time, he'd been careful to spend himself outside of Pearl. It was a small victory, perhaps, but it made James feel like he had control. Like he wasn't pushing himself upon Pearl, forcing her to bind herself to him if she didn't want to be there. He needed her to feel wanted, just not obligated. Or worse, scared.

They had finally made it to her room last night, dinner forgotten. They slept entangled, flesh pressed against flesh. He awoke at some point in the morning, the fire already going in the grate. A maid had been in. Now the entire household would know that the master and mistress had consummated their marriage.

But what of it? Surely there was other gossip more worthy. He glanced at Pearl, sleeping on her stomach, her red hair spread about, wild and snarled from his hands.

He knew this feeling, even if it had never before been this powerful. He loved his wife. What a lark. Of all the outlandish, unlordly things he could do, he had fallen in love with the woman he'd married. In a way, it was like kicking his father's gravestone. In fact, he decided, he would go so far as to spoil his wife. Not only would he love her, he would buy her jewelry and dresses, take her to the theatre or wherever she wished to go. Indulge her whims.

As he contemplated her sleeping figure, he realized that more than presenting her with finery, he wanted her to be proud of being on his arm. She didn't have an enemy to crush or need protection from a brute—she'd capably dealt with all of that on her own for years. But he did have a power she could never wield. He had influence that couldn't be bought with all the ill-gotten gains in the world.

James extracted his arm from underneath Pearl's head. He needed a pen and paper and some food.

The idea of feeding her breakfast in bed came with further ideas that he would definitely need sustenance to perform. He crept out the adjoining door and into his room—his, not his father's. For there was no reason to think of that old dandiprat now. He was finished believing he could atone for another man's sins. In fact, if he could ever exact vengeance upon his father, it wouldn't be by the man's destruction, which had already occurred—it would be by changing the minds of every maid that shrank from James's face. James should endeavor to make the Andrepont name synonymous with generosity, tolerance, humility. Revenge wasn't negating his father by erasing his lineage. It was erasing his father by negating his cruelty.

James smiled. Perhaps Lady Teeton would get what she wanted. The best way to undo his father's cruelty was by embracing all of his power. If he didn't take up the mantle, how else could he protect friends like John, like Mr. Worley and Bess? *His wife* was right. Those words amused him. His wife.

He grabbed a banyan to cover himself and dashed off a note to Lord and Lady Teeton to please give specifics on their country retreat. Then he rang for a large breakfast tray to be brought up and to have no one disturb them until they were summoned.

There was no reason to return to Pearl's room, other than that he wanted to be near her. To smell her. Touch her. But she needed her sleep. He crept back in, thinking to take up a position in a chair near the fire so that she wouldn't be disturbed.

But she raised her head, blinking those large blue eyes at him. "What you doing all the way over there for?"

"I wanted to let you sleep." She reached her arm out, which he took as an invitation to approach. The bedsheet came to her waist, exposing a freckled back that had the most elegant lines of muscle and skin.

She propped her head on one hand, her breasts pressed against the mattress. One eye was closed, the other barely open. "What you wearing clothes for?"

"The servants."

"Bugger 'em."

He grinned. "I thought you might be more interested in that."

Her eyes popped open. "You want a buggering? Never done it, but I can learn. There's a shop down on the Strand what sells those sorts of—"

He laughed and pushed her onto her back. Her pink nipples tightened in response to the air. God, he wanted all of her. Every second of every day.

"Oh, you mean I'm interested in where you put your cock. Well, yes. That is an area of my interest. Do you have any further research I might do?"

He kissed her neck, hoping for those gasps he'd heard last night. And he couldn't wait for the nonsense she spewed when she was about to find her climax. Some words were incomprehensible, and others strung together as obscenities that would make any sailor shift his breeches. He didn't think she even knew what she was saying, which, though she wasn't hoarse from screaming his name, he still appreciated and viewed as a stamp of approval.

A scratching at the door indicated that the breakfast tray had been delivered. He sprung off her while she made sounds of acute disapproval.

"We need food, pet."

"Please don't call me 'pet,'" she said.

Her tone was light, but the nickname stopped him cold. He hadn't meant to say it. There was nothing inherently wrong with it. But it was what his father had called anyone he was abusing. It was a word to shush and silence. To hurt and disable. But he didn't want to tell her that. He hadn't meant it like that.

"What should I call you, then?" He opened the door, hoping whatever servant delivered the tray had enough sense to quickly make themselves scarce. James had no intention of putting clothes on today.

"I'm not sure yet. But nothing quite so...broad. I like specifics." Pearl eyed him as he brought in the tray. "Specifically, what is happening behind those grapes?" She pointed at the tray, which happened to strategically cover his cock. His body responded to her interest without hesitation. A feat he didn't think he could manage at his age, frankly. But such was novelty.

The clock downstairs rang the hour. He watched her counting out the bells. "Shitballs."

"Pardon?" he asked, barely containing his laughter. Her vulgarity was funnier than anything he'd ever encountered. She was so dainty, so delicate, so elfin, even. And then her mouth was as foul as a guttersnipe.

She shot him a look. "I'm supposed to be at home today to receive callers."

James set the tray on the bed, revealing himself and his exact intentions. "You certainly may." He pulled the sheet back, yanking her leg over to the edge. "But I make no promises of what state I will be in when visitors arrive."

It didn't take long. Such a boost for his self-worth. A few licks of her honey and she was gripping his head with her thighs, arching her back. It was marvelous. Simply marvelous.

CHAPTER 16

Time passed faster than James had ever experienced. He received a note from Freddy, clearly fishing for a dinner invitation. And of course, James had accepted the formal invitation to the Teetons' country home, where he would no doubt be hounded for his political absenteeism.

But he had plans now, and Pearl's delight when he told her he'd accepted the Teetons' invitation had made everything worthwhile. The world could be in flames and he wouldn't care. She practically glowed, and he had done that. He had made her happy.

Their days fell into a predictable pattern of bedding each other, eating, and then returning to bed. She took her at-home hours very seriously and received callers from three until five. His cousins arrived, her chums from boarding school—sometimes even Lady Teeton made the rounds. But James was all but pacing outside the door, waiting for her to finish so he might carry her off to his study and do filthy things to her.

He'd never been so enamored. Once or twice, he tried to assist his mother in her gardens. She looked so pleased with herself that he couldn't bear it.

"You could just tell me how right I was," she'd

called after him the last time he left her greenhouse. The woman was insufferable.

Pearl's courses came. James was relieved, and while she tried to keep him from her bed when she bled, he couldn't stand to be parted from her. He still brought her to her breaking point again and again, and she admitted that it helped her cramping. They slept entwined, and she kept his hands over her womb as if it were a balm to the ache there.

Suddenly, it was time to go to the country. They collected the luggage at the front drive and Smithy strapped it to the back and top of the carriage. When Pearl arrived at the front step, looking beyond fetching in a brown-and-blue traveling gown, James waved off the footman. He would hand Pearl up into the carriage himself.

Pearl gave him a saucy look, dropped into a curtsy, and took his hand. "Thank you, my lord," she murmured as she stepped into the carriage.

His body was all but thrumming. They'd have a six-hour ride, and he knew exactly how they would occupy themselves.

Mrs. Foraker approached and handed him a hamper. She didn't look at all pleased with him. "This is for your journey. I've given Smithy, Mr. Phillip, and Miss Lily their own. Goodness knows they're not going to want to look inside that carriage during this journey."

James accepted the hamper from her. "It's quite heavy."

She grimaced. "You've got to keep up your strength, my lord."

He started laughing, looking to the male servants to see if they found the humor, but they all were studiously occupied in their tasks. His wife's maid was already staring straight ahead at the horses. James hauled himself inside the carriage.

"Apparently we've managed to scandalize the servants," James announced to his bride.

She gave him one of her wicked smiles. "It was only a matter of time."

He opened the hamper.

"What have you there?"

James pawed through it. "Chicken, pâté, bread, cheese. Oh, some eggs and asparagus."

Pearl laughed. "I don't think we need that anymore."

James gave his best impressions of a dubious look. "Mrs. Foraker said I needed to keep up my strength. I believe she fears you're wearing me out."

Pearl's eyes took on a wicked gleam that made his blood heat in return. "I can't wait to see if I can." She glanced out the windows, proving they were still sitting in front of the house.

James leaned out the door, banging a fist on the carriage wall. "What's taking so long? Are we ready to leave or not?"

⚬✿⚬

JAMES THREW UP HIS HANDS. "I've done my best, but you still look as if you've been thoroughly—"

Pearl cut him off with a harsh look. Her hair was a mess. And her gown was so oddly fixed on her body that a blind nun would know what they had been up to during a six-hour carriage ride. Truly, what else was there to do for so long in a private carriage? Read?

"Fortunately, it's dark out."

Pearl sighed, hoping the pattering rain covered her sound of exhaustion. "Will we be expected to go to dinner?"

James shook his head. "Not likely. They'll ask if we feel well enough, or if we'd prefer a tray in our rooms."

Pearl swiped at her hair. "Normally, I enjoy the

jostling." James gave a chuckle, letting her know he appreciated her vulgar allusion. "But I have to say, the carriage ride is more exhausting than I thought."

James frowned. "Have you never been for a carriage ride outside London?"

"Of course not. Where would I go?" Ah, yes. Had James forgotten his wife had been raised a gutter orphan?

"You know, I do own properties in a few counties. We are always free to reside in those whenever we desire."

It was her turn to frown. "What do you mean? I thought your family didn't go to the country."

"We don't. At least, we don't now. We used to be there constantly. My mother and her sister were raised in the country, and they loved to be out in the fresh air. We'd all go together: my mother and I, often my sister Margaret and her mother, and of course, William and Lydia and Agnes with their mother."

"William?" She didn't remember meeting a William. Or hearing about a William, for that matter.

"Lydia and Agnes had an older brother. He died when he was not yet twenty, and the girls were quite young. He was the heir, of course. Another brutal blow. We had all gone out to the country to help him recover, and then he didn't. And that was when my father—"

Understanding dawned. That was when James's father had hurt Lydia. Of course. Because they were together in the same house and people were grieving, not watching a monster as carefully as they should have been. "I understand. It makes sense that your family wouldn't want to return to the countryside after so much tragedy."

"I think it's time for a change." James shrugged. "The man is *dead*."

He said the last word with such conviction. Pearl's heart swelled with pride in him.

"He has no power over me. Over us." His big hand snaked out and grasped hers as the carriage turned onto the long, muddy drive. "Thank you."

Pearl didn't even try to control the blush of pride that covered her body. She not only belonged here, with James, but she had made a difference for the better. She squeezed his hand. So this is what it felt like. To be needed. The carriage heaved against the uneven gravel, which had no doubt been made all the more menacing by the deluge that had tormented the countryside, if the over-full rivers they'd spotted between bouts of cramped love-making were an accurate sign.

The carriage rocked to a halt in front of the manor house. While the staff tried to keep them dry as they dashed in, the wind and rain still chilled her. Pearl was grateful for being shown her room and almost cried when a maid suggested a bath. The maid pushed the empty bathing tub in front of the fire and disappeared.

James appeared at her door, looking tired but still dark and handsome despite his rumpled and mud-splattered clothes. Hers likely didn't look any better. He leaned against the door jamb. "Want to cause an absolute scandal?"

Her body warmed all over again and the exhaustion disappeared. She bit her lip. "What did you have in mind?"

"How about you send away the maid and I bathe you? And you bathe me." He stalked towards her, freeing the doorway for the two footmen hauling in buckets of water.

Pearl eyed the footmen, waiting for them to pour out the water and take their leave. The maid came bustling in with scents and oils for her to choose from. James looked at her expectantly, then stared down the maid that was laying out Pearl's choices in an elegant display.

"You can't forget them, can you?" James asked.

"Forget who?"

James gestured to the maid. Pearl shook her head. Servants, while trained not to divulge the secrets of those they helped, were still extra ears. She couldn't continue with the outrageous flirting while other people were present. Even if they were paid to be there. She'd grown up as barely more than a servant in many of the households she stayed at, trying to keep herself welcome and fed. It was hard to forget.

"Thank you." James plucked the final bottle of bath oil from the maid's hands. "You are no longer needed for the evening. Please tell Lady Andrepont's maid that she is also no longer needed this evening. You will need to find quarters for her elsewhere."

Pearl's cheeks burned. Lily was supposed to stay in the corner of her room—there was a cot made up for her, at the ready. Where would Lily sleep? Philip was sleeping in James's room. The maid curtsied and left, not meeting Pearl's pleading gaze.

"Don't worry, love. They'll find a place for her. Big houses like this? There's always space." James crept towards her.

Did he just call her love? Oh, she couldn't think about that and worry about her maid at the same time. "But Lily—she depends on me. After all, she is supposed to sleep right there." Pearl glanced at the cot, expecting to see Lily's small carpet bag.

"I took the pleasure of directing her bags downstairs as we disembarked the carriage."

Pearl put her hands on her hips. "Mrs. Foraker thinks I am wearing you out."

James snaked his arms around her waist, letting his hands cup her bum. "I have so many plans." He kissed her, slow and deep, as if they hadn't spent the entire carriage ride doing precisely that. "You taste like sunshine. And happiness. And all that is good in the world."

She undid the knot of his cravat, exposing his neck. "I believe you once called me a sunshine hellhound."

He smiled against her lips. "I stand by it. Get in the tub."

৩১৫৩

JAMES AWOKE in Pearl's room. The curtains had been opened and the fire in the grate was merrily burning. The sky was gray, but Pearl lay next to him, her red hair flung about, tendrils strewn across his bare arm.

He had never been a man to think about luck. But the contentment he felt, the *rightness* of it all, struck him. This was what men killed and died for. This is what his mother had aimed for and missed. No wonder she'd wanted him to get married.

Rose had also wanted him married. Is this what she experienced with Henry? Was that why she wanted him gone? He waited for the stab of pain that thoughts of Rose should bring, but it didn't come. If Rose had this with Henry, then he wished her well. In fact, he hoped she had this level of joy.

He leaned over and kissed Pearl's bare shoulder, but she didn't even stir. He really had been wearing her out. He grinned. He wasn't so old then, despite their decade-or-so age difference. Mrs. Foraker, indeed.

His stomach growled, urging him to dress and go down to breakfast. But he loathed to leave Pearl in bed alone. She was so warm. And beautiful. And she was *his*. Maybe he could ring for a tray without waking her. Bestowing one last kiss on her arm, James slid out of bed and crouched on the floor. He waited a beat, listening to her breathing to make sure she wasn't disturbed. Once confirmed, he crept towards his shirt and tossed it on. He held his breath for a moment, listening once again to ensure her breathing hadn't altered. Satisfied, he crept out of her room and into his next door.

Phillip was up and bustling.

"Ah. My lord," the valet greeted him.

James shushed him and the valet's eyebrows flew up. "Pearl is sleeping next door." James had never been good at reading another man's expression, but he could have sworn that the valet let amusement skitter across his face before controlling it.

"Of course, my lord," Phillip whispered, handing him a piece of heavy paper. "The events for today. I'm afraid you've missed shooting."

James waved at his valet. He didn't care about shooting, especially in these muddy conditions. He certainly didn't want to lose a boot to a mudhole. Besides, how many times had he been out tromping in the woods with a rifle? He far preferred the company of his wife. *His* wife. His *wife*!

"I'll dress for the morning, that's fine. But please ring for a tray for two to be brought next door. We shall break our fast together."

"I'll see to it."

Not long after, he was dressed and ensconced in one of the chairs in Pearl's room, reading the paper, sipping bitter drinking chocolate, and reading an issue from last week's *London St. James Chronicle and Evening Post*. He didn't care for chocolate first thing in the morning, but it wasn't bad, considering they were in the country.

He took another big sigh. The country. Friends. Love. Perhaps that dusty old poet was right: Living well was the best revenge.

Pearl stirred in bed, and he all but dropped the paper. The tray was laden with delights of orange marmalade and honey. He put the bread in the toasting iron and held it to the fire, knowing she took a few moments to fully wake. There was a certain satisfaction in toasting something for her.

"What time is it?" she called, her voice scratchy.

"I believe the clock last chimed ten."

More rustling. "I can't believe I slept so long."

James risked a glance over his shoulder, which treated him to the sight of his wife pulling a chemise over her head. She dug through the chest of clothing that would have been unpacked by her maid last night if James had allowed the maid into the room. Pearl wrapped herself in a dressing gown and joined him by the fire.

"Is this drinking chocolate?" She picked up his cup.

"Have it, by all means." The toast looked almost brown enough. He didn't even know how she took her toast. There was so much to learn.

She made a luscious sound of contentment. "I love chocolate in the morning."

Noted. "You never mentioned. We've had tea at home."

"Oh, whatever you prefer is fine," she said, waving her hand, shaking her head. All those things she did when she wanted something for herself but couldn't quite figure out if she deserved it.

"Pearl. You are a viscountess. And it's only drinking chocolate. Tell Barton or Mrs. Foraker your preference, and it will magically appear whenever you ask for it."

"That just seems..."

The toast was done. He stood and pulled the lever. Two pieces of beautifully toasted bread slid onto the breakfast tray that sat between the chairs. He looked at her, waiting for her to either finish her sentence or applaud his antics. She did neither. Of course.

"What kind of jams do they have?" she asked.

Amazingly, this woman was more vocal about her needs in bed than in actual life. It was strange, and not at all what he would have expected, but Pearl was anything but predictable.

She spread butter and orange marmalade on her bread and murmured a mouthful of thanks to him. He'd placed her itinerary of events under her side of the tray. She pulled it out and studied it. "Will you be going to the afternoon salon?"

He smiled, forgetting how inexperienced she was. "No, gentlemen have a separate agenda. We will not have the same activities until the evening. In the next few days, we will likely have a few activities scheduled with both men and women, but by and large, we will be separate."

Pearl frowned. "But I don't like that."

He took her hand and gently kissed her knuckles, setting up a joke he knew would send her howling. He looked deep into her eyes and said, "But darling, how can I miss you if you never go away?"

He was rewarded with her laughter and a roll tossed at his head. He laughed and tossed it back, knowing his aim was wide.

⚭

SITTING WITH LADY TEETON, Lady Kinsley, and two new acquaintances, Mrs. Aguilar and Mrs. Shumaker, Pearl felt less buoyant. She hadn't meant to become so reliant on James's company, but during the last few weeks, she'd grown accustomed to his presence.

"I have, of course, shared my husband's work with all of you." Lady Teeton shifted, taking them all in. "Forgive me for being so blunt about our gathering this afternoon, but I would like for us to have a salon of sorts. What did you think of the proposals in the bill? Would they work in a practical manner? Do you find them cruel at all? Is there anything the bill overlooks?"

The ladies looked at one another. Pearl studied

Mrs. Aguilar. She was dark eyed and dark haired, thin and watchful, which contrasted with Mrs. Shumaker's doughy paleness. The plump Mrs. Shumaker seemed to take the opulent drawing room in stride, which Pearl desperately tried to imitate.

The overt luxury no longer made Pearl nervous. Rather, it was the home's understated nature that gave her pause. In the hall, the paintings of ancestors stretched back farther than there was available room. Every object was beautiful, well-maintained, and clearly very old. This was a house full of old money. And Pearl was new money freshly ripened.

"With all due respect, Lady Teeton, your bill is very well and good. But there are more pressing things than harsh punishments for criminals." Mrs. Aguilar looked about at those present, as if searching for support. "For instance, my family cannot even involve themselves in government, should they wish."

Pearl watched the silent argument of subtle gestures happening between Lady Teeton and Mrs. Aguilar. Lady Teeton had an agenda that Mrs. Aguilar was disrupting, and Pearl was beginning to notice that Lady Teeton didn't care for surprises.

"Can you elaborate, Mrs. Aguilar?" Lady Kinsley asked. James's former paramour wore her spectacles today, through which she peered with absolutely no acknowledgment of her friend's distress.

"It's the Anglican question," Mrs. Aguilar said, holding her hands out as if it were obvious.

But Pearl didn't follow politics and had never paid attention to political discussions. Her mind had always been focused on a floor that needed sweeping or a baby that needed soothing, assuring that her next meal would be provided. Mrs. Aguilar's reference didn't sound like anything Pearl had ever heard of.

Lady Teeton sighed. "No one calls it that."

"They should," Mrs. Shumaker said quietly.

Pearl thought she might like Mrs. Shumaker more than anyone else in the room.

"I'm afraid I don't understand. What is the Anglican question?" Lady Kinsley asked.

"Mrs. Aguilar is speaking of the requirement for all public servants to be Anglican. Mrs. Aguilar is of the Jewish faith, and Mrs. Shumaker is Catholic. Neither of their husbands can vote, despite their land ownership or their wealth," Lady Teeton explained tersely.

Once elaborated, Pearl recognized it. Of course. Yes, she'd heard about that. Some of the Irish families she'd stayed with were Catholic. Pearl hadn't cared overmuch. She might have been baptized Catholic— it was certainly a possibility. Given the nature of her itinerant upbringing, it was far easier to be Anglican.

"I'd never heard it referenced as the Anglican question," Lady Kinsley said. "I understand now."

"Then you agree that there are more important things than discussing punishments of criminals. They are criminals, after all." Mrs. Shumaker sniffed.

Pearl's cheeks flushed, and she forced herself to take a breath before speaking. "If I may, what makes a criminal?"

Lady Kinsley locked eyes on her, as if she were the most fascinating creature alive. "Oh, yes. Excellent question, Lady Andrepont."

There was no shift in tone as the woman said her name. No jealousy or acidic demeanor. Pearl had expected something from the woman, but there was nothing. They were just...strangers. Who had loved the same man.

Lady Teeton held up her hand. "No, we do not need to debate what a criminal is."

Lady Kinsley looked visibly disappointed. "Why not? It is pertinent to the discussion at hand as well as your proposed legislation."

"Why should a criminal be discussed when the

rights of upstanding citizens are ignored?" Mrs. Aguilar countered.

Pearl didn't have an answer for that. She had committed crimes herself. And yes, crimes that could have seen her transported or hanged. But she wasn't a criminal. She'd had no other choice. And the law was very unforgiving to those stealing handkerchiefs.

Lady Teeton smiled and stood. "Mrs. Aguilar, Mrs. Shumaker. I appreciate your position. I do. But I have a strategy, one that is decades-long."

Pearl watched the blonde woman pace. She was graceful as she walked, but the fact that she moved at all was evidence of her frustration.

"I am sorry that your families have hardship. I'm sorry that your husbands suffer the same lack of rights that we women do. But I also know that advocating for their rights, in this moment, will do nothing. Just as if I advocate for my rights, we will end with nothing."

"I hate politics," Mrs. Shumaker grumbled, her plump form shifting.

Pearl caught her eye and smiled. The woman returned it with a sheepishness. She hadn't meant to be heard, evidently.

"This year, we ask for a reform of those laws calling for the blood of those committing minor offenses."

Pearl giggled and glanced at Mrs. Shumaker. "Bloody laws."

Mrs. Aguilar gasped, but Lady Kinsley laughed aloud at Pearl's curse.

"Quite right," the marchioness said. "Bloodied Bloody Laws."

"Please stop the obscenities," Lady Teeton said.

"Why? It's quite accurate, don't you think?" Lady Kinsley said.

"Quite," Mrs. Aguilar nodded, as did Mrs. Shumaker.

"But we achieve nothing if men find us vulgar," Lady Teeton protested.

"Aren't you saying this is your husband's work?" Pearl frowned. "So if he calls them 'Bloody Laws,' won't they find him clever and humorous? At least, that's been my experience around men."

"The men know I am heavily involved. They won't believe my husband thought of it."

"Then have another man introduce it," Mrs. Aguilar said with a shrug.

"I'm afraid it doesn't fit the character of my husband," Lady Kinsley said. "He's much too gentle-hearted. But it would fit Lord Andrepont quite well, I believe."

Pearl found the women staring at her.

"Will he finally be taking his seat?" Mrs. Aguilar asked.

Pearl swallowed hard. Did everyone know about her husband's absence from Parliament? Though, if anyone had a remote interest in politics, it would be obvious. "We haven't discussed it."

Mrs. Shumaker gave her a lusty smirk. "When might you find the time?"

Pearl's cheeks colored once more. The other women froze at the allusion to Pearl's marital bed.

"Even if he doesn't take his seat," Lady Kinsley said, "James is an excellent candidate to refer to them as 'Bloody Laws' elsewhere. At his club, for instance."

"Pardon?" Pearl wasn't sure she'd heard correctly.

"I said that it doesn't matter if your husband takes his seat—"

"You said *James*."

It was Lady Kinsley's turn to blush. "Of course. My apologies."

Pearl's heart beat fast and hard in her breast. She didn't like her husband's Christian name on this woman's lips. She'd given up her right to him, pushing him aside and breaking his heart. James belonged to

Pearl. Her hands shook and sweated. If she didn't get out of there, she would say something far worse than *bloody laws*. She stood. "If you will excuse me, ladies. I think I need some fresh air."

"But it's raining," Lady Teeton protested.

"Only a sprinkle," Pearl countered.

"I think better while I'm moving," Mrs. Shumaker said, standing. "If you don't mind, Lady Andrepont?"

Pearl smiled, sensing an alliance with this easy-natured woman. "I'd be delighted."

"I would love to hear any advice you may have regarding the wording of the bill or the speech to introduce it," Lady Teeton said to both of them, but Pearl felt that she was mostly talking to her, not Mrs. Shumaker.

"Of course. Perhaps after I take some air. Excuse me." Pearl smiled and curtsied, given that Lady Kinsley, the one she truly needed to escape, was higher ranked.

Lady Kinsley gave a brief nod of acknowledgment but didn't look at Pearl. She knew what she'd done.

☙❧

JAMES WENT to the library to smoke, despite the fact he rarely did. It was early afternoon, and Pearl would be busy writing peace treaties or whatever it was that Lady Teeton had organized for the ladies. Henry was already there, playing a chess game against himself at one of the tables. No one else was in the room.

The last time he'd seen Henry was at the Haglund's soiree, a time when James was still begging for scraps of Rose's attention. How distant and unreal that time felt now. Instead of offering a greeting or even a retreat, James cleared his throat to gain his former friend's attention.

"James," Henry said in surprise. "You're here. I didn't know if you'd attend."

Henry looked well: happy and at ease. But there was strain in his voice. The situation was damnably awkward, after all. "I'm sure you heard of our invitation here," James said.

"I knew Lady Andrepont would come. I wasn't sure if you would deign to join her."

James bowed to Henry, his acquiescence to Henry's higher rank. Since he referred to Pearl by her rank, he figured Henry wanted the distance that formality gave.

"You don't need to do that," Henry said, looking at the chessboard. After a moment, he moved a white pawn out.

"Seemed like I ought."

Henry looked up, studying James.

"It's been a long time since you absolutely humiliated me at chess. Would you care to do so again?" James asked.

Henry motioned to the empty chair. "By all means. The misanthropist in me welcomes the degenerate in you."

"You aren't a misanthrope, Henry. I think that's the trouble." James looked at the board. Henry had just started, but it was as good a start as any. James matched the white pawn with a black one.

"I don't think you are a degenerate, either."

"Any more emotion and you'll be grabbing my hand and pressing it to your cheek. Move." James flicked his hand at the board.

"You're a good man, James. And you seem happy. I'm glad." Henry moved a knight. "So prepare yourself. I'm betting your chess game is still atrocious."

James grunted and matched the knight. He'd had enough practice to know he could usually block Henry long enough to foil his opening gambits. "Well, shocking as it may seem, Rose was correct again."

"Hm?" Henry stared at the board for a moment,

proving that James had foiled at least one plan. "Correct about what? She usually is. If I were half the man I am, it might bother me."

"It was good to marry. And Pearl is..." What could he say without mortifying them both? "More than I could have hoped."

Henry glanced up from the board, his blue eyes full of warmth. "I'm so pleased, James. Really, I am. You deserve it."

James felt their old camaraderie return, and it eased an ache he hadn't known he'd shouldered. They'd been friends since boyhood, and they had seen so much together. "Stop the gushing sentimentality," he said. "You'll embarrass yourself. Get on with the slaughter."

ॐ

IT WASN'T until dinner that Pearl saw James again. She was nervous about her dress and interrogated James multiple times about the propriety of her dark burgundy gown. James patted her hand and made lewd innuendo, and she had no choice but to believe she was in good company.

The other guests were already assembled when they arrived at the drawing room, and Lady Teeton took her around to introduce her to the men she'd not yet met.

"I do hope your walk was invigorating," Lady Teeton said with a smile, though clearly steering Pearl away from Lady Kinsley.

"Mrs. Shumaker is insightful." Neither Pearl nor Mrs. Shumaker had spoken during their soggy tromp through the gardens. The damp gown had been a delightful reason to lounge in her room in her shift, reading all afternoon. Lady Teeton returned her to James, who was speaking with Lord Teeton.

"Your bid to take your seat will go uncontested, of course," Lord Teeton was saying.

Instead of looking peevish, which Pearl expected, James seemed to be listening and considering the man's words. Perhaps change could occur.

In fact, Lady Teeton flicked a pleased smile Pearl's way, as if thanking her. But Pearl hadn't done anything at all. This was the first she was hearing of it.

The dinner gong rang and interrupted them all. Without thinking, Pearl started for the back of the room, ready to process into the dining hall last. James caught her arm. "Where are you going?"

Pearl shook her head. "To dinner."

James shook his head and gently guided her to the middle of the group. Ah, yes. Because she was no longer the untitled orphan. She was a viscountess. She was more than just Pearl.

At least dinner was a prescribed dance that she understood. Mrs. Tyler had drilled them nightly on etiquette and manners. This was no hardship. No, the worst was when dinner had concluded and, stuffed full of a delicious bread pudding, Pearl was expected to converse over tea with the rest of the ladies.

Lady Teeton led the way back to the drawing room, and chamomile was served to help them digest. Lady Teeton made a few attempts at casual chatter, but the conversation was clearly tarnished by the afternoon's awkwardness. Pearl felt sorry for her hostess, and for her part in making the company uncomfortable.

"If I may, I wouldn't mind sharing some thoughts on your legislation, Lady Teeton." Pearl cleared her throat and smiled at the rest of them. "As you have previously said, I am well acquainted with the people it affects most."

Lady Teeton perked up and Mrs. Aguilar looked at Pearl with interest.

Pearl outlined her concerns, which included the definition of "criminal," protests notwithstanding. She discussed a childhood acquaintance who had been hung for stealing at the tender age of nine, and the difficulties for children who were not rounded up for a London workhouse or an industrial mill in the north.

She spoke on conditions that might compel a person—particularly a child—to steal. How a lethal sentence wasn't an effective deterrent if the person already faced death by starvation.

Lady Kinsley found some foolscap and scribbled notes. Lady Teeton kept an unwavering eye contact that Pearl found unnerving. Mrs. Shumaker listened with her head cocked and her eyes on the floor, and Mrs. Aguilar sipped her tea and nodded when Pearl hit a point she agreed with.

The group was deep in discussion when the men joined them, interrupting a rousing conversation about transportation, the shipping industry, and the economics of slavery.

"We tried last year to abolish the trafficking. Another group will introduce the legislation, slightly altered, of course, this year. If it still doesn't get approved, we'll take it again," Lady Kinsley explained.

"Shockingly," Lord Teeton announced as he entered the room. "My wife is discussing political strategy."

Lady Teeton smiled at him indulgently, the way one would smile at a child, but said nothing.

"And your conversation, Lord Teeton?" Lady Kinsley asked, her tone edged in annoyance.

"Shooting! Conditions tomorrow should be drier, let's hope. I'll have all the men with me, no exceptions." He gave a sly smile to each of the women. "So no lazing abed. It's an early start!"

It wasn't long until the couples dispersed. Pearl

and James walked back towards their rooms, enjoying the paintings of dour ancestors along the way.

"I've heard nothing of your day," Pearl said.

"Nor I yours," James said. "But first, my room or yours?"

"Can you not be separated from your wife for even one night?" she teased.

"I could, but why would I? I have a hedonistic reputation to uphold. Besides, nothing would please me more than making you walk funny and making all the other wives jealous."

Pearl barely held back a howl of laughter. "You cannot possibly think you can make me walk funny."

He stopped, pulling her to a stop in the middle of the hallway. "Is that a challenge, my lady?"

Pearl laughed, not knowing what to do. She let him push her against the wall, caging her between his arms. "You know I could have dodged that."

James's grin grew wider and more feral. "I know that it means you like it."

The door next to them opened, and a very stern-looking Mr. Shumaker peered out of it. "My lord. My lady. Good night." And then he shut the door.

James burst out laughing, as did Pearl. They hurried down the hall.

CHAPTER 17

J ames had not expected to enjoy himself this much at the Teetons' estate. Shooting with Lord Teeton had hardly seemed worth leaving Pearl's bed that morning, but he did find that he enjoyed the excuse of joining her before dinner as a time for another round of love-making.

There was a bit of pride that Pearl looked flushed and glowingly postcoital at dinner. Petty of him to want to show that off to both Henry and Rose, but he had never been accused of humility.

So James spent a wet but invigorating morning tromping through the woods with Teeton on one side and Henry on the other. His boots were soaked, and his nose and cheeks burned with cold. The last time he'd been shooting had been well over a decade ago. The last time he'd been in the country was the same.

"Will you really take your seat then, Andrepont?" Teeton called through the curtain of fine mist.

James glanced at the man whose land he was trampling. "I thought we were supposed to be quiet in order to find game."

Henry snorted. "That's not why we're out here."

James laughed in agreement. It was true. He didn't care if they shot something or not. He didn't care for game meat anyway, but it was a way to feel alive without killing his knuckles on a sand-filled bag. "You know I like to play coy, Teeton."

"My wife will be disappointed to hear that."

"That is why your wife is a better politician," James called back, prompting another snort from Henry.

Up ahead, birds flushed out of a copse of trees. None of the men bothered to raise their guns. They weren't prepared, and it was far better to watch their graceful escape. James took a lungful of cool air, stopping his forward progress. He felt as if he might find a way to fly as well. Who knew that happiness had been standing so close to him after all these years?

The other men approached.

"So you'll take your seat in the new year?" Teeton asked as the last bird winged its way to safety.

"Don't tell your wife yet. I enjoy her overtures." James felt powerful in a way he hadn't throughout his entire life. Like he'd been holding his father's oilskin overcoat all these years, waiting to slip into it, but he hadn't. Not only could he let go of it, he got to discard it. His father was dead. He could let go of the past. And not just him—his entire family could live the way they deserved.

The vengeance he would wreak on his father's legacy—generosity, kindness, advances for the disadvantaged. Perhaps even greater rights for women. His father would turn in his grave.

They set out again, but before they got too far, Henry leaned over. "I'm proud of you, James," he said quietly.

James didn't say anything—couldn't say anything what with the lump in his throat.

PEARL WOULD NEVER DESCRIBE herself as a vindictive person. Or a jealous one. But she'd spent time imagining punching Lady Kinsley square in the nose. Just a quick rabbit-style jab. In and out. Walk away.

It wasn't one particular thing. And Pearl was *trying* to like her. Mostly, in fact, she could like her. But then things would dribble out of Lady Kinsley's mouth and there was that thought again: in and out. Dainty, really, as far as punching went.

Calling Pearl's husband *James*. Talking about him as if she knew him. And tonight, playing cards as a foursome with her was all Pearl could handle.

"How dare you suggest a men's team and a women's team," James asked across the table to Lord Kinsley, "when you knew very well that we would lose?"

Kinsley shuffled the cards. "It was as Lady Teeton instructed. You know I follow orders."

Across the table, Lady Kinsley preened and smiled at Pearl. Because of course this was the woman whose favorite compliment was not of her dress or her beauty, but her intellect. Which, after so many drawing room conversations, Pearl had seen quite enough of over the past few days.

"Don't listen to them, Lady Andrepont. They only talk like this when planning something devious."

The familiarity made the hairs on the back of Pearl's neck stand up. But she smiled sweetly. "I'm well-acquainted with my lord's tactics."

James gave her a heated glance, which she returned, knowing that even Lady Kinsley might pick up on the innuendo.

Kinsley coughed and dealt the cards.

"The rain should let up soon, don't you think?" Lady Kinsley said. "We've been talking of taking the carriage into town tomorrow."

Lady Teeton walked over. "How is the game

going? No betting, I see. How do you make it interesting?"

"By incisive conversation, of course," Pearl said, looking at Lady Kinsley, whose weather conversation had been anything but scintillating. Lady Kinsley blushed in response. Pearl should have felt guilty about the jab, but she didn't. James even gave her a look of disapproval.

"Should you go to the village tomorrow, you may take our curricle. Michael had it built for these muddy roads. It should be ideal. But it only seats two, so choose your companion wisely." Lady Teeton had the audacity to wink at Lady Kinsley.

If that woman invited her husband in the curricle tomorrow, Pearl didn't know what she'd do.

Pearl picked up her cards and shifted them into order of suits and numbers. It was a hand that could go either way. Neither high nor low. A supporting hand. Because of course that's what she was dealt. Nothing that might help her forge her own path forward, but rather, everything to help someone else find glory.

What rubbish.

EVEN THOUGH SHOOTING was cancelled the next morning, likely because Teeton had overindulged in spirits while playing cards, James went on a ramble in the woods alone. The day was technically dry, though how long it would remain so was anyone's guess. How long had it been since he'd spent time in the fresh air like this? When he was young, the family was in the country constantly. He couldn't wait to join them during school breaks. He and William would go out walking, or even he and his uncle's friend Vasily.

For years, he'd hoped Vasily was his real father, given the close attention Vasily paid to James's mother. As a child, it had seemed to him that the adults were constantly together, minus his father, who was off committing some dark deed elsewhere. It seemed natural, his aunt and uncle, and then his mother with Vasily. But as James got older and grew to resemble his father more and more, his paternity was under no cloud of doubt. He was his father's son. And all the natural curiosity that Vasily had encouraged on these long walks vanished. The hard edge became important. Necessary, even, to keep people at bay, so they wouldn't get hurt when he eventually became a monster, too.

He turned, watching gravel and muddy water fly as a curricle with absurdly tall wheels went down the long drive. James saw that Henry held the reins, and Rose clutched her bonnet as the horses galloped. If that was Teeton's idea of engineering for muddy roads, the man was a damned fool.

It was hard to tell how late in the morning it was from the overcast sky. And they planned to leave tomorrow, so this was his last ramble. Good for Henry and Rose to go to the village. Now, without him, they seemed stronger somehow. He hadn't been their third leg, as if they were a triangle. He'd been a wedge that had gotten between them.

Now that he had Pearl, he understood what a fool he'd been. He thought they could be happy that way, and perhaps others could, just not Rose. She couldn't focus on more than one thing at a time. And she was right—Henry deserved a wife if they were going to be a political couple. Like Lady Teeton, Rose needed to put that tremendous focus and intellect on the task ahead. He wished them well.

James turned back to the manor house. Pearl would be up by now.

The day moved quickly. Pearl was in much better spirits after being strained last night, even to the point of making sharp comments at Rose's expense.

Pearl and James even managed to leave their room and play chess in the library. To be fair, both played distracted and mediocre games, and they returned to Pearl's room shortly thereafter.

By midafternoon, with them freshly abed and sated, a storm moved in, and lightning cracked across the sky. Heavy rains pounded the house.

Pearl snuggled in tightly under his arm. "I love weather like this when I'm safe and warm."

James grumbled his assent. Her words made him think—he'd never had to add that caveat to his thoughts. He'd always been safe and warm. It had been his greatest guilt that the women around him had never been safe. He pressed Pearl closer and kissed her head. He swore she'd never have to worry for her safety.

They dozed until the clock struck seven. The storm's onslaught hadn't lessened, but as Pearl said, they were safe and warm. James forced one eye open. "I should go back to my rooms and let you dress for dinner."

Pearl murmured her assent. "If the food wasn't so good, I wouldn't budge."

"You just like the pudding course." James slid out of bed. "You have a sweet tooth."

"With a childhood like mine, you're lucky I don't hire a French pastry chef whose sole job is to make me puddings three times a day." Pearl covered herself with the thin sheet, but it was a paltry shield from his gaze.

He let his eyes drift to her breasts, barely covered. So tantalizing and soft. She caught him staring and lowered the sheet further. "Minx."

"Could we not call up for a tray?" she said, her voice thick with desire.

"It's our last night. We leave in the morning." He would rather have a tray as well, but frankly, he was beginning to wonder if Mrs. Foraker had been onto something. His desire and his body were finding themselves at odds more and more often. James pulled his shirt on.

Pearl pouted, but she nodded. "I would hate to disappoint Lady Teeton. She has been very kind. And cordial."

He sat on the bed, facing away from her to slide on his breeches. She came around to sit next to him, still covered in the sheet. "What about any of the others?" He asked because he wanted her to like Rose. He really did. Not that he had any designs on re-entering an arrangement with Rose and Henry, but he cared about Rose and wanted Pearl to feel the same way. The women seemed as if they could be friends.

"I like Mrs. Shumaker. She's very funny, in her own way."

"Anyone else?" James knew better than to name Rose, but Pearl figured it out and moved away.

"Don't." She emerged from the sheet and slipped on her chemise.

The only real strategy here was to play dumb. "Don't what?"

She gave him an annoyed side eye. "Don't try to force a friendship with your former mistress. It's ugly."

"I'm not forcing anything." James pulled on his boots, which had been drying next to the fire. He really ought to escape before anything went terribly awry.

Pearl didn't say anything more, just wrapped her dressing gown around herself. It was his dismissal, then. "Shall I fetch you before I go down to the drawing room?"

She gave him a tight smile. "That won't be necessary. I'm comfortable enough here now to go down alone."

Ah. He returned her tight smile and left. She

erected her defenses so swiftly. But he was certain he could breach them tonight, after dinner. Some flirtations, some kisses. They would be fine. And she was probably correct. Orchestrating a friendship with Rose was too much for him to expect.

Phillip was ready for him. Indeed, James was washed and dressed in a thrice, and he ambled downstairs long before anyone else should be ready for dinner. He wandered into the library, half-hoping to find Henry there behind the chess board. He poked around the shelves until he heard a commotion in the passageway. With nothing better to do than be of assistance, he went to investigate.

Lord Teeton stood with two footmen who still wore muddy boots and wet oilskin overcoats. Their low tones were laced with urgency.

"Might I help?" James said as he approached.

Lord Teeton nodded and looked to him with a stricken face. "It appears we need to form a search party."

"In this weather?" As if on cue, lightning cracked nearby, flashing the house full of momentary light. A second later, a loud boom wracked them all.

"Precisely because of it. Lord and Lady Kinsley have not yet returned from the village."

"But surely they would have holed up at the local inn or tavern?" James frowned. He didn't like the idea of either Henry or Rose stuck in the elements. They were lovely, smart, resourceful people, but neither was particularly familiar with the out of doors. Despite Rose's childhood in the countryside, she'd had an intellectual's upbringing.

"My men have just come from the village," Lord Teeton said, nodding to the men dripping on the carpets. "They were seen earlier but left not long after midday."

James felt a weight settle onto his chest. One that

wouldn't be dislodged until both Rose and Henry were safe again.

"Would your driver be available to join the search? I think we might be able to pull a few more men together. Take the four cardinal directions. Do our best. It will get cold tonight and I—"

James held up his hand—he didn't want to hear it said aloud. "Of course. My driver and I will be one team. I'll change while he readies the horses." He didn't wait for approval. James turned and bolted for the stairs, tearing at his dinner jacket.

☙❧

DINNER WAS SOMBER with only the ladies present. Even though Mr. Shumaker was not in the best of health, he still went out in the storm to look for the missing couple, much to Mrs. Shumaker's worry. All the women picked at their food. Lady Teeton in particular seemed devastated.

Pearl felt a stab of guilt over what she'd said to James earlier that day, about enjoying this kind of torrid weather when she was safe and warm. His friends had been out in the elements, neither safe nor warm. Not that their disastrous trip had been Pearl's fault, but she felt guilty because she'd been feeling unkind towards Lady Kinsley and had enjoyed the weather which tormented Lady Kinsley.

As they all stared at their pheasant courses, picking and rearranging food, Lady Teeton finally admitted defeat. "If anyone else will eat, I am happy to stay at the dinner table. But none of you have managed a morsel since the soup course."

It was true.

Lady Teeton summoned her butler and ordered the table cleared and sherry to be brought to the drawing room, where they would retire. "Honestly, what kind of charade must one perform? Our friends and husbands are out and in danger. We will do as women have always done from time immemorial: we will sit vigil. Come."

Pearl wasn't quite sure what the lady meant by her speech, but sherry would be welcome. Actually, whisky would be preferable, but Pearl didn't dare ask for it. They filed into the drawing room as sullen as they'd been in the dining room.

Pearl stood next to the piano, one hand on the dark wood-finished lid. She wished James were there to play for them.

And there it was again, that stab of jealousy. James was out searching for Lady Kinsley, not looking after Pearl. Which was completely reasonable. Pearl didn't need looking after, and clearly, Lady Kinsley was in trouble. But James needed to protect his loved ones, and Pearl wasn't in need. Would she lose his regard because she was so capable? She was sickened by the idea that Lady Kinsley provided him with something she could not. Because Pearl felt something for him. More than something. It struck her: she loved him.

When had that happened?

She'd married him because he offered, not because of love. It was a way to have a life to call her own, not dependent on the charity of others. And now she was back in another dependency of her own making. Her chest felt tight and panicky, like she was running from a magistrate and dodging through the small alleyways of St. Giles.

The enormity of it struck her all at once and she faltered. She'd rather have him return safely with Lord and Lady Kinsley and leave her unloved than have his friends lost.

"Lady Andrepont? Are you well?" Mrs. Aguilar was by her side in an instant.

Pearl nodded but allowed the other woman to guide her into a chair. James must return to her. Even if it meant he would be wooed back to Lady Kinsley's bed. Pearl gulped down the proffered sherry, but it wasn't enough.

"I'll ring for some strong tea," Lady Teeton said.

"Perhaps some stronger spirits as well," Mrs. Shumaker said.

"Here, here," seconded Mrs. Aguilar.

"Please," Pearl agreed.

Mrs. Aguilar held her hand. "You're still newly wed. You've every right to be worried about your husband."

Pearl nodded, though she wanted to protest. It wasn't just that she was worried for his safety. She wanted to tell him that she loved him. That she wanted the best for him.

Another crack of lightning flashed through the room and the thunder boomed. A maid appeared with a tea tray, and the aged butler rolled in a drink cart laden with a variety of spirits. The footmen were out looking for the missing marquis and marchioness.

"I think it's time to tell stories, don't you think?" Mrs. Shumaker said. "Anyone have a rousing past we need to know about?"

Lady Teeton poured a cup of tea for each of them, and the butler followed with a tumbler of their choice of heavier spirits. None of the ladies volunteered. But Pearl felt emboldened. She felt as if she had nothing to lose while James risked his life.

"I have a story that might captivate you," she said, accepting her tumbler of whisky. "But I'd prefer it you all down your glasses first and swear not to repeat what I am about to tell you."

The other ladies laughed and complied, sputtering and coughing their way through drinking the heady liquor. The butler went around refilling tumblers once more. The man stood at the ready, but Pearl stared him down. No extra ears for this.

Lady Teeton gave her butler a look. He put down the carafe and left with a bow.

"I was not born into nobility, as you may already know. In fact, I was born to an Irish immigrant and a handsome chairman who, of course, ran off before I was born. My brother is an infamous prizefighter, but before he made his money, I lived wherever would offer me shelter. And I stole things. Many things."

Understanding dawned on Mrs. Aguilar's face. "A criminal!"

"Precisely. But I argue, and submit myself as evidence: I am reformed. Why? Because I am safe. I am loved." She almost choked on the word. "And I have everything to lose. I am not a criminal. Nor was I ever."

"This isn't a courtroom, Lady Andrepont," Mrs. Shumaker said, snuggling back into her chair with her tipple. "I think what we need now is a good yarn. A tale of intrigue and derring-do. Perhaps lost loves and almost-captures."

Mrs. Aguilar smiled, leaning against her end of the couch. "Quite, Mrs. Shumaker. I won't hold you to the truth, either. In fact, I'd prefer it if you made it up. I'd worry less."

Pearl felt a chuckle bubble up. The stories she could tell: tales of Mrs. Coldcroft, or training with Bess Abbott. Even the love story of her brother and Lydia.

"Even Lady Andrepont's own love story is quite the tale, from what I understand," Lady Teeton said, peering over her tumbler.

"I can tell you it is, from what I've heard through the walls," Mrs. Shumaker said.

Pearl blushed as the other women shrieked with laughter.

Mrs. Aguilar put her hand on Pearl's wrist. "No need to be embarrassed. We were all young once."

"On with the story!" Lady Teeton commanded, holding her glass up.

Pearl was glad she'd insisted they all drink the first glass quickly. It helped them forget their friends in trouble, and it gave Pearl courage to speak. As the storm raged, they could be a balm for each other in the dark.

❦

JAMES COULD BARELY SEE in front of him, the rain came down in such torrents. He was colder than he'd ever been, flexing his fingers to keep them from going numb. The roads were muck, and his horse was stumbling. There was no visible moon, but James could just make out Smithy ahead, his horse faltering as well.

They needed to head back to the manor for fresh horses. Perhaps another group had found them. James shook the water from his face. Smithy crossed the bridge ahead of them, the river below swollen and churning.

One moment James could see the bulky shadow of the man in front of him, and the next he was gone. Smithy's horse slipped just after the bridge, both horse and rider tumbling. Over the torrent of rain, James heard Smithy's yelp. Cursing, James dismounted while still on the bridge. He couldn't afford his horse following Smithy's. Leading his horse around the shifted mud, he threw the reins over a branch and called out.

In the dark, James inched down the embankment towards the other man's voice. And then Smithy shouted, "I found them!"

James startled and slid down on his bum. He stopped when he hit the bulk of Smithy's wet oilskin coat. A horse whimpered below him.

"James?" Rose's voice called in the darkness.

"I'm here!" James got his bearings and steadied himself.

"I'll hand her up," Smithy said. "You take her back and I'll stay with Lord Kinsley."

The big man moved and the lightning flashed, giving James a sudden picture of his surroundings. The stone bridge still had space underneath it as the river swelled. Figures were huddled against the posts.

"Why can you not take his lordship now?" James shouted over the rain.

Rose crawled into his arms, soaking wet in her woolen pelisse.

"Their horse was swept away. And my horse is injured." Smithy moved towards the shelter of the bridge.

James was loathe to leave either man. He paused while he considered any other option, but there were none. They all perished together, or he left with Rose and sent riders back.

"I'll send riders as soon as I can," James promised. Rose's teeth chattered. "Can you walk?" he asked her.

"Yes," she whispered.

It took them a few tries in the mud, but they got to his horse. He helped Rose up and then sat astride behind her. He would have to be careful navigating the roads. His instinct was to bolt, but the conditions were treacherous. He needed to get to civilization quickly. Rose reached back and clutched his sleeve.

"James." She shivered violently. "I'm with child. Keep me safe."

The weight of her words settled like a heavy stone. "I will," he promised through gritted teeth, then urged the horse forward with a cautious nudge.

They rode towards the village, the darkness surrounding them feeling inescapable. He dared not gallop with abandon even though Rose's body shook uncontrollably. He drew her closer, trying to warm her. Inwardly, he cursed. Could this child be his?

It pushed him to think on whether he could welcome a child. He wasn't sure—and when he tested the thought, imagining dandling one on his knee, he found that he wanted the mother to be Pearl. Regret coursed through him.

James rode through the meager town square and out the other side, praying he wouldn't miss the turn to the estate's long drive. "Hold on, Rose."

She nodded stiffly. But he still took it as a good sign that she could do that much.

When they were together, they'd been so careful not to conceive. There was no way the paternity wouldn't be openly questioned because of his dark features and Henry's blond good looks.

And how unfair to Pearl if he'd fathered a child before he thought to propose to her. That a mistake of the past would so color their future together. It would positively kill her to watch another woman raise a child that could have been hers.

It wasn't fair. Nothing was fair. It wasn't fair that there was a child. It wasn't fair the life that any of them had lived, especially his family—deprived of the countryside, irrevocably hurt and damaged through actions that James had been helpless to prevent. It wasn't fair that he was galloping across the countryside in a dark storm with a woman he'd once cared for, all the while his wife—the woman he loved —likely worried.

He hoped Pearl had gone to bed, faithful he would succeed. He remembered what she'd said: *I love this weather when I'm safe and warm.* He couldn't wait to love it, too. And he would, despite this, if that's what Pearl wanted. He would give her anything, if only they could all make it through this alive and in one piece.

Thankfully there was a stableboy at the turnoff with a lamp, holding vigil. James stopped briefly, giving directions for riders and a carriage to retrieve Henry and Smithy, and then continued on to the manor house amid shouts.

James all but threw the reins to the groom that stood by the front door. He slid off the horse, reaching up to help Rose, only to find her barely conscious. In the dim light, he saw that her lips were blue and her skin was far too pale. He lifted her into his arms and shouted directions to any maidservant available to bring warm towels and prepare warm baths in his room, Henry's room, Rose's room, and the servant's hall.

In the light, she looked far worse. Her skin was far too pale, tinged with a terrifying purple. Not knowing which door was hers, he carried Rose to his own room, kicking in the door when no one accommodated him quickly enough. Rose didn't have time. He sat her on the bed, murmuring to her, talking, trying to hold her attention. He stripped off her sodden pelisse and bonnet. It was a laughable joke of a hat now. He ripped at the buttons on the back of her dress, sending them flying. He stripped her down and shoved her under the covers.

"Phillip!" he shouted until the valet appeared at his elbow. "Bed warmers. Now. As many as you can find. Bricks, whatever they have. Now."

"My—" Rose murmured, disoriented, kicking her feet.

"Fuck," James said, noticing her wet stockings. He stripped them off as quickly as he could, then shed his clothing as well. Dry warmth was the best he could offer her and whatever promise of a babe was inside her. He slid into bed with her, rubbing her shoulders, murmuring to her. "Come on darling, come on."

"The babe—" Rose said in a sob.

"Does Henry know?" James asked, his lips in her hair. It was familiar. It was the man he'd been who had held her like this.

Rose sobbed. "I told him today, it's so early."

James shushed and calmed her. Phillip arrived

with bed warmers and James helped cushion them around Rose. "Henry will need this, too, when he returns," James said. "Please direct the staff."

Rose calmed, and her uncontrollable shudders ceased. James sighed and finally let his head rest against a pillow. As he closed his eyes, he felt rather than saw the shadow move in his doorway.

৩৵৪

PEARL'S HANDS SHOOK. She'd only ever felt this way after running from the magistrates. Her heart pounded and she felt cold all over. No, this was far worse than the magistrates. The wall felt cold against her back, but she swore she was sweating. Her husband was in bed with another woman. And not just any woman. His former mistress, who, according to the conversation she'd overheard, was pregnant.

Since everyone knew about the marquis's predilections, it wasn't likely to be Lord Kinsley's child. It was true then—James needed to protect, and he regained that in the form of his mistress and unborn child. The woman really had taken him from Pearl. It was because of her that James had asked Pearl to marry him. A sham marriage. He'd only asked because Pearl was sitting in the same room with him. It hadn't been love. Not even a pleasant feeling. It was merely proximity and the idea that she would be easy to set aside and ignore.

She couldn't bear to peer into the room again. She'd shoved herself into a wrapper as soon as she heard him bellowing in the hall. But she hadn't expected to see this—to see him climbing bare-arsed in with that woman.

Her chest hurt as she returned to her room. Blimey, there had never been a pain like this before. It was like the deepest, darkest shadows of London were inside her body, swallowing up every bit of joy and light she'd ever possessed. She gasped, and a great sob emerged unbidden.

She knew he wouldn't want children. But this already-married woman would have his child instead. And Pearl would watch as someone else got to have her family while she lived in a big empty house utterly alone.

How foolish had she been to fall in love with a man she knew, *knew*, was incapable of the emotion. He'd told her in so many words. Why hadn't she believed him? Why did she force the idea of a real marriage? One with physical intimacy and laughter and late-night piano concerts?

She would rather be stabbed. She had been once, on accident. Missed the important bits, healed nicely, barely a scar. And she'd rather have ten of those. With dirty knives or done on purpose. It would feel better than this. She sank to her knees. What was she to do now?

This was ridiculous. There were far worse things in life than being broken-hearted. Pearl scrubbed her face with her hands. No. There was no giving in to this weak despair. It was pointless.

God, she wanted to clean. Give her a floor and it would be as freshly polished as a mirror. She rang for Lily instead, despite it being well after midnight. Might as well let her know the expectations.

Pearl was going home. And it would be her home. No more running, and no more silly romantic expectations. She had traded happiness for a large house and security and a title. It was time for her to take what was hers.

※

JAMES STIRRED, coming out of his drowsing. Rose slept peacefully beside him, the healthy flush in her cheeks reassuring him. He slipped out of the warm cocoon of the bed, hurriedly donning his clothes. Now that Rose's danger had passed, he wanted there to be no uncertainty about his intentions. For him, nothing could be clearer: Rose was not the woman he wanted to wake up next to every morning.

Pearl was his friend, his coach, his sparring partner, someone who could make him laugh. She understood James in a way that Rose was fundamentally incapable of doing. And Pearl was incredible in her own right. Far more than one expected from her demure exterior, which he'd learned was hard-won. He respected her compassion and insight. And it made him want to be better to earn her respect.

He'd invite Freddy to dinner when he returned to London and then take his rightful seat in Parliament at the next convening. Pearl had been right: he had been a coward, and now he would do better. He would use his voice to give the powerless a chance to speak. That, at least, he could do. A feeling of clean, pure power surged through him.

While he was at it, he should also call his estate manager. There were likely issues he should take care of for the tenant farmers. And upkeep to the houses. There was much to do since his father's death. All obligations he'd pushed off to anyone who would take up the task. Mourning damage wrought by the former viscount was over. What a fool he'd been.

James left his room and found Phillip already up in his nearby quarters.

"Yes, my lord?" Phillip seemed inwardly appalled that James had found him.

"Lady Kinsley is still abed, but when she wakes, she will no doubt be embarrassed and disoriented. Please have her maid sit in my room so that she might arise to a friendly face. And might you also point me to Henry's room and Smithy's? I'd like to check on them both as soon as they are awake. If it isn't too early, I'll be in the dining room, begging for a morning tea or coffee."

Phillip nodded. "Of course, my lord. I will have someone notify you when the men are up."

James left Phillip's small room and scratched at his wife's door. He hoped she was well, and not too overwrought. But she was no wilting flower. She was likely waiting for him. Yet there was no answer at the door. Perhaps she was still abed. It was early, after all. And if it was that early, perhaps he might join her in that bed. He grinned and opened the door slowly, trying to be quiet.

Instead, he found an empty room. The bags were gone. Her perfume bottles had disappeared from the dressing table. James frowned. They'd been planning to leave today, but she couldn't have possibly roused Smithy after that ordeal. How cruel could she be? James thundered down to the dining room, encountering a footman on the way.

"Who has left today?" James demanded.

The footman was young and seemed cowed by James's demand. "The Aguilars left in their carriage."

James raised his eyebrows, waiting expectantly. Nothing came of it. "Was it only the Aguilars that left in that carriage?"

"I…I…I'm not certain, but I believe perhaps Lady Andrepont and her maid also?" The boy was practically bent in two trying to lean away from him.

"Fine." Pearl had left without even saying goodbye?

James stormed into the dining room. He no longer wanted tea or coffee or even breakfast. Well, at least she'd let Smithy convalesce. And that meant James might leave with the carriage at his own leisure. He took a deep breath. It was oddly rude for Pearl to not at least leave a note for him, but it had been a strange night. No, this only meant he could aid Henry and Rose as long as was necessary.

He found the good in it and breathed through his hurt.

And now he could have the leisure to check on Henry and play another round of chess with him, if he was up for it. Well. Since no one was awake yet, he would ring for tea and the newspaper and try to enjoy himself. He could trust her good judgment.

৩৯৫৩

THE DOWAGER LADY Andrepont appeared in the doorway of her late husband's study. The curtains were flung open for the first time in likely decades.

Pearl refused to acknowledge the older woman's entrance, continuing her discussion with Mr. Peabody. "And the bookshelves feel heavy, don't they? I like the space for books, but is there a way to make it feel less overbearing?"

Mr. Peabody wasn't willing to go along with Pearl's charade that they were the only two people in the room. "My dear lady!" he cried when he noticed James's mother in the doorway, immediately sweeping into a bow so low he almost touched the top of his hanging toupee to his feet.

Pearl turned and gave a short curtsy of respect. "I didn't hear you come in."

Lady Andrepont gave a tight smile. "Mr. Peabody. So lovely to see you. The last time I had the pleasure, I believe you were just out of leading strings. Your father helped me greatly when I first remodeled this house."

Mr. Peabody brightened with her acknowledgment. Lesson learned, Pearl thought. To be a great lady, to garner respect and aid—remember. Remember the people. She could do that.

"Lady Andrepont, forgive me. There's two of you now!" Mr. Peabody reddened. "I'm so pleased you remembered my father, let alone me."

Her mother-in-law gave a demure nod but then focused her stare on Pearl. "Now that I am the elder, I find myself less informed."

Pearl suppressed her embarrassment. But she was not going to relinquish the one thing she'd earned in her trade. This house was her home, and as mistress of the domain, she was reclaiming any and all territory. Starting with the dank domain of her husband's dead predecessor.

"Not to worry, dear Mother Wallingford."

The dowager winced. "Mr. Peabody, might you excuse us? I'm sure Mr. Barton will fetch you refreshment in the drawing room."

Mr. Peabody froze. The power dynamic couldn't have been clearer. Pearl moved to the fireplace and employed the disused bellpull, her eyes locked on her mother-in-law. There were aspects of her life that she would give on, but this room was non-negotiable. The verbal contract had been clear: the house was hers.

Mr. Barton and Mrs. Foraker appeared within moments, both wide-eyed and out of breath.

"Mr. Barton. Please see Mr. Peabody to the drawing room and fetch him some refreshments." Pearl's eyes never wavered from the dowager.

Mr. Peabody gave curt bows and hurried after the servants, who disappeared as quickly as they'd come. No one wanted to be in the middle of whatever was about to happen.

"I'm surprised you opened this room," her mother-in-law said, taking commanding steps into the room.

"Well, the occupant is dead. The room is available. I'm claiming it."

"For yourself?" She stopped short of the heavy oak desk, as if she couldn't manage to touch it.

Pearl squared off with the woman. "For myself. I need a place to work. To function. This is my home now. I intend to occupy it."

"So militaristic."

"What is marriage if not conquest?" Pearl didn't believe it, but it was a well-guarded repartee that would be difficult for the other woman to counter.

But instead of marshalling an offensive, her mother-in-law softened. "I hoped that wasn't how your marriage would function. You seemed happy enough when you left for the countryside. May I ask where my son is, since he didn't return with you?"

"I know not. The last I saw your son, he was in bed with his mistress." Pearl tried not to spit the words, but they left her mouth before she could check them.

James's mother hung her head, hands clasped in front of her. The dust, disturbed from years of collection, floated in the air, the mild light from the tall windows highlighting its unhurried drift. "I'm sorry Pearl. I truly am."

"I had hopes," Pearl admitted, turning to observe the bookshelves she'd advocated tearing down. Her heart was nothing but a bricked-up wound, a naked void impossible to access. "But I know better now."

"I hope you give him a chance to explain."

Pearl whirled around. "Explain that our marriage is a sham? That she crooked her finger and he came running? I'll not play a fool for him. I've too much dignity."

Lady Andrepont gazed about the room. She hesitated, but then ran her finger through the dust on the desk, streaking a clear path of burnished wood. "Tear it down. Turn it to firewood. It's better than he deserved." She trained her emerald eyes on Pearl. The color she'd gifted her son. The one feature of hers that shone through his father's face. She and Pearl were mirrored, both hurt, turned to stone by different circumstances. "After all, you're Lady Andrepont now."

Pearl dipped a shallow curtsy. The older woman

left the room, her shoulders still back and proud, but somehow more relaxed than they had been when she entered. This was no longer a domain of men. Pearl would rule here.

Mrs. Foraker appeared in the doorway. "Begging your pardon, my lady. Shall I fetch Mr. Peabody down?"

Of course the housekeeper had been listening at the door. There was likely not a single secret she didn't know.

"Yes, please, Mrs. Foraker. Thank you. I'd like to get started on this project as soon as possible. It's about time we begin our future, don't you think?"

"Of course, my lady."

Pearl turned back to the looming bookcases. She put her hands on her hips. Who cared about that man's secrets anymore? He was dead. And the devil take him, he could rot.

CHAPTER 18

James took an extra two days of the Teetons'
hospitality. Smithy's pallor was deathly and he
couldn't stop coughing. James didn't feel that a
return to London should cost a man's life.
Henry also suffered a rattling cough, but Rose
regained her robust health within a day, thanks to the
cook's broth and fussing in general by Lady Teeton.
James's own health was impeccable, though his mood
was anything but.

He missed Pearl. But he couldn't miss her if he
didn't stay away. It would make their reunion all the
sweeter. James sometimes fantasized about the
bathing room, the gymnasium, even the gardens as he
trod through the Teetons' estate. The country air felt
good in his lungs, pushing him to think more of
reclaiming his own country manor.

In the evening, after dinner, he entertained the
party at the piano. Mr. and Mrs. Shumaker taught
Rose and Henry a type of country reel they hadn't
known before while Lord and Lady Teeton
encouraged them. James had...fun. He wished Pearl
were present because her laughter would have shaken
the house. And who knew what other dances she
could have taught them?

On the carriage ride back to London, James

realized his heart ached to bring his reconciled friends and his wife together. And his family. In his years of self-indulgent sulking, he'd let them fracture and wander away. Pearl wanted a family—she'd said as much. Why could they not become the house of weekly dinners and casual visits? The kind of household that was filled with witty banter and full bellies? The safe repository of their familial love. He could invite Margaret in from the countryside to stay once a year, if not more.

As for children? Well. If Pearl wanted them, and they happened, then he was no longer opposed. Not welcoming, of course, but the idea of children raised by Pearl didn't threaten a recurrence of the kind of monster his father had been. If James could be redeemed, then perhaps a child, only a quarter of the blood of his paternal line, could be a happy, healthy, productive member of society. Or at least not a menace.

As they bounced along the road, James let himself picture this new world where the house didn't feel like a mausoleum, but rather a bustling hive of light and color. He hadn't known how well he'd chosen when he first proposed to Pearl. But he knew now that no other woman could have shown him this kind of future.

They arrived in Mayfair after dark. James got out, stretching his legs. He'd grown accustomed to walking for miles in the countryside, and now it viscerally hurt to be in a cramped space.

Mr. Barton met him at the entry, looking relieved to see him. Odd, but not unwelcome. Perhaps Pearl had a difficult time in their two-day separation. That was easily solved.

"Welcome home, my lord," the butler greeted him.

"Thank you, Barton. Good to be home. I would welcome a bath, if the footmen would be so kind. It has been a long day." James watched as the footmen retrieved his trunk. Phillip followed the trunk, and James was grateful for his valet. He was grateful for all of them.

"Of course, my lord."

James peeled off his overcoat after handing over his hat and gloves. He'd had ideas about that bathing chamber, specifically, inviting his wife into it.

"If I may, my lord, there is a matter that I would like to bring to your attention."

"All these *my lords*, Barton. Are you nervous?" James teased. "I know I don't leave town often, but the house is, in fact, still standing. It can't be that bad."

Barton inclined his head. "Quite. However, there is a matter that her ladyship has undertaken—"

"I'm certain it can wait until tomorrow. I'm famished, I'm covered in dust, and I would prefer a dram of whisky, a bath, and then my bed. Tomorrow morning, I promise I will be up and about to solve all the problems."

"Certainly, my lord. I will have a tray sent to your room."

"Thank you." There were scandalous and tantalizing things he planned with the whisky and Pearl. By the time he trudged to his room, he felt the weariness of the journey. He had worried for Smithy and Henry and Rose's health. And Rose had reassured him that, in fact, the babe that she carried was not his. She'd had a cycle between the last of their romps and this. If Rose was certain the babe belonged to Henry, then James trusted her. She was meticulous and careful by nature.

Three nights ago, he'd galloped like a madman through a storm, certain his world was ending. And now, it felt like his ship had righted itself.

Phillip was finishing the unpacking when James entered the room.

"I'll be done in a thrice and stow the trunk," Phillip said, tidying everything as James unknotted his cravat.

"Have I ever said 'thank you,' Phillip?"

Phillip blinked and straightened. "I don't believe so, my lord."

"Then thank you for all you do. I know it's your job, but I can be a bit of a bear. Thank you for your patience."

Phillip paled. "Am I being let go?"

"Of course not!" James threw off his cravat. "Don't mind my happy rambling. I'm simply glad to be home."

Phillip nodded and finished his task. "Then may I say that financial incentives are an excellent way to thank your staff."

James chuckled. "Consider it done. In the meantime, good night."

Phillip latched the trunk and carried it to the door, pausing to say, "Good night, my lord. Also, Mr. Barton anticipated your desire for a bath, so it is ready. As any good, well-deserving-of-a-bonus servant would."

James waved him out, but smiled. He shucked his clothing and went to the bath. He wouldn't fool himself—he hoped the splashing might alert Pearl to his return. But there were no sounds coming from her room at all. Surely, someone had informed her of his arrival?

He finished, a tad disappointed there wasn't an excessive amount of rose oil or orange halves in the water. He dried himself, tossed on his banyan, and tried the adjoining door, only to find it locked. That was odd. He knocked softly, but there was no response.

She must be elsewhere in the house. James tucked into some slippers, grabbed a candle, and went wandering. The earlier bustle of his arrival had calmed and the house was quiet. It should have been easy to detect her, but then again, she was stealthier than he had initially given her credit for. Not in the drawing room. Not in the dining room. He went to his study, and it was then he noticed the open door further down the passageway, meager light spilling out. The door that should have remained shut and locked for the rest of time.

Lamps were lit in the room. He crept in, finding her sorting through his father's books. Upending some, rending pages out of some, tossing the remnants into two piles.

Panic flooded him. "What are you doing?"

Pearl glanced over her shoulder, giving him barely a nod of acknowledgment. "Taking what's mine." She continued her project, grabbing books from a great pile in the middle of the room. The empty built-in walnut shelves loomed over them both.

Memories assaulted him. His heart pounded twice as fast as usual. The urge to cover his head with his hands was overwhelming, but the internal warning that he shouldn't move kept him from it. His mind stuttered as it clawed for logic, his body screaming deep in his belly, that this was wrong. More than wrong, it was dangerous. "But—" He swallowed hard.

"Oh, but I am doing it," Pearl said, tossing yet another book. Her plummy accent had faded. "This pile here's for selling. This pile here's for burning."

"You can't burn books," James sputtered.

"These bits of filth I can." She whirled around to spear him with a look. She was livid. "Did you know about these?" She held up a nondescript tome.

He shook his head, inexplicably terrified.

She stood and opened the book, flipping pages until she got to an illustration, shoving it under his nose. "Recognize this?"

He lifted his candle to study the illustration. It

was unmistakably Lydia as a girl. His cousin's likeness in a book.

"Or this one?" Pearl spat, turning the page. Another illustration. The girl in a state of undress, looking over her shoulder, coquettish, as if she were a grown woman. James thought he might cast up his accounts.

"Did you know about this?" She flipped pages again.

"Stop," he begged.

"*Frolicking with the Innocents*," she read. "By an Anonymous Gentleman." Fury colored her cheeks. "I think we both know who that might be."

James's chin wavered. "I didn't know."

Pearl hurled the book into the burning pile. "If your mother hadn't already assured me that the publisher is long dead, I'd burn down all of London to find them."

"I knew nothing of this," he whispered.

"Did you not? Because you were the one who ordered this...this...this dungeon preserved!" Pearl spun back to her pile of books. "If you want to save them, you may put them in your own house, because I will not stand for it in mine."

James's brain tripped over her words. "My own house? Pearl, I cannot emphasize enough, I didn't know."

She planted her hands on canted hips. "Do what you like in your own home. Where you may play father to your bastard children. Really, James, I underestimated you."

James's blood ran cold. "I don't have any bastard children."

Pearl laughed. "S'all right now. We made a deal, you and I. I'd be a poor sport if I sulked over getting exactly what I asked for. You gave me a home and a title. So I'm claiming them. But you will be living elsewhere, I'm afraid. I haven't the stomach for the antics of men like you and your father."

"That isn't fair, Pearl, and you know it. I'm not like him." James deposited his candle on his father's wooden desk, which was streaked in heavy layers of dust. "And I am not going anywhere. Pearl, I will help you burn this house to the foundation if that's what will please you."

"It isn't about what I want," Pearl insisted. "It's what I can stomach from the likes of you. I'll not be sharing a house with a man who has already got a family wif' another woman. A married woman at that. But then, we all know about Henry Parks, don't we?"

James hated the look on her face as she said Henry's name. It was the same as all the bullies at Eton. "Don't talk about Henry like that," he warned.

"I don't condemn him. But I read the papers, like everybody. He don't seem to favor his wife. So pardon me if I expect the next heir to the Kinsley line to sport green eyes."

"That isn't the case," James growled.

"Isn't it? Because last I saw, you were naked in bed with your former mistress, cooing about a babe. Tell me. What is the part that I don't understand? I'm not stupid, James, so give me the dignity of our arrangement." She stalked towards him.

"That isn't the full story. That's not the—"

"Stop whinging, you selfish cunt," she spat. "You want everything for yourself, without sparing a thought for the rest of us. Thinking only of your pleasures, like your despicable papa. The devil may take you, but I won't." She stomped out.

James stood frozen in his father's study, taken to its bones. Only now did he notice the missing curtains, the rolled-up carpets, the absent chairs. She was gutting it. Excising the monster like a surgeon. Because she hated him. His father. Interchangeable titles, interchangeable men. His stomach roiled.

His hands shook, his body gone cold. Nothing made any sense. Everything had been fine. Better than fine. And here. Now. The blackguard was rising from his grave to punish him once more. How could James not have seen this coming? The man had trapped them all, outsmarting them at every turn. James would never be free of him.

۞

PEARL RIPPED her carpetbag from under the bed and dumped out her things. She marched over to James's bedroom door, not caring about her feelings. She didn't care about anything. Her insides had been ripped from her. The only thing left was that brick wall in her chest, the one surrounding her heart, the one that protected her and wouldn't let her melt.

This threadbare carpetbag, which had once been her salvation, was now to be her deliverance from her husband's evil. She shoved trousers, stockings, and a waistcoat into the bag and threw it down the passageway.

There.

Now her intent couldn't be mistaken. This was her house. He could entertain all the mistresses in the world elsewhere, for all she cared. Back in her own bedchamber, she slammed the door and slid down against it until she was on the ground. It wasn't until she heard his footsteps and a heavy sigh, and then those footsteps retreating, that she let herself cry.

He could be damned.

She let out a howl that a wild dog would understand. A howl of inevitable loneliness and pain, the kind of which she should have expected. She should have known. But she was a fool to have believed in something greater. That she'd had a partner. A husband. A marriage.

No, the world was very much as it always had been: the only constant she could rely on was herself.

※

"Good God," Corinthian John's butler spat, surveying James on the doorstep. "Begging your pardon, my lord."

James held up a hand. "No need. I've got nothing beneath the banyan. May I come in?"

"I'll roust the master at once," the butler said, making room for James in the foyer.

"I will be begging for a place to stay the night," James said, holding up the carpetbag.

"I'll put you in the study while I ready a room."

If there was a time for James to poach some of Corinthian John's gin, this was it. The humiliating walk from his house in Mayfair to John's in Marylebone was enough to pull himself together. His hands no longer shook, and the inexplicable terror had subsided. He poured himself some of the clear liquid and held it up to the flame of the candelabra. Very suspicious.

"What have you done?" John croaked from the doorway. The man was also wrapped in a banyan, his face slack with fatigue. Now that he knew Pearl better, James could see the family resemblance. It was the coloring, but there was also something in their smooth mannerisms, the fluidity with which they moved through the world.

"Being born, apparently," James answered, then knocked back the glass. The gin burned his throat and mouth. Lord, that was unpleasant.

"What bit of mingle-mangle is going on? You've plenty of rooms in that monstrosity in Mayfair."

James poured himself another measure of gin. "Your sister told me it was no longer my house, as per our marriage contract. As the person who drew it up on her behalf, I must ask you, is it true?"

John rubbed his eyes and stifled a yawn. "How'd you cock it up?"

"Did no such thing." James sipped at the gin. The juniper flavor was starting to grow on him. Still burned. He coughed.

"Fuck off," John said. "Pearl can turn right nasty if she needs, but not without reason. So?"

"She's ripping apart my father's study," he murmured. His hands began to shake once more. That dread feeling welled up: the feeling that nothing was right, that it all was wrong, wrong, wrong. That he was in danger, as was everyone he loved.

"Good fer her," the prizefighter said, dropping into a chair. "Cold in here, yeah? Get on wif' it. What else?"

"It's not right, John. She can't do that." James set down the glass to prevent his friend from noticing his shaking hands.

"Sure she can. You told her as much. Said that house was hers. She was the viscountess. Gave her a wide permission. Don't know why it's a surprise."

"But he'll be, he'll be..." James couldn't stop shaking, nor could he finish his sentence. Helpless terror settled into him, the familiar demon that had sat with him all his life.

"He'll be nuffin'. Prolly dust by now. Some bones, rat droppings, and a slick of tar where his heart done sat."

"Who?" Lydia stood in the doorway, bound in her wrapper, just as sleepy as her husband.

"Go back to bed, love," John cooed.

"What's the matter, James?" She frowned, and somehow it felt like they were children all over again.

"I can't," James said, his teeth chattering. "Lyds, I can't."

She made her way to him, embracing him. She shushed him, holding him. He couldn't stop it. He tried, God, how he tried. He had failed Lydia, and now he'd failed everyone else as well. Nothing he did was good enough. He was as helpless as he'd always been.

"I can't protect her, I can't. I can't. I tried." Hot tears streaked down his face. The world rushed by him in a panic, a stream of relentless, unfixable problems.

"Protect who?" John demanded.

"Pearl," James said. "She's in there, and she doesn't know him. She doesn't understand—"

Lydia whispered soothing sounds at him as if he were a wild horse. "He's gone." She repeated it until James's shuddering stopped. "He can't hurt her. He can't."

"But I'm just like him, and—"

"You aren't. Not at all." Lydia pulled back and forced him to look at her. She put her cold hand on his face. "Are you listening to me? Not. At. All."

James looked deep into her eyes, blue like her father's. If she could get past it, anyone could. He steadied his breathing. She nodded encouragement, concern so clearly etched on her face that he could see it in this low light. He was coming back to himself. The panic ebbed. He shuddered as the feeling evaporated.

"If you had a drop of that monster in you, I wouldn't have let you take Pearl," John said. "I knew you didn't love her, nor she you, but we figured," he glanced at Lydia. "We figured you would find the good in each other."

"We have," James said, clearing his throat and reining in his rampant emotion. "Or rather, we did."

"So, what changed?" Lydia asked softly.

"Rose," James admitted. "Rose is pregnant."

John swore and turned away.

"But it isn't mine. Pearl saw me in bed with Rose and—"

"Have you lost your mind?" Lydia demanded. Gone was her soothing, mothering side, and the blunt-edged weapon of her personality returned.

"It isn't what it sounds like," James insisted.

John folded his arms. "This had better be an outstanding explanation."

"There was a storm."

"Still not an excuse," Lydia tossed over her shoulder to John.

"Hear me out," James insisted. "Henry and Rose were lost in it. I found them, out on the road, and I took Rose home while Smithy stayed with Henry."

Lydia narrowed her eyes as she listened, but John's face was an implacable professional mask.

"As we're riding home, Rose tells me about the babe, but she's been in the rain for hours and is blue all over. We get back, and she begs me to help her save the baby. I whisk her up to my bed, strip off her clothes—"

Lydia threw her hands up. "What is wrong with you?"

"What am I supposed to do? Let her die?"

"You call her maid, you fool!" Lydia shouted.

"But I was there! I protected her! I saved her!" James roared, pointing to his own chest. When would they understand? He did what he could, but most of the time it wasn't good enough.

John sat on the arm of a chair, looking skeptical. "Then?"

"To get her warmed and not let her die of hypothermia or lose the baby, I stripped down, ordered my valet to bring in bed warmers—"

Lydia snorted.

"And I held her until I accidentally fell asleep. We both fell asleep."

"Can you hear it, mate?" John asked.

"Hear what? Hear that I saved a woman's life? As well as her unborn child? I'm a fucking hero is what I am."

Lydia's pointedly unimpressed expression remained unchanged. He glanced at John, who looked as if he felt bad for how stupid the person standing in front of him was. Which was him. James thought about it. Could that evening with Rose have gone differently? In his opinion, no—at least, not to be as efficient. Would Rose have survived if her maid had tended to her instead? Possibly.

But he hadn't wanted a maid to care for Rose. He had wanted to make sure she was safe because he cared for her. Ah, yes. There it was. Pearl was upset because she'd seen or heard about his naked former mistress in his bed. Well. Perhaps. It hadn't *needed* to be him under those sheets. It had only needed to be someone with body heat to spare.

"It was only to save Rose's life."

The two merely waited.

"Nothing happened."

Lydia rose an eyebrow at him, which only made him think of Pearl's comments about the expression. It didn't matter what he thought. What mattered was that Pearl believed he wanted to be with Rose—and believed that Rose carried James's baby. "Now that you mention it, perhaps Pearl's concerns are legitimate."

"Not exactly the sob story you thought it was, is it?" Lydia asked.

"You two are miserable at making a chap feel better." James picked up the tumbler of gin and shot the rest of it back. The pine tree flavor made him cough.

John held his hands up. "Just so I am understanding the situation. Pearl is remodeling your house, yeah?"

"Yes."

"She's safe?"

"Of course."

"Yer the arse in the scenario?" John took the tumbler from James's hand and set it on the cart. He slid his arm around James's shoulders and started guiding him towards the door.

"Presumably."

"Yeah, right. That's fine, then. Need a bed for the night?" The butler was in the passageway, signaling that the guest room was prepared.

"I'd like that." James was suddenly very tired.

"Apologize for it all tomorrow?"

"Absolutely."

"Not gonna work, tellin' you now."

"Not helpful."

"You'll have to do somefin' big."

"Oh, fuck off." James felt immensely better.

❧

PEARL FELT a fat drop of sweat release down between her shoulder blades. She'd never worked a hanging sandbag this long, but she could see the appeal. Sometimes, the only solution to pain was inflicting it on a stationary object. Even her thighs were aching from the time she was putting in, but she welcomed the distraction.

Today, Mr. Peabody had returned with some very large men, and they were pulling down one of the bookcases. The other was being painted white. She didn't care that it was a "crime" to cover the fine-grained wood. The heavy oppression needed to be exorcised from the room, and that was one way to do it. Besides, Pearl planned to line the shelves with an entire collection of novels where women triumphed in whatever way they wanted. If she couldn't find any, she'd write them herself. Women like her deserved to win.

A coin landed near her feet with a plunk and a rattle as it circled its way to lying flat. Pearl stopped her exercise and looked towards the doorway where James stood. There were dark circles under his eyes, his hair was raked up, and he wasn't wearing a waistcoat. His shirt hung open at the neck, exposing skin that Pearl found more alluring than she'd like to admit. He looked determined.

She looked down at the silver coin. "What's the half-crown for?"

"It's a challenge." James sauntered in.

"You seem awfully sure of yourself." Pearl turned back to the sandbag, hoping to resume her exercise, but she found herself suddenly unable to choose which combination to throw.

"We spar. I win a round, you must listen—really listen—to what I have to say." James pulled his shirt over his head.

Pearl couldn't even look at him. She knew what was happening over there. The smooth skin, the broad shoulders, the dark hair that retreated from his navel into his breeches. The skin that had been laid next to his mistress the last she saw. She threw a right uppercut at the bag. "And if I win? Because I will."

"Whatever you want," James said.

She turned, raising her eyebrow. "And what if it's something you don't want?" He wasn't the only one who remembered their first sparring match.

The tight smile on his face wasn't one of pain or controlled humor. It looked like softness—like something she hadn't seen before. "I don't mind."

Pearl's stomach tightened. She wanted to hurt him. Badly. The pain that had clung to her like black tar wasn't fading. "Fine. Into the ring then."

James threw his shirt on the ground. She watched him move, noticing the muscles in his back. Maybe her demand would be to have him make love to her, just so she could get up and walk away afterwards. He could see how it felt.

"Do you need to warm up?" Pearl asked.

He gave her a smirk. "No, but thank you for asking."

Pearl remembered what her brother had said about his technique: he had creativity, but he was slow. She toed the line and settled into a shallow crouch. Across from her, he echoed her movements. Her heart thudded, unsure what she was feeling. Anger, humiliation, heartbreak.

"We need a bell," she said, ignoring her conflicted emotions. "Countdown from three?"

James nodded.

"Three, two—"

"I love you," he said.

Pearl blinked. And before she knew it, he'd grabbed her by both arms and tackled her to the ground.

"I win round one," James said, his face a mere inch from hers.

"That's cheating!" Pearl struggled in his grasp, but his weight blanketed her. He wouldn't move. "You can't do that!"

He smiled, which irritated her to no end. She struggled, knowing it would tire her out. "Do what? We're on the ground, and you can't get up. I win."

"You can't *say* things like that." She squirmed. The idea that he believed he loved her was absurd. It wasn't true and it wasn't real. As if he even knew what love meant.

"I mean it. Pearl." James waited until she met his gaze. "I love you. I do. Give me five minutes to explain everything."

"You don't and you can't," Pearl said, trying to wrest her wrist from his grasp, but she couldn't manage. His hands were too big for her to break his grasp easily. She couldn't see straight, as if a red haze covered her eyes while she struggled against him with absolutely no plan. Finally, realizing it was easier to listen than to think, she gave in. "Fine. I'll give you five minutes, but no lies. I can't stand you lying to me."

"Pearl, I've never lied to you. Not once. Of all the horrible things I am or could be, I am not a liar." His green eyes bored into hers.

"You just did." She pulled her leg up, hoping to shove him off, but she couldn't raise it. He was too heavy. "Love. You don't know what it means."

"That is where you are wrong. Someone like me, raised in a loveless home? I know all the things that it isn't. It isn't attending parties, or fancy trinkets. It isn't children or a new carriage. It's something else, both bigger and smaller, both extravagant and simple. I realized that I loved you weeks ago. I knew from the moment you let me in that I couldn't bear you shutting me out. And I needed you to be proud to be with me, to be my wife. You said it: I have to be the man I want to be, not the one I'm afraid I could be."

"Get off of me." Pearl didn't want to hear this.

"Five minutes," James reminded her without moving.

"Fine!" Pearl pushed at him, and his body eased off of hers. She sat up, letting the backs of her legs stretch while she gave him a look of disdain. She didn't want to believe that he loved her when it would hurt so badly over and over. There was no possible way she could live through another heartbreak like this.

"Will you listen?" James sat across from her, one hand reaching out but not quite touching her.

She raised her eyebrows. What else could she do to signal that his five minutes was starting now?

"You are absolutely within reason to be angry. I had not thought about what the situation that night would look like to anyone else. My only thoughts were to save my friend."

"And saving her conveniently meant disrobing."

His head drooped. "Oddly enough, yes?" He grabbed her hand. "Please. That night, hauling Rose out from underneath a muddy bridge, more than anything, I wanted to get back to you. I wanted to show you that I was safe so that you wouldn't worry. And I wanted to tell you about the search, about how lost I felt, how Smithy's horse went down, and how scared I was. But to get to that point, I had to help Rose. I couldn't go as fast as I wanted to that night—not with her in such terrible condition. She was blue, convulsing uncontrollably, soaked through, and unable to keep herself upright on the horse. When we returned, my only thought was to save her—and the unborn heir to a powerful title. All I could think was to warm her up as quickly as possible, which meant sharing body heat. There wasn't time to get a bath going. No time for other people."

It was the talk of the babe that was the millstone around Pearl's neck.

"But she also assured me the babe is not mine. You know her well enough now to know that she is many things, but above all, meticulous. She is not the kind of person to declare anything with certainty unless she has facts."

Pearl couldn't look at him. Tears welled in her eyes. She wanted it all to stop. That brick wall was not as sturdy as she'd believed. Couldn't she hurt in private?

"She carries the heir to a marquessate. She is my friend. She is my best friend's wife. I would do anything to save a life—I hope you would believe that. If nothing else, I am doing my best to be a good man."

"It isn't about saving lives," Pearl sniffed. Oh, bugger off. Tears threatened.

"It's about seeing me in bed with another woman?"

"Without clothes!" Pearl shouted. "What would you think if the situation was reversed? Would you believe me? Would you think so kindly of my life-saving efforts?"

James seemed to think about it, which gratified her. "It would be hard. But, in the end, I hope that I would trust you. I hope that you would say, 'James, I am not the father of that baby' and I would believe you."

Against her will, she snorted. She shoved his shoulder away from her. He responded by scooting closer and putting his hand on her leg. Her tears spilled onto her cheeks. "I don't forgive you."

"That's fine." He scooted closer. "But can you believe me?"

Tears kept coming, no matter what she did. "It hurts."

James nodded. "It does. And I'm sorry. I hurt, too."

"Why?" He was making this about his pain, his hurt, his victimhood, and she wasn't having it.

"Because I love you. And I think you love me too. And if you make me stay away, then not only can I not show you how much I love you, I also cannot protect you. I know that there is something of me that cannot stop the need to keep the people I love safe. Lydia explained it to me last night, more or less."

"Lydia?" Pearl sniffed.

"That's where I stayed last night. With Lydia and John."

"I kicked you out and you went and stayed with *my* brother?"

James nodded. "Turns out, they're my family too."

Pearl couldn't have said why, but it was at that comment her tears became a torrent. James gathered her in his arms and set her on his lap. He rocked her as she sobbed. Her tears and snot became slick on his shoulder until she couldn't bear it anymore and wiped it away with the dress sleeve she'd tied around her waist.

"I love you, Pearl Wallingford."

She looked into his green eyes and saw the truth. Finally. His handsome face, his love, his hope. Her future. "I believe you," she said, and she kissed him.

He pulled back, tracing his thumb along her cheek. "Do you love me?"

She saw it there, his vulnerability, his fear. What he had gone through to get to this point, and what a miracle it was that he could feel anything at all, let alone love for her. "I love you, James Wallingford. I'm sorry I said those things to you last night. I never thought for a moment you were like him."

He searched her gaze and offered a smile. "I know."

She leaned into him and kissed him, a salty mix of tears and sweat, frustration and fragile hope. And also love.

"Now, I think it's time for a bath." James stood and pulled her up.

"You already called for a bath?" She asked, following as James held the rope up for her to climb out of the ring.

"Do you not remember me being overly confident when I first walked in? Of course I did. Because I have been thinking about you and me and that tub for ages." He climbed down next to her and scooped her into his arms. "I mean to take our time. My wife is very demanding, and I am nothing if not thorough."

EPILOGUE

"Perhaps it is vulgar for a wife to give a speech for her husband," Pearl said, standing and raising her glass. "But you all must know by now that I don't care if you think I am."

The dinner table was lined with friends and family members who chuckled at her remarks. Hosting weekly family dinners with Lydia and John and Agnes and Jack had ballooned into far more. Tonight, they hosted a dinner party larger than any that had been hosted at the house in decades.

James's mother, his uncle and aunt, and even his half-sister Margaret and her husband, the earl, had come to stay with them for the opening session of Parliament. In addition, Lydia and John and the Worleys joined them, as did James's childhood friend Freddy, and Mathilda with her parents, who were distinctly thrilled at being so near the aristocracy. Agnes and Jack attended, as did a few of their friends, including Miss Persephone, whom Pearl liked immensely. Indeed, watching Miss Persephone take on Lady Teeton's politics made for the most diverting table talk. Lord Teeton kept his eyes on his dinner. Even Henry and Rose had come round for the momentous occasion, and Pearl was surprised to see the rapport between Henry and Freddy, who were also renewing their acquaintance.

"Here, here!" shouted Bess Abbott, who also responded to the title of Mrs. Worley. Pearl liked to hear the accent she had been lured away from. It made her feel grounded and real because it melded who she'd been and who she was becoming.

"But my greatest sin," Pearl continued, "is not vulgarity, but rather pride. I'm exceedingly proud of my husband, James Wallingford, the viscount Andrepont, for taking his Parliamentary seat tomorrow morning. A decision that was wrought by pain but emerged from devotion. You will do us all justice, my love. Thank you for being brave enough to make the world a better place."

She held her glass up to toast him, and her guests mirrored her. "Oh! And Freddy too!" She added, blushing as she sat down. Freddy had become enough of a fixture at their household that Pearl often forgot his actual title. An earl of someplace? Freddy was in want of a wife, and Pearl kept inviting Mathilda Perry over, but Mathilda kept bringing the insistent Mrs. Tyler, who seemed to quash every conversation attempt at a dinner table. Hopefully Mathilda's parents weren't as vigilant.

James leaned over and kissed his wife. "I have no sins," he whispered. His breath smelled of the sweet claret they were drinking. "Except the thoughts I have of you."

"You're the very devil himself," Pearl whispered back. "And I love you for it."

❧

HISTORICAL NOTE

This book contains references to much of the history of women's boxing. For those who have not read my historical notes for my previous books, may I recommend those for your historical edification on the best boxer of the 18th century, Elizabeth Wilkinson Stokes. Here, I will assume you know about those prior references.

What is new in this book is that I've made Pearl Arthur a bit of a history buff. She knows the history and is emulating Elizabeth Wilkinson Stokes by using her boxing costume of short dress, white stockings, low pumps, and a white jacket for a top. This is how one of Stokes's fights was described in an advertisement, to assure the public that it wasn't anything indecent. That said, based on my research, as years went by, the Regency era would have had women boxers taking down the tops of their dresses and tying the sleeves around their waists. They did not wear stays, and thus would have only had their shifts/chemises on underneath. These were likely made of undyed linen, as cotton would be expensive.

The purpose of a shift/chemise was to absorb the oils and sweat of a body, keeping the outergarment clean. However, because this was considered underwear, many writers of the time talk about the women being "topless." I don't believe they took their shifts down as well, mostly because I've tried it. However linen is transparent, and there would be very little left to the imagination. A small jacket, as referenced in my book, and by the advertisement of Stokes's fight, would cover the fighter and also keep her contained in such a way that might be construed as a pre-cursor to the modern sports bra. That last part is speculation from me.

As for Andrepont's fighting, this was a very popular sport for young men of the aristocracy to participate in. There was a gym on Bond Street called Gentleman John Jackson's, which many young men visited. They could spar, train, and in some satire from the Regency era, they could give themselves black eyes that might make them appear tougher than they actually were. A home gym for the wealthy is also not unheard of, however, transforming the ballroom is excessive. My hope is that in my novel, it shows just how unbalanced Andrepont can be.

To move on to the political aspects referenced in the novel: Pearl's recitation of knowing a nine-year-old hung for pickpocketing is fact. It did not matter the age of the criminal, punishments were meted out with a harshness that a large chunk of the populace found abhorrent. The collection of these harsh laws were begun in the 17th century, but more were added over time, so that eventually, there were a hundred and sixty infractions that were considered to be so egregious that not only did they incur the death penalty, but that the death would take place without the benefit of clergy (last rites). In 1717, the Transportation Act allowed judges to commute the death penalty to transportation to either the American colony, or later, to Australia. This is pertinent to the plot of Daniel Defoe's famous book <u>Moll Flanders</u>.

Of these offenses, everything from treason to impersonating another with intent to defraud was considered deserving lethal repercussions.

There were attempts yearly by coalitions to have the penal code overhauled over the years, as it stated that anything stolen worth over five pounds warranted the death penalty. As inflation occurred over the centuries, by the Regency, a well-made, ornate handkerchief could be worth five pounds. There were people, women mainly, who sold used clothing, and the unscrupulous would pay children for whatever wares they came across. Handkerchiefs were a common item to be resold, and easy for children to find in the streets. They were also easy to pickpocket.

After the Regency, this penal code became known as the Bloody Code, though it was not referenced as such during the time. Hence, the conversation of the women at Lady Teeton's country home. Also of public debate was the Catholic Question. I rephrase it here in my book as the Anglican Question, because of how upset Mrs. Shumaker is. But it comes down to the fact that Catholics had been barred from holding any public office in England or Ireland since 1672, and an even further limited of their voting rights in 1728. This was not repealed until 1829. So during the time period of this book, a Catholic could not vote, regardless of his status. Of note, a Catholic is still barred from becoming the English monarch, or marrying into the royal family (this took effect during Queen Anne's reign in 1701). Modern audiences might first think of the Jewish Question, as it was phrased from Nazi Germany, but the population of Catholics was far more threatening and had the weight of historical upheaval. Jews, like Catholics, also could not vote, and would not be granted the right to vote until 1835, and not able to be in Parliament until 1858, but even that was with conditions.

All of these political questions, the Bloody Laws, the Catholic Question, the Jewish Emancipation, and even the abolition of slavery, all took many years of bills not being passed by Parliament. When Lady Teeton argues over a strategy, and different groups lobbying behind specific causes, this is what she is referencing.

Pearl's debate about what makes a criminal is also a philosophical debate—and continues to be one. The belief then (and some hold this to be true now) was that criminals are made: some people are inherently bad. But Pearl sees this very differently, as she has had a marked change in circumstance. At what point is a criminal forgiven? Only if they've paid penance by going to jail? Or can we forgive some crimes, but not others? I give this debate to you as well, gentle reader. In the U.S., there is still an on-going debate about how former prisoners are rehabilitated, and many with a criminal record will not admit to it because of how society will see them. After serving jail time and parole, is that person still a criminal? Or are they only a criminal if they get caught? Does it matter the nature of the transgression?

Pearl argues that her crimes are of need—perhaps you have violated the speed limit, or lied by omission to a teacher, a partner, or even the IRS. I'm sure you had a very good reason for what you did, but does it make you a criminal?

ACKNOWLEDGMENTS

First of all, thank you, reader, for joining me on this journey. We have one more book in this series—explanations of that tricksy teapot will come, trust me. I also hope you enjoyed some of my egotistical self-references in here, like the fact that John and Lydia also consummated their engagement on the floor of a ballroom-turned-gymnasium.

Some of my other references that I found funny include the fact that *The Pearl* is the title of a Victorian era erotica book. I got endless cackles about that as I wrote.

Of course, thank you to the insightful and amazing team that help me put this book together: Anya Kagan of Touchstone Editing, Signe Jorgenson of Signe Jorgenson Editing, and Fiona Jayde for the cover. He really catches the eye.

Thanks to the Paper Lantern Writers who helped support me on this entire journey, you guys are great.

And thanks to my beta readers and Street Team: Ana Brazil, Kellie Dunn, Nikky Rossini, Jen Kimber, Lisa Friedman, Nicole Hatch, Stephanie MacDonald. I'm sorry if I missed anyone.

Lastly, thank you to everyone who has bought one of my books. It makes me feel like what I'm doing is worthwhile. You have my gratitude.

ABOUT THE AUTHOR

Edie Cay writes award-winning Regency romances. A LADY'S REVENGE (2020), THE BOXER AND THE BLACKSMITH (2021), A LADY'S FINDER (2022), and A VISCOUNT'S VENGEANCE (2023) focus on the history of women's boxing and themes of misfits and found family. As a speaker, she has presented at Historical Novel Society, Regency Fiction Writers, History Quill, Chicago-North Spring Fling, Toronto Romance Writers conference, and the Historical Romance Retreat. She regularly contributes to the HNS quarterly journal. She is a member of HNS, The Regency Fiction Writers, ALLi, and a founding member of Paper Lantern Writers. Follow her on social media @authorEdieCay.

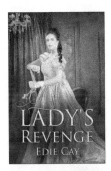

A Lady's Revenge (First in When the Blood is Up series)

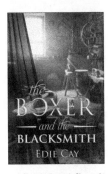

The Boxer and the Blacksmith (Second in When the Blood is Up series)

A Lady's Finder (Third in When the Blood is Up series)

A Viscount's Vengeance (Fourth in When the Blood is Up series)

Also available by Edie Cay

In Her Element, a contemporary romance novelette

A Soldier's Medal (Flash Historical Fiction)

CPSIA information can be obtained
at www.ICGtesting.com
Printed in the USA
BVHW050955130323
660180BV00014BA/1037

9 781734 439779